Comanche Is Not My Name

2: My Mithersome Progress to the Little Big Horn

William Fagus

Fagus Press

Editor's Note

This is the second instalment of the story of Comanche, the self-styled, 'one and only living survivor of the fight known as the Little Big Horn.' A break was created in the original narrative at the author's own, as he might himself put it, contumacious edict. The general reader, therefore, is best advised to turn initially to the first volume, *My Jeopardacious Life on the High Plains*.

If you are a newcomer to the account, there is still be much to enjoy and edify in *My Mithersome Progress to The Little Big Horn*. It forms a self-contained account of Comanche's life in the US Seventh Cavalry during the years 1868-1891 — the final days of the 'frontier' and the traditional lives of the West's native inhabitants — and no doubt students of military history and the Plains Wars in particular will relish picking over the details and debating new and controversial assertions. In this respect, the author's appraisal of the character of George Armstrong Custer springs to mind.

For new readers, a note on authenticity: the narrator is given to whimsy and digression. He supplies details of minor characters and undocumented events which have a ring of truth but are impossible to verify. When the narrative touches on documented history, however, there is a remarkable correspondence.

The text: I have made only minor changes to the text, and strictly to the end of clarifying syntax and structure for the reader. The narrative and its pungency, its circumlocutions and at times exasperating vocabulary, remains, to the best of my endeavours, untouched.

William Isambard Fagus, 2024.

Part Two
My Mithersome Progress to The Little Big Horn

ONE

I expect the Sozodont is now a big deal with you humanos. Mac, least while he was still in full possession of them items, why he had the whitest teeth you ever saw, and you can imagine the heightened effect, them choppers shining out that sunburnt face capped by that all that fiery hair. He were quite the sight. But the odour of it were always mithersome to my highly refined nostrils, and I never partook, despite my jockey's efforts.

He were in a state of intoxication, and it was, Here laddie, take a wee nip of this, it'll cure that halitosis of yours I'm obliged to endure. But my butcher-block head in pendulate motion is quite the weapon, and the bottle went spinning away to be cast upon the prairie and lose the balance of its contents. He got the mulligrubs with me for the remainder of that day.

Anyhow, you ain't here to get inculcated-up on the prevailing dentifrical prophylactics of the Gilded Age. I got to get you up to the Powder River country and that creek the Indians call the Greasy Grass and the altercation thereon, of which fight I was the one and only living survivor.

So, my first day on active duty with the Seventh US Cavalry furthering the cause of civilization and commerce, and I done run off, albeit at the behest of my new jockey. Now we was joggling along, the plain spread out before us in all the glory of its spring raiment, goddamn birds tweeting, toward the wisp of smoke that denoted the furthest extent of that civilization and commerce. No plumes of dust to our rear communicated hasty pursuit by our former comrades, so we kept to the higher ground, the railroad in our sights. I'll adjunct that on the equitatory side Mac weren't no Comanche, but he were Pinkey Barnes compared to the Cornishman.

Come the late afternoon, a hailstorm busting through, God's fingers delving the prairie, Mac reined me up and dismounted, fetched out of his saddle bags a change of clothes. The hail pimpling his lard-white flesh, he stripped off them cavalry duds and cast them to the winds. As they flew away he yelled, Get it right up ye, right up ye, ye goddamn US cavalry, and he thrust his dexter fist in the air and clapped the sinister palm to his bicep, keeping his poorly thumb out the way. As sign language went, it possessed an admirable lack of ambiguity. The new habiliments was about as nondescript as you could find in a frontier dry goods store, and hence not worth the mither of descript. What is worth describing was his top coat, if that is what you'd call it.

A blanket it were, with a hole cut in the top to poke his head through, and it was when he remounted I twigged the gumption of it. It covered the saddle, Prop. of US Gov., and similarly titled accouterments. We was about to head down to the railroad when he said, Shit, and peered over my shoulder. The brand. Goddamnit.

He took a metal fork and attempted to tease up the burnt hair. You can imagine the efficacy of that. He trotted me over to a wallow, slapped on black earth, rubbed it in, and stood back. That'll just have to dae you Rab, he said, and we meandered down to the end of the line.

NOW I GUESS it is worth the inconvenience of supplying a description of this feature, the terminus of the Kansas Pacific Railroad as it were back then on that spring day long forgot, being you and your progeny ain't likely to be seeing such an item in your lifetimes.

It is right peculiar to stumble on an entire town in the middle of the blasted wilderness. I say entire, but you'd say its mercantility were a good bit skewed. There were a dentist, a lawyer, a land agent, a quacksalver with an undertaker handy next door, a grocer and a dry goods store, but these was single establishments. I'd guess five-to-one, maybe even ten, they was outnumbered by the dance halls and the drinking emporiums.

The names of them establishments have faded some now, but I'll supply these what have stuck in the old noddle. Two Silver Dollars, a Bucking Bronco, a White Elephant, an Occidental, a Crystal Palace. For aspirationals there was the Grand Hotel, for nostalgics Ma Smedley's Eating House, a Holy Job for religious types. Salty Mae's catered for indeterminate inclinations.

If you was a parvenu walking down that street you might figure it a permanent town, what with all that carpentry evident. But they was mere frontages and you'd stroll round back and see the balance of the edifices was the work of needle and thread. Ease of conveyance were the motive behind it. The railroad progressed, and them purveyors packed up, piled their towns on a flatcar, and progressed with it.

I'd say though this town ambitioned perpetuity. Sticks was knocked into vacant prairie, some was even little crucifixes, and in lieu of our Lord being affixed street names was daubed on the crosspieces and I ventured maybe auriferous ores been discovered roundabout.

Beyond this enterprise spread a village of white tents, like them back at the forts, only the straight lines was crooked. I conjectured they was where the labourers abided when at rest, and despite it coming on late in the day, the tents was unoccupied.

Off yonder the railroad line furcated off to a dead-end, a couple of fancy cars parked there. Sundry trumperies framed the windows, tassels and swags and such, and I bottomed it out that was where the gubernators abided. They was occupied, and I caught the stink of fine brandy and the fumid currents of cigar smoke.

On the main track stood the iron horse, hissing steam, stink of oil and charred wood, unexplained clankings and tickings that emanate from such mechanicals in repose. In front of it, where the iron equine had shoved them, flatcars was lined up, loaded with split logs cut to the same length, iron rails filmed with rust. Empty flatcars was tipped over at the side to make way for more full examples. Teams of burlies was hauling them rails off and carrying them forward to join to them already stretching back to the Mississippi, where they pried them into position and went back for more. A bunch of other fellows come along then and set the spikes and banged them in, their arms windmilling slender picks, and you never saw them miss. That's what repetitive labour does to a man I guess. The spike drivers, they worked in pairs, and it were a sight to behold them working in rhythm like that, one clanking while the other began his descent. They'd got a little song going, to help them keep tempo I guess. I done forgot that song now.

Them toilers not singing was jabbering, and here were yet another means of English locution to get my lugs around. In this example, the words started off high and tumbled down low, in the manner of a waterfall, and the words, when you was able to pick out a particular example, was bent over at the end like they'd been struck by a shovel.

Beyond the rails, the crossties stepped off toward the high sierras I knew was out there, though yet invisible. The ties ceased, and then only shorn grass and levelled dirt indicated destination. Two waggons was parked there, and crossties was getting unloaded in readiness, a man on a horse telling them how to do it, the mules with their heads bowed, staring off occidental at the expanse of unsullied wilderness like they knew it was the last time they'd see it.

I calculated Mac fascinated at the sight of this labour and enterprise, being we dallied no little time watching that bustle, until he come to hisself and licked his lips and said, You know what Rab, I got a hell of a thirst on me.

We moved off back toward the street, and my lugs was glad of it. Even though them clangours had paused waiting for another rail to be brung up, them sensitive organs was still dinning with Sunday church bells. Off from the fancy frontages a waggon was parked, afore which the owner had set up a wooden counter. Glasses was set up thereon and displayed in bottles and barrels in the waggon behind was a range of intoxicants. The range were limited, mainly beer and busthead, bar a dusty bottle of champagne, kept back for celebration purposes. Him being a fugitive, I calculate Mac wanted to avoid them more salubrious groggeries, so we appropinquated ourselves thereto.

He tied me to a rail considerately installed at back of the waggon, hooked the bag of oats over my nose and said, Back soon Rab. Dinnae do nowt I wouldnae do.

Pitched behind the waggon was a tent commodious enough for two with extra room to jag out a limb or three. Outside a female sat on a camp chair, topped by a blonde syllabub coiffure and ruddled cheeks. She evidently didn't feel the cold given her sparse skirts, albeit her teats stood out through the corsetry she scarce filled, hard as the rivets keeping that iron horse together.

Her eyes was set deep in little caverns their depths grey as old musket balls, and the ruddle scarce concealed the hollow cheeks. Jesus, if you was female back in them days and discovered yourself located on the peripheries of the civilization, career options sure was limited, and I would have pondered on the concatenation of life's contingencies what had fetched her up there, if I was able to give a damn.

While his mouth took care of his whisky, Mac's eyes slavered over the female. She smiled and nodded and blew him a little kiss, said, Hey there Honey, like a taste of sugar? Mac hesitated, and I remember thinking, well after all that fleeing we done across the blasted plains, if you ain't going to take up the offer, I sure will. But I was callow in the ways of humanos back then, how they like to disguise the act of coitus like it ain't the naturalest thing the Lord gave us to do in our spare time.

Mac exchanged a word with the barkeep and handed over a coin of small value, drained his glass and strode off toward the tent. En route he stopped by me and rummaged in the saddlebag and took hisself a slosh of Sozodont.

I calculated that barkeep had got hisself a lucrative enterprise going there, him handling the financial end of things, polishing tumblers while she handled the physical labour, and I pondered how he'd arranged it thus. His forearms, like ladies stockings packed with earth, I guess appertained to the agreement.

That goddamn nosebag. A patch of fresh grass stood untrampled adjacent, mocking my incapacity. By then I could shuck off a hopple, worry away a tether, tease out a picket pin, so, why not. It took a deal of head tossing, and at one juncture I was obliged to put my muzzle to the ground and trap the bag under my hoof and pull, but I got the goddamn thing off of me. Tore a hole in it to boot, which was a crying shame.

I FIGURED us to pernoctate in the hereabouts, but once he'd took his few minutes tupping the strumpet Mac mounted me and we trotted off toward the low sun. That vulgarity ain't my invention. I am quoting my jockey. Having satiated a brace of carnal desires, I guess he wanted to put some distance between hisself and his erstwhile comrades. But his taste of sugar left Mac depressed, and he said how that demimondaine wasnae worth the slosh of Sozodont, leave aside the federal currency. If you are going to take up that trade, he said, ye might show a little enthusiasm about it.

We trotted on by the two waggons and the mules and the last of the cross ties, the low sun turning the grass to gold spikes. Beyond that, they'd dug away the prairie some, filled some in, and we come to the bunch of toilers what'd done it.

Chinamen they was in the main, and If that ain't the polite designation for them fellas, I don't mean no disrespect by it. How they'd got to the Kansas plains all the way from China, wherever that is, well you probably know better'n me. But they is enterprising types them Orientals, and I figured the whites best watch out or one day they might get out-enterprised.

At that point the prairie fell away into a dry gulch, and them Chinamen was filling the gulch with rocks, packing the gaps with smaller geologicals. Now, this will strike you as curious, given my extensive prior dealings with locomotives, but it clubbed me only then. Iron horses was incapable of climbing even the gentlest inclivity, and was thus obliged to have the merest hump and hollow ironed-out, otherwise they'd stand huffing at the bottom like a retired coke-stoker partial to cream cheeses and Cuban cigars. My estimation of them mechanicals declined further.

Carts and barrows, they was the principal forms of geological conveyance, thenceforth shovels and rakes was scraped about to form a ridge for that feeble train to chuff along. They possessed a further means of conveyance, kind of pole with a bucket either end, the pole lodged on the shoulder and springing according to the weight of the dirt packed in. It struck me as a fine method of shifting dirt, if you was inclined to such activity. Despite its evident utility, none of the whites present was using it.

Speaking of them latters, I saw that the white workers gave these Chinamen a wide berth. Some even directed a gobbet of spit in their direction. But if you dress yourself in long shirts and baggy drawers, braid your hair, wear non-standard headgear and own eyes what ain't of the orthodoxy, you is apt to draw unwanted attention from malefactors. That, and they worked cheaper than the whites. Why, I expect if some fellows showed up from Mesopotamia, wherever that is, and offered their labour for a spoon of slumgullion a day and a crack in the dirt to sleep in, them Chinamen might have been similar aggravated. I observed this in my earthly. When humanos is desperate for a grubstake, they is apt to abase theirselves to any kind of life, which is exactly how the gubernators like it.

The railroad bosses, they couldn't give a damn them Chinamen was sallow skinned and narrow eyed. For all they cared, they could have been from the moon and complected purple with yellow polka dots and possessed of the eyes of a goddamn owl. They laboured cheap, ate little, viewed sleep as optional, foreswore spirituous liquors, and owned no ambition of being invited to dinner with the missus.

Now, the headgear. I glossed over them items but I got to go back being them apogees of the milliner's art. Like upturned dishes they was, with a pimple on top, and I don't know how they arranged it, but they appeared to stand off from the head a piece, leaving a space for the air to circulate, what struck me as an ingenious modification. They'd never win no prizes in the sartorial stakes, but for hard labour out on the plains they was the acme of practicality. Mac should have purloined hisself one to protect his scorched face, but he never, and I saw nary a white wearing one of them items, though blistered noses and lips were in ample supply. The only downside I saw to them hats was they was made of straw and could not be left unattended adjacent to mules.

We didn't linger at that that scene of utter drudgery, Mac wanting to use up the balance of the daylight, I guess, and as we proceeded on I whittled on what the Comanche male would have made of all that toil, them disdaining such as unmanly, fit only for females and slaves. Why would you bust your back shifting dirt all day, just so as you could get to a destination a day quicker, a destination what probably ain't no improvement on where you is presently located, when meantime you could be copulating with your woman, lying outside your tipi gambling with your friends chawing on buffalo tongue, racing a fine horse out on the plain, humbling a bull buffalo with a single arrow, or enjoying a fine coup on your enemy and taking his scalp as souvenir. To hell with all that. I'll go shovel some dirt to make some other bastard rich.

We loped on into the night. Lucky for Mac, I never saw no Indians, him being alone in the wilderness and in possession of that hair. The hoary old dictum that Indians don't attack at night can generally be relied upon, albeit it ain't down to no superstition. It's just they don't own no flashlights. As the almedra moon rose copper, an orchestra of wolves struck up. The din spooked Mac and he said, Jesus Rab, and kicked me to go faster. I ignored him.

You might not know this, but wolves generally don't fancy humano meat for repast purposes. Buffalo and elk and deer is more their line, the occasional equine. A humano ain't likely to run fast or far, and maybe the chase is part of the fun. But you never know. Could be one of that bunch was independent minded, and if he'd come after us I'd have been obliged to buck Mac off and proceed alone. Wouldn't be no sense in us both getting et alive.

Shortly thereafter he said, Christ I'm tired, and he pulled me up and dismounted, gathered hisself a fazzle of brushwood and set it ablaze. He spread his tarp on the ground, wrapped hisself in a blanket and set hisself to sleep, a saddle bag under his head. I never heard no snoring. Indians and wolves circumambulating about is apt to promote insomnia.

At dawn's first glimmer he rose, farted, took his boots and socks off and worked a digit between the toes. He held that finger to his nose and sniffed, then wiped the grease on his britches. I told you, you witness all manner of things when you is accounted a nothing but a dumb beast, although I admit to licking my lips contemplating the saltiness of it. After the podalic maintenance, he stood and stepped on a prickly pear, an act what made him howl and hop and put him in a vinegary mood the remainder of the morning. He limped over to the fire, stirred the embers, melted a spoon of grease in a tin cup and dipped a cracker, said, Wish I'd bought some coffee, then hopped off to attend to his toilet. The foot he'd injured turned out to be his mounting foot, a misfortune what delayed our departure, what my jockey accomplished with the punctured foot unshod.

Come the middle of the morning, them not generally being early risers unless threatened with massacre, a bunch of Indians showed up. You know it, they'd seen that blazing brushwood the night previous and come see what made it. The encounter weren't much of a scrape and hardly worth the telling, but I'll tell it anyhow.

We'd no sooner passed by a draw when half a dozen Cheyenne come a'larruping out of it. Mac said, Jesus Rab, and kicked me hard. I put my legs into an easy lope. This evidently weren't rapid enough for my jockey and he said, Jesus Rab. Come on, and kicked me anew. I can forgive him that. He were ignorant of my prior life as a Comanche and concomitant experience in the fugacious arts. I held my pace. Them Cheyenne nags was already blowing anyhow, having just galloped up out that draw.

Them boys was all whooping and shrieking, and one let off a rifle shot, didn't bother me none. Don't believe what you read in the dime novels. Ain't no jockey, white, black or indigene, who can make an accurate shot from atwixt the ears of a galloping horse. They hit you, though they will doubtless claim otherwise, it is pure luck, and out on them plains you is just as likely to get struck by a giant hailstone or a bolt of lightning or a precipitating prairie dog.

So there I am, loping along, letting them gain on me a little, Mac up top panicking, picturing his ballocks excised and roasted before his eyes, chawing on his own privy part. I allow them to get in twanging range, but I don't want to get no projectile in the arse like that Ute boy done to me, so soon as them arrows commence clattering about my posterior, I put in that little spurt I been holding back.

Now you know by now I ain't no speedy horse, but it takes them by surprise, and I open up a little distance. So they larrup their ponies and regain the ground, and I repeat my previous. Now my wind comes into play. I can hear them ponies is blowing like that blacksmith's bellows back at the big fort, and me, well I'm only just beginning to open up my lungs. That little distance, this time it don't close.

Them Cheyenne pull up, and I leave them chawing on my dust, what satisfactions me no end I can tell you. I spy a rocky outcrop and lope on up to it, criss-cross around and leave a few false trails on the peripheries like the Comanche taught me, and head off occidental. But looking back from my eyrie, I realise those latter actions was for showing-off purposes.

You can imagine, Mac, he is overjoyed, him departing bodily intact a lone encounter with a bunch of Indian braves, and he slaps my neck and yanks on my ears and says, By God, Rab, I owe you ma life. I was shitting masel so I was. How did you manage to avoid all they prairie dog holes? I'll buy you a bucket of apples when we get to town.

Step in a goddamn prairie dog hole. Like I'm some dumb cart horse.

LATE IN A PM and us on a good trail, no trees roundabout and the topography nice and flat just the way I like it, the circle of the sun flitting between clouds of resemblances, I saw the first of them big sierras showing theirselves through the haze. Mac was taking regular slugs from his canteen, but I hadn't had a decent sup of Adam's Ale since the eve previous, if you'll pardon the wordplay there. So I was right cheered when I clocked a shanty ahead, stable off to the side, a well out front, no mules.

The establishment had been subject to recent aboriginal attack, arrows poking out the dobies and attempts at combustion the prima facie evidence. No humanos was about, not even the deceased variety, and I estimated they been carried off for leisurely disobligements. The only live items was the twirling dirt devils.

Mac called out but the only reply was the squeak of a rusty hinge. He dismounted and stretched hisself and limped off toward the cabin. He neglected to hoist a pail of water out the well for me. Mac, he weren't never an unkind humano, but he were goddamn absentminded. Me, I gazed down the well a stretch and smelled the water and got vexed, then went for a sniff around the stable to check for a forgotten pail or green herbage. The roof had been tore off and the timbers was smoking, but fresh horse shit steamed from a pile up to my shoulder, so equines had been lately present, and now be starting new careers as Indian ponies.

I heard Mac clattering about in the cabin and I dawdled round front to see what he was about. Hey Rab. We've struck it rich! Bottles of intoxicants was hugged to his chest, chinking together, and if there is a sound what betokens future merriment to a humano, that'd be it. He leans on me and un-toggles a saddlebag and packs them in. These'll see us through till Denver, Rab, he says, and goes back for more. I feel the heft of them. Like I said, he weren't never the acme of empathy.

Twere then my saviour comes.

Two

I t were a good bit in their peripherals, but my highly refined optics saw the earth move, saw it twist and rise. Maybe the Comanche was right after all and we'd found the spot where the buffalo sprouted out the depths and I was being humbled for doubting their religion. But that hole weren't big enough to shove a greased hog through, lay aside a full-growed buffalo, his beard and pickle-jar knees. Maybe a giant worm, and I couldn't picture no giant worm being friendly disposed.

Humano arms and hands appeared. They held that mushroom of earth aloft and tossed it aside. The limbs disappeared an instant, then the twin barrels of shotgun poked forth, them prior hands holding the operational end. A bonnet followed, crumpled and printed with daisies. The headgear was maintained in location by a head of the female variety I guessed, albeit at this juncture in my earthly I weren't placing no bets on it. The female, if that what she was, propped her elbows on the dirt and squints down the barrels.

Mac, him stowing away intoxicants, remained unaware.

You mind telling me why you is making free with my ardent spirits? The voice of a woman, the timbre of which puts me in mind of a stone in a paint can shook about.

Mac drops a bottle. It falls onto his bad foot and makes a donk noise. The impact occasions him to howl and hop on the good foot. He bends and rubs the foot now glowing red as that branding iron, and I swear I see it pulse. At these events, the woman neither moves, nor allows the level of that shotgun to fall. Mac composes hisself and turns slowly. He has the Coltses holstered, and I see his fingers twitch.

You go for that sidearm mister and you and that sawed-off nag's innards will be spraying the plains.

Sawed-off nag? Goddamnit. And why you dragging me into this?

Now you'll oblige me by unbuckling that pistol and letting it fall, and I'd advise avoiding your poorly foot. Meantime you'll maintain your hands in clear vison. Otherwise this shotgun is liable to go off. It's an old piece and my man is short on gunsmithing.

Mac did as he was bid, and spread his arms and held the palms out. Forgive me madam, is his opening gambit. I thought the post deserted, what with the hostiles rampaging about and us not seeing a single stage during our journey. I therefore concluded the service was suspended. That Cornishman would have had a word for this manner of speech. Oleaginous. That'd be it.

The woman, she rejoindered with, You deprived of olfactory faculty?

Madam?

You can't smell horseshit? Why'd there be all these fresh turds laying about if we wasn't still in business. She began to pry herself out the hole. We just deposited ourselves in this sanctuary here till those Cheyenne boys wearied of their pillaging. Doesn't give you the right to be making free with our ardent spirits.

Keeping one hand on the shotgun, she gathered up her skirts for the final push. You saw a bare knee in the dirt, a long boot with them tiny buttons. I heard Mac say, Jee-sus. To complete the disinterment she pushed herself up on the butt of that shotgun, head well clear of the business end. Mac took off his hat, spat on his hand and smoothed down the copper hair, detached a flake of old blister off his face. If it weren't for that prior instruction to keep the hands in full view, he'd have been delving for the Sozodont.

She was standing tall now, legs apart, that shotgun hoisted on wiry arms what looked in no danger of giving way. She said, State your business here, if it was not to rob me and mine. She pushed a strand of hair out of her eyes, and I'd never seen a humano face set so stern, and if she was so minded she could have embarked right then on a career as a funeral preacher, supposing females was permitted to enter that profession.

Mac opened his flytrap to speak, but a kerfuffle issued from the hole and curtailed the nascent locution. Another head popped up. This example was of the male variety, a beaver-toothed example, although lacking that creature's whiskers, contenting itself with bushy mutton chops what concealed the lugs and what'd be right delaying in the plains wind if you was mounted and attempting full chisel. The whiskers compensated for the upper portion of the head, disappointingly bare of headgear, and smooth as a river stone. The beaver teeth parted and it said in a penny-whistle voice, Is it safe to come out now, Stella?

Stella said, You can come out now Enoch, and a torso naked save for twin suspenders followed, a torso what recollected me of that hog washed-up on the Cornishman's erstwhile dam, albeit that hog weren't wearing no suspenders. Enoch's britches was attached to them suspenders, thank the Lord, and thenceforth a half-dozen more humano heads and bodies took their cue and clumb out, all of diminishing height and all stopple thin, the final example carrying an infant as big as itself and what commenced squawking. Far from the music halls Stella and Enoch had evidently found a way to entertain theirselves out on the blasted plains.

Stella gave the shotgun to Enoch, and went to pick up the pistol, Mac leering down as she did. She said, I'll be keeping this till you leave. Vaginated tother side of me was that Spencer which could have done some damage if Mac was minded. But by then I estimated him not the type.

Mac, he stated his business. Told her he was a miner on his way to the Nevada silver mines and had lost his companions and their waggon of moveables in a dreadful Indian attack perpetrated by fifty or so sneaky and cowardly heathens of the Cheyenne, Arapaho and Sioux nations combined and had been grievously injured in the foot but had managed to escape and was proceeding on alone in terror of another attack and with scarce a bite to quell his protesting stomach since, Ma'am, the oleaginy lubricating the tale.

The woman rubbed her chin and said, Mister, you tell a colourful tale, and in a strange accent to boot. You should embark on a career writing dime novels, make yourself a fortune. She shouted back, Enoch, I figure this specimen harmless enough. Go ahead and un-cock the fowling piece.

Mac and Stella then jabbered a stretch, exchanging reports and forecasts on hostile activities, her preacher face slackening off as they conversed. Enoch watched on. Them kids started to poke each other. Mac restituted the bottles and Stella invited him to share their evening repast. I calculate that she calculated an unarmed, short-arsed, blister-faced Scotsman reduced to one leg presented but little danger, and it'd be handy to have another shootist around if the Indians came back.

Mac said, well I'm obliged to you ma'am, and to you Enoch. You are fine people. Stella said, Thank you for the obsequies, but you'd best water that nag of yours if you don't want it to give out on you tomorrow.

I can't supply many further particulars of this visit. Yours truly, I was left standing there with my tail up my arse until a shaver come out and led me round back and gave me a further bucket of water, a clump of herbage and a kick up the rear end. Some shavers is like that. So I was deprived of the conviviality, and you'll just have to use your imagination to conjure their gay discourse and

Mac's roving eyes. That's the downside to being an equine, you ain't deemed worthy of such cordialities, although doubtless were I present I'd have made a hurra's nest of the dinner table and its condiments. The upside, I guess, is you don't have to keep no posterior disbursements corked up.

I didn't think he would, but Mac plumped to pernoctate, I estimate him preferring further survey of Stella's mammiferous topography over mileage from the US Seventh Cavalry. But he finished bedded out in the roofless stable adjacent to yours truly, an accommodation he got depressed about, Enoch chucking an extra blanket in his direction, and I figure by then that latter done clocked the leers. He apologised, but said there just weren't enough room inside what with all the kids. After he bid us goodnight, Enoch paused and placed a hand on my shoulder, where that bastard done branded me, and rubbed at the wallow mud.

Enoch. It just smote me now. He were the one the Lord took in them antediluvian days when the giants was knocking about, not even a fare-ye-well to the missus.

YOU KNOW RAB, now that was a fine woman. A fine woman. Why can't I find masel a female like that. I find a female like that, I'll settle down. Stop drinking and gallivanting. How'd that beaver-toothed baldy managed to land her, Rab? Now my Molly, she were a fine woman, but she lacked the adventurous spirit and wouldnae accompany me across the big ocean. Mind you, I got a wee roll in the heather out of her as a fond farewell, so I suppose I shouldnae complain, eh Rab. Aye, a fine woman was Mollie, knew her since she was a lassie, and they all said we'd wed, us being such a handsome pair. But you cannae live on fresh air and fine scenery, can ye Rab.

He'd been going on in such vein all morning, Jesus, ever since they said their goodbyes at the stage station. I reckon Stella'd doctored his foot up some, being he was walking easier. Enoch went off to attend to a distressed pig, and with all the shavers watching on Mac said, I dinnae suppose I can cajole a wee kiss on the cheek out of a beautiful lady this fine morning? Half an hour's time I might be lying on the scorched prairie bristling with arrows.

Stella's face softened and she approached. She were devoid of headgear and the wind was blowing the hair about her face and if you was of them inclinations you might say she were right easy on the optic nerve, albeit you'd have to be partial to knobby joints and sinew. Mac closed his eyes and puckered up. Stella grabbed his cheek and pinched it, though it couldn't have got no redder.

Nae, wee man. Ye cannae, she said. First off, I'd have to send Ulysses there to get a box for you to stand on. Mister, I enjoyed the twinkle in your eye, and your tall stories more than make up for your short stature. You probably play the banjo for all I know and I expect you'd be entertaining company if we were ever snowed in. But I am a respectable woman. You have to stick with the life you made for yourself, better or worse. At this juncture she cast an eye in the direction of the squealing pig.

Mac climbed aboard, tipped his hat and set it to a jocund angle. To the next life then, Stella, he said, and we toddled off, the wind whisking her dress, Stella looking out from under her eyes, an awry smile trailing us.

I AIN'T MENTIONED Mac's headgear. That is remiss. Weren't no sombrero, but it owned a wide flat brim downturned at the front, him needing that brim complected as he was, and a tall stiff crown with a kind of ravine running down the domed centre. No band. Colour of Stella's knee it was.

Dawdling along, Mac offered various conjectures of vulgar cast, which I won't recount here, pertaining to the dimension of Enoch's privy member and it being the only likely reason to account for his successful wooing of such an exquisite woman. He referred to the appendage as, Enoch's knob, what elicited a roaring laugh. Well good for him.

All the time them snow-capped sierras was growing bigger, putting me in mind of a foam-crested wave about to engulf the plain, of the Lord's deluge what induced old Noah to invent intoxicating liquors. That's what it must have looked like back then, the Lord's great waves sweeping over the land, annihilating the giants, all the creation he got wrong first time round and regretted and had to start again.

Mac prattling on, I got my legs to maintain forward motion and got in some shut eye. I calculated danger of aboriginal attack to be fading now. We was then close to a town called Denver, and them current denizens' policy to the former denizens was shoot-on-sight. I know it was called Denver because one day we passed a wooden sign and Mac said, Look Rab, Denver.

I took to Denver right off. It captured the embranglements of life in true perspective. The first institution you encountered when entering were the graveyard. A brace of hombres was engaged therein in dispensing funerary sacraments. One had hold of the ankles, the other the wrists, and they had worked the deceased into pendulum motion. On three, one said, and on three they both let go and the deceased arced into the grave. A stubborn foot lay hooked onto the edge, so they kicked that in and sundry prior excavations to boot, wordplay intended, and got to work with the shovels. Wonder who he was, Rab, said Mac. Following on from graveyard were the garbage dump, and ripening up good it was too, the snows now all melted, a limpid sky and a souther blowing.

Denver weren't no city like that burgeoning example back on the Mississippi, albeit all them construction materials dumped roundabout you could see they was aspiring. I'd say the most notable aspect to it was that most of the buildings was made of stuck-together bricks, and yet you saw all that timber bristling the hills yonder. Sure, shacks and shanties was sprinkled about, carpentered store fronts, but the brick examples held the majority, and I figured the citizens wasn't fixing to up-sticks no time soon and itinerate off after the buffalo.

Mac ticked them off as we passed by: saloon, tailor, tinsmith, eating house, pharmaceutical emporium, saloon, meat market, land office, saloon, print shop, hotel, flour mill, brewery, insurance broker, grocery, saloon, saddlery, church, newspaper office, saloon. Straight lines, they was already present, them edifices all laid out in neat rows, and I calculated Denver weren't going to be a city with no dearth of corners to play a banjo at, though they wasn't all painted white, least not yet.

We fetched up at a crossroads, on one corner a bank, on tother a lawyer office.

The builder of the bank had fitted round-headed windows, stone pillars flanking double doors you had to climb stone steps to get at, above, another arch and carved in stone therein a shaggy-headed panther like I never saw before standing on its hind legs. I guess he wanted to convey it a secure place to deposit the product of your subterranean moil. Relax. We got goddamn exotic panther over our door. Ain't nobody going to mess with that, and the emolliented barbered bespectacled men presiding in such a fine edifice, well if you can't put your faith in them who can you? They ain't likely to be a bunch of chisellers thimbleriggers, fragglers and picaroons. Are they.

The lawyer's office, it was bestowed of a glass window and calligraphy had been applied thereon. Mac read it out.

Thaddeus M. Spurgeon.
Attorney at Law.
Honest and fair treatment guaranteed
Partiality is our watchword
The Lawyer is your friend
Put your trust in him

Mac looked back and forth between the two buildings a number of times then let air out of his lungs and said, Jesus Rab, it's all fucked now.

We was in the hereabouts of the river by then, and them whites, despite all the enterprise, had yet to subdue that natural feature. Such had been its late inundations, the street suggested a buffalo wallow of many and frisky visitations. It was lucky them buildings was elevated and furnished with a raised boardwalk, otherwise the whites'd have been haggling and dickering with their ankles plugged in mud.

Sufficient whites was hurrying about nonetheless, and planks was laid across the mire to expedite it, but few risked that rude carpentry, laying aside sporting shavers. They was leaping off the planks up to their thighs. Tiring of that, they propelled gobbets of mud at the hurryers. One aimed a shot at a preacher in a frock coat and knocked his hat off, got hauled off by the ear for it. Lucky for him it weren't the Old Testament days or the Lord would have sent a bunch of grizzlies to devour him and his pals like he done to revenge old Elisha.

I felt Mac come slack in the saddle. He said, You know Rab, I've got a hell of a thirst on me.

He wheeled me around and we departed the mire for a livery yonder. Presiding was a single-toothed fellow of short stature and puppy belly, bald bar for two saddlebags of hair flanking his shiny crown he kept in middling condition. He didn't appear to own no overshirt being he wore two undershirts. I won't mither to describe this individual further. He ain't germane to the narrative and I don't know why I gone this far.

Mac gave him a couple of coins and said, I know he dinnae look much, but you look after this lad. He has served me well. Mac turned to me and I noticed his blisters was clearing and I saw his face were fernytickled with dots the size of blood-swoll ticks, colour of fresh-cut straw, a day dried. They congregated around the bridge of his nose, although outliers had decamped below the cheekbones. I had seen their ilk once before, but couldn't recollect where.

Mac grabs an ear and says, Now Rab, I'm just off to take a few of them fancy cobblers and play a hand of cards, win us a wee grubsteak. Dinnae do anything I wouldnae do. I knew by then that last behest left a degree of latitude on the scruples side. He took a swig of Sozodont, fitted the bottle into his hip pocket and slapped my rear end. It were two nights and a day before I saw him again.

Cockshut of the next day, yours truly making inroads into a bucket of tolerable oats, albeit I'd have preferred the spring grass, the single-toothed fellow telling me about his widely distributed offspring who considered him an idiot, I heard a bunch of equines clomping by. Due to the boarded carpentry and my location, my highly refined optics was unable to identify the clompers, so I pressed my lugs into duty and directed them rearwards and away from the dynastic history. Iron-shod hooves clicked and tack jangled and accouterments rattled and sullen horses snorted deject-edly. Nobody makes a racket like a goddamn bunch of cavalry.

MIDDLE OF THE NEXT DAY, me thinking on the mudslide-bellied boy and recollecting he were similarly befreckled and wondering how he was making out with the Comanche, the other set of freckles showed up. By the look of him Mac'd overdone them cobblers, whatever they was. Glassy-eyed, puff-faced, hair what looked like it had been tousled and twirled and tweaked by a succession of greasy-fingered females, shirt buttons fastened askew, likewise those of his pantaloons, and his hat was absent. You got the picture. His knuckles was all bloodied up to boot, though his face scarce showed a fresh mark.

He took a circuitous route toward me, like he wanted to delay the moment of arrival. Off yonder a tall man with a thin mous-tache and a bootlace tie stood waiting. He wore a flat-crowned flat-brimmed hat, and at the sight of it my heart thudded and my foot kicked out and sent splinters flying and I whinnied some. I couldn't see them particular items, but I guess my eyes was rolling too.

Mac come over directly then. Hey lad, what's got into you, he said. I told you I'd be back. He reached up and rubbed my ears. Tears was in his eyes. He started slowly.

I have a wee confession to make lad. He stops rubbing my ears, rubs his copper hair instead. I was on a real good run. You never seen aught like it. I'd been winning all night, and the currency, it was piling up all around. Then I lost some, thought I'd play one last hand and call it quits for the night. I was dealt two pair. Two pair, Rab. Queens and nines. And then I drew another queen. Can you imagine that Rab. Prile of queens, a pair of nines. Jesus, you get a hand like that maybe thrice a lifetime. What I'm trying to say is, you'd have done it too lad. It would have set us up, both of us. I could have bought us a piece of land, built you a nice wee stable, imagine that. I had to do it Rab. The pot was piling up and I was out of cash and I had to do it. I'd never got another chance like that. He is blubbering now, so much he can scarce enunciate.

Now you can imagine, I ain't getting the complete purport of all this display, being no card player and all. All I know is he perpetrated some act what ain't propitious to my future prospects, and that act that connects to the hombre in the flat-crowned flat-brimmed hat waiting yonder. I dare to raise my head to see if he is wearing a conchoed belt, but the stall is blocking the view.

I'm sorry Rab, he says, and rubs my ears again. He turns and nods to the man in the hat.

Now that speech had held me so rapt, and what with the man in the flat-crowned flat-brimmed hat bringing the panic on, my ears never heard the other'n arrive. He is standing behind Mac now, and as Mac turns to go I hear a swish followed by a clang, and recognize them combined phonics as the swing of a shit shovel interrupted by flesh and bone and gristle of human physiognomy.

Mac's head jolts backwards, but the rest of him delays and his feet fly into the air to compensate. His shoulders hit dirt and I hear a clunk as the head does. His nose, what formerly possessed a dainty upturned character ill-fitted to its proprietor, is now mashed across his face in a mess of blood. His mouth lolls open and a see a couple of teeth missing, a brace more at a curious angle, and I ponder the dentifrical powers of Sozodont, and whether they will be up to the task.

The sergeant stands over him, cap pushed back so he can better see his handiwork. He bends over and bellows, Mac now being hard of hearing in his unconscious state I guess, You goddamn sign up for five years with the Seventh United States Cavalry, you goddamn do your goddamn five years with the Seventh United States Cavalry. You goddamn son of a bitch.

As he bellows he sprays Mac with spit, and I notice his locution is now accompanied by a whistle, both new features by dint of his own lately removed dontics. He stands over Mac, bracketed-arms swinging, fists clenched, his mouth working but silent, frustrated I figure at Mac's deafened state. He fetches Mac a good kick in the clackerbag and yells off into darkness, Get this sack of Scotch shit out of here, and a trio of troopers appear rubbing the backs of their necks.

Now I don't know if the man in the flat-crowned flat-brimmed hat was the same horse combuster what near sent me under them days since. From my earthly observations I do know that certain styles of hat are predilected by certain styles of character, and I never met an occupant of that type wherein the milk of human kindness abided. But then again, maybe I just ain't met enough. Anyhow, I looked up, and he done vanished.

THREE

E arly in the pm, the sun burning to wilt the flowers, and we was back on the blasted plain retracing our trail. Mac, he was folded over me, belly where arse should reside, although he'd regained some wits by then and begun salty remonstrations. We dawdled along, them troopers disinclined to hurry back to the fort and resume chasing Indians, and it weren't until the next afternoon that we paused at the stage station for respite and a refresco.

They'd allowed Mac to sit up in the saddle by then, and with his spread nose and concave mouth he looked a poorly sight. Stella came and looked him over. She said, Well mister, you sure are prone to personal injury. Mac kept his eyes downcast and the oleaginous speech corked. She carried an axe. Blood stained the blade, and on a stump yonder lay the head of a rooster, the rest of it at locations unknown. Enoch, he lingered by the stable, feigning the repair of an undamaged wheel hub. He fired a sly nod at the sergeant, what got reciprocated.

Stella said, Looks like he's been subject to some rough treatment Sergeant, an edge in her voice, the funeral preacher face back.

Yes Ma'am, said the sergeant, and he should count himself lucky. There's some as'd shot him.

Stella said, You object if I doctor him up some?

Yes ma'am. I believe I do.

Then I believe my bar is no longer open for business.

AIN'T MUCH MORE to report apropos this excursion. The Lord sent us one of his deluges and the sergeant refused Mac a slicker. He dies of pneumonia, be good riddance to bad rubbish, he said. Lightning forked the plain so frequent a permanent glow dwelt roundabout, despite the sun blotted, and a smell of burning infused the ether. It thundered in a continuous roar like we was located in the midst of a waterfall, and you looked about and such we were, the air comprised more of agua than aught breathable, and come a point I wished I were one of the fishes of the sea.

Nearing the fort, the sergeant clocked one of the troopers what had been sent out to catch the deserter had hisself deserted. Nobody had seen him go so they couldn't say exactly when he'd absquatulated, and they couldn't divide the force to go look what with hostiles in circulation. That sergeant, he quirted Mac in the face for it, an act I considered unwarranted being Mac weren't no paradigm of desertion worth emulating. For the remainder of the trip the sergeant contented hisself with muttering malediction, which appeared to assuage his wrath not an jot.

The creek had bust its banks, and the white tents, they was all dishrags, and what troopers as was wandering about was up to their knees in the mire, what sure stymied marching about in squares. They threw Mac in a squat stone building they called the guardhouse. I heard the splash as he landed, and didn't see him till a good few days after.

They give me a new jockey, Buster, him of the rocky locution who'd applied his palms to Mac's arse cheeks that first day. His speech were the goddamnedest thing. How can I express it. It were constructed of a rapid pap-pap-pap-pap-pap. Imagine ambush gunfire, the attackers profligate with ammunition. Maybe like the speech was constructed in a line of pointed rocks is better, but the hardness of it softened by the cadence, what went up and down in a sing-song. Anyhow, weren't no English that I recognised.

I guess I ought supply a description of that humano, albeit this renewed acquaintance were to be another of the truncated variety. He were a good bit taller than Mac, but weighed a good bit less. He was surmounted by a glossy slab of tar-coloured hair devoid of undulation. His face, it commenced at an infundibular chin, its form attenuated by coulee cheeks what rose to high cheekbone bluffs. Facial hair were scant, eked out to a thin moustache located a good bit distant from the nostrils. At a glance you'd think it charcoaled on, but it were indeed bristles and must have took some time to barber. His other features was unremarkable, including them windows into the soul what the Lord provided in his wisdom. The curiousest aspect to his lineaments was his eyebrows. These wasn't curved like the standard examples but was straight as fence posts and was permanently wigwamed upwards, imparting a look, how can I express it? Dejected embranglement, that will have to do her. So I guess it was them features taking duty as soul windows, for such was his character. He sported a domed turd-coloured hat of medium brim and no distinguishing features.

Now obviously, I would know nothing about that man's character if it was left to his vocables. I only recollect a smattering what cropped up frequent, my noggin being chock full of Comanche and Taibo words by then with no room for more, unless they was fancy examples. Vafanculo were one. Kay cadzo? That were a frequent interrogative. He could make hisself understood English-wise to his comrades apropos the basics, and he got them goddamn bugle toots nailed to a tee.

We was sent out chasing Indians again, although we never cocked an eye on no particular example to give chase to. When we got back Mac was mounted anew, but it weren't on no armchair swayback. They called it the Spanish Donkey, although it bore no resemblance to that latter beast, and I never did cipher the Spanish part to it. Two boards fastened together to form a downturned vee were its contrivance, picture them tiny tents but of a more severe inclination, a quartet of legs affixed to the boards to supply further elevation and prevent feet from touching the ground. You humanos'd never perceive it, but I smelled the blood atwixt Mac's legs. I calculated it a contraption to garner plaudits from the Comanche, and had they the lumber and the carpentry acumen they'd have knocked up a few examples for sure, and got a few Texans mounted.

Mac's head was hanging but I could see the hollowed cheeks and I pictured the gritted teeth, them as was left. As we jangled past he looked up. He rasped, Rab, my wee laddie, and the head fell back to his chest.

An officer strode up to him. I'd seen this individual about the fort, pernicketied up and yapping out commands in the euphonics of a pampered lapdog. He carried a cane, that officer. He weren't no cripple, and that cane possessed no propping function, slender as it was and of insufficient length, but like I said in the heretofore, gubernatorial types got to have their affectations. Anyhow, he strode up to Mac, us all watching on, and called him a, Goddamn craven coward, which I considered tautological construction, but that ain't the point. Mac raised his head to offer riposte, and the officer struck him across the face with that cane, the crack echoing around the low buildings. Our jockeys, they all turned their heads and looked away.

WE PASSED the summer chasing Indians about the west Kansas plains, sometimes as far west as the headwaters of the Smoky Hill. As implied in the hereunto, we rarely saw any actual Indians, even though the scouts was on a hundred-dollar bonus if they located an Indian village for us to massacre, and I guess the Seventh was short of aboriginal trackers back then to get the job done right. In all that time I recall only one shot fired in anger, and that example missed its intended target, the embarrassing part to it that boy was flaunting hisself close range trying to draw fire so as to show off his bullet-deflecting medicine.

Reports was always coming in of the Cheyenne and Arapaho and Sioux nations raiding a farmstead, firing a few shots and scaring the poultry, making off with beasts of the field. Sometimes a settler or railroad worker got shot, a captive or three carried off, a female subjected to lewd conduct. Now I weren't present personally to witness these incidents and so cannot testify to their veracity or otherwise, but I will say this. Them settlers and railroad men was trying to shove the Indians off all that land they was squandering so they could monetize the hell out of it theirselves. That's all I'm saying.

Now you can wax on all you like about acts of combustion and rapine and bovine kidnap perpetrated back then, but you weigh it all out, I'd say in general the American Indigene was over accommodating to the shoving whites. But could be the Comanche in me talking.

To get back to the point, I can't supply no escapades or adventures to entertain you, unless you count talking to disgruntled farmers an adventure, although throughout my earthly I never met a member of that species that weren't disgruntled and I often pondered why they took up the life. I guess I could describe the plains for you, but I believe I have already done that to surfeit. I expect I could make something up. But ain't nothing in this narrative made up.

You is wondering what became of my erstwhile jockey. Well after he got tortured and done his time in the jailhouse, I guess his hindquarters weren't in no condition to bounce on no equine, so Mac was put on what the US Cavalry called fatigue duty. Fatigue duty is so nominated because after performing them duties you is apt to feel fatigued. Digging latrines, emptying latrines, digging up clumps of prairie and building sod shacks, scraping the grass off the prairie and heaping up stones to build roads, painting stones white to demarcate roads, digging latrines, chopping timber for lumber and fuel, collecting buffalo chips for that latter purpose because no trees was about, painting carpentry white, digging latrines. The sort of labour the Comanche'd give to slaves, although I never saw no Comanche avail hisself of a latrine nor enter no sod house, unless to perpetrate bloodshed.

I'll say one thing for that Scotsman, he went about them labours cheerful as a canine with a string of sausages. I guess you would call Mac one of life's optimists, believing whatever the current miseries, things was sure to improve, notwithstanding mounting evidence to the contrary. A bit like religion I guess.

I'll supply an example. Late that summer, we was trudging back in from some patrol, and even my highly refined optics couldn't figure it. At first I saw some globular cactus done took root in the parade ground. But it were Mac's head sprouting out, and I estimated him having engaged in further contumacious conduct. He appeared none too discountenanced by the interment and as we passed by his head it called out, Hey there Rab, how you doing? Hope that Eye-talian is taking care of you. You take damned good care of that horse, Buster. You hear? He'll save your life one of these days.

You guessed it. He'd absconded hisself anew, took a mule and headed off hesperian-wise. By God but that Caledonian was undiscourageable. That mule though, couple of hours from camp he'd planted his hooves and decided that were it, like they is apt, he weren't progressing no further, and Mac weren't the type to apply a fustigation. I never obtained no confirmatory evidence, but that intractability were typical of the bane of my life during them days.

I imagine you is expecting me to fill in a few curiosities about everyday life in a US Cavalry camp back in them days long departed.

Us nags, we was kept tied to rope laid out in a straight line, goddamn nose bags suspended come chow time. If aboriginals was guaranteed distant, maybe they'd picket us out on the prairie and we'd chaw a perfect circle of grass. But we was always attached to some object. Back in them days horses was to Indians what Delilah was to old Samson. Samson, he was a holy man and he couldn't resist, and neither could the Indians. At the risk of flogging this analogue to death, they done brought the house crashing down on top of theirselves to boot.

Sometimes the troopers mounted up and marched us equines about in squares. We did this generally when the dirty-mouthed moth-moustached officer were in residence at the fort, him now present more frequent what with the Indians in a rising state of indignation, though no Indian I ever knew got demoralized by obscene speech, them being well versed in such arts theirselves. That officer, turned out he was a big general. The troopers, they called him Little Phil.

The band might provide musical accompaniment to our marching, and I believe we was expected to keep some kind of rhythm to the whistles and toots and bangings, though I never got the hang of it myself. The troopers, they all polished up their buttons and buckles and the like to the extent they could have doubled for signalling purposes. They even shined the leatherwork up, belts and straps and cartridge boxes, and that lapdog officer demanded that the cartridges within them boxes was shined-up too. Even took a look inside to check. Jesus. Could be they is more accurate if they is shiny.

Me, I never comprehended what such primping and marching activities had to do with our mission of exterminating indigenes. The Comanche seeing it, well they'd have tossed dust in the air and laughed theirselves silly. But they got whipped by the end. So shows how much they knew. I cyphered it down to the bald fact them generals thought it looked right pretty when we marched out the fort in them squares of fours, and on the battlefield them neat squares advancing slowly upon the enemy must have made a great spectacle, if you is observing from a hilltop.

More soldiers was deserting, them usually waiting till after payday, and if you think I am exaggerating their dedication to this pursuit then you best go drink some black coffee and consult the history books. You have to remember most of them boys was what they called the dregs of society. Recall that unshod gunny-sack-clad shaver what stole Ahithophel's fruit knife? Well he were the exemplar. Others was from foreign parts, and might have been Friedrich Von Schlegel hisself, whoever he was, but they couldn't speak the lingo so they was buggered. I believe others was outlaws on the run, but I can't prove it.

What I'm saying is them boys didn't join up with no noble ideas of expediting the white's destiny of turning the plains into folding currency. Them dregs, they joined up to get fed, shod and sheltered, to learn the lingo, get a ticket out west, and when they done got what they wanted, they absquatulated theirselves.

Neither were desertion prompted by terror of aboriginal arrow and war club. You was more likely to die from the inclemencies or a rattlesnake bite or the squirts or a surfeit of Baldface. A few took to the life, mainly them fleeing lives of destitution. Okay, cavalry grub weren't up to much, but they got enough pay they could get theirselves wistful at the groggery and copulate with a whore. There is worse lives for a humano to live. I heard one fellow tell Buster that he never took a bath until he joined the US Cavalry, although going by the olfactive coming off of him I'd say he'd not enamoured hisself of the habit. Buster he said, Say un myalay sporco. And no good you looking that up in no dictionary of Italian words. I done rendered it phonetically.

Black soldiers was knocking about, and they'd lived the destitutest lives of all, but as to whether they was similarly inclined to abscond I can offer no comment. Our bunch kept well clear of that bunch, in actuality the officers camped us on opposite sides of the creek, and no few insults was lobbed over, mainly originating from them what had fought in the big slaughter back east in gray uniforms. A shanty town they called a city was located nearby. I only passed through once, but you never saw such a municipality of gougers, fragglers, freebooters, hornswogglers, honey fugglers and betrumpers, and they was the acme of the citizens. But that was where the fun was, and was where the black and white troopers come together, and where scores got settled.

One day I shucked-out my picket pin and strolled over to the river for a drink and change of herbage. On the opposite bank a black boy was fishing and, goddamnit, he shouted across at me. Hey there horse. Hey there horse. You know me.

I was occupied chawing on a clump of herbage at the time so I oriented my auricular receptacles in his direction. Curiosity got the better of me and I added an optic. Hey there horse. Remember me? You want an apple? I got an apple.

An apple. I raised my head and emitted a nicker. He launched it across, There you go horse.

I did know him. It was Pervis my de-ballocker, in a blue uniform and a canted forage cap. He done achieved his ambition.

The apple plunked in mud, but made no difference to me. An apple is an apple and I soon slavered off them alluvials. Ain't you a fine horse, Pervis said. Always said so. I sure am sorry I cut your balls off. I wish I got me a fine horse like you. They give me a scrub. Barely raise a canter. I've a mind to swim over there and come get you, take you for my own. Can you swim horse? You a good swimmer?

Can I swim. Jesus.

What they named you fine horse? Me, I'd call you Flash. I know you is fly and windy. Bet you could tell me some tales.

I don't know why, maybe it is some aspect of my mien, but throughout my earthly it were always them dregs what could read my former life, see the mustang and Indian in me. I estimate Pervis now figured the blandishments and the apple a fine trade for the use of my lugs, what he presumed was listening, and he uncorked them hereunto mentioned aquifers.

He pointed to a plum-coloured bruise on the upper part of his cheek. Got beat up the other night. You believe that? Beat up, by God. How can it be? You tell me. How can it be we is out here chasing their Indians for them, protecting their property, and they won't allow us into the saloon to wash the dust out our gullets. He was staring on off at the tip of his fishing pole, which remained motionless.

He was quiet for a spell. Then he said, You know horse, I sure do miss my ma. Oh Jesus, here it comes. He said, It hurts something terrible, down here in my gut.

Well, it all come pouring out, them bedtime stories and the smell of her clothes when she hugged him tight, the little swing they had in the yard where she rocked him back and forth when a shaver, singsongs around the stove, the castrated granddaddy sat on the rocking chair picking on a banjo, him finding it easy to cross his legs I guess, even the whippings was related with fondness, and going by the inventory of delicious repasts, the ma was George Crum hisself.

Sure enough, them ocular lubrications welled up and coursed down his cheeks, the chup-chuppin kicked in, and he dropped his fishing pole in the grass, whereupon he got a bite, and the pole and line got drug into the creek, not that he noticed through them obfuscated eyes. Me, well the apple was long gone by then, and Pervis didn't appear in possession of more such items, so I got my head down and relocated the herbage.

I HAVE one final curiosity to report before we get back to the action, what I am sure you is all hankering for after this history lesson. A male humano proceeded about camp dressed as a female.

He wore a moss green dress and black hair stretched back and tied into a bun. He generally wore a gauzy shawl as headgear, to furnish disguise I venture, and it doubled as a veil obscuring the lower regions of his face. You could still trace out the contours of a considerable beak under there and when the light was right whiskers sprouting through the powder. He wore it, he told anybody who asked, due to an over sensitivity to the sun's rays what prompted pustules to bust forth.

Nobody paid him the slightest heed. In the end I bottomed it out I was the only one who clocked the peculiarity, me being fitted with the high-tuned olfactive apparatus to detect the particular stink what arises from a male and knowing he ain't done been de-ballocked like yours truly. All them troopers treated him like any other plank-chested strong-featured female of their acquaintance. With indifference and condescension.

He kept hisself to herself, performed female chores, laundered, swept the officer huts, polished knick-knacks, darned socks, and I believe him content with his life. He said his name was Mrs Cash and that he was a widow to a kindly man who'd met a tragic end, an end he could never speak of for fear of emotional collapse, although camp talk was it involved a Comanche and a picket pin.

One time when my jockey was off marching about in a square and showing his weapon to a lieutenant, Mrs Cash come over and shoved a sugar lump atwixt my choppers and curried me. He was right tender about it too, whispering up my nose and rubbing my ears. She said, What a pretty horse you are, though I doubted his opinion on such matters, him being no paradigm of beautification herself. For reasons unknown he was ingratiating hisself. Maybe like Pervis he saw some kind of kindred spirit in me. I can't say why, and humanos have their whimsies. His voice, well he must have practiced hard, being it were that of a female's right enough, although if you was possessed of the same refined auricular apparatus as me you'd detect the bass notes it were founded on. He'd clipped his nostril hairs real short, dusted his face with peach-coloured powder and wreathed his neck in a high collar, so you could scarce see that Adam's apple bobbing up and down.

Me, I never let on. She could have been male, female, or any of the stops between. As long as she showed up with sugar lumps and rubbed my ears, he could have been accoutered up like Lola Montez doing the spider dance. Maybe in a former life Mrs Cash'd been some kind of theatrical, and with such proficiencies and that high-toned locution he could have pulled off a career as a Cheyenne chief.

I know for a fact later in life Mrs Cash married a first sergeant of the US Seventh Cavalry, a bunioned, slack-bellied disciple of Bacchus, possessed of quick fists and a slow train of thought. So either he was in on it, or he was in for a big surprise come the wedding night and them preliminary fumbles.

I done detailing curiosities. One day in high summer come a big kerfuffle and we was out on the plains again.

Four

It barely gets dark that time of year out on the plains, and it seemed I'd only just commenced my shut eye when that goddamn trumpeter begun tooting and they accoutered us up and kicked into forwards motion. They didn't risk the Scotsman. He was bound to make another run for it once we was on the blasted plain. He was digging out a ditch when we left and he waved his hat and yelled, Rab! Rab! Don't you worry yasel. That Eye-talian is only keeping my seat warm. Best pals eh? Best pals.

Buster jabbered away, although his locution that morning consisted mainly of a single surly phrase, cadzo di merda. I don't figure it no benediction and I venture he were commenting on the inconsiderate hour of our departure. By the way he spat it out I don't advise you consult no dictionary of Italian words.

Mac told me one time how he got his name. Buster, that is.

I expect you are wondering how that Eye-talian came by his name, he said. I weren't. Buster, now that's a strange name to be giving a grown man, don't you think Rab. I had never considered the matter. All Italian males was called Buster for all I knew. It was when he first joined the troop, Mac went on. Everyone gets a good hazing when they first join, but he took it personally. Especially when we took him to that doctor who wasn't really a doctor who made him drink jalap for his hangover. It were the straw that broke the camel's back, and I tell you, he directed no few harsh phrases at us that time, between trips to the privy, flinging his arms about like he does, but the one word that stood out was, Basta. Basta, basta. Said it over and over. So it kind of stuck. Nae idea what it means. What do you make of that Rab?

Me, I made nothing of it. In actuality I come to learn the bona fide nomenclature of that fellow, and I estimate I were the only creature in the entire US Seventh Cavalry what did. Slow days out on the chase, or if he was brushing me and out of earshot of them others he'd slap his chest and say, My name is Fabridzio. Me kiamo Fabridzio. Capeesh? Fabridzio, capeesh? Well eventually it sunk in, though it made no difference to me. Fabridzio Capeesh, by God. In my entire earthly I never heard of another named likewise. Frenchmen included.

Now you can go off to some glum library and blow the dust off of the Seventh's Muster Rolls for them years, but you'd be wasting your time. You won't find no Fabridzio Capeesh, an upshot what might elicit from you a smirk and the ejaculation, Ahah! Got the bastard! Thenceforth you will proceed to doubt the veracity of my memoirs and the existence of the protagonists therein. But them thin-armed army clerks would have yapped out, State your name, and their reaction would have been akin to Abendego's turnip going full chisel suddenly confronted by a water-filled ditch. They might have got their quills around the Capeesh, but they'd never have arrived at that juncture, having already balked at the Fabridzio. So you best be looking for a Frank Smith, somebody of that ilk.

Course, Fabridzio Capeesh had give me a name back when Mac were interred. Trasandatino. Jesus. Don't exactly trip off the tongue does it, and if it has a meaning, I don't know it and not sure I'd want to. Still, on the bright side my tenure of it were but of short duration.

I believe that fellow to be birthed in the mountains or by an ocean. The blank grasslands and then endless skies disturbed that fellow's psychological equilibrium. When we was out chasing Indians his mouth was like a faucet set either full-on or full off. Following them blessed bouts of silence he'd gabble. Two things he repeated ad nauseum still lodge in my old noggin. Me mankano lay montanye. Well I estimated that appertained to mountains, being it akin to the Spanish for them topographies. The other thing he said was, Me manka eel maray, which I cyphered out as some encomium pertaining to his Ma.

Rare days he was in of good temper he sang songs, but not like you'd hear in the dancehall. Feegaro-Feegaro-Feeeeeeee-garo. That were one example. Let me whittle on it. Cherubino, alla vittoria. Alla gloria militar, were another. La donna ey mobilay. Yep, but that's me done, and he sang the songs in a voice redolent of mosquito whine on a sultry night.

I got bifurcated there by nomenclatural matters of them of the frivolous arts. The patrol. This was no small patrol we was going on. Big bunch of us there was, quartet of supply wagons in tow, teams of mules hauling, all the officers up on their nags, them latters prancing about showing off to us inferiors. A brace of Gatling guns and a howitzer headed the waggon train. They was for flaunting or exterminating purposes depending on the upcoming exigences. In actuality, they was only intending to take one Gatling along, and then somebody yelled out, Are we likely to meet any Comanche? We even took the band along, and I could hear their instruments clattering and clinking as we left camp, us in neat columns, four abreast.

Little Phil, he must have been suffering from the lumbago, being he never pried his back off his bed to see us off, though that bunch of baying canines in tow must a disturbed his slumbers somewhat. Indeed, I ought supply whenever a cavalry column set out in them days, a bunch of canines showed up and tagged along. To this day I don't know where they all came from.

We headed south, the sun just blistering up on our sinister side, the prairie birds tweeting, a coyote yipping off yonder, goddamn owl chorusing in. Fabridzio Capeesh stared about at the wind-scoured flats growling, Kay brutto, Kay brutto, and I figure him recollecting the mountainous regions of his homeland and finding the vastnesses discombobulating.

Turned out a general was leading our party, but a lesser example than Little Phil. I never did cipher out how they arranged these matters. He must have been scant on the equitatory side of things, either that or the Lord had struck him with haemorrhoids, because he rode along out front behind the scouts in a kind of stagecoach they called an ambulance, a sullen expression writ on his countenance.

We paddled through a bunch of creeks. We dusted through a bunch of dry creeks. Tom Custer, he went off with a trio of troopers and brought back a half-dozen buffalo tongues for him and his cronies to supper on. Come the day the land folded and bluffs rose up and I felt my body stiffen, my heart thudding and my knees quaking of a sudden. I know this country. It was around here that degenerate about abused me to death.

Fabridzio Capeesh, he feels that change in demeanour surge through me. He rubs my neck and utters felicitous words, Calmati Trasandatino, Calmati, bello. Ecco. He takes his canteen and pours water into his palm and leans forward. But that agua just falls away from my lips and waters the grass.

We top a swell and on the line of the horizon I see a bunch of elk grazing. Nobody else sees them, they is so distant, and something about that sight, what's existed since Noah's floodwaters drained off, calms my heart some. But them elk shift, and my eyes drift over to a line of cottonwoods marking the course of the Arkansas. Jesus. We is close to where that Indian worshipped the burning rock.

Now I am ashamed to admit, I kicked and shied at the sight of that river and my recollections, and for a minute Fabridzio

Capeesh struggled to hold me. A need to flee had seized me, and you know me by now, I ain't no panicker. It were the voice of that lapdog officer what brung me back to my wits.

You better get that nag of yours under control soldier, or you'll be digging latrines tonight.

Well I couldn't let that cane-toting bastard best me and land my jockey in dudgeon to boot. I dropped my head, and my jockey, he allowed it, and I plodded on, staring at the dirt like I done in that other life on the Llano, when I saved Looks At The Sky from the spirit Apache.

We struck the Arkansas, more sand than agua, and turned west a hair to follow it. My nostrils caught the odour of a big Indian camp, and I mean a real big. They must have been holding a convention. That olfactive drove off the nightmares crowding my mind. My peepers came into play, and that completed the cure.

I'LL SAY this for that bunch, unlike most Indians when the US Cavalry is appropinquating itself, they weren't attempting fleeing or ambush. It were the biggest Indian camp I ever saw in my earthly, and I'm including the example up on the Greasy Grass years hence when I became the only living survivor of the fight known as the Little Big Horn. Erected by a creek the whites called the Pawnee, countless tipis and wickiups bristled up afore us, and Tom Custer piped up and said the savages numbered 20,000 and you had to admire the rapidity of his tallying.

Off yonder was tipi-sized scorch marks. A general had come through the year previous and burned a village, but an Indian ain't one to quit lightly on an ancient and munificent camping ground. I forget the name of that general now, but it weren't Little Phil or the current example. Custer were involved somewhere along the line, but he weren't the boss of it. Had the male privy member as a component of his cognomen did that general, what the troopers advantaged for aspersionary purposes. So could have been a Dickson or a Cockburn or a Johnson or some such. Look it up in some encyclopaedia of the plains wars. That'll tell you.

The lodges, they was all arranged in circles, according to families is usual, the doors all facing the sunrise. I don't know why, but the sight of them circles and the ponies picketed yonder emolliated my heart further. That instant I longed to be back with the Comanche, out in the waving grass with Looks At The Sky, her chiding me for some misdemeanour whereof I was blithe.

We didn't line up, wait for the toot and charge into that camp for massacring purposes. Reason being the camp was adjacent to a fort, and were that the strategy them occupants would have made a prior start so as to bag the glory. I knowed the name of that fort but it's another item from them days done faded. The degenerate shunned that fort. I'll say this for it, it knocked the Hays example into a cocked hat as an exhibition of the stone mason's art, and I noted one of them erections was a fancy six-sided affair, a shape what put me in mind of a prairie rose.

A thought nagged me like a blackfly evading my choppers on a sultry day. An Indian camp, a high summer's day like this, well it ought be a'buzzing with activity. The females should be fleshing hides and hauling firewood, the children sporting, splashing in the creek, firing blunt arrows, racing ponies. The males, well the males don't serve to sustain the point I'm trying to make here, but I didn't even see any of that persuasion standing about jawing, or hear a whoop when somebody won at gambling or wrestling.

A lone Indian was banging on a drum, and a right ponderous rhythm it were. Doom was the theme you'd extract out of it, and I wondered why his kin hadn't told him to knock it off. The crepuscular coming on, the Comanche by God, they'd have got a dance going by now.

The Cornishman'd have a supplied a fancy word for the ambience of this camp, but smothered is the best modifier I can supply.

In an effort to cypher it out I raised my muzzle and twitched my hairy nostrils, but no stink of sickness crept therein.

Then it smote me like Samson's donkey jawbone an uncircumcised Philistine. Where was the meat hanging to dry, the skins pegged out, the smell of roasting buffalo and boiling puppy dog? And looking on, scarce few of them canines was toddling about. They'd already done been et. By God. This crowd, they was short of their chuck. Fabridzio Capeesh, he said, Kay vista pietosa.

First thing the officers did was get the artillery hauled to a prominent spot and the business ends pointed toward them aboriginals. Talk was they had gathered at the fort to collect the rations promised them at the Medicine Lodge, what the whites called annuities, and they was in for bad news.

My bane, I ain't mentioned him for a good bit. He were between the shafts of the howitzer, and if I was to plump for one vocable to decoct that mule's disposition when in harness, it'd be aggrieved. As he trudged by he must have caught my stink, being his ears pricked up and he drug his head up to the horizontal and nickered a greeting. Could easy have been, Don't you wish you was back with the Comanche. I nodded in return, though I tried my damnedest not to.

All them myriads of aboriginals knocking about, I was hoping maybe to cock an eye on an old acquaintance. A Comanche, he can sniff out free grub a day's ride away. But I clocked nary a one and it was a Gatling gun wasted. They was probably off with the Kiowa at the feet of the Christ Bloods warring on the Ute, again.

Before I departed that Pawnee Creek, I saw a lone Kiowa female staring off west. She was chanting and shifting her weight from foot to foot to a rhythm unique to her head, that gaze never shifting. She'd took a knife and slashed her forearms, likewise the forehead, and I ventured that expeditionary force ain't done returned victorious.

THAT EVENING, a soft breeze, thunderheads boiling purple on the horizon, the officers fished the gold braid out their travelling chests and smacked the dust out. They shined up their boots and girded cummerbunds about their bellies, hoisted boxes of intoxicants and went chinking on down to the fort.

I'd prior seen a fazzle of furbelowed females bustling into a long building and, them not being of the aboriginal variety, I venture they was the incentive. The band struck up and you heard that polished footgear clattering on the wooden floor as they stepped out the beat, tinkle of polite laughter. The beverages kicked in and the steps become stomps, the tinkles whoops and shrieks, and the jollifications fingered out amongst the tipis, mingling with the thin smoke of them famished families' meagre fires.

That sullen general, he evidently weren't the sociable type. Maybe it were the haemorrhoids. He got his ambulance towed up a knoll where he could look out over the Indian camp and the river, on towards the Rockies and the cinnabar sun and the purple thunderheads, spokes of amber light radiating out. He must have considered it a sublime belvedere, being he got his striker to unfold a chair, got him to open a box and take out a wood frame akin to the fixture the bumbershooted prairie painter had. That general, he didn't own no umbrella, but he fetched out his brushes and got to daubing. He'd pause to gaze at the vista a spell to fix it in his eyes. Then he resumed. Sometimes he cocked his head and sucked on the end of the brush, the dry end.

You got to hand it the whites, how they can conjure the picturesque out of desperation. Slow times I wonder what he titled the piece, and if it is nailed to the wall of some gallery of fine art back east. Sunset of the Starving Savage. Yeah, that'd be a good one. It got alliteration to it. Or is it sibilance. I done forgot. Maybe I never knew.

WE WAITED for something to happen. Nothing did. The general and a retinue donned their best bib and tucker, trundled down to the fort for a parley with the indigenes. Being a nag yours truly weren't party to them discussions, so I cannot report their nature.

But I'd guess discussion were scanty and one-sided, like it or lump it comprising the peroration, and if the Indians was gloomily disposed before we showed up, soon it were beetled brows and downturned maws and bent shoulders galore. Weren't going to be no rations. You can't go off raiding the rustics and expect us to donate campaign rations and powder and shot to the enterprise. That'd be the gist of it, and I expect the chiefs deployed the bad-apples defence, but no sooner they got the news, the womenfolk started howling, wondering how they was going to feed the kids, and there ain't no sound on this earthly like a bunch of aboriginal women howling out despair.

Five

I ain't done yet with that camp on the Pawnee.

By God but them days was tedious. I was chawing on a bunch of bunchgrass, watching a quartet of boys polishing the artillery, that's how bad it was, when out the corner of a highly-refined optic I saw a pair of children leave the camp. I turned my head from them titivations and watched the children move on up the slope. The troopers, occupied as they was, and anyhow feeling secure in the possession of artillery in the face of primitives, never saw them, and even if they had, alarm would have been excessive reaction, that pair being shavers. Holding each other hands they was, and was taking a right circumambulatory route too, one stooping to pick prairie flowers and fixing them into a little bunch. But they always resumed their course, and soon it come evident the big gun was the destination they got in mind.

A bird sprang out of the grass and steepled up into the sky, spooling out a thread of song. They halted. They stared on after it and pointed, palming their brows, until it were a dot, until only the Here-I-am what-you-going-to-do-about-it song remained to signify it abided in that expanse of blue. Now, Indians is amenable

46

to signs from nature, and I suspect this pair interpreted that avian eruption as endorsement to proceed. Don't ask me why.

I recall being with Looks At The Sky one time up on one of them creeks what flow south into the Canadian. She nudged me, Look Brother, and pointed to where a panther slipped into a stand of timber. Course, being an equine, I'd clocked it long ago when that panther was mere riffles in the grass. Only a glimpse she had, a rare sight indeed, them felines being partial to their privacy, but it convinced that Indian she had been granted the magic of great stealth, and she spent the rest of the day experimenting it.

That magic made no difference that I saw, least not at first. She tried to sneak up belly-down up to a prairie dog town, but them vedettes clocked her right off and started yipping. The jackrabbits too was singularly unimpressed.

But she killed an otter, and you know how shy of humankind that creature is. Laying on the flat rock it were, sunning itself, licking body parts to which I wish my tongue enjoyed access. I believe Looks At The Sky scarce broke a blade of grass as she slunk along that creek bank. She lay watching it a stretch and then, with her eyes still fixed upon it, she raised her head real slow. That otter, well if it saw her it gave no sign, but I estimate by then she was invisible, that panther magic now kicking in. Naturally, she apologized to the otter.

Otter skin is real soft, and after she performed the necessaries, she cut it into strips, wrapped a strip around my halter where it rubbed across my cheek. You know I don't own no refined sensibilities, but the feel of it was right agreeable. The remainder, she wrapped strands of silver about it and wove it in her hair come special occasions.

Forgive my divarication there as a fine memory of that girl come bundling into my mind. Took the ginger out the episode I guess, but you'll just have to go with it.

Where was we. Them Cheyenne kids meandering on up that rise. When they was a decent arrow shot away, a polisher finally clocked them. A boy and a girl it were, stopple thin, and an exponent of the glockenspiel could easy have knocked out a ditty on them ribs. Age-wise, I'd estimate the older you could sit atop a pony going at a trot with no danger of it falling off. Fabridzio Capeesh said, Vedee Trasandatino, kay poveree sono. The polisher said, Hey fellas look at this. Best get that Gat loaded.

I believe now the remark was made in jest, but you can never be sure with the US military. Another fellow shouted up, Hey you kids, you go home now, you hear. This ain't no place for you. But that pair gave no sign of hearing, let alone understanding English, and they kept right on coming, although one dallied to chase a butterfly a spell.

Them troopers looked at each other. One shouted up, Lieutenant you best come look at this. They done eked out their initiative.

Turned out the lieutenant were Tom Custer, and he adjacentized hisself and stood tall and put on that gubernatorial voice and repeated the instruction to go home. Lest they be slow on the uptake he pointed in the direction of the Indian camp. But them Cheyenne children evidently weren't awestruck by bombast and slanty headgear, and soon they was at that weaponry and fingering them fresh-polished barrels and giving each other a leg-up to peer down the muzzle of the howitzer.

The troopers, notwithstanding all the finger marks on their burnishments, well they was grinning by now. My jockey extracted a piece of hardtack out his pack and held it out to the girl. Ecco bella. Prendeetela, but she weren't that hungry. The boy, he was back adjacent to the Gatling now. He shot a shifty glance at the trooper and reached up to pull on the crank.

Tom Custer said, Put a stop to that now trooper.

That trooper stepped forward and put a hand on the boy's shoulder. Right gentle about it he was, and I truly believe his only intent was to chivvy him away. But at that instant a wailing arises from the camp yonder, the origin of it a woman standing outside of her tipi, eyes gaping in our direction, pulling at her hair.

An infant cradled by the lodge choruses in, and a male stumbles out the tipi, glances up at us and races for his pony, a grey flecked with black like windblown embers. In the time it takes a humano to draw half a breath he leaps aboard and gets it in rapid motion.

The troopers, they go for their rifles, and Tom Custer, his facial features have composed theirselves into a smirk and he says, We got the nits. Here comes the goddamn louse. Remember boys, aim low, and squeeze them triggers.

He races on up that rise and I see that Cheyenne wears a buckskin shirt and leggings of the same. I see he wears no paint and bears no arms, saving a knife fixed to his hip, and he ain't whooping his war cry neither. I believe now it was the absence of them particulars what saved him.

Hold your fire. You let that buck come on now, men. Another officer had stole up behind to watch. He sported gray hair he affected to wear long, though he looked no older than Tom Custer. I reckon he were another of them telling Tom Custer what to do, being I see them trigger fingers relax, though the troopers glance at each to see if they is all doing it.

That Cheyenne ain't had time to fix his braids and his hair flames out behind. He larrups that pony right on up till it is almost clambering atop that polished ironmongery. The pony don't complain as he pulls it up hard, and I see tears coursing down that man's cheeks. He yells out the names of his children, the pony wheeling, dust spiralling up, his voice cracked. They come running and his wiry arms sweep them up. The boy straddles behind and the girl he cradles in his arms. He jabs his heels into that gray who, being an Indian hisself, knows what to do.

Apropos this summer excursion along the Arkansas, ain't much more to report. The troopers marched about in squares or loafed about praying for action. The officers held a footrace, and Tom Custer finished down the field and wore a face like a smacked arse. Fabridzio Capeesh attempted to learn the trumpet and I distanced myself. The troopers hit a ball around with a club and others chased after it. But no massacres was forthcoming. The Indians got told they could have grub but no ordnance, and consequently got the mulligrubs and told the general where they could shove their slimy beef and mouldy meal and went off with naught.

We departed back to our fort and transpired no sooner we'd gone a kindly Indian agent arrived and beseeched on their behalf, and a bunch of Arapaho was give both commodities, a few days later a band of friendly Cheyenne. But it come too late for them Cheyenne already umbraged up. They'd turned their ponies north and had gone off to smoke a few homesteads.

Mac read out the headlines to the illiterates. Hundreds killed along the Saline and the Solomon. Homesteads Burned. Children Carried Off. Women Outraged. That were the gist of it, and being writ in the newspapers it were all gospel. The Indians, well they said they was just going about their business like they done since times forgot, heading off to make war on the Pawnee, and it were the whites what'd done shot first.

It'd been a good bit since I'd studied the Mac close up, and he bore the marks of his adventures. His nose was bent sideways where he'd been struck by the shovel, and when he opened his flytrap to speak I saw he was yet to be subject to remedial orthodontics and his diction carried a shushing component like a soft brush being swept over a hard floor. In idle moments I pondered whether that ostler's shovel carried the indent of the Scotsman's face, and if one day he might gain possession of it and pour plaster therein and make a replica of hisself.

Mac, he greeted the news of rapine with glee, and one crepuscular he snuck over to articulate that feeling into my ear. This'll do it, Rab. You mind. They'll be relieving me of my shovel and giving me back my Spencer, and you and me, we'll be reunited. He tousled my mane. Partners again, ey Rab. How does that sound?

Fine, so long you stay clear of the goddamn cards and cobblers.

The malefactors was centred on a small bunch, led by a chief who'd been a boy at Sand Creek four summers previous, although, far as I can bottom it, witnessing your ma and pa and brothers and sisters get slaughtered, their privy parts made into souvenirs, is apt to make you vengeful.

We found a child one day wandering about the plains. A girl, maybe eight summers old. She was red, but she weren't no Indian, the sun burning hot and her poorly attired for the conditions, skin and lips blistering up, her feet blood-shod. She was talking, and being no other humanos was about, I figured she were conversing with the doll she clung to. Fabridzio Capeesh dismounted and stooped and said, Chow bella. Cosa fi qui, ragadzeena, and gathered her up.

I swished my tail as a disparate bunch of fellows was fitted out at the Hays Fort. Fifty or so they said there was, and they called theirselves the Solomon Avengers, so you can imagine the unassuming character of them individuals. A mixture of soldiers and scouts comprised the party, them latters strangers to the barbershop and attired such you'd think they been drug backwards though a mesquite thicket and detoured on the way out to roll in mire. No waggon train, no music band, no artillery in tow, and their equines looked spry enough, for army nags. They was to travel light and fast.

Could be they had a chance. Might even find some indigenes to shoot at. That bunch with the Sharpses had chased us up onto the Llano and de-existed Walks Slowy, and they was accoutered similar. Nearly rubbed us out by God, and we was Comanche.

Yours truly, they sent me off on a far more wearisome expedition. I'll try spice it up best I can, leave out the tediousest episodes, but it will truly be an onerous task.

Six

I admit that farewell salutation of my last weren't exactly roping you into this next chapter of my earthly, but you' just have to lump it if you want to get up to the Greasy Grass in possession of all the facts.

The Solomon Avengers was out whipping the Indians up north, so we was sent back meridional for like purpose. We should have remained on the Pawnee Creek and saved ourselves a deal of shank's. We didn't dally at the fort but proceeded on, following the settler trail till we come to another fort my horse-abusing degenerate eschewed, located where the Arkansas elbows off occidental. There we decamped. A few days previous, a bunch of troopers was near wiped out in the hereabouts, their corpses despoiled, and our bunch was looking for revenge.

We rode about the plains looking for Indians to massacre, but I bottomed it out revenge on that particular bunch weren't the real intent behind our presence down there. Something big was afoot. Talk was the generals had concocted up a plan to crush the indigene once and for all, and the Seventh US Cavalry was to be its St Michaels, which I guess would make the Indians all dragons.

The sullen general showed up trundling along in his ambulance, towing a column of cavalry in his wake, and day or so later Little Phil followed, though him too proud to ride in a waggon. He was mounted on a big bay, of easy gait I noted. Our bunch, they all took this bi-gubernatorial advent as confirmatory evidence of the magnitude of the afootedness, if you is catching my drift here.

I guess time is ripe to delineate that ambulated general, being as he has already cropped up in our tale and is about to figure in this next episode.

His eyes, they was a notable feature. Dead like a fish's is, they was, like they was constantly being forced to regard something his head were indifferent to. I do believe they was furnished with the ability to blink, though I never saw them perform that action. They looked out over a slumpen face and one of them beards that ignores the cheeks and only warms the top lip and the chin, the lower part worn long, a style signifying vanity and a degree of leisure time. Attempts had been made to divide the beard into a fork and curl up the ends of the moustache, but they was also slumped. Further affectation was located in his hair but remains difficult to describe. Imagine he had wove-in two turkey beards above the ears and dyed them to match the rest of his hair. These he teased forward so they extended beyond the temples. Corniculate, the Cornishman'd call it.

As for the regions below the beard, well he struggled to fill out that uniform, and his fine worsted sagged and rumpled over the absent parts of his body. The sagging apparel expressed his comportment, and if I was plump for a word to describe that item, I would go for the Cornishman's favourite modifier, knackered. Must have been all that Indian burning he did up north he bragged about. I'd venture massacring Indians is a wearisome business, and maybe that was why he took up the liberal arts. A hobby like painting pictures must be relaxing when you is in that line of work.

He had a big reputation for being adroit in the arts of profanity, that general, though you'd scarce believe dirty words could struggle out that slumpen face, and him holding them artistic sensibilities. I never heard him going at it personally, but I was rarely in range. I done forgot the name of that general now. I'm inclined to call him General Sullen, but I know that ain't it.

I'm pleased to report that the copper-headed Caledonian formed part of the escort for that weary general. So they believed they done tortured the wanderlust out of him. After completing the bicep-punching hair-tousling formalities with his cronies, I saw him turn that speckled face of his over to us nags. His eyes followed the line of them dozing heads until they alighted on that belonging to yours truly. Rab, he called out, Rab, and waved, although how he expected me to rejoinder that salutation I cannot say. He fired a word in his sergeant's ear, who flapped a lackadaisical hand, and he ran over.

Rab my boy. How ye been? He reached in his pocket and extracted an apple and shoved it in my choppers. There you are ma boy. That'll do ye fine.

Him now lacking the central examples of dentigerous fixtures, I figured he had little further use for such vegetation, and that apple sure tasted good, despite the hint of Sozodont, and a picture of the Cornishman flitted through my mind and that Christmas Day. Mac slapped my neck and rubbed my lugs. He walked around me and ran his hands down my flanks, slapped my arse, the suddenness of which made me flinch.

Aye, that Eye-talian hasnae been treating you too bad. You havenae put any fat about you have you. Must be all that chasing about the prairies.

The felicitations done with, he recounted at great length and in jocular fashion his own recent discomposures, including the interment. He said that while he was buried up to his neck the sergeant come and poured Jalap down his throat, kind of joke. You can imagine the state I was in can't you Rab, he chuckled. Well I couldn't, and to this day I remain ignorant of the nature of Jalap.

They say if I do it again they are going to brand a big D on my forehead. He chuckled and enunciated, Tsssssssss, for emphasis, and jabbed a finger at his forehead, lest I might be ignorant of its location.

There's hundreds what have made it, he went on, and there's barely a man here who wouldnae try it afforded the opportunity and the balls to do it. I guess I'm just unlucky, Rab. I mean, look at that last hand I got dealt, for Chrissakes. By now he was directing his speech to his own hand and another apple he'd extracted.

After such extended discourse he went silent a stretch, and contented hisself with twirling a finger in my mane. Then he said, Where's that damned Eye-talian. He gave me a last slap, shoved the apple into my mouth, shoved his hands into the pockets and toddled off. That apple, I made clumsy work of it, and got my lips to slabber up the mush off the dirt.

They jabbered, him and Fabridzio Capeesh, that latter gesticulating with tremendous vigour and variety, until he whittled the gesticulating down to a single curious movement, his thumb and forefinger tips held together so as to form a circle. He extended the remaining digits and waved the construction in Mac's face. Mac, he stood unperturbed, hands still in his pockets. He withdrew the dexter. In it were a thick wad of federal currency of small denomination. Fabridzio Capeesh quit talking. His mouth stayed froze open and the bottom lip pouted out such that you could have dibbled a tune on it. He gazed down at the cash. He glanced about and in one quick movement trousered it, and I went from Trasandatino back to Rab.

———

RIGHT RAB. That'll dae you for five days. Mac, slapping the sack of grub he'd just stowed behind the saddle. He proceeded to strap on a sack stuffed with his own chuck. From the knobs and bumps protruding I ventured it also contained a bottle of tangle-leg and the same of Sozodont. More items followed, a frypan, a tin cup, a canteen, articles of cutlery, couple of boxes of ammunition, sundry lariats, a picket pin, a blanket for cool nights, a tarp for wet nights, a brace of pouches the contents of which I remain ignorant.

When he clambered athwart, his carbine dangling from his shoulder, his Coltses holstered and a box of shells fixed to his belt, his goddamn sabre dangling and poking me in the goddamn nethers, my back sunk and my disposition went with it.

By God, you should have seen that column forming up around me. All us nags and jockeys was encumbered likewise, and to be extra certain we got everything we needed for the trip, a waggon train snaked back, teams of four and six sumpters hauling. How many waggons? Well for once I can supply the precise arsmetrick, being Mac looked back and said, Will ye look at that Rab, and he tallied up them to thirty, not including the artillery and the general's ambulance. They must be bringing the kitchen sink along, he said.

A peculiarity. A number of waggons was occupied by soldiers, the non-riding type, what they call infantry. What use them fellas'd be out on the blasted plains was beyond my noggin, and I estimate our jockeys was of a similar outlook and first opportunity they got they heaped derogation upon them.

I checked the sun. Late in the pm. A curious time to be heading out for a massacre. Like I told you, to make life more exasperating they generally had us reveilled up in the wee hours with only the moon and stars to illuminate the preliminaries, the breath of life steaming out afore you. But I guess that slumpen general knew what he was doing, him being a famous Indian fighter and all.

The boy tooted and the jockeys mounted up and formed us into straight lines. He tooted again and we got kicked and duly walked forwards, and the sergeant yelled out, Forward, like otherwise we'd all have gone backwards.

Now I alluded to this before and promised to enucleate on it. You should have heard the racket, them tin cups and fry pans and picket pins and steel swords and Spencers all clattering and clanking, waggons enunciating likewise, axles squeaking, iron wheels grinding, wainwrightry creaking, reluctant mules chorusing in and the general's chickens and a goddamn pack of dogs supplying harmony. I tell you, we couldn't have made more noise if we was the Kansas branch of the Callithumpians letting the New Year in. The Comanche. Well you know by now what them high plains Indians would have made of it.

We proceeded on up the Arkansas at a walk, and now I done got us into forwards motion on this trip I might as well intelligence you up on the purport behind it.

Wearing out us nags chasing about the plains perscrutating for will o' the wisp warriors, well the beadledom had consigned that idea to the dung heap. We was to locate them warriors' villages and families, and we was to attack them specifics. We was to destroy their moveables, massacre their ponies and any humanos who resisted and some that didn't. We was to render them impoverished. That way, them families, if any was left alive, and the warriors out raiding, they'd be forced back onto the reservation to live in draughty shacks and eat reesty beef and dream out the rest of their days on rotgut.

Now here you might rejoinder, Hold on there. Them aboriginals you is about to pillage ain't the ones perpetrating the depredations on the yeomanry, and there's probably a goodly number of friendlies disposed among them to boot. Why should they all get massacred along with the guilty? And you know what, them aboriginals remonstrated with them very same words. But you ain't figured the genius part, the glory of a religion featured of an omniscient God and an afterlife. It don't matter. You can massacre the whole bunch, infants included, and leave it to the Lord to sort them.

The one thing the big generals never got their heads around was the Indian chain of command. There weren't none. Well, least as the whites with their systematized denominatized gubernatorial tiers would consider it. As I have intimated in the hereunto of this essay, an Indian chief's role was purely advisory. He could advise his bunch not to go out raiding, explain to them the likely repercussions, that them repercussions might ricochet on the rest of the tribe while they was taking their ease. But weren't naught enforceable about it. Them boys got to display their manliness somehow. They can't do it by acquiring federal currency and buying furbelows to flaunt. So they paint their bodies and ride off to count a few coups. Not a goddamn thing he could do about it. Maybe get the females to chide some.

Twere likewise on the field of battle. A chief might advise, Okay fellas, this ain't going to be like all them other times. This time we is going to sneak up through the long grass and only fire when we is in range. You all got that? And they'd all nod, Yeah, sure. But you'd guarantee some club-twirling tyro would spy his chance for glory and plunge forward shrieking his war cry to draw the requisite attention to hisself, and that prior stratagem would crumble like a desiccated coyote turd subject to my hoof. But the tyro, he wouldn't get hung up by the thumbs for it, get flogged or buried up to his neck. If he survived.

I'm losing the discursive thread here. I guess what I'm trying to say is back then the whites needed a culprit, and if the genuine article weren't available, well them redskins was all the same anyhow.

All this philosophizing is befuddling my noggin. I'll switch back to the narrative and supply some colour.

To help us hunt down them families, a number of white scouts was on this trip, including one who'd got hisself nomenclatured-up as California Job, although seemed to me the Kansas variety of them items would be more use on our forthcoming circumambulations about the Cimarron River, and indeed his knowledge of the country proved indifferent, though his tracking abilities was tolerable, being about half that of a middling Comanche adolescent.

Apropos his sartorial propensities, I refer you to my previous comments about them scouts comprising the Solomon Avengers. As to his physiognomy, well I'm obliged to leave you in a state of ignorance, being his face was obscured by a full beard what left only a knob of pickled-beetroot nose protruding forth, the result of bibulous imbibance, and the orbs of his eyes, eyes what darted about seeking signs of offence. A bit like the Lord I guess. The beard itself held congealed particles of comestibles and displayed all the signs of being self-barbered with a butcher knife, a dull example to boot.

As to the important topic of headgear, he wore a tan hat of broad brim and domed crown circumscribed by a leather band, disappointingly devoid of the décor you might expect of such a colourful character, in the manner of Indian beadwork or eagle feathers, snake rattles, porcupine skulls. I'll append that the hat's appearance betokened frequent usage as a larruper during episodes of fleeing.

His vices, well besides spirituous liquor he was a devotee of the tabaccy, as he dubbed them desiccated foliations, to the extent he maintained a plug of it fixed inside his left cheek what prompted red juice to ooze from atwixt his lips and flow into the beard to lubricate the comestibles, all while simultaneously puffing on a mundungus-stuffed corncob pipe. He picked his teeth with a big knife, I'd guess the same used for barbering purposes. For equitation he favoured a mule. Jesus.

Talk was California Job had demised a number of white men for perceived offence, acts what elevated him to a position of veneration among the troopers. He'd even killed a man for kicking his dog, and upon receipt of that intelligence I determined to curtail my canine-kicking habit, least for the time being. No aboriginal scouts was in our party, what struck me as a sin of omission on the tactical front.

I done wasted enough wind on that blatherskite.

IT WAS COMING on crepuscular when we reached the point where the settler trail furcated off. The whites dubbed that location the Cimarron Crossing, which you might consider confusing being we was about to cross the Arkansas. It sure confused me.

Off to the flank a bunch of officers was coming in what'd gone off to harvest a few buffalo tongues, while ahead a group of troopers was waiting atop a knoll. I squinted and saw Little Phil's moth moustache working up and down, no doubt issuing a stream of invective.

Now I figure our slumpen leader clocked the presence of Little Phil, by dint he leaned out his window and halted the column and called for a horse. I didn't even know he possessed one of them items, and a heavy-haunched doe-eyed sorrel what looked fresh off the farm was towed over. The general got his striker to give him a leg up, which took a prile of attempts, one thereof involving that striker's hand shoving on his arse. He set his headgear, a stiff example of medium brim and a valley running down the centre of a shiny-banded medium-tall crown, to the prescribed angle, and trotted on off to the front of the column, that trot joggling his body to the extent you'd think he'd got St Vitus' dance.

The slumpen general made it on up to Little Phil. He saluted and Little Phil saluted back. I saw the facial hair of both parties working up and down, and I pictured them trying outdo each other in the cussing department, upping the maledictory ante until they was deploying scatology, obscenity and blasphemy combined, until one or the other reeled back and admitted defeat, confessed the other the better man. Anyhow, they saluted each other anew and the slumpen general kicked the palfrey.

Little Phil, he lingered atop that knoll, so the slumpen was constrained to remain ahorse as we splashed across the Arkansas, what that sorrel balked at, an act what occasioned daylight to appear between the slumpen general's arse and the saddle and knocked his hat awry, even though the Arkansas ain't more than a chain of puddles at that season, and it weren't until we rounded a hogback that he were convenienced to dismount and retreat back inside his ambulance.

Before he did that, he took advantage of his mounted condition to allocutate his officers, figuring I guess being ahorse added more gravitas to them utterances than if his head were poking out the window.

He puffed out his pigeon chest and placed his dexter hand across it. He fixed his fish eyes off yonder and loosed off. Gentlemen, now we have crossed the Rubicon. That is what he said.

Where was that goddamn Cornishmen when you needed him? To this day I remain ignorant of the nature of a Rubicon, especially being it were the goddamn Arkansas we just done paddled across, via the Cimarron crossing.

He held his gaze yonder-wise, and I was obliged to follow the line of his eyes, trying to figure the source of his rapture, maybe a smoke signal or a bunch of savages lined up along a ridge, but all I could spy was a coyote urinating against a stump.

He come to hisself and went on. Gentlemen, tell your men to maintain strict silence. Our quarry is cunning and watchful. We must not alert him to our presence. Henceforth, there will be no bugle calls, no verbal commands. Furthermore, there will be no campfires. Any man who so much as strikes a match is to be castigated. Dismissed. I misheard that final punishment as castration and considered it extreme for a petty crime.

Now, think on it. At the same instant he was injuncting thus, our jockeys' assorted metalwork was clattering and tinking together, their mounts horses was all nickering and snorting, them nags un-tutored in the arts of clandestinity unlike yours truly, being Comanche, and them thirty waggons was lurching and crashing over the river bottom, iron tires grinding on the rocks, paraphernalia banging about, mules complaining like only them equines can, goddamn canines howling, the general's chickens squawking. A crate of the general's canned peaches fell out and crashed onto a rock and the cans all spilled out and rolled off. Imagine a bunch of apes let loose in a hardware emporium. That'll get you somewhere close to the din.

Two things I got get off my chest here apropos that allocution. How dumb did he think them Indians was? These plains we was lumbering onto they'd circumambulated since before the conquistadores was tramping about. They knew every cutbank, creek, crest and rill (I done exhausted my c-words there). They'd glance at a patch of herbage and see the half-dozen antelope what had tiptoed through and when they done it, at which creek they had slaked their thirst and to which next'n they was directed. Come a fall night they'd hear the cranes whistling overhead and know which beaver lake it was time to sneak down to and take their portion. To think the entire Seventh United States Cavalry clattering along on their overfed nags, a bunch of infantry, artillery, and a rumble-bumble waggon train of comestibles would make no impression on them aboriginals' sensibilities, notwithstanding them troopers told to wheesht, like we'd be able to sneak up on them and catch them at their toilet, by God, well that was just plain goddamn ignorant.

The other thing. Them officers what'd gone out to get the buffalo tongues, well an Indian hunter had been out there too, albeit he was going about the task less flashy. They saw his dust as he absquatulated hisself, but they never let on about that encounter till decades later when they was telling their stories to the leisure magazines for whiskey money.

Two other incidents was the final nails in the coffin of our general's plan for total silence. An hour or so further on, the Lords lanterns twinkling down but the moon absent, goddamn owl yicking away yonder, the general leaned out his window and signalled for a halt. The signal was passed to the captain in command of them in the van, and he forgot hisself and bellowed back, Troop Halt!

Well, that captain, he missed his vocation as an opera singer, very least a newspaper boy, and that holler were in receipt of a rejoinder to boot. A mule, evidently affronted at its hauling duties at that unsociable hour, let out a bray and thenceforth commenced kicking and bucking, the sound of splintering wainwrightry following on. My ears pricked. I knew them equine ejaculations. The timbre of it were identical to that I heard that day up on the headwaters of the Purgatoire.

Next day me and Mac was shunted back to the rear to guard the waggon train, and my bane come huffing past, that aggrieved look on his face, and going by them stripes on his flanks he'd been subject to a good fustigating to recompense his tantrum. He clocked me, and his eyes brightened and his ears pricked and he nickered a greeting. But I averted my eyes and maintained ignorance of his acquaintance. You got to keep some standards in life else all goes to perdition.

SEVEN

Course we never saw no Indians, that day nor the next. A scout come barrelling in, reported sign, but then the Lord drew a curtain of rain down upon us, and that were that. Yours truly, my highly tuned nostrils told me they was about, watching on, though no piles of rocks was in evidence for them to peep out behind. They was drawing us in. Getting us to the location most convenient to their intention.

Being no Indians was knocking about, the general gave permission for a bunch of officers to go off and shoot some buffalo. At that juncture he must have chucked in the sponge on the inaudibility front.

My jockey, he commenced singing incomprehensible songs. You bairnt their hames and garred them wainder. Gor a' waid a stayed wi' the deil himself, is an example of them lyrics.

He continued the concert in camp, for lubrication taking a sly pull on the bottle he'd brung along. Shut your goddamn caterwauling, yelled over his nemesis sergeant. You sound like some whore squaw at the pup.

Mac quieted. He stared off at the sergeant a spell, chawing the corners off a cracker. He threw the cracker away and said, Enough.

He delved in his pack and extracted a bottle, shaped different that that other, and strolled over to the sergeant. The bottle was filled such that no air remained between cork and liquid.

Sergeant, I believe you and I we got off on the wrong foot. He took up a whisper, Here's a token of good will. The sergeant uncorked the bottle and sniffed and said, I could have your arse whipped for bringing this on campaign. He glanced over to a bunch of tented officers who was already well along in their libations and grinned, But what hell. He took a sip, held the bottle away and studied it from under beetled brows as though to divine its ingredients. Where you get this?

Made it masel. Grandmammy's recipe from the auld country.

Well Jock, we finally discovered you a calling. He tilted the bottle and poured a draught down his throat. You could hear the glugging from where I stood. To the non-coms of the Seventh US Cavalry, he toasted, and drank again.

They couldn't wake him. The column formed up ready to head out, and he snored on. The empty bottle teddy-beared to his chest, his countenance wore a look of such serenity you'd believe it composed by an undertaker. He weren't deceased. But it took a pail of that salty water to rouse him and when he opened his eyes he claimed to have gone blind. He tried to stand, and indeed at one point he managed to get hisself up on two pins, but he soiled hisself and the legs buckled and dumped him afresh. Him soiled like that, the only waggon that would have him were the one conveying the cannon balls, so they dumped him atop and left in a posture I'd describe as angular. While a degree of vision returned during the day, he spoke gibberish and repeatedly ordured his britches and hence was held as an object of derision. He rode in the cannonball wagon the rest of that trip, and the Captain said when they got back to the fort he'd be subject to the severest discipline for drunkenness on duty.

Mac regarded him slumped in the waggon and murmured in my ear, What dae you reckon to that Rab, my lad. My granny sent off many a laird's factor with such a gift, and they never came back. The clever part is it turns your brain to crowdie and you retain nae memory of how you come by it.

I'll adjunct that that sergeant, he were a pugilist, and never scrupled at using that faculty to enforce his will. But even weeks hence when apparently recovered from that ministration, he never found the range, and his blows merely grazed whiskers and dusted eyebrows, and many an opponent's sogdologer went unreciprocated.

WELL IT WEREN'T PROGRESS to set the grass waving. Old Isaiah reported the Lord saying, I will make a way in the wilderness, and I will make the crooked places straight, but he ain't done got around to it here, no disrespect intended. You get a day's ride south of the Arkansas and the country breaks up into gulleys and gulches and scars and ravines, the ground crumbling sandy, the geological reasons thereof I remain ignorant. So you can imagine them thirty waggons and their advancement, having to be winched down and hauled back up, them infantry all debouching and rebouching theirselves, the mules complaining. A bunch of troopers they called engineers, they took rocks and timbers and built up roads, filled in holes, like them Chinamen done for the fire waggons, but you lost count of the delays while they repaired a broken wheel or fashioned a new axletree.

We struck the Cimarron. The Cimarron ain't much of a river at that season, and right salty to boot, though come a pickle yours truly can hold it down. A storm upstream had filled the channel some, had turned the water blood red, but you know I ain't one amenable to meteorological portents.

On exiting its banks a pair of waggons foundered in quicksand. I saw them teams approaching it blithe, but what could I do? Mac, he stuck his heels in and I galloped him off to render assistance, him being of generally obliging disposition.

Now, me birthed out on the Llano and an erstwhile wanderer of its breaks, I was fully savvied up on the nature of this fluvial adhesive, and I spied out its margins and halted at appropriate time of my own volition. That didn't satisfaction my jockey, him being a neophyte in the ways of quicksand so unable to distinguish the soft dirt from the hard. Maybe they don't get quicksand in them heathery Highlands. He mentioned bogs one time but as to their nature I remain ignorant. Anyhow, them mule whackers was vocalizing their panic and their beasts was bucking and braying, one already about to go under, and Mac, he dug them heels in again. Come on Rab. Dinnae let me down.

Well, alright. Don't say you didn't ask for it.

I was a colt. Us bunch was out in the breaks, following a creek up toward the crumbling red cliffs. I don't recall which creek, though it were a spring day and I reckon we must have been heading up onto that topographical billiard table to crop some sweet new grass. My Ma, who was generally the acme of wilderness providentiality, she plunged into a patch of quicksand.

I recollect my jawbone dropped open at that point, and me being naught but a sprout I reacted much the same as them drivers and mules was doing now. My Ma though, she never.

Mac scrooched his arse back and forth and dandled the reins and I trotted on up. My hooves sank, and before Mac knew it I was up to my combusted belly. But I knew what were afoot, so to speak.

Jesus, Rab. Jesus Christ. You could hear the panic rising in his thropple. Now at this juncture, I'm ashamed to admit, I opted to crank up the tension. I floundered about and threw my eyeballs up into my skull, pumped my bellows, snorted and whinnied and flattened my ears, just like I was in true jeopardy. Then I did what my ma did all them summers since.

I flopped over on my side and commenced walking. Walked

myself in a kind of arc, working my legs in a steady rhythm until I was back out to the margins of that quicksand, just like my ma done when she laid over on her flank. Mac, he weren't a dumb example of humankind, and he shifted position to lay along my upside flank, hanging onto the reins. Him normally an eloquent fellow, his verbal arts was now reduced to, Jesus Christ, Rab. Oh Jesus.

My hooves poked something solid and felt around. They gained purchase, and them horny fixtures, in unison with my shankses, hauled me on out. I stood on tierra firm and shook the sand off of me and I elected to stare off into the middle distance, adopting what I considered to be an insouciant bearing. Quicksand ain't nothing if you is prior apprised of the correct remedial procedure.

Mac, he fell off. He sat on the dirt and gibbered a spell, until a pair of troopers rode up and aspersionized his manhood whereon he pulled hisself together. But when he remounted them knees still knocked into my flanks.

They unhitched a team of six and got them fastened to a bemired team and managed to drag them out, waggon and all. They cut free a quartet of the others and got them out, but it were too late for that remaining pair. They was dug in deep. Panic will do that that to you, which is why I endeavour to steer well clear of that mountebank. Them goggle-eyed mules was knackered from the struggle and I knew they wasn't long for this earthly, although their vocal chords was still spry.

They cut the waggon free and tried to haul it out, but it were fast. They got a line out to the driver and he tied hisself on repeating to the Lord, I promise never to sin again, and they hauled him off, him ploughing sand into mouth and nostrils. Engineers showed up and laid planks out and tottered across and got off what commodities they could, them mules still shrieking. Turned out them commodities was powder and lead, so it was no surprise the waggon sank, and it turned out to be a propitious retrieval, given events pending.

We was obliged to listen to them mules the whole goddamn time. Mac said, Jesus Rab, I must end this, and hoisted his carbine. He was still shaky, and even at such reduced distance I'd have laid no bets on him making the shot. Officer shouted up, Hold your fire soldier, him I guess either a staunch disciple of the clandestine tactic or parsimonious on the ammunition front. So we watched on as the sand engulfed them sumpters and quieted their braying, and the last thing you saw to evidence the affair had ever took place was a pair of them big lugs twitching in the sand. Those of a certain cast of mind, not me you understand, might have considered that auricular farewell a good bit comical.

Two loose ends germane to this incident to tie up. Unbeknownst to me, an officer who was to figure large in my future earthly and become famous hisself at the fight known as the Little Big Horn, of which I was the only living survivor, he had been watching on. Second, and it only smote me now as was in the act of telling the tale, I believe now my ma done thrown herself into that quicksand on purpose.

WE FOLLOWED that string of red puddles on down some miles, and still we ain't located no aboriginals. I saw yonder the grass had been cropped by what could only have been a tolerable large pony herd. The scouts, well they missed that sign.

I ought intelligence you up on an aspect appertaining to a US cavalry campaign in them days you probably ain't aware of, and what may go some way to explaining our slow progress. A good deal of the time them troopers was mounted on the Shanks's brand of equine. Come the middle of the afternoon, order would come back to dismount, and they'd all get off and walk a spell. It was to give us equines a rest, keep us in fine fettle lest any mayhem bust out. Among the soldiers the command produced a deal of begrudgery. Me, I couldn't get enough of it. The Comanche, well you can imagine what them Indians'd have thought.

Anyhow, it was during such a period of afootedness we found the Indians, or better is they introduced theirselves. The three white scouts was out front as per, when a dozen or so Cheyenne bedizened for battle come barrelling up over a knoll, cut off the scouts' retreat and began circling. I was located back in the column but I saw the gunsmoke and heard the reports and the whooping. The general leaned out the window and told a bunch of troopers to mount up and charge forward to render assistance. Weren't but a minute before they trotted back whacking the dust off of theirselves and reported that the scouts remained unmolested and they done killed two savages, though yours truly saw no warrior fall. And that were the sum of the overture.

Them scouts, well now they was seeing Indian sign galore, pony-cropped grass, scratches of drug lodgepoles, old campfires, discarded supper bones. No hot pursuit was feasible, what with them thirty waggons of movables in tow, minus two, so we proceeded on at the former ponderous pace, the plan being I estimate to lure them indigenes out to get massacred via the weapon of boredom.

Come the crepuscular and us camped, sundry arrows began swishing through, a musket ball or three. Mac, he picketed me close and he hunkered down behind his saddle and feigned jocularity with his fellows. Us nags, weren't no cover for us, and while the others panicked some, I knowed the Indians held no interest in killing thievable horseflesh, albeit I admit you couldn't guarantee their marksmanship.

Next morning two soldiers got kidnapped. Like I said, that previous eve them boys did not assign due gravity to the projectiles flying about, and come time to break camp a brace of cooks dallied to scrub their culinary paraphernalia and ensure all was present and pristine. We was in the rear at that time nursing the waggon train along, and I heard a cook call out, You boys go on ahead. We'll be but a minute, which in the circumstances I considered a foolish injunction.

Sure enough, we marched on a stretch and them chefs never caught up. Soon as we was over a brow, bunch of Cheyenne and Arapaho showed up, brained the pair of them, tied them athwart their horses and dusted across the plains, intentions unknown but presumable.

Us bunch heard the whoops, Indians generally not inclined to clandestinity, and we heard the cries of the ambuscaded men. The mayhem might have been out of sight, but my highly attuned lugs caught the clong of an iron frypan employed for non-culinary purposes.

We was ordered to go out with the rescue party, a task my jockey accepted with glee, that excursion getting right tiresome by then. I venture, like most of them troopers, hereunto he'd only ever clapped eyes on the tamed Indian, and he said, Right Rab, let's go see what these wild heathens are all about.

We race back to the camp and see no bodies is in evidence, though it appears a number of utensils have been purloined, along with a quartet of nags. The troopers surmise them boys been carried off alive, and all manner of conjectures bust forth as to their fate, the balance concerning the combustion and excision of bodily appendages. Not necessarily in that order. They kick us hard.

Now I weren't savvied up on the Cheyenne and Arapaho brand of Indian back then, but I knew the Cheyenne to be a snooty bunch, believing theirselves superior to their fellow aboriginals. They always claimed they took no part in torturing activities, although obviously they could never speak for all the tribe, there being bad apples and such, or whatever the Indian equivalent of that dictum is. Prairie turnips, maybe. They said such disobligements was conducted only by men of low character, ignorant of honour and true manliness, and hence worthy of contempt. Any rate, that's what they claimed. Now I cannot vouch personally for that Cheyenne assertion, and apropos the Arapaho, no wordplay intended, I have less knowledge of them than of Frenchmen. All I can say is the females of them tribes always had a high time with any white corpses they come across.

So picture it. Spanking over that broken ground, leaping ditches and plunging in and out of ravines, kicking up clods, them boys all trying to keep their hats on, big plume of dust. Me, I am at the rear, letting them horses chisel on, Mac, knowing my wind by now, is blithe.

We sight the Indians, and them troopers start firing off their Coltses, as much to succour-up them boys we is on the rescue as for death-dealing purposes, and none of them Indians fall. Mac says, Okay now Rab. You show them lad, and I ease on up through them blowing nags just like I done in that Comanche horse race with Looks At The Sky aboard and she painted me up after. I feel Mac extract his pistol and I flatten my ears to attenuate the bang.

We hear a shot. But them Indians ain't making a stand. Getting massacred by a bunch US cavalry gingered up on vengeance ain't part of the deal. They dump one of the captives. He tumbles and flails like a rag doll and rolls to a stop.

Besides the lead he has been ventilated by a couple of arrows. He ain't dead yet, but his head has a concave aspect where that fry pan connected, and going by the blood bubbling forth from his mouth and the air whistling out where the ball exited, I figure him lung shot. He is conscious and he attempts speech, albeit the result garbled. I discovered later he were a Hibernian and hence powerless to stymie that activity.

Our officer dithers and a debate breaks out as to whether they ought continue the pursuit. This little chase ain't nothing to me, but I can see them army nags is blowing and sudorated now, and them Indian ponies, well this is all part of the quotidian routine for them, and if the Lord had seen fit to endow me with the powers of locution I'd be putting my penny-worth in for a postponement. The officer and moiety of the troopers is of similar mind, but the rest, comprising my jockey is for larruping on and rescuing that poor chef from his grisly fate, although the way they was all aspersionizing his gastronomic talents the night previous, they'd be saving more lives if they let him go.

Another bunch of cavalry is coming up behind. Maybe somebody among them can tell us what to do. Officer is among them, an Irishman, but by the way he talks a more pedagoguerized example than them burlies laying track on the Smoky Hill. Our officer intelligenced him up and he told our officer to tell his sergeant to tell us that we was proceeding on after the other chef. While the sergeant relays the order that new officer is studying yours truly to the extent I have to turn my head away. I weighed it later and bottomed it out it was by dint I weren't lathered up and blowing like them other nags.

A topic crops up in that former that maybe I ought break off and exposit. In the US Cavalry officers never spoke directly to the men. Not even if they was standing half a horse length away. They always told it to some sergeant or corporal and they told it for him, even though that bunch being told had already heard it.

We was about to larrup off when we heard a bugle toot from the column. Naturally I was ignorant of what that toot implied, but it resulted in rolled eyes and tight lips, wherefrom reproachful remarks was directed at the general. The upshot to the toot was us nags was wheeled around. So it must have been the recall. That Irish officer told our officer, Quiet your men lieutenant, but I read on his face the same begrudgery. He looked away to where them Indians was dusting off. Pity, he said. Those savages are worthy game.

What dae you think of that Rab? chuntered my jockey as we trotted back. The Seventh US Cavalry leaving one of its own in the clutches of a gang of butchering redskins.

Well he were only a chef. We never did see him again, but look on the bright side. Maybe he took to the Cheyenne life. Some did, and could be he inculcated the Cheyenne in the gastronomic arts, and they lauded him for it and he graduated to great medicine man and took to strutting about in a buffalo-horn hat. Anything is possible.

THENCEFORTH WE WAS under more or less constant attack from them Cheyenne and Arapaho, although constant attack makes it sound more jeopardacious than it was in actuality. Bunch'd come whooping on up of a draw or appear atop a knoll and fire off a few shots, arrows if they was close enough, bunch of us would ride off and chase them off, and then they'd show up atop another knoll or ride on up out of another arroyo, and the whole affair would begin again. I never saw no combatant get demised in all this yo-yoing, and when party to such doings I intuited the Indians thought it all grand entertainment. The indigene generally ain't got no racetrack nor dancehall nor billiard parlour to resort to for amusement.

You can imagine, to the troopers, this was fighting cowardly. Come out and fight like men you goddamn red vermin, you'd hear them yell, meaning come out and fight like they just done in the big slaughter back east. Now, the whites never understood the Indian mode of fighting and the Indians never understood that of the whites. So I'll enucleate on it.

What you got remember is them Indians was, like yours truly, birthed and reared on the plains. On them plains, the wolf is king. Now you might kink your nose at this bald assertion and say, Now you hold on there squire, I think you'll find the Grizzly..., and I'll interrupt you there to save you from embarrassing yourself.

In a one-on-one altercation, I admit, a wolf will find itself airborned and dumped in the dirt to discover its belly torn open. But such a conjuncture never cropped up, unless that wolf was maybe a hydrophobic example. As you know, a wolf don't hunt alone. He hunts with a bunch of other wolves.

What that bunch of wolves do is, they loll on a knoll and watch their prey, and they is right patient about it too. They is watching for weaknesses. When they spy a weakness, a bunch will go out to test it. See if that young'n or old'n is as feeble as it appears. Maybe they come back bloody and thwarted. Maybe they don't, and when they judge it right to go for the kill, it is the goddamnedest thing.

They don't wait for some trumpet toot. They don't wait around while a comrade goes get final orders. All them individual canines fuse into one canine of a single mind and purpose, that being to kill and eat that animal they done picked out. I seen it out on the Llano. They cut an old mare out of our bunch one time and you knew it were the end for her. The rest of us stood there with our tails up our arses watching it play out. We could have grazed the herbage for all the jeopardy we was in.

Now, I tell you what don't happen. A bunch of buffalo or elk show up one day and one of them canines pipes up, I know what we'll do this time fellas, we'll form ourselves in a straight line, bare our teeth and walk very slowly towards that herd of buffalo or elk. I'm pretty sure we won't get the shit kicked out of us.

So the Indian. He done grown up observing these tactics since a shaver. They got an enemy come into their territory threatening their families. First off, they don't form theirselves into line and pootle on towards them in the manner of the whites' mode of warfare, like they just done in the big slaughter back east. They'd get theirselves all shot to hell. Where'd the sense be in that? Remember, the Indians wasn't populous like the whites was. The whites get a bunch of boys slaughtered, they just send back east for a bunch more to shovel onto the battlefield. The Indians get a dozen or so braves killed, well that's maybe a quarter of a band's fighting and hunting force, and they can't send off to the depot for more. They got to wait for the copulations to fruition out and the next crop of boys matures up.

You is getting the picture now, the Indian, he copies them

monarchs of the plains. He lays belly-down on his knoll and studies for weaknesses, goes out and tests them, and when he strikes, he strikes hard and without pity.

Now I have to admit, like most of them items, this ain't the perfect analogue. Where the wheels come off is here. Them Indians ain't of a single mind like the wolves is. Like I said in the hereunto, there's always a couple of characters what'll break off and pursue independent ventures, generally for motives of personal aggrandizement.

EIGHT

We stumble on an abandoned village, by the looks of it late and hastily departed. Cook fires was still smoking, horse turds steaming. A parfleche hurriedly secured had tumbled and lay open, contents spilling out, culinary items and a blanket and a brace of buffalo robes, pair of moccasins, size small, a miniature bow and arrow and a drum. The officers went over and collected souvenirs and I expect some kid back east tied a band about his poll and stuck a feather therein and played cowboys and Indians with that weaponry until he broke it one day and he cried and his ma chucked his chin and said, That's alright, we can get you another'n.

The white scouts squatted, palmed their eyes and gazed off at where them drug lodge poles had corduroyed up the flora. California Job, he took a stick and poked at a fresh turd, to gauge its friability I figure. He fingered a pony track and put them digits to his nose. He stooped and picked a broken stem and studied it like it were a conquistadore's callous parer. He looked up and surveyed the sky and sucked in the air. He opened his flytrap, and spat out a gobbet of tabaccy spit, the bulk of which spilled down his beard and took up residence there. Sounds issued forth from that orifice, what might have been the euphonics of a snuffling hog, but what I ciphered out vocables. This is what he said, honest to God, Them red varmints is close. Close enough I can smell 'em, their goddamn bitches and their lousy stinking whelps.

Jesus Christ and all the Saints in heaven. On slow days I wonder if that fellow ever begrudged the life he chose. If given the chance he would have chucked it all in, took a bath, got hisself professional barberized, Sozodonted the tabaccy out his mouth, and put on a fancy frockcoat and sat of an evening afore the fire reading hisself a mess of Trollope. Maybe squirt on eau de parfum, whatever that is, pomade up his hair and take hisself off to the ballet or the lyceum to get cultured up, quit talking in that goddamn ridiculous fashion. But I guess when you done knocked yourself up a persona like that, you is stuck with it and you just got go on gutsing it out.

That aside, you can imagine, as intelligence goes this was poor stuff. We all knew the goddamn aboriginals was close. We'd had their ordnance buzzing about our ears most of the day, by God. But them ignorant words and the abandoned village put the ginger in the troopers, them all convinced the long overdue shellacking of them red varmints imminent.

We trundled on following them lodgepole gougings, and hour or so later they got their chance. Big force of Indians showed up and attacked the van. At that point that slumpen general'd gone trundling up for a confab with the scouts, and I venture maybe the Cheyenne done spied out his ambulance, adjudicated it our weakest part and aimed to carry its occupant off as trophy. Jesus Rab, There must be a couple of hundred of them, said my jockey. Us bunch was still doddling along at back guarding the waggons against sneak attack.

The Indians was gingered-up and making repeated charges. Some boys was riding back and forth in front of the lines, drawing fire to get the troopers to empty their Spencers so the rest of them could pile on in. But they was out-gunned and out-ammoed.

Troopers later claimed them Cheyenne and Arapaho was in possession of repeating rifles what they got as part of their promised annuities. But I never heard nor saw any of them items. Single-shots sure, which they fired off once and then employed for clubbing purposes. Somehow they had got theirselves revolvers, and the best modifier I can select to articulate their employment of them firearms is, gleeful.

The troopers in the rear all cheered every time they saw a warrior slump on his horse, figuring him demised. But I knowed to avoid the fire they was swinging down on the lee of their ponies Comanche-style. They was fine riders was them Cheyenne and Arapaho, but they weren't the Comanche, and I'll spit in the eye of any mortal says different.

Now, after all I said in that lofty manner about wolves and such, here was the Indians fighting front on, charging fixed positions, though weren't no strolling involved. Only one reason they'd be so reckless. California Job was right in one aspect. Them families was real close, and this was a rearguard action to afford them women and children fleeing time. Them troopers called them Cheyenne and Arapaho cowards and sneaks, but like I said in my discourse on the Comanche, there ain't nothing braver on this earthly than an Indian defending his wives and kids.

Being them Indians was fighting fair this time, the infantry boys decided time to pitch in. They trotted off front in little squares, got themselves settled in a couple of straight lines and after a delay while an officer got round to telling them they could, they fired off a couple of volleys. But by then the Indians had lost interest and was melting into the knobs and ravines.

The infantry, they got their wind back and cheered and slapped each other's backs, claiming dozens of hostiles killed, but as we trudged across the battlefield I only saw two corpses, both divested of their hair.

Off yonder in the brush, a pony nickered and I cast a glance to investigate. Mac said, What is it wee man, and trotted me over.

They'd left a couple more behind, one dead, judging by the position of his head in relation to his torso and the hole in his face, his fellow alive though gut-shot. Mac trotted me close and looked down. I estimate he wanted to see a savage close up. I'd doubt he wanted to render medicaments.

On his knees, was that fellow, his pony huffing close. He said a word of valediction to that pony and commenced chanting his death song, one hand attempting to staunch his belly, the other spread heavenward. A beadwork band circumscribed his wrist, a finer example adorning his neck, and I saw tiny turtles was worked into a pattern of red and white and turquoise chevrons, the fashioning of which must have required nimble fingers and an eye for design.

I hear an equine trot up behind, the sound of a man dismounting. I recognize the stink of California Job and his mule, hear his jaws working away at that tabaccy. He strolls over, them big Mexican spurs jangling. He says, Goddamn stinking savages. He sticks his big knife through that necklace and takes that man's hair, puts a bullet through the brain of that pony. My Jockey, he mutters, Jesus Rab.

You might think I ought feel guilty, my curiosity leading that scout to terminate the Cheyenne's existence like that. Well, you never saw that belly wound, and furthermore, I ain't capable of feeling guilty. Thank the Lord.

———

WELL THAT FRONTAL assault served its purpose. It was no little time before we got the column trundling into motion, and I pictured them women and kids up ahead, hurrying along hugging their bundles and cradles, firing off rearward glances, the ponies hauling on them travoises, yappers hauling on miniature examples, paragons of begrudgery.

Me and my jockey didn't take part in that fight, us being

guardians of the waggon train, and I sensed feelings of thwartation in that diminutive Scotsman. But he were about to get his chance. No sooner had we got them conveyances into forward motion and through the battlefield, the Indians attacked our rear.

I never did understand why the Indians didn't make more use theirselves of the clandestine approach. They was sure practiced at it, what with them always sneaking up on game. Anyhow, them Indians sprung on up out of a scrubby crack and came at us quick, a score or so I reckon. Us bunch was pretty much on our lonesome, them forward troopers smug as pelicans in their victory and proceeding blithe.

Our jockeys galloped back and dismounted and formed a straight line and shot off a volley or two, but them aboriginals swept on through like we was elsewhere located. I saw what they was about. The wolf, chasing down a buffalo, he slashes its hamstrings, renders it incapable of speedy motion. That way he can bring it down at his leisure. These Indians, they was intent on the waggons and mules, cut the lines and drive them quadrupeds off. If that failed, kill them. That way our column would be without its chuck and ammunition and the general deprived of his peaches and his chicken and dumplings, unless we stayed put.

Our jockeys swivelled and raised their carbines. But the Indians was now in amongst the waggons and mules and whackers. A stray shot, and all that ammunition what might go off. You can imagine how inconvenient that'd be.

The Indians cut the lines of one team, and a pair of boys drove them off. They was occupied sawing at the lines of another, when I heard a toot. From ahead, them done heard the ruckus, a bunch of cavalry was charging down waving swords. Them infantry boys was likewise astir, affixing bayonets. Them Indians clock these developments and cease their sawing, whip out their revolvers and begin shooting the mules.

I search the noggins of them beasts. My bane were located out front. He'd got his lines cut and was cropping the herbage while dropping apples on the grass, a fine trick if you can pull it off, especially with the mayhem busting out roundabout. He'd picked some dry old stuff to chaw on, the Lord knows why, and when he raised his head the straws was sticking out his maw suggesting a cat's whiskers. Close by, some trooper been cold-cocked and he lay grasping his rifle, that item butt-planted and pointing at the sky. That mule goes and scratches his belly on the muzzle, scratches till that rifle topples over. He catches me watching, goddamnit, and his ears prick up.

The aboriginals absquatulated theirselves, that other cavalry coming on, all them swords and bayonets glinting, similar I guess to when the wolves got a calf surrounded and the rest of the herd bundle in to save it, which let's own it seldom happens, them ungulates being dumb and oblivious to danger when it ain't exsanguinating them directly. Anyhow, them boys went off whooping and that were the end of it.

No Indian fell in that charge, and only one of us bunch was injured, that trooper taking a rifle butt on the skull, what that useless cap did naught to mitigate, that boy whooping as he counted his coup. We lost, what, maybe half-score of mules shot or drove off, that trooper his wits.

BEFORE FURTHER MAYHEM busts out I'll opportune myself to intelligence you up on an aspect you is likely ignorant of apropos the Indian wars back then. This'd be it.

Laying aside sundry notable exceptions, for example the Little Big Horn, of which fight I was the only living survivor, there was never many killed outright in them battles. First off, as adduced earlier the Indians wasn't looking to get theirselves killed and saw no shame in fleeing if the need arose. Second off, the combatants in both parties was all such terrible shots.

A bunch of raw recruits show up at the depot destined to fight the Cheyenne or Sioux or some such indignant indigene. Now you might think it'd be a matter of priority to find out if them boys could shoot. But we are talking the US Military here. They was more interested in getting them marching about in squares and holding out their rifles for the lieutenant to look at. It is a little known fact that the average US cavalry recruit received zero training in the fusillatory arts, and even less in equitation. I witnessed it. First fracas a recruit got sent to, he got propped on his horse and told to keep calm and aim low.

There being such a lack of marksmen, exceptions was always noted. A Kentucky boy were in our bunch who had been raised from infancy to shoot squirrels for the pot, what he called squirls, and these individuals got their talents exploited as the need arose. Hell, first thing goddamn Custer did when he showed up was hold a shooting contest and assemble hisself a company of sharp-shooters.

The aboriginals, well they could hit a doorknob at fifty paces with an arrow, but when it come to firearms they was equal inept. Jesus, on hot days when the troopers discarded their jackets, yellow suspenders and a shiny belt demarcated the ideal area for them to ventilate, but even that visual aid never improved the aim. Withal they was frequent supplied with weaponry of antiquated or inferior quality, prior used, and hence often featured of bent barrels and askew sights. I never shot a gun in my earthly but I imagine them defects demand a deal of habituating yourself to if you was planning to hit anything other than a barn, and I refer you back to my earlier remarks about them aboriginals' gunsmithing abilities. But even if they had been equipped with the finest Remington sporting rifles and bountiful ammunition to go out and practice with, a psychological aspect strangled any budding aptitude. Forgive me if I am repeating myself here, but to the Indian, shooting a man with a rifle from long range was fighting unfair. Braining him with it while breathing his stink and looking into his eyes as his life dwindles is their style.

So, I guess to the casual observer them battles looked impressive, all that lead flying about, the gunsmoke billowing blue, but I remain of the outlook it was mainly the birds of the heavens in mortal danger. Barring for when they got the howitzers out.

AFTER THAT WE saw no Indians a piece. Their guts, both literal and metaphorical, had allowed their families to flee on ahead and put some distance atwixt us.

Their trail cut away from the Cimarron and headed south, and come late in the pm we was on the banks of the Beaver. Here two more waggons got stuck in quicksand and become subject to the laws of gravity and embarrassment. We camped and I tumbled into the embrace of Morpheus, once more to the sound of zipping arrows. During the night they stole in and drove away half-dozen horses, and I pictured them boys acting out the telling around the campfire, them stealing them nags right out from under the noses of a fully munitioned US Cavalry camp, all them sentries posted, every one wide awake as goddamn owls.

That night the wind shifted. I caught the odour of the Llano. First time for a year or so, and I never realized we was this close. I saw that huge expanse, the clouds boiling on the flat horizon, my old bunch cropping the herbage, their tails whipping about in the implacable wind, a fazzle of new foals I never met engaged in high jinks. I saw their manes flaming as they galloped off, some jeopardy presenting itself, the tumble of stones as they picked their way down a ravine, the incline thereof you'd think to render progress impossible, heard the nickers and snorts as they settled theirselves and butted and nudged in.

I don't know what it's like for you humanos, but my picturing were so strong I was recollected of my lustful days. The urge came upon me to take off, like Mac'd done, gallop off to my old stamping ground, nicker a greeting, nuzzle into that bunch, sink my choppers into an old rival's arse. I truly believe I would have made a run for it that night, that red line on the horizon and river of stars pointing the way home. But I weren't tethered to no picket pin I could shuck out easy. I were knotted to Mac's ankle.

It crossed my noggin to chaw on through that cordage. But it'd be a task of no small duration and my slabbering would doubtless stir my jockey's auricular nerves, and it were unlikely I would have made it through our perimeter without enquiry. I know now I should have licked my choppers and gone for it, being that were the last time in my earthly I caught the scent of that eternal wilderness.

In downcast moments I think myself truly a coward. All the heroic deeds they said I done in my earthy, carrying Looks At The Sky to safety, surviving the fight known as the Little Big Horn, &etc. Well these events was thrust upon me. I had no say in it. Possessed of my own volition, opportunities like fleeing the degenerate, absconding the Seventh US Cavalry and running back to the Llano that night, I let them slide. I can't say why. You think you'll always get another chance, but you don't, and you watch the chance drop away irretrievable like a packhorse pin-wheeling down from a mountain trail.

That said, in cheerful moments I conclude myself merely lazy and of curious disposition.

We was ordered up front next morning, don't ask me why, but it got us out of chawing on them other nags' dust. The Comanche, when they travel they fan out across the plain so they ain't chawing on everybody's dust, and get called a rabble for it. We proceeded on down the Beaver, that creek scarce flowing, though the agua when you found it were right quenchsome.

We toddled along adjacent to the slumpen general's waggon. The way it lurched and jolted, well he sure must have held a strong antipathy to being ahorse. I considered them bruises he was accumulating a poor trade for an intact arse, and I heard a profanity issue forth from them windows with every jolt, what I took as validation of my adjudication. But then I remembered for some misdeed the Lord done struck him with haemorrhoids.

No sooner we got underway, we heard shots as the Cheyenne renewed their efforts to slice our hamstrings, but us bunch never galloped back to render assistance.

Around noon we must have been closing on them fleeing families afresh, being Indians struck the front anew. We galloped forward and our jockeys dismounted and got down on one knee and formed their redoubts, filled the air with the stink of cordite. But they weren't diminishing our numbers none, riding back and forth in front like that, whooping, twanging off arrows, a few single shots zipping through, and I'd peg it more a delaying tactic.

I ought intelligence you up on another aspect of cavalry tactics back then, being it figures large at the fight known as the Little Big Horn, of which I was the only living survivor. To save Mac the nuisance while he was shooting, some trooper I didn't know hung on to my reins along with a trio of other nags. This is standard cavalry procedure when a fight busts out. I ain't never fired no firearm, but I imagine if you is taking careful aim at a vengeful aboriginal chiselling down on you waving a war club and some terrified nag is yanking on the reins you got wrapped about your wrist, it must get right exasperating. So they generally give a quartet of nags to the ineptest marksmen to hold, which is no easy selection let me tell you. Now, while I maintained my insouciance, that other trio was all eye-rolling and spinning and pitching, to the extent that boy had difficulty holding on and nearly got drug off. Me, I saw a shadow ranging over the grass, and for something to do and take my mind off the din and smoke, I looked up to see what occasioned it.

A hawk rode the wind, wingtips flicking, head craned down, eyes locked onto some item below. I followed the eyes down, and it were the goddamnedest thing. A rattlesnake were engaged in that very same activity. It were observing a rat. The rat, unusual for that creature, was still as old Lot's wife. It were observing a beetle. The beetle, well it were in motion, and was carrying a grub off to locations unknown. Time it right, and that hawk could go home with a four-course meal. If this interlude is a parable appertaining to the United States Cavalry and the American native, don't be looking at me for no interpretation. I'm just reporting what I saw. You can solve it yourself and swank about it.

The slumpen general, I estimate he too was finding that din irksome, being he poked his head out the window and told an officer to tell that Irish officer to tell a sergeant to ride to the back and tell somebody to get the artillery brung up.

NINE

I'd never witnessed army artillery in action. Day before when the mayhem bust out it'd been bemired. The Comanche always spoke of such ordnance in tones of fear and awe, and were any encountered advised circumvention as the appropriate action. So you can imagine, when them two mules come clattering up with that howitzer I took an interest. Now, it arrived close on the tail of another waggon. That latter they parked in front, lateral-wise.

Well they got that big gun settled and pointed in aboriginal direction. A trooper were standing by holding a stick. He shoved it down the barrel, withdrew it and scrutinised the end. He nodded to his fellow, who nodded back and shoved powder down the barrel, and the former poked the powder down to the bottom of the barrel with the stick. They then got a tin can and shoved that down.

The tin can, that I weren't expecting, and I concluded it a matter of pure luck if that can was to interrupt the progress of an Indian riding by, though the hole it created would sure knock the example that Sharpses made in old Burnt Stick Glowing into a cocked hat. Them troopers now stood aside and looked over at an officer to tell them what to do next. A further trooper was standing by. So it was going to take four of them to do it. This latter were holding a smouldering Lucifer, but it weren't no example of them incendiaries you'd be conflagrating your pipe with, being it was half the height of him what held it.

That officer yapped out a command, and the whacker belly-down in the lead waggon leapt up and yee-hawed them mules and got that rude screen drug out the way. The officer nodded and the man with the big match touched it to the knob end of the barrel. A burst of smoke and a bang louder than the biggest clap of thunder I ever heard in my earthly issued forth and lifted all four of my hooves off the plain and whipped my head back. When I finally regained mastery over that latter, it were the goddamnedest sight.

Now if you is the type titillated by details of guts and splintered bone laying about, well you is about to be disappointed. I ain't about to supply no depiction. The recollection of that sight makes me feel discomposed in myself, and it resides in my head like a day-old campfire, a heap of damp buffalo chips piled atop. One poke and it'll explode aflame.

All I'll say is this. A mess of man and pony fanned out from before that gun. Reason being that tin can had been packed with musket balls, jagged stones, broken bottles, scraps of metal, any small item, hard and preferably sharp, they had laying around. Imagine the vengeful Lord had sent a squadron of angels down, and it were a last-minute affair and they ain't found time to sharpen their smiting swords. Even the grass was flattened, by God. I'll stop there, and leave the picturing of the scene to your own minds.

Well, who can fathom the creativity of you humanos. You know what Peaches, we just ain't killing enough mankind with our artillery shells. Pass me that pencil and paper and mind the kids. I'll go figure a while.

The troopers, well they was all cheering and tossing their headgear in the air. Some rushed forward to take trophies but was barked back by the officers. I'll say this for the Scotsman, he never took part in them celebrations. By the way he was breathing, I could tell his mouth was starched ajar, and when he finally got it closed, it were a good piece before it cranked it open again and words issued forth.

The Cheyenne wasn't finished. A brave bust out the scrub and rode back and forth before us on a piebald pony, shaking his lance. Considering what had just happened I'd say he was the acme of dignity, and that dignity could be why nobody shot him. He didn't yell nor nothing. Just spoke loud enough so everybody could hear, his eyes ranging over them what'd done it. I would like to report that speech verbatim, but I didn't know no Cheyenne then, and if I was to guess at the purport of those words, I'd say they was intended to shame.

It were at that time I first got the trouble with my bottom lip. I looked away from that scene but the pictures was still in my head, a pony or three still shuddering, and I apprehended that my bottom lip was flapping about and I had no control over it. Them flappings played havoc with my herbage-chawing and I went off my chuck a spell. In later events of bloody mayhem, while the remainder of my body remained unperturbed, that lip would always flap, especially after, and became the source of considerable embarrassment.

———

WELL, they left their dead in the field that time, did them Cheyenne and Arapaho, though not as many as you might conjure, being them Indians ain't dumb. They'd spied that howitzer get unveiled and begun to get the hell out, albeit not near quick enough for a goodly portion of them individuals. On the plus side they'd put us further behind them families, which were the point of the exercise, and I guess them boys was spirits now, lolling about with their Gods, their earthly sorrows and sufferings and pains now passed away. Jesus but ain't religion a comfort in times of calamity. I was right glad that Cornishman put me on to it.

We'd trundled on after them families a good stretch by the time Mac started talking again. In the interim I heard him sobbing some, though he kept it well hid from his comrades, making out dust was in his eye or a ladybug done flown down his throat.

He kept saying, Why didnae I fight? Why didnae I fight? Those fucking bastards come with their fucking arse-lickers and drive us off our land, our land, what we'd worked for centuries. That cunt in his fancy clothes sat atop his fucking thoroughbred, looking down his nose as they drove us away in the rain like beasts to the slaughter. Why didnae I fight? Tears flowed again at this juncture, and after discharging them lubricants he was silent. Then he snorted up his snot and said, You dinnae need pay nae further attention to me, Rab. I'm nae kind a man.

Now obviously, I had no cognisance of the events to which those comments was germane, never did, and my sincerest apologies to those of you delicate of sensibility for rendering the speech faithfully, least as I recollect it. But I wouldn't be respecting that man's cast of mind if I diluted it. He evidently saw something in the plight of them Indians what unpicked a scab from his own history, a scab he thought calloused over.

Now, I'm losing track of the days here on this excursion, it being so long since now. All I can say is I think it were around noon the next day when I spied something awry with that families' trail. It was fresh and clear, as the officers kept remarking and the men was gingered up by. But it were a mite too fresh and clear in my estimation, though them white scouts riding back and forth gave no indication they smelled aught piscatorial about it.

I tried to figure when they'd done it. It must have stormed the day previous on the headwaters, and overnight I'd heard the stream filling, and come dawn the Beaver was running steady and clear. We'd come to a ford, and you could tell by the way the ground was stamped they'd paused there to water up. A clear trail curled away, and it was there, I knew it, them families had dropped off.

I pictured them as they unloaded the necessaries off of the travoises, gathered up their bundles and cradles and a moiety of the pony herd, and splashed off down the stream. I figured them now heading south toward the Wolf, or maybe they was all hunkered down in that timber off yonder, their kids and ponies and yappers keeping silent like they been inculcated. The males meantime had chunked a bunch of rocks on to them travoises and was now leading us bunch along on a trail the Cornishman could have followed.

Old Moses come stomping into my mind, waving his rod about, his wild hair flapping about in the Lord's wind, albeit I am assuming he possessed them bodily fibres and weren't bald like old Elisha who got aspersionized by them adolescents for it. It could be we was old hard-hearted Pharaoh's army. The wheels of our chariots was about to fall off and we was to be engulfed by a red sea. It ain't the perfect analogue I know, and don't bear detailed scrutiny. But it's all I got.

The trail drug us into a country of knobby scrub-clad hills and runty trees, country the like thereof I'd never laid my eyes on before, and the topography discountenanced me no little, like any country that ain't billiard-table flat and scant of goddamn trees. As we plodded along I felt the ground crumbling beneath my hooves, which I took as a poor augur for any pending equitation. Course, they was still harrying us, like they done since we crossed the Cimarron, nipping at our flanks and hams, but as we got deeper into them crumbling furuncles, the attacks grew in frequency and ferocity, and soon we was busier than a one-legged man in an arse-kicking contest.

They wasn't no Julius Ceasars, whoever he was, but they was refining their tactics. They'd even got a bugler by God. He'd made up his own toots and he were directing the action thereby. They'd pop up at the top of one of them knobs, rain down the combined ordnance of arrows, lead, rocks and pejoratives, and when a troop was sent out to truncate the activity, they disappeared into a ravine to appear atop another knob further on up the trail. There they repeated the action. I guess the counterpart to it would be hunting prairie dogs.

Now you is all ejaculating, Why don't you cavalry just whip out your swords and go off smiting with the edge of them items. Well, this is where your ignorance and the friable ground comes into play. Soon as us nags attempted to scale them knobs we plunged into sand, that pulverized geology being the stuff of them humps. We'd flounder, even yours truly, and no amount of pitching and bucking occasioned a rapid exit, and thenceforth we'd come subject to a lengthy spell of projectiles and insulting discourse.

Now if this was the nature of us nags' progression in that country, you can imagine that of the waggon train. Them engineers was spending half their time digging them conveyances out, only for them to slough down further on, the mules all braying, the whackers cracking their whips and issuing futile invective. One time as they was winched up a slope the rope snapped and the waggons precipitated back, dragging their animals tumbling back with them, and you never saw such a tangle of equine limbs. I hold to the opinion that them conveyances, they'd have been better off fitted with square wheels, a refinement what'd have thwarted all forwards and backwards rolling and smoking brakes.

We couldn't leave the waggons behind, what with them toting all our chuck and ammunition and the general's poultry, so our pace through them knobs become reduced to that of the hereunto mentioned funereal gila monster, this time wearing clogs. As for the howitzers on them narrow wheels, they was now redundant, unless you was able to corral up a bunch of Indians and request them to hold still.

These attacks, well they didn't bother the slumpen general much, him ensconced in his ambulance, the arrows rattling off the roof, a portion penetrating the coachwork and remaining erect, and I expect the stationary interludes was saving his haemorrhoids some. But the other officers was getting right vexed. It was all a big embarrassment, a bunch of heathens running about in their underwear dictating terms of battle to the Seventh United States Cavalry, the aboriginal bugler further confusing the ranks.

Come the point when that Irish officer came barrelling over on that fine steed of his. Tall, the colour of Mac's hair, all four legs white up to the knees as if it had paddled through milk, broad nostrils and de-ballocked, that's the sum of it, and hoity-toity to boot to the extent it uttered no greeting to yours truly. The officer opened his flytrap and I could smell the whiskey on him, him being Irish, and he says to Mac, Trooper, give me your horse. You knew he was meaning business being he didn't get no sergeant to do his telling.

Well, Mac, his spirits was fair busted by then what with historical clunking into the contemporaneous and crushing his self-esteem atwixt the buffers, so to speak, and he remonstrated none, and it'd done no good if he had. So, bunch of troopers in tow, we dusted off toward a ravine, wherein a number of Indians had lately absquatulated theirselves. To put me into forward motion that Irishman dug his spurs into my flesh with undue force. But he weren't acquainted with my disposition at that point, and would never know my history as a Comanche, so I let it go.

Now, I figure this maybe the juncture to supply a description of that Irishman and his affectations, being he figures large in the episode and crops up again on the Greasy Grass, of which fight I was the only living survivor, albeit once the goddamn Custer showed up no little photography took place of them officers, Custer being partial to having his likeness preserved. So I guess what I'm saying is you could go find a picture of Captain Myles

Keogh in some book someplace and render the following redundant. I don't guess you'll find one in this volume.

Tallsome, slightsome, brownsome hair, the facial variety of them fibres similar to that of the slumpen general, to wit, owning no flanking whiskers to unite it to the scalp. I noted he trimmed the beard into a point, and some attempt had been made to curl the opposing ends of the moustache to the perpendicular, what the mayhem had occasioned to droop. The history books tell you that he had piercing blue eyes. But I never saw no blue in them. They looked gray as musket balls to me, not that I paid much attention to them orbs, but maybe the whiskey had dulled their lustre.

His hat. Now that item was of the broad-brimmed slouch variety, tan in colour, and you might think it not worth the mention, them being items worn equal by the commonality. But it possessed a distinctive refinement. The dexter side of the brim was upturned to the vertical. It must have been pinned to the crown by some device, being I never saw it depart from that arrangement. Clearly it was some kind of affectation, and I cannot deny it lent him a dashing air. But I believe a practical aspect lay in it. It allowed room for him to flourish his sword, an item he weren't never leery of evaginating.

His voice, well he was Irish, but he come from a rich family so his words weren't bent up like then railroad workers', and I venture them smithed flat by elocution lessons and poetry readings. But they was still delivered in that pebble-bouncing-down-a-hill cadence. Me, I was sure grateful for that education, being it allowed me to expand my compendium of fancy words. The timbre of his voice was of the middle range, and contained a feminine aspect, which maybe explains why he was given to acts of recklessness to prove manliness.

He were a soldier of fortune that Irishman, a vocation what always prompted confusion in my tiny intellect. They said he fought for the Pope, whoever he is, in some war in Europe, wherever that is. Down there, his sword going rusty, he heard about the big slaughter about to kick off over here and joined up with the Union. I venture they paid better wages and he figured them boys in blue a better bet for victory. That done, out west indigenes was needing exterminating to make way for civilization. If he'd not got demised at the Little Big Horn fight, of which I was the only living survivor, and we'd licked the Indians that day, he'd have perused the newspapers for the next big slaughter about to bust out. Mesopotamia or somewhere. But I saw his corpse when that altercation was done, and he couldn't have survived it less.

So bloody mayhem was his profession, and he was from a fancy family and I guess knew his Shakespeare from his Virgil, so he weren't forced into it, not like them desperates who was my usual associates. Me, I never bottomed it. By dint of bad luck and poor life choices, I was always pressed into it and afforded the option I'd have fled from all that killing, like the goddamn wind.

Here's a curiosity for you what illuminates the ironies of life. Up on the Little Big Horn our drummer was an Italian fellow, not Fabridzio Capeesh who was a cobbler by then, but another example. In the pope's war he done fought on the opposite side to the Irishman, for them what was fighting the pope, under a general they named a biscuit after. Make of that what you will. Back to the action.

Well that knuckled ravine wound on along, and we rounded a bend and the Indians was vanished, the trail disappearing into a defile pregnant with the prospect of ambuscade. The Irishman called a halt and said he'd go for a reconnoitre, and he told a sergeant on a roan and a boy soldier on a swayback they was coming too, both of whom none too smitten by the idea. That roan was possessed of heavy belly and white socks akin to my own, but unlike yours truly owning the full complement of them features.

We drove on up to the top of a knob. By God, but it was mithersome, us plunging in and out of that sand up to our haunches and elbows, creating our own little avalanches, detouring the shrubbery, but superfluous to say I arrived atop the summit ahead of them others, me being spry and eschewing the corn and oats, albeit my bellows pumping and I'd slicked up some.

My God, said my new jockey as we topped out, an ejaculation that weren't occasioned by the presence of bellicose indigenes. It were the goddamn nature of that knob. That crown of it was the curiousest topographical article I ever saw in my earthly. It owned no summit to it in the traditional manner of summits, but was composed of a circular ridge what formed a steep-sided cup. At the bottom of that cup, what, maybe a dozen horse lengths down, was the top of the tree, bald as a January hickory on a wind-blasted promontory.

My God, my jockey said again, The wind must have built this hill around the core of that tree, and then excavated later it by some freakish contrivance. He was of an enquiring mind was that Irishman, like Looks At The Sky, a feature I admired about that individual, and it sure saved me working it all out. He said, I wonder if trees form the kernel to all these sand hills. The recent-arrived sergeant and the boy, they contributed naught to the debate.

I never heard the conclusion to them musings, being arrows commenced swishing about and truncated the geological enquiry.

Indians was popped up on the next knob along, and had their bows inclined toward the sky so as to achieve the trajectory required to negotiate the intervening distance and them projectiles was raining down at an angle just shy of the perpendicular. The sergeant and that boy eyed that sandy decline, and I saw they was thinking, why ain't we taking cover down there. But the Irishman stood blithe, like them missiles was a spring shower, and I guess that other pair was loath to display unmanliness, so they stood fast too. I never smelt no ardent spirits on that pair, so they was being manly fully facultied up.

A ssssudd arose from the hereabouts of my anterior hooves, and I looked down to see an arrow sticking out the sand. Now, this event furcated my mind along two paths of enquiry. The broad and spacious path was wondering why my Jockey wasn't digging them spurs in and getting us the hell out. The narrow and cramped path was wondering, Now, what is so damned familiar about that arrow?

I looked over to them Indians and back down at the arrow, and was in the act of repeating the former action when it clubbed me. They was Comanche arrows, by God.

So, either Comanche arrows had been purloined by the Cheyenne on some raid, an unlikely permutation being they was currently on friendly terms, or they was Comanche on that yonder knob. Done ciphering out that logic, my heart skipped, I can't say why, and I squinted over for optical affirmation.

Now in the history books you can read them scholars saying that the fight in them sandy knobs along the Beaver was conducted between the whites and the Cheyenne and Arapaho tribes, and them alone. But I was present at that altercation, and them dandruffed specimens wasn't. So I'm telling you, a bunch of them Lords of the Plains partook, and did so with gusto.

I'll further append, you can take yourself off to some library and blow the dust off some official report, but you won't find it writ therein. Reason being we was under strict injunction from the generals not to engage with the Comanche nation, who at that time was pretending to be friendly. They had enough on their plate with the Cheyenne and the Arapaho, not to mention the Sioux up north and didn't want to antagonize the finest light cavalry the world has ever seen.

Now, back over on the broad and spacious path of enquiry, the reason my jockey wasn't chiselling us back down that slope, aside from his bibulous blitheness, was the mass of them arrows was falling short, intelligence what soon sunk into the aboriginals' noggins. They ceased fire. Thenceforth they contented theirselves with firing off an old musket every minute or so and discharging volleys of obscene derogation. That gun were as long as its shootist were tall, and he had no little difficulty holding it horizontal for aiming purposes, till he had to get a boy to prop it up with a stick. Anyhow, the hiatus in deadly missiles afforded me the opportunity to confirm my prior mentioned squints.

I saw that they was in the main, a short, somewhat portly bandy-legged bunch, and the paint and the headgear sure had a Comanche aspect to it. The final prop in the scaffold of evidence was, while all the other Indians was running about afoot by dint of the sand knobs, this bunch was all ahorse.

Having reported them aspects, as though to prove me wrong, a quartet of them Comanche dismounted. They turned their backs to us and raised their breechclouts and bent over, a concatenation of actions what displayed their arse cracks, and they proceeded to jab at these apertures with their thumbs. As sign language goes I'd adjudicate it crude, but possessing an admirable lack of ambiguity. The balance performed the activity while standing on the backs of their ponies, which I took as further corroboration apropos their identity. Then something else happened, which removed all doubt.

An Indian shouldered to the front of that afoot bunch, and he weren't no shy type, him being painted yellow from head to toe like that.

Well, Jesus Christ and all the Saints in heaven. He'd lost some off that lard off of his bones, but his noggin was still fronted by that wide-featured buffalo-sat face and his chest by the inset nipples. But the cornerstone upon which I founded my identification was his diminutive privy part, which by dint of his gyrations was flapping about. Because, save for pair of moccasins and a bonnet of eagle feathers, Slow Turtle was, as was his habit in trepidatious moments, stark-ballock naked.

Ten

By God. Who'd have thought it. Not me. He bore a lance adorned with eagle feathers, and they was flapping in similar manner to his member. Sundry skulls of deceased creation dangled from it, couple of scalps, and he commenced waving it in our direction in a manner I'd describe as belligerent. His other hand bore a shield, the yellow plain and an azure sky depicted thereon. A horizontal line bisected the two, interrupted by a domed red sun fitted with buffalo horns. The eagle, the rattlesnake and the humano had contributed further décor, in the form of feathers and skulls and rattles, a scalp. He was shaking it with full vigour, but at such distance you could scarce hear them rattles. His discourse though, well that were another item.

Maybe the voice is like a muscle. Maybe you can train it to make it stronger. How the hell would I know. But I pictured him saying goodbye to his ma and pa of an evening and heading out on the open plains, going through his lexicon of invective to warm up the thropple a little, and letting rip. I tell you, hearing him that day, he could have found employment in the circus ring in a red coat and stovepipe hat, maybe a livestock auctioneer or a stump speaker, had he been a white.

First thing I learned from his oration was that boy undergone a change of moniker. I am Isatai, he said in Comanche, I kill whites like the chiggers they are and rape their women as is my wont, though their slack [I'll omit the vulgar term he applied to this item here] fail to satisfy my lust, and I devour their children though the meat is not that of the buffalo.

Well, good for you. You done growed up.

Before we proceed with his disquisition, item here I ought enucleate. His new cognomen, well I believe it to be a vulgar term for the privy member of a she-wolf, which you might consider a curious item to eponymize yourself after, but there ain't no ciphering the mind of a Comanche, and doubtless his cronies would have deemed it a fine selection.

I'll precis the remainder of the speech to save time and print-er's ink. He weren't no weak and blind seven-sleeps-old puppy. He were the Lord of the Plains (I wondered how long that would take to crop up) and as strong as a bull buffalo. He was born where the wind blew free under the unbroken light of the sun. He had growed up within by the eternal circle of the sky where no fences or cows interrupted the view. He knew every blade of grass and spring and hummock and hollow between the Arkansas and the Rio Grande (a goddamn exaggeration if ever I heard one). He had lived as his forefathers had lived and killed buffalo and counted coup on his enemies. Now these whites show up and tell him where to pitch his tipi, tell him he must eat bacon and plant corn.

A good deal of the usual stuff followed about the whites scaring off all the buffalo and their habit of breaking treaties when them latters got inconvenient. His concluding remarks was reserved for questioning the dimension and potency of his adver-saries' privy members thereof they was shortly to be divested (I considered his argument founded on sandy ground here, his example at that point resembling an under-ripe chilli hung out to dry), and outlining further disobligements they was about to perpetrate on them troopers whose blood would soon be staining the grass and draining into the sand.

Now obviously, this was all pearls before swine, the Irishman and the sergeant having no Comanche and hence understanding not a jot of this discourse, and that jimble-jawed boy didn't appear no likely linguist. But given the hostile manner of the delivery I figure they got the gist. At about the halfway point, the Irishman turned to the boy and said, Shut that savage up boy. That boy, he replied in a curious accent, Be like barking squirls in the woods, Sir.

Now, he was so thin I reckon his ma must have thrown him fully attired in the creek and left him to soak a spell just to get them garments to fit, and that dangling jaw didn't auger too well in my judgment. But the Irishman had faith in him, so he must have possessed some talent pertinent to this injunction.

He didn't keep no carbine dangling from a strap. His firearm was ensconced in a scabbard strapped to his scrub. This he evaginated, and it weren't no carbine. It was a rifle, of consequent longer barrel, and of the single-shot variety, like you wouldn't be needing more than one to get the job done.

He belly-slid down the rim of the cup, whenceforth he took a deal of time getting hisself comfortable, scrooching his hips and elbows about in the sand and such. But I guess he had to have something to buttress the recoil of that rifle, or he'd finish tangled up in that tree down there. He licked his trigger finger and held it in the air. He lowered it, examined it, and nodded at it. Evidently some aspect of evaporation had satisfactioned him. He reached round the back of his head and pushed the cap forward so the peak shaded his eyes, an ineffectual action on the practical front, being the sun were at his back, and I judged it an affectation. A trickle of sweat had evidently accompanied the hat and he wiped it away with the trigger finger. He licked the sinister counterpart, and smeared spit down the front sight. Then he blew on his fingernails.

I ain't spinning this out to crank up the tension. He took his own time about the task, and I figured he best make haste or Slow Turtle will run out of words and absquatulate hisself. But he were still going strong, that Comanche, the topic now his ability to send lightning bolts against his enemies. That boy going through his fusillatory preamble, I calculated him another possessed of narcissistic proclivities, apt to bulk out his role to convey hisself more important than what he is, like humanos is given.

At goddamn last he settled his cheek along the side of that firearm and said, Your speechifying days is over, you goddamn red varmint, what struck me as an odd remark, Slow Turtle painted yellow. He sucked in a deep breath and exhaled over his trigger finger what he'd poked out for that express purpose. Then he squeezed. The rifle banged and I looked up to see the upshot, so to speak. Well, my highly refined peepers witnessed it, although I doubt them poor examples owned by the troopers did.

Now I need to adduce a detail here so you know what in goddamn hell I am talking about. I mentioned Slow Turtle's feather bonnet earlier. Well don't be imagining the standard example, wherein the feathers is composed such as to convey the wearer galloping full chisel into a headwind. His feathers was erected perpendicular. Picture a king's crown. Maybe an angry porcupine's hindquarters. Back to the bullet in transit.

At the side of the crown a feather hinged and toppled. This event prompted a hiatus in the Slow Turtle's lucubration and he dropped his shield and felt at the plume's former location. He snapped it off and studied the feather like it were a Frenchman's face powder applicator.

Goddamn it, said the boy. He raised his head and pushed his cap away from his eyes and stared out. His bottom jaw fell open and dangled a spell, before he hoisted that feature and added, I'm sorry Sir. I was sure me and Betsey had him. I don't get it.

Don't go for a fancy shot soldier, said the Irishman. Just take him out easy. The boy fished about for another cartridge.

Now, Slow Turtle over on that knob. I'll say this for him.

Rather than viewing that lead-felled plume in a discouraging light, the event gingered him up no end, and he began ranting anew.

I am Isatai, he yelled over, three times. To spare the hereunto mentioned articles, take it as read he uttered the following sentences in triplets. I have ascended to heaven and been bestowed the power of the gods (ditto, ditto). You may fire your rifles (&etc.) I am impervious to your bullets.

Oh Jesus, not another one. Hadn't that boy learned anything. He was bodily present that day on the Llano when Walks Slowly had communed with his spirit, taken the identical outlook and gone whooping off toward that Sharpeses. He'd heard the report and witnessed Walks Slowly knocked off his pony and get deposited a jumble of limbs. But there just ain't no helping some folks.

You could do naught but admire that yellow boy. At the very moment our white example was inserting in another cartridge into Betsey, he'd got his back turned and was thumbing his own arse crack, which I noted was untouched by the yellow, and I pictured his ma's demurral when requested to complete the job.

Bang. Another cloud of gunsmoke swam into my nostrils, that boy dallying over the task not near so much as that previous. A red mark appeared on Slow Turtle's hip, about the same length as the bullet what made it. The boy said, Fuck it. The mark commenced oozing blood, an outcome Slow Turtle took as further encouragement.

He spun round and leaned back and thrust his loins out so the privy parts was now the furthest extent of him. His body quaked and them parts kept rhythm, the privy member jiggling and the ballocks clacking about in the manner of twiddled castanets. A challenge issued forth from his throat, the timbre thereof you'd believe that boy incapable, lay aside any other mortal thing. Like a spirit bear done entered into his body, Legion crowding on in there to boot, and I cannot report them words, being they was of no earthly language I ever heard.

Bang. Another cloud of gun smoke and another oath from the boy. Sorry Sir, he said, Betsey's sight must have got knocked out of line during a skirmish. Just get it done boy, said the Irishmen, his tone now brittle as hardtack.

Now you probably won't believe this part, but like I said in the hereunto, the outrageousest parts of this story is them what is truest, and your credence don't matter to me none anyhow. First thing that Comanche does is make regurgitating motions. Picture a housecat troubled by a fur ball. He retches up the expectoration and captures it in his hand, holds it aloft for all to see. It is a bullet. I'd doubt it'd be the same calibre and form of that propelled by Betsey, but it is a bullet. So together with his vocal exercises, Slow Turtle been practicing prestidigitation.

You can imagine, his cronies cheered and hopped about at the sight of it, but he weren't done yet. That fellow had developed a taste for showmanship. Maybe he were about to fetch a hen's egg out his ear, saw a companion in half, produce a bunch of flowers out the rear aperture.

Slow Turtle shouts back and a boy runs forward. He carries a pouch and water and a metallurgical item. The pouch and water appertain to paint, and Slow Turtle gets him to paint a black circle on his chest. He truly did. He even puts a red dot in the middle, roughly where the pump'd be. Then Slow Turtle puts on the hat, the metal hat we took off the desiccated Spaniard you all forgot about. He's got a female to scrape the rust off and polish it up and the sun twinkles off it. The boy retires and Slow Turtle makes sure the hat is set right and spreads his arms and bellows anew, him now the apogee of conspicuity.

Twice more that Kentucky boy tried to make that shot. After that he was obliged to quit by dint of a ruckus coming up from below.

Now, you know I can't explain it. I don't know if that rifle sight had been knocked awry in some incident, or whether that boy had received a bang on the bean hisself. Maybe he got dazzled by the conquistadore's hat. All I know is they reckoned him to be the troop deadeye, and he missed every shot. It weren't no great distance and no great wind was blowing. What can I say.

Maybe them shots did hit dead centre, and they just bounced off. Maybe his bear spirit really had decided to render Slow Turtle impervious to the whites' bullets that fall day up on the confluence of the Wolf and the Beaver. But then you is obliged to ask whyn't he perform the same salvifical action for Walks Slowly. That latter done took a knife slashed his chest, by God, and you can't get more devout than that. But these things is beyond my feeble noggin to bottom out, so you just got to run with it, or go mad. And you can't go demanding answers from the Lord or you just end up like old Job and scraping yourself with broken crockery. The Lord got his whimsical wonders to perform, and them heathen gods, well they probably got whimsies too. Best not dwell on it is my take.

Now, that truncatory ruckus below. The din of shots and shouts was arising from the valley, so they got remounted and soon we was plunging down off that sandy rim so the Irishman could go tell them what to do about it. Them prior mental excogitations had disturbed my concentration. And I believe that is why I now got shot. Twice. In the arse.

An arrow plunked into that fixture dexter-wise. The part where that degenerate stuck his knife when my body was used up. The pain was alike, and in rejoinder my rear legs kicked out and I about bucked off the Irishman. He hadn't clocked the advent of the arrow, and I estimate he figured me of obdurate mind, now confronted with the negotiation of the sandy declivity. He gave me a good quirting and said, Git on you.

So we pitched on down that knob and soon the toil of it made me forget the pain pulsing out my hindquarters, but I guess that's what replacing one pain with another does to a body.

We rounded a scrubby swell and saw the fount of the ruckus. Bunch of Comanche had snuck up the neighbouring knob and was now raining missiles upon our comrades in the manner the Lord done precipitated fire and brimstone, whatever that latter is, upon the citizens of Sodom and Gomorrah. Them troopers had tried to shelter theirselves best they could, but no boulders was laying around, and scrubby brush might snarl an arrow but it won't deflect no fifty-calibre shell what these Comanche appeared in possession of.

Two equines mortally injured, one standing head down, blood pulsing out its neck, the other already laid out, chest heaving, flanks juddering, terrified eye, one rear peg kicking on in defiance. So you can imagine, I couldn't see why we had to go down and join that fracas and put ourselves in equal jeopardy. What could us trio contribute? But the Irishman, he were as impervious to such logic as Slow Turtle to bullets.

He dismounted and yelled out orders to them hunkered against the arrows and bullets and rocks and antique turds raining down, and figure this, he commenced using yours truly as a shield. I'll repeat that for emphasis. He commenced using me as shield. Jesus Christ and all the Saints in heaven. I looked about and no few of them troopers was doing likewise, and I ciphered it out. Such must be standard procedure as recommended in the cavalry manual, and I admit this act shocked me, me having always been treated fair to middling by them troopers. But I guess when the indignant indigene munitioned-up with ancient and modern ordnance is set to de-exist you, kindliness to dumb beasts gets sent to perdition.

Now you think back to when I was a neophyte in the Seventh, to that Phaeton and the marble road and my high trot. Well I'd had my suspicions, but now, them shrieking shuddering nags bleeding out roundabout, my true station in the military slammed into me like that ostler's shit shovel done Mac's face. Us nags we was boots and britches and forage caps and fox-hole shovels. Goddamn disposable sundries.

Exasperated at the Irishman's egotistical conduct, I whittled out a solution. I'll turn the tables on the bastard, work my way on the lee side of him, get some shelter from him, least my lower frontal portions. But he weren't having none of it. He vituperated the hell out of me and snugged my bridle down tighter, so I had to content myself by rolling my eyeballs and dancing my rear end about best I could. He was firing off shots from his Coltses, and the adjacency of it caused my ears to whistle and my teeth to rattle. Gun smoke flooded my nostrils producing a sensation you'd think a bunch of fire ants had clambered up there, and that conjunction of mithers were almost the worst aspect to the mayhem.

He emptied his revolver, thank the Lord, pushed his hat back and looked about, licking his lips while at it. His mind were working through the permutations, and it evidently calculated the only option left were the fugacious example, being he searched out the bugler and told him to sound the retreat.

That boy, however, was inconvenienced, having got an arrow in the cheek, lately extracted, leaving a perforation you could shove a German sausage through. So when he put that trumpet to his lips no sound issued forth. In lieu, the hole in his cheek whistled and flapped and the effect were a good bit comical.

He handed the instrument to a comrade. This fellow looked at it a stretch, turning it about in his hand like it was an antique come all the way from Mesopotamia, until a malediction from the Irishman jolted him into action. He pursed his lips and pressed it to them regions. The strangled euphonic that exited resembled no musical command I ever heard, but by then them troopers was desperate and would have construed a fart as the retreat.

The Irishman, I calculate either he wanted to see his troopers get away safe or flaunt his manliness, being we was the last to flee, him slapping them nags on the arse as they galloped by, some with two aboard. He'd got the sword out by then, and for an instant I worried he intended to return and smite them Comanche Amalekites single-handed and become famous. Him being a soldier of fortune and all, such action would make a fine addition to his resume. But when he swang atop me he wheeled me around to follow them others. Them Comanche hurled derogations after us, no few turning to raise their breechclouts.

I said I got shot twice and you are thinking my addled brain done disremembered the other'n. But I ain't. It quieted a good bit by then, I heard the shot what done it. In actuality, I calculate it the final projectile of the whole engagement. I pictured the Indian what done it, pointing his rifle to the sky and firing it off in my general direction, him having prayed for special medicine that day. Well his orisons was answered in grand style. The lead by then had travelled far, and was well along on the downward slide by the time it united with hours truly. Nevertheless, it was like one of them burlies had took his spike hammer and swung it into my arse, sinister side. So I'd got me a pair.

ELEVEN

The blow buckled my rear legs, and it took me a good bit to get some sense back into them pegs. It punched the wind out of me too, which as you know ain't me, and I come discombobulated. I floundered a good bit in that sandy ground, bellows pumping, the pain redounding about my body, my front legs trying to drag them posteriors back to verticality, and I pictured that Indian raising that rifle anew, smearing spit down the sight.

Despite my flounderings the Irishman was still ahorse. He glanced back and saw my wounds and said, Feck. Come on now boy. Get on up. Go on now. You can do it, and I'm pleased to report that while he waved that quirt about, he never applied it.

Well, I might as well truncate the trepidatious stuff, being you all know I progressed on to become the only living survivor of the fight known as the Little Big Horn, which altercation my jockey also attended, though he didn't share my luck and the Lord's providence that day up in the Powder country. So I'll tie up sundry loose ends germane to that engagement.

Those of you slow on the uptake might be asking why the Irishman come over and kidnapped me from the Caledonian that day to go on the mission to chastise them insolents. You all know I ain't naught on the pulchritudinous front, not like that fine gelding what befitted his status, so what could it be?

I'd conjecture he'd witnessed me walk my way out of the quicksand, noted my unmithered state after we gone chiselling off after them two chefs when all the other nags was sucking and blowing like the breath of life was going out of fashion, heard how I'd got Mac over to Denver in record time. We was about to chase after Indians through all that sandy ground, God knows how far and for how long. He'd have thought, I need me a nag with wind. And he don't need to be no Plato, whoever he is, he just got to have the smarts.

Now, you'll read in the history books that around this time I become the Irishman's personal mount and his favourite horse. The sources for these histories was frumpty-brained old soldiers telling their stories half a century later for whiskey money. Them doddering raconteurs never paid no attention to a nag like me at the time of these events, why would they? I was just another disposable nag among hundreds. They wouldn't have knowed me from Adam and the snake. It weren't till a decade later, when I become a celebrity and had poetry wrote about me, them geriatrics started taking notice and inventing fanciful stories.

And cogitate on it. Why would the Irish officer choose this dirt-coloured, sawed off, butcher-block-noggined nag, who, come the spring, his hide looks like a billiard-parlour rug subjected to cigar butts, spittoon slops and rapacious moths, why would he pick him to be his favourite mount? He got to go prance about on the parade ground giving orders. He got go meet the generals and have his picture took. He got go dispense justice to obstreperous troopers like Mac. He needed a nag to articulate his status, and he already done got one of them items. Athwart yours truly, he'd have become subject to hilarity.

So thenceforth what he did was, he come and took me as and when necessary. As and when he calculated depredations lay afoot and he'd need a nag with wind and gumption. Like that day up on the Greasy Grass. To commemorate our engagement with them boorish Lords of the Plains, however, he did give me a new name, albeit he were the only one what ever used it.

You all know it. Comanche. Life don't get no more ridiculous than that.

APROPOS MY BATTLE WOUNDS, I guess you could say the Lord smiled on me that day. The arrow turned out to be that of the beast-killing variety rather than the man-killing. So it weren't equipped with no barbs to impede withdrawal and tear flesh, and I remember the shhlupp when it came out. The bullet, well I guess it had lost most of the penetrative force and was relying chiefly on the laws of gravity to achieve final destination, that destination being my sinister arse. Insertion-wise, they said it penetrated to a depth equal to its diameter. So neither of them wounds threatened my earthly prospects.

But like I said into the hereunto, I was never much of a hand at getting my wounds doctored up, and they had to snug me down tight to the side of a waggon, tie off a foreleg and a rear. The surgeon what done it, a mule whacker of vulgar speech and gherkin fingers, kept yelling, Shut your —— belly-aching you —— cry-baby or I'll put a bullet in your —— brain.

In mitigation I'll adduce that arrow might have been intended for a creeping thing, but it was in right deep, and it took a deal of excavation to get that bullet out, and they never give me no whiskey to dull the pain like they do when they is sawing the leg off of a trooper, though that whacker were taking a pull or three. So I admit to a good deal of kicking with them free legs, to the extent that to protect his person the skinner was obliged to complete the surgery standing on the waggon bed, and I vocalized to boot, what I know some called shrieking. Of these actions I am not proud.

Turned out I was some kind of hero, along with my jockey. We'd got them troopers out of that gulch with only a quartet wounded, and I'd got my jockey back unmolested despite getting shot twice in the posterior. Mac, when I got restituted back to him, said, Well Rab, looks like ye've done it again.

A shade of regret coloured his tone, I noted, and I venture he was chagrined at not being part of it. But truth be told that Scotsman was never the same after they fired off that canister shell and minced up that indigene flesh, them personal recollections barging in contemporaneous.

WHAT ELSE CAN I report about this fall expedition to massacre aboriginals and degrade the survivors what ain't already been said, you all possessing a picture of it by now, them days long since forgot.

I been dropping in references to the general's chickens on this trip, kind of device to keep curious them uninterested in bloodshed. What about these goddamn chickens? I best keep reading, kind of style. Well this burlesque is nearing its end so I ought exposit. The slumpen general had special waggon brought along on the trip. Fitted with chicken coops, it was. He favoured a soft-boiled egg of a morning, the occasional roast, and the blasted wilderness weren't about to stymie the predilection.

We got back from that engagement in the knobs and the slumpen general's ambulance had broke a wheel. I guess this'll form an amusing interlude. Bunch of burlies had got it hoisted and propped on logs but he never stepped down from his carriage to temper their toil. He'd poked his head out of the window and was issuing maledictory encouragement, and I saw with some excitement he was wearing headgear the like of which I'd never seen before, nor since. So I'll describe it.

I pictured it the type of hat you'd wear to accompany a stripy jacket and a bonneted lady on a stroll along the bank of a tame river, her with her parasol unfurled to protect her fragrant complexion from the ravages of Helios, you with your cane, pointing out riparian features of interest, the conversation gay. Clearly no aboriginals could be about or they'd be making off with them three appurtenances. You can tell I was grateful for the sight of the headgear, the contemplation of it distracting my mind off of my wounds as it did.

Constructed of straw it was, and featured of a low crown, perfectly flat to the extent you could set it on a table and rest a gravy boat on it without spillage, the base of the crown circumscribed by a ribbon banded yellow and blue. The crown formed a perfect circle, the brim broad and formed likewise to match, and I tried to recollect the shape of that general's head and whether that too was circular, or whether he'd be stuffing wadding in there to keep it located. The sun was burning hot and the day had heated up by then, and I figured that straw hat a right boon in that type of meteorology, possessing that brim, and it being but light in weight. But he better watch out if he set foot out that waggon lest the plains winds carry it off to Mexico. I guess he could pierce holes in the brim, pass string through and tie it under his chin. That'd fix it.

But I never saw the slumpen general step out of that waggon when we was in transit. It was fitted out with curtains, which was generally closed, to shut out the embarrassments what was occurring outside. I speculate he had a chamber pot in there, commode even, and a striker tasked to empty it for him, being I never saw him micturating out no fenestration or his arse hanging out.

Speaking of the general's toilet habits, a fine memory come bundling into my mind. That Cornishman told me about a King of England. Could have been France. That king owned a servant whose only job was to wipe the King's arse. Even had a proper title to boot did that position, which I done forgot now. Jesus but you got to be desperate to assume that as your vocation. It sure is hard to come up with any perquisites appertaining. And you wouldn't be let right in to minister to the King's arse. By God no. You'd have to go practice on somebody else's arse first, maybe get a letter of recommendation. And what would you tell the kids when they asked, What did you do at work today daddy? But humanos always seek to amplify their lot, and I reckon he'd have puffed his chest out and said, I'm an intimate of His Majesty the King now. They call me a groom. How about that for your old daddy? Whack the side of his nose with a forefinger and leave it at that, go fish a morsel out the stewpot.

In our expedition there was a heron-like individual who acted as striker for the general, a position what entailed laying out his clothes, cleaning his boots bringing him his chuck and cups of tea, wiping the corners of his mouth after he done ingurgitated for all I know, applying emollient to the haemorrhoids. I do know it entailed little actual Indian fighting.

But I think that Cornishman may have been jangling my chain with that whimsical story, himself being a frequent target of the Lord's whimsies. Maybe it were some kind of allegory to illustrate the nature of humano endeavour. You got somebody to wipe your arse for you, you done made it to the pinnacle.

I tell you, you got to watch out for the gubernators. Give them the chance, that is what they will do to you.

I done with them circumambages.

The burlies finally importuned the slumpen general to get out the ambulance. It being being such a rare sight the Kentucky boy yelled out, Hey, lookie yonder. The ginnel, he is vacating his vee-hickle.

He might have had an egg banjo in one hand and a cup of Darjeeling in the other, but his temper had declined further. Maybe the haemorrhoids was playing hell. He looked about for somebody to complain to and his gaze alighted on the boy lieutenant who'd led out first expedition to the railroad them months since. The lieutenant caught the gaze and kicked his horse to leave. But the action proved tardy, and he got on the wrong end of a speech.

The general waved an arm at the broken waggons the wounded troopers and broke-down nags. This expedition, its modes and objectives are a shambles, he said, the calibre of troopers involved in its execution a rabble. You can fill in the malediction for yourself. None of this were his fault you understand. Little Phil had lumbered him with it.

We never had this trouble in the Dakotas, he said. Piece of advice, son. To defeat the savage it will be necessary to exterminate everything clad in a blanket. Mark you, the bleeding hearts back east will never allow it. The cheapest and easiest way to exterminate the wild Indian is to shoot all the buffalo. Thereby you will force him into civilized country, get him dependent on the fruits of modernity. Then get the whiskey traders in. The men will soon become drunkards and the women whores.

The waggon fixed, he ceased hortating and climbed back in and made hisself a decision, got the officers gathered around the window and issued the order. Turn north back towards the Arkansas and the forts and away from the sand hills and these goddamn savages who weren't fighting fair. That were it, and it weren't naught pertaining to no fleeing, you understand. No sir. We needed to go get provendered up and our wounded attended to.

You can imagine, this decision produced a deal of gabble. That general was already in dudgeon for leaving that chef to his fate, and now we was retreating from a bunch of naked heathens nostalgic for the stone age. They looked back at all them waggons and chuntered there was enough chuck to keep them in the field for another month, and if only he'd just stick with it, they'd soon have the vermin exterminated. But I don't reckon a single trooper weren't relieved at the decision, though they'd never admit it to their fellows and so gainsay their manhood.

Bar Mac. He let it be known to all and sundry that he was glad to be getting out and leaving this Indians to themselves. He said, Here we are tramping all over their land uninvited, evicting these families from their homes. What would you do in their situation, ya bastards.

Now you can imagine such independent thinking elicited surly rejoinder, the principal examples being, Injun lover, and you — — coward. Him being Scottish and copper-headed and diminutive of stature, he answered these slurs with his fists and boots. I tell you, he won most of them bouts, barring the one when a trio set upon him in the crepuscular. He lost a further dontic and nearly an eye in that one. His heretical remarks come curtailed a stretch, but I saw on later occasions we skirmished with the aboriginals, he aimed high, save for when where his life was in personal danger, or that of yours truly. Our partnership was shortly to get truncated. But I'll delay the telling of it.

WE TRUNDLED on north out of them sand hills into rumple-ridged country. Them attacks never ceased, and we was continually obliged to go chasing them off, but they never dallied long enough for us to get the howitzer out and fertilize the grass. Times, they even got ahead of us, and they'd stand atop a knoll and watch us go by, indulge in further sarcastic bodily manifestations. Got so they didn't even shoot at us, which were the biggest insult of all.

I done lost count of them equines we left behind, shot to death, wounded, lame. You might expect nags to die in battle, but just as many died on the retreat. You come up claudicated, they don't doctor you up, they leave you on the trail for the wolves, maybe for the Cheyenne cook pots. I guess it ain't considered manly to be considerate to dumb animals, who the Lord done give

117

you dominion over. No spare ammunition were available to end them nags' misery, although I witnessed a couple of troopers breaking the rules, and I'm sure Mac would put one in my own noggin if the incumbency arose.

They sure ain't done kept up with their bible-reading or they'd be aware of Deuteronomy 21: 4. But throughout my earthly I learned that scripture was akin to Indian treaties and horses, dispensable when inconvenient.

I walked directly by two nags one morning, a bay with a white face, the other a skewbald with a mud-brown muzzle, their heads dangling. The skewbald, he were the putative farter of my subterranean days, though I never proved it either way. You might say they was right handsome equines. I had been picketed adjacent no few times, and I can tell you that pair was no embarrassment to their kind. I nickered a farewell, and had I been so furnished, I'd have wished them good luck.

North of the Cimarron we looked back and saw a big smoke on a hill and a big bunch of Indians gathered to say farewell. My highly refined optics told me they was waving weapons and making gesticulations I didn't infer felicitous.

Shortly thereafter, small herd of buffalo showed up. Tom Custer and a bunch rode off and shot them, every last one, and they returned with near a hundred tongues and humps, according to Mac's arsmetrick. I conjecture their intended quarry had embarrassed them and they done articulated their exasperations on a dumber example.

ONE FURTHER CURIOSITY I can append to the tale of this expedition. No bloodshed is involved, so those of you of certain proclivities may wish to skip to the next chapter.

We come to a creek what fed the Cimarron, well-timbered and the water dulcifluous. Some might call it a pretty spot, but you know my base opinion of arboreal features. Beyond the trees a thin smoke spiralled up. Mac and half dozen troopers under an old sergeant was sent off to investigate.

The sounds of manual toil, and we come to a clearing where a white was building a log cabin, off to the side a tent serving as temporary residence. He'd already built hisself a corral wherein a mud-coloured scrub and a splay-legged mule abided, a pen wherein a brace of hogs rootled. Sundry poultry pecked about, and stretched across a wooden frame were wolf pelts, a brace of them, so he'd already begun making inroads in the local varmints.

Other sounds of toil originated from a reed-limbed Indian female, pregnant with child. She were rendering corn to atoms by pounding a pole into a stone bowl. She weren't no local, that girl, and I estimated her to be of them parts yonderward of the Llano, though going by her agreeable attire she weren't no Apache.

I guess by dint of the sounds of them labours and the popple of the creek, they hadn't done clocked our arrival, and no yapper nipped at our heels, an omission I figured augured ill for their prospects. The old sergeant went over for a parley. The girl saw him and screamed and ran into the tent.

You folks alright? The sergeant he called over to the man.

The man stuck his axe into a log. He was middling age, disappointingly hatless, though topped by a flat pate of brindled hair which deputized for shading duties. His lips was clenched over as if to hold in loose teeth, but when he pried them items apart he was in possession of a full set. They was as white as fresh tombstones, and I wondered if he too were a disciple of the Sozodont. From atwixt words issued forth, Sure sergeant, why wouldn't we be?

Well, just that you is in hostile Indian territory, he said, pushing his cap back over his grey hair with his forefinger. We done left several hundred of the bastards behind this morning.

You get them whipped?

The sergeant demurred. Why, sure we got 'em whipped.

Well that's alright then. We'll be just fine.

The blithe response derailed the sergeant's negotiating tactic. He inspected his fingernails a spell, and then the sky, patted his nag's neck, actions what put it back on track. He said, If you like, we can accompany you into the fort. It's just that you is a hell of a long way from civilisation out here. He looked about, scanning for telegraph poles.

Thank you kindly for the offer. But like you just said, you got the red devils whipped. And if they do show up I got my squaw, bought and paid for. She can parley for me, and they ain't likely to be killing one of their own.

I knew him then to be an enterprising fellow, but illiterate in the ways the indigene. Like they all spoke the same language just because they was ruddy of hue, Jesus, and it was unlikely the presence of a Navajo female would confound any Cheyenne fiendishments. Most likely it'd put the mustard up them.

The sergeant stiffened hisself up. Well I can't order you to come in with us. But you know them red bastards, they never know when they is whipped. You'd best —

The man cut in. Look around you sergeant. The sergeant looked around. We all did. See that grass, that timber, that sweet water in that creek. Well I got here first. It is all mine. No heathen savage and no white man is going to take it from me. I'm going to build myself up a ranch here, get myself a wife, and by the time I get to your age I'll be living easy.

That old sergeant, well he was insensitive as my horny hoof to the derogation, and he sighed and said, Well leastways I recommend you get yourself a hound and you keep your firearms loaded and to hand.

Obliged for the advice, sergeant. We got ourselves a dog. But just the other night he done vanished. You go well now, he said, and picked up the axe.

So that were that. I told you there weren't much to it. Maybe it is illustrative of some greater truth, but you'll have to go figure what.

The Lord was pouring rain upon us when we pulled into that fort on the Arkansas, though due to some meteorological contrivance you could perceive the watery orb of the sun through the nimbus. The troopers, glum as Methodists, tethered us up in a straight line and went off to get some hot chuck leaving us with our tails up our arses. Later, them not expecting no Indian trouble, couple of boys took us out on the plain to get some good grass.

I saw that mule getting released from his shafts. He got out from atwixt and free of them lines and kicked and pitched and hee-hawed in joy, to the extent they had difficulty holding him. He caught sight of me, and quieted up. He let out a single bray as greeting, ears standing up like soapweed spikes.

The quietude were a ruse. Soon as them whackers was blithe he kicked and broke free, and next thing he were oriented towards yours truly going full chisel, that dexter rear flicking out. He planted his hooves. Crimps of mud sloughed up what soon covered his hooves and progressed on up the ankles but served no braking function that I could see. He clattered into me, winding me some, but being subject to previous such greetings I was prior braced for impact, so least I never finished in the mire. He butted my head and sank his teeth into my mane and yanked on it, his front choppers nipping my neck.

Naturally, I ignored him best I could, yours truly being no goddamn draught animal, a course of action he took as encouragement, and he clamped his choppers around my tail and leaned in. Past experience had taught me there was no rectifying that action, so I was obliged to tow him out to fresh pasture, them other nags looking down their noses as we passed.

Now I get to the part I been delaying. I'll take a run up.

We got back to the fort. Mac absconded hisself anew, and this time he triumphed. Hid hisself in back of a sutler's waggon en route to Santa Fe. I content myself with the thought he'd sure have been happy in there, all them bottles chinking about, although whether there was a crate of Sozodont included I cannot say and consider unlikely. But steadily relieved of his dontics as he was, it wouldn't be long before he'd no longer require that dentifrical comfiture.

I know all this because he come to me the day before he done it, eyes brimmed over with tears what inundated the freckles, told me the particulars of his plan, apologised for not taking me along. I cannae. I just cannae. He said, I wish ye luck Rab. You're a damn fine horse. Best I ever known. He choked on that last phrase and was obliged to turn his head away.

His departure left me discomposed in myself, notwithstanding he'd got drunk on cobblers and lost me in a goddamn poker game. I cannot say why. I never saw that Scotsman again and often wonder what became of him. Slow times, I picture him struck it rich, standing on the steps of some fancy saloon he just bought, wearing a costly suit and a waistcoat of contrasting colour, the swagged chain of a silver pocket watch diving into one of them tiny pockets, the screw top of a fancy flask poking out a hip pocket, Sozodont decanted therein. His mouth is set in a grin, the cat what got the cream, set of dentures gleaming out. He wears a hat of the type not easily bent, the crown oval-shaped and deep-ravined. The band is silk, the brim edged with similar to prevent fraying. The brim is up-curled, except the front, him being no idiot, and narrow, it no longer required to shade his fair skin and freckles from the plains sun. He wears it set back a tad, and canted. A pair of furbelowed females is on either arm, smiling down at him.

You know what, scrub that last part. He goes off and steals Stella away from old beaver-toothed Enoch. That pair was made for each other and they both knowed it.

KIND OF FIZZLING out ain't it, this account of that fall Indian-exterminating expedition, but that were the feel of it back then. Only one loose end remains germane.

That slumpen general, well he exited the ambulance claiming glorious victory, but soon the officers and men got to talking otherwise, and he finished with his reputation as great Indian smiter a good bit sullied. I do wish I could remember his name. He were soon shuffled off the whites' frontier and I never heard of him again, although if you was to look, I reckon he'd be found resident in the vicinity of an apothecary well-stocked with haemorrhoid preparations. The troopers, they soon forgot him, being the raids started up again.

Talk sparked up of his replacement. Gossip and rumour turned to hearsay. Some trooper said he heard Little Phil say it. The Seventh's reputation had been dragged through the mire and were in dire need of redemption and reinvigoration. Now, rub your chin and stare off into the firmament. Maybe jut out your bottom lip. Who might we get to accomplish that task? Some modest, unassuming fellow perhaps, without a self-glorificatory thought in his unremarkably coiffured noddle. A man dedicated only to the restoration of The Seventh and its glorious future.

Well screw that.

TWELVE

The return of the golden-haired prodigal. At goddamn
last.

Now if you is reading this expecting some kind of
insight into the psychological disposition of the goddamn one,
well you is about to be on the end of short shrift, whatever that is.
The bastard already got enough publicity, what was his main vocation in life, and yours truly ain't about to add to it.

Nevertheless, I admit, that the bastard is pivotal to the forthcoming events recounted herein, so I am henceforth prepared to
relate a number of lesser-known vignettes from his earthly what
will elucidate the character of that popinjay. Then to perdition
with the bastard.

Now before I begin I picture some of you possessed of a
pernickerty character wrinkling your noses and exasperating, How
does this goddamn joker know this stuff? He can't read no history
books.

Apropos that latter statement, ain't never a truer word been
uttered, and I feel no lacuna by dint of it. Apropos the former
enquiry, well no sooner that bastard's name cropped up as the
messiah to save the Seventh United States Cavalry from ineffectual-

ity, ineptitude and ignominy following the fiasco to destroy them Cheyenne families notwithstanding us bunch bestowed with the blessings of modern technology, them troopers never shut their goddamn flytraps about him.

There's some as sneer at alliteration, but it don't half ginger up a slow passage.

Item: The First. The goddamn Custer were out on them Kansas plains the year previous attempting to exterminate Indians like we just done, and he too done failed. Mid campaign, the Indians mithersome and flighty, the mulligrubs upon him, he decided best course of action was to go off and copulate with his wife, who was safely forted-up some distance to the oriental. He must sure have had the ache on him, because he destroyed no few equines and got a brace of troopers killed in that pell-mell dash across the parched wilderness. They say they covered 150 miles in two and a half days to satiate his lust. But I don't believe it, that being near-on the rate of travel that degenerate horse combuster about drove me to death.

Item: The Second. His apparel. He decked hisself out in a fringed buckskin suit and a pair of knee-high Apache-style moccasins, ported a big sombrero hat and grew his scalp hair in a golden mane, omitted to wipe his arse for all I know. He wore his twin pistols reverse-wise, butt forward, the true sign of the self-admirer. A confection intended to convey the mien of the Great Plainsman.

But that first year out in that wilderness he went out alone shooting buffalo and got hisself lost on three occasions and shot his own goddamn horse out from under him on two of them occasions, had to sit and wait to be rescued. Jesus Christ and all the Saints in Heaven. How do you conspire to shoot your own horse out from under you, twice. I'm even cutting him some slack here. Some troopers maintained he even went off and did it a third time.

Lucky the Comanche wasn't about, else he'd a got give nicknames more derogatory than Yellow Hair. Man Who Shoots Own

Horse Twice, maybe. Or, given them golden tresses, Woman Who Shoots Own Horse Twice, which would be the greater insult. I'll add this to the account of him as a Great Plainsman from my own personal stock. Twice he mistook a herd of elk for a party of hostiles, and he and a bunch of officers evaginated their swords and charged off to administer correction.

Item: The Third. He were the one who invented burying errant soldiers up to their necks, but that ain't the sum of it. He was also partial to flogging and executing deserters. I conjecture now the prospect of capital punishment was why Mac opted to abscond hisself around that time, what with all the talk of His advent. And so to the next.

Item: The Fourth. Custer condemned two men to death, not a remarkable act for that individual, but the enactment of the sentence possessed a convolution.

One was an officer who had circulated a paper proposing another officer's resignation due to incompetent and cruel behaviour. The other were a deserter.

The day of the executions Custer got a big bunch of soldiers to come out and watch, arranged them in straight lines on three sides of a square, the executioners in the middle. He'd got the band out too, this being a signal occasion, and the conductor waved his little stick and they struck up the funeral march. The drummer beat out an appropriate rhythm, and the men was marched out to their coffins what was already laying there convenient. They was blind-folded and told to take the load off and sit on them coffins, a command some might view as considerate, their legs quaking as they was. It were the usual procedure, officer telling them boys how to do it. Ready. Aim. Fire, always one shooter a little behind the others.

Only the deserter fell back dead. The other remained alive, and then crumpled over in a faint. The record don't state whether he soiled his britches. I know I would if I wore them items. That fellow were a popular officer, and goddamn Custer was scared his troopers might take it amiss if he went right on and executed him, fearing assassination hisself.

Custer, he considered the whole pageant a fine practical joke, and you can imagine the you-shoulda-seen-his-faces over dinner that night. He were right partial to such japes, provided they weren't perpetrated on hisself personally.

This ain't part of the items but I judge it appertains. One time Custer wanted to display manliness, so he and a party of officers including Tom Custer took some ladies out on the plain so they could watch them kill buffalo. While the slaughter was proceeding a bunch of Indians showed up atop a nearby ridge, accoutered up for rapine. Now you can imagine the terror of them fine ladies at this vista, the pictures their minds was conjuring of filthy savages perpetrating libidinous acts upon their pale and fragrant bodies. One fine lady dismounted and dropped to her knees and commenced beseeching the Lord. Custer, he spurred his horse and he and Tom Custer went off with a brace of other fellows to chastise them hostiles, and soon them fine ladies heard the shots and the whoopings and watched on as the gunsmoke billowed up and them sharps and blunts whirled about. You can imagine their relief when they saw the savages tumbling off of their steeds and the remainder break away and gallop off whipped, picture their shiny-eyed adoration as the Custer boys come trotting back slapping the dust off, saying it were nothing.

All were bogus. Custer had paid a bunch of malefactors to bedizen theirselves as aboriginals and comport theirselves accordingly.

Item, The Fifth. Custer strangled his own dog. Out chasing Indians one time he located a camp and plumped for a sneak attack. Like that slumpen general done before him, he told the retinue to stay quiet so the Indians wouldn't get wind of their forthcoming massacre. All obeyed except his hound. Enlivened by the imminent mayhem, that canine proceeded to bark and wouldn't be shushed. So Custer got his lariat and strangled it. He didn't ask no other to do it. He did it hisself. Make of that what you will. Some say he pushed a picket pin up through the roof of his mouth.

That's all the intelligence you are getting out of me about the bastard.

———

OUR R N' R at that fort on the belly of the Arkansas were but of short duration. We only remained there two days before we was retracing our steps back meridional to the hostiles. I have a curiosity to report appertaining to my short sojourn there.

One morning Mrs Cash out for a stroll meandered toward the horse herd. Her eyes roved over us nags until he saw me and he came over for a visit. Like I said before, she saw some congruence between our natures, in the manner I guess of a mountain creek flowing into a muddy river and their waters flow side by side for a spell, though which was which in our relationship I never took the trouble to ponder, and in truth I never saw no congruence myself.

She'd brought a brush with him, which I considered thoughtful, but I sniffed about his crevices and found no apples, so I guess it is swings and roundabouts in this world, as Mac was prone to say. She brushed and jabbered, me taking no notice of the words but enjoying the feel of them hog hairs de-knotting and de-bugging my coat, although I determined not to show it being he ain't brung no apples. She worked her way down my flanks till she come to my arse wounds. Jesus Christ, she said, What the — and though the phrase was truncated the sight of them wounds had rendered her forgetful and the voice dropped an octave.

That very morning my wounds had been mithering me. I reckon it were that unguent that mule whacker had slapped onto me. I'd reached back and tried to bite it off and clean out the wounds with my tongue, but the consistency of it was like tar. Maybe it was tar.

What have they done to you? Mrs Cash said, regaining her wits. Those brutes. It looks like tar. Christ almighty. It is tar. Her timbre of voice put me in mind of an oak beam what been adzed by a dull iron, them fibres shredded and poking up rough. I can't say why, and generally I ain't poetic of nature.

Anyhow, so tar it was. She dropped the brush and marched on back to the fort and come back directly with a pail of steaming water and an Indian female of the fort variety. I don't know why she just didn't lead me over there to spare the return trip. They regarded me and jabbered a spell, arms folded. The Indian poked at my wounds and tutted and went off and come back with a pouch of herbs. I winced some when they cleaned my wounds, but it weren't like the whacker's ministrations, well leastways not until they was about done and they conferred, the upshot thereof Mrs Cash said, Now Rab, this might sting a little. In my experience humanos underestimate when it comes to the pain of others.

Well, I don't know what it was she sprinkled on them perforations but it elicited the standard motion form my posterior hooves. My head jerked back concurrent and my eyes rolled and I let out a squeal, only a tiny one, but by then Mrs Cash had regained his womanly pitch and was speaking mollifying words. These calmed me some. The pain had been but of short duration, and now a kind of ease was spreading through my wounds like warm treacle. Maybe it was treacle. There, she said. That wasn't too bad was it. The Indian departed back to the fort. She had a long blanket wrapped around her such that only the movement of the moccasins indicated forward locomotion.

After that, I estimated might be Mrs Cash was a humano I could trust, them items being in short supply, the first since Looks At The Sky. What about the Cornishman, I hear you cry. Well he might be the acme of acumen when it come to digging holes in the ground or hoicking pilchards out the ocean, but he were a neophyte when it come to life on the blasted plains and shouldn't have been let loose unaccompanied. Way I saw it, it was more me taking care of him, and what with his partiality to blasting powder there was always a chance he would blow us both to perdition. As to the Caledonian, many laudable qualities abided in his soul, but constancy weren't one of them.

Mrs Cash come round front and resumed his jabbering. Well there is always a price to pay, I guess. She'd let her veil drop a little, being no other humanos was about apart from a boy guard off yonder, and I saw she'd let the barbering slide some, a dark shadow on her chin, sundry whiskers poking forth, but she kept the voice well hoisted. I guess if you are living a lie you got to stay in practice.

I'll be discovered one day, Rab, she said. I'll slip up one day, then what will become of me? They'll throw me out and I'll have to start over. That's what. Yeah, I thought, and they'll kick the shit out of you to boot, no wordplay intended.

Then come the chup-chupping.

I wish now and could go back in time and tell her it would all be ok, that she'd marry that bunioned toper of a sergeant, and have a fine time together up on them northern plains exterminating Indians, though I still try not to dwell on the particulars of the nuptials. Back then I didn't know them facts, laying aside the Lord ain't done blessed me with the necessary powers of locution, so I got my head down to chaw on the herbage, turned my lugs around and endeavoured to shut them lubricated words out.

She said, Oh Rab. You are incorrigible, I do love you. You put everything in perspective. You're right, nothing really matters does it, Rab. She patted my bent neck and with the other hand pushed the shawl out from his eyes. She took out a snottinger and blowed them tears out and was silent for a spell, gazing off in wistful manner to some buffalo-hump hills located to the orient, toward a prior life.

Now apropos them prior utterances, I knew she weren't trying to elicit no philosophy out of me. When humanos talk to dumb animals they ain't looking for no debate. They is after concurrence and consolation, of the silent variety, and yours truly had supplied them items in spades. As to the I love you part, well during times of emotional friability humanos is prone to frivolous words. They is generally of the evanescent variety and I paid no heed. I were more interested in that brace of new vocables to add to my collection.

A stretch of inactivity, the only sounds the wind hissing through the grass, my chawing and a slack flatus, mine not hers. She let out a gruff cough and glanced about. She raised her skirts and petticoat and ferreted about, trying to locate some item. Maybe she'd brung me an apple after all, and my nostrils done let me down. The male member when she extracted it, well the Lord sure had smiled kindly on her, and it'd be of a dimension to sure send Slow Turtle off in dudgeon. She held it forth and hosed down the prairie a spell.

Life sure gets strange don't it. Some say the Lord don't own no sense of humour, but I beg to differ. I stood by enough tedious campfire discourse to acquaint myself with the items men set great store by.

An example from up on the Powder. Trooper pipes up one time and says, What would you wish for if God gave you three wishes?

How do you mean?

Well, I just spoke plain English and can't put it no different. You got three wishes. Wish for whatever the hell you want.

Why, how would that happen?

Jesus, I don't know. Maybe you did him a big favour. Saved an angel's life or something. We is just supposing here.

I don't get it.

Just goddamn do it.

Well, let me weigh it.

The answers was always the same. Riches. Health. A giant pecker. And not always in that order. Sometimes, they'd debate.

What about the end of war? You could wish for that.

Nope, I'll pass on that. I'll be going for the giant pecker.

What about the end of pox and diphtheria?

Giant pecker.

Cure all the crippled children?

Giant pecker.

I never bottomed it myself. And there was Mrs Cash, who had no need of that item, who viewed it as an encumbrance, wished to disguise it and be rid of it if developments in chirurgical affairs allowed, toss it out for the hogs to fight over, well she was blessed with an appendage of the type I once saw a fireman use to extinguish a barn fire. The Lord. Jesus, you got to hand it to him.

In the quiet times with which the Lord has now seen fit to bless me, I wonder what the Comanche would have made of Mrs Cash, had they kidnapped her in some raid, tore her clothes off to take back as gifts. They'd have staggered back, sure, scratched their heads a spell, trying to cipher it. But you know what, in the end I reckon they'd have admired her for it. Any halfwit can mosey on along with the herd, live the life the others expect of him, not brush no fur the wrong way. Them Comanche'd have took him in as one of their own, and she'd have embarked on a new life of scraping hides and chopping wood.

KAY CADZO FI, stronzo? My jockey, he were always dyspeptic of temper when tramping about the plains were in prospect. The remark which, I knew by then weren't no benediction, were addressed to yours truly, and you can piece it together. Rampaging Indians, the Seventh injuncted to head back south for admonishing purposes. Mac departed. They done give me back to Fabridzio Capeesh.

It were a minor offence what occasioned the remark. Me distracted and daydreaming. Bunch of recruits was getting trained in equitation, the usual stuff, them shoved on to slide off the other side, trotting along dandling reins bouncing in the saddle like bundles of laundry. The scene recollected me of Ahithophel, when he first sat atop me in that three-horse town they called a city, how we did the spiral dance and I nearly walked him into that saloon, but I got diverted somehow and walked off to commence the rustic life. The Cornishman were now consigned to fickle memory, and Mac, he too were heading that way.

Smettila! Smettila! Feelio dee puttana! I weren't holding my foot up right.

Thirteen

The Messiah showed up.

Things was slow that day. The boys had a baseball game going. The officers was sitting outside their tents taking pot shots at local creation. Another bunch was off someplace harvesting buffalo tongues.

Column of dust puthered up from the north, and they all snapped their suspenders up and ran for their guns thinking it was Indians, until California Job come a'larruping in athwart his mule. He yanked it to a halt, its hooves plowing dirt, and spat out a stream of tabaccy juice to clear the road for diction. It's okay boys. It's ar'n. It's ar'n. It's the Ginnel. It's the Ginnel. By God, what an ignorant fellow.

Naturally, Custer being Custer he made us wait. He knew we'd spy his dust, and so set about taking his sweet time. Rode off with his dogs to shoot hisself a buffalo or three for all I know. Got his camp table set up and wrote a letter to the missus. They plodded on until at the base of the cloud you could make out a bunch of riders. The bunch resolved into individuals, one tan coloured. He weren't riding in no ambulance. He were ahorse at the head of the column, first time I ever laid an eye on the bastard.

You know, I do believe he missed a trick there, making his advent from the north like that. It was the middle of the pm by then, sunny to boot, and if he'd thought on it he'd have circled round and appropinquated hisself from the west. That way the sun would have been at his back and maybe created a halo, at least dazzled our gaze so we'd be forced to squint like the begrudged Israelites did at Moses fresh down off the mountain.

But he never, and there he was, still distant, though his haughty mien was manifest even at that range, the erect manner he sat his horse, elbows high, ditto the chin. No humano caught it, but my highly refined optics saw him take off a gauntlet and slap the dust off of him, saw him extract a tiny mirror out of that buckskin jacket, and smooth his moustache, readjust the cant of his hat, about which more shortly.

It was then you heard the damned canines. These specimens weren't no Indian ankle-biters. These was hounds. Point-nosed, bony affairs, with combed-backwards coats, and their yolfs emanated forth as though from the bottom of an empty barrel. They trotted along at the heels of his steed, a shiny chestnut with a high-stepping gait. Me, I considered its head too small for its neck.

Well, they come rattling in. He holds up his hand to indicate to his sergeant time to shout Halt, like otherwise they'd tramp right on through, and I take in the apparition in all its glory.

That hat. The campfire tales ain't done done it justice. Say what you like about the bastard, he had an eye for headgear. It possessed the biggest brim of any hat I ever saw outside of them worn by Mexicans. But the brim to it weren't circular, it were oval, a refinement that ensured the face and neck received more shade than the shoulders. Nice. The brim were upturned, but only about them narrow parts, meaning the precipitations would debouch not onto the shoulders, but be directed to them anterior and posterior zones, to spill harmlessly out beyond face and neck. The crown. Well you'd think that feature might be trying to outdo the majesty of its cousin below, maybe in the manner of them domed affairs ignorant cowboys favour. But it were the antipode. Low and flat it was, and you might think it a betrayal of the foregoing aesthetic and experience a puncturing of your anticipations. But I tell you, it were the Eve to the Adam of that brim. Circumposing the crown was beadwork of intricate design, what he must have pillaged off of some Indian female. Behind the band, on the sinister side, he'd planted an eagle feather, not too big nor too small, and set at the perfect angle. I tell you, that were some headgear.

As for the rest of that bastard's habiliments, well it was the buckskin composition as reported in the hereunto, and set against the headgear unremarkable, bar for its spotless condition what communicating recent departure from a sporting goods emporium. That's fine. I'll wear it home.

Now something were awry in the composition, like when the bugler hits a bum note, but I couldn't quite put my hoof on it. Then it clubbed me. The yellow locks. Where was all the goddamn golden tresses cascading down we been promised? The crown of that hat weren't sufficiently capacious for him to have stuffed it all up there.

By God, he done cut it off. And when they clocked that aspect, you heard a murmur arise from among them troopers who was now standing to attention, albeit some was still tucking in their shirts. Could be recollections from their Sunday School lessons was tramping through their minds, pictures of old Samson and Delilah, her hoorawing him into getting barbered up, and the enfeebling consequences.

Could be the tonsorial curtailment were to show he meant business in the pending vengeance on the aboriginals. Could be he didn't want to afford them Indians increased incentive for a scalping. Could be he'd tired of being called Fanny by the men and no few of the officers, though never to his face.

Now, the physiognomy. I ain't going to supply no detailed description, being, as alluded to in the hereunto, photos of the bastard ain't exactly on ration. I'll point up such particulars as struck me at the time, and what may not been rendered well by them silvered plates.

He took that hat off and you saw why he'd kept them golden locks flowing all them years. I tell you, out on the prairie he'd no need to cup a hand to an ear to catch a faint sound. Them lugs stuck out like the prairie wind was blowing from behind and they lacked the rigidity to resist. They recollected me of cabbage leaves, in miniaturized form.

Further maltreatment were administered to the optic nerve via the nose. Long and thin it were until you arrived at the end, at which juncture it bolused out, like he got an incipient carbuncle under there. That tumescence were cahooted up with the bottom lip, what stuck out like that of an adolescent told to go tidy. I venture in moments of intimacy Mrs Bacon had a fine old time dibble-dibbling on it. Assemble them features together and you get some idea why he lived a life of over-compensation.

I'll mention the facial whiskers being they held an item of interest. Typical moustache to scalp arrangement of the period, all of luxuriant growth and well-tended, the chin bare. Bushiness was most marked in the moustache part, what was doing its damnedest to conceal that blubber lip pouting out. Below that pout resided the salient feature appertaining to this interpolation, a square of golden hair. As to its purpose, other than affectation, I cannot comment.

So to synopsize this discourse on his physicality, I'd say knock his hat off and reduce him to his underdrawers, Custer'd be an ordinary sort of a fellow.

His gubernatorial style. He spelt it out right off so any was slow on the uptake could allow it to soak in. Things-are-going-to-change-around-here, were the substance to it. He looked out over the camp and until his eyes rested on a trooper lashed to a waggon wheel. Why is that man tied to that wagon wheel? he barked out to our officers what had recent adjacentized theirselves for fawning purposes. Desertion Sir, one said. That man is to have thirty lashes, Custer said. See to it immediately. Yes sir.

Custer dismounted and walked a long a line of troopers what was standing to attention. He studied each one, employing the line of that knobby nose for aiming purposes, his head pecking up and down in the manner of a chicken just discovered a tribe of termites. Them rigid boys, licking their lips, trying to stare dead ahead, you'd think they was about to undergo a procedure pertinent to the clap doctor.

He paused. What's your name soldier. That boy had dressed in haste and them jacket buttons didn't correspond with the preordained holes. His Adam's apple leaped about and he stammered out his moniker. Custer struck him across the face with the back of his hand and shrieked, You are in my army now soldier. You will not disgrace me or your uniform by dressing like an inebriate. I have to say, his locution at that juncture sounded like that of a pampered female in a tantrum, and I felt embarrassed for the man. He turned it down a notch and said to the officer, See this man leads his horse when next on patrol, and carries his full kit. Yes Sir.

As I may have alluded to in the hereunto, we is about to arrive at an hiatus in my sojourn with the US Seventh Cavalry, but in them few days I was present at that camp, I witnessed some hard penances exacted from them boys. An individual minced along wearing a whiskey barrel for britches. Turned out he had been purloining whiskey for his fellows. Two men was paraded about with their heads shaved on a single side only, so that if you observed them from one side they was bald, while if they was turned about they was normally coiffured. They recollected me of that canine the medicine man banished from camp to save Looks At The Sky. Transpired they'd been out shooting prairie turkeys without the necessary paperwork. A further fellow was tied to the wheel and flogged, misdemeanours unknown.

Now, our saviour newly arrived, the Cheyenne, well they must have consulted their spirits, maybe exchanged words with a far-sighted eagle or three, being come the crepuscular they struck the camp. First time they'd ever done so directly, but somehow they knew old Yellow Hair had showed up, and they wanted to serve up a few antipasti.

Weren't much of a fight, that bunch engaged in their usual tactic of riding back and forth firing off shots, both lead and feathered. But you can imagine, this were dumplings and gravy to Custer. Those of a distrustful nature might even declare he arranged the attack hisself, paid those boys off so he could display his martial prowess. He clumb up onto a waggon, tipped that hat back, stood tall, one leg cocked on a barrel so everybody including Indians could see him, and you never knowed, a photographer might be loitering, hoisted that fancy rifle and commenced firing. Toward the end of it he even got his sword out and pointed out which ones to aim at.

Say what you like about goddamn Custer, and I have, but he weren't no coward. I witnessed it, and some judged him reckless in battle, yours truly included. I have applied my admittedly limited intellect to it and have whittled it down to this nub which I will now impart to you. The part of his brain what ought conjure terror at the prospect of bloody battle, personal dismemberment and death agony, that part was missing.

Anyhow, none of us bunch was hit in the fight, and I didn't see no Indians drop, so I guess you'd call it a zero-zero tie, assuming them braves wasn't whites ruddled up. Custer, he tried to bluster it out, but you could tell his humour were knocked awry. It'd have sure embroidered his advent if he'd knocked an Indian or two of his horse, sent his striker out to go get the scalps. He thumbed the rifle sight as if clearing impedimenta, and issued an expiatory statement. Well boys, may God damn those savages. It was like shooting swallows on the wing.

Next day, as we was heading out to serve up admonishment to them insolents, I saw troopers lined up on one knee engaged in target practice, first time I ever saw such activity, and as I said in the hereunto Custer was to assemble hisself a company of sharp-shooters. He'd also got troopers riding about waving swords and decapitating rude scarecrows. Me, I never got to take part in them inculcations, but you got the idea something big were pending.

I AIN'T GOING to describe us riding about the dusty ridges and gullies looking for Indians led by a young lieutenant laying the foundations of a career. Needless to say, we saw none. Come the crepuscular the lieutenant told us to camp by a creek the Lord had seen fit to furnish with sweet water. Me, I judged the decision to be founded, like our camp, on sandy ground. That stream had a tolerable flow to it, and it roiled around rocks and splashed over tree branches, and the associated din would render us deaf to aboriginal approaches.

I speculate it a day or two since that boy had been laying around camp, watching the womenfolk at their chores, feeling his privy part engorge, maybe even sneaked down to the creek to peep while they was at their toilet. Enough, he'd thought. Time to prove myself a man and get noticed. A US cavalry horse, now that'd would be a fine start. Right from under their noses. That'll show them females. Yep, I'll go get me one of them.

The morning star was lodged atwixt the horns of the moon when he showed up, the sky milking over to the oriental, the moon gleam answering it on the opposing quarter, the camp all snores and flatus. The Indians ought dub it, The Hour of the Sleeping Sentry, though I never heard no particular Indian utter that dictum. My nostrils and lugs caught him contemporaneously, his odour, them stalks of grass stirring, though no humano could have perceived them intimations. A nag off yonder nickered, having clocked the new presence. Yours truly, I stayed silent, being curious to see what were afoot.

Why he plumped for me I have no clue. Maybe I was closest

and he didn't want to push his luck. Maybe he'd picked out that fine grey picketed nearby, but the dim light and the shifting nags had confused him. Fabridzio Capeesh, well he was partial to his shuteye, and he didn't want no fidgety nag tied to his ankle disturbing such repose, so he'd picketed me in that sandy ground.

He'd been inculcated up good, that boy. He quit crawling and rose to his feet and strolled right on over, a stoop to his walk, his hands spread to show he weren't carrying no weapon. He said, Quiet brother. I do not come to harm you, which got him on my good side. He stoked my neck all gentle, blew up my nose, and you know what that does to me, whispered nonsense of like quality. He took my bridle. He said, Come brother, let me free you from these uncivilized soldiers. He stepped away, and I followed. Well, what the hell.

FOURTEEN

The sun was half way up the sky, and we'd dusting along all that time, him taking the usual detours of rocky outcrops and stream beds, albeit them troopers wouldn't take much confusing what with no savage along to do the tracking. We stopped and he stood on my hindquarters and palmed his eyes and searched the posterior plains, grunted satisfaction, set me off again.

At that juncture he figured it appropriate to sing his victory song and I was obliged to orient my lugs in contrary direction. I'd got my famous wind, and by the way he was slapping my neck and wailing out that ditty that pulmonary feature had impressed him and I estimated him convinced he'd purloined winged Pegasus hisself, had he ever heard of that nag. Done singing, he stopped by a creek to water up and inspect his prize.

Well, he'd never make no poker player. As he surveyed the sawed-off, butcher-block headed, turd-coloured apparition, I'd say crestfallen about nails the expression. What with the recent exertions my arse decided time was to answer a call of nature, and them apples spilling out behind about completed the confection. He opened his maw and bent his body backwards and emitted a sound a housecat might make if held by the tail and whirled about. He picked up dust and threw it over hisself. He squatted, slapped his hands to his head and leapt about in the manner of a frog, and I venture he was picturing his courting prospects dusting off over the horizon.

He arose and reached up to pull at an absent ear lobe, and it was about then we recognised each other. Last time I saw that boy was on the Purgatoire River in a state of health I believed terminal. It was Hears The Moon, the Shoshone-Ute-Comanche boy what done led the convoluted life.

Now you is casting your eyes heavenwards. What is this joker up to now. You done told me he was dead of the cholera. Well such I believed he was. You can check back, but I don't recall confirming his demise. It were an assumption, and given my cast of mind, my jockey breathing out her last, pardon me if my thoughts was otherwise occupied. Any number of possibilities might explain this new manifestation. Well, two.

His god had resurrected him, him being destined to perform some future act of great magnitude, the absence thereof would reroute the course of Comanche history, an entirely feasible and unremarkable explanation to the Indian mind.

He done survived.

So I admit it. While I waited around up on the Purgatoire to be certain Looks At The Sky had breathed her last and her sprit was safely departed, and I was pretty sure that Humps a Lot with his stoved-in head had gone under, I hadn't perambulated around to check on the residue of that feculent bunch. I do recall the stillness of Hears The Moon's chest, and I don't remember hearing his pump working, but maybe them organs was working but leaving no sign. I ain't no quacksalver. Being of practical mind, I'd plump for this latter explanation.

Now this thought made my own pump quicken and skip a beat or three, and a turbidity entered my mind, as when the muddy stream swirls about some submerged obstacle, and my thoughts tumbled through that turbidity and wouldn't be corralled, if I might mix my picturing.

Jesus. What if I ain't done waited long enough. What if Looks At The Sky's bodily organs had give no indication of their continued function. What if she was back at the camp right now with the square ma, or out on the plains talking to otters and studying the flight of avians. What if she got a new fancy pony what usurped my position. But then she had saved me when she come to me incorporeal that time, in the rain after the degenerate horse combuster near sent me under. But if she'd said the right prayers and performed the correct necromancies, that appearance could have been arranged. This was some tough figuring.

He approached, eyes and jaws widening in concert. He pawed my white star, walked about me and felt the white sock, ran his hands over my scars. He stood back and scratched his head. His locution, when it finally showed up, were fractured.

Why, he said in Comanche, I believe you are Yellow Crow with One Foot in the Snow. You are the pony of Looks At The Sky, Looks At The Sky, of the mother we call Brays Like a Burro. You got that right, I thought, but he ain't done yet. You are the horse of the great wind who carried Looks At The Sky to safety after she killed the cunning but poorly attired Apache.

Well, apropos his perspicacity, this boy was burgeoning in my estimation. He walked off to the stream and turned and rubbed the back of his neck and said, I see you. I know it is you, but how this came to be, this I do not understand. He saw my shoulder and the US burnt thereon. He come back and ran his fingers over it, said, Hummm.

Well, you whittle away at it. You is a bright boy blessed with a broad life experience. You'll cipher it out.

I guess it appropriate now to describe this fellow being he figures large in the upcoming. This I will proceed to do.

Corporeally, well the Comanche tend to portliness, and a pure-blood is a squat and bandy-legged affair, but pure-bloods is in short supply and anyhow if you remember he weren't no Comanche he were a Shoshone. Lissom and wiry I'd precis it, and I expect a white'd judge him in need of a sow-belly and dumpling supper. Tall, but not so tall you'd be leery of standing adjacent during an electrical storm. Physiognomy-wise, don't be picturing no moon-faced indigene. His face comprised a series of angular slabs, brows, nose and chin and such, though these wasn't sharp featured, and you might say they'd been subject to the action of eons of wind and water, if they was items of geology and you was of poetical cast. Departing this geological vein was the lips, what was fleshy, maybe in the manner of some desert succulent I never heard of after a rainstorm. I venture ignorant types might describe them as unmasculine and aspersionize him for it. Now taken independently, you might adjudicate them features economy-sized, and such they was, but they was arranged in harmonious concert, and in my brief acquaintance with that boy, I never knowed him short of female admirers.

He weren't no devotee of the eyebrow plucking neither, being he owned a brace of them items to tempt a shoe-shine boy, and below resided them windows to the soul. Dark they was, so you humanos might scarce discern any border atwixt the black circle and the coloured ring. My eyes discerned it, the colour of charred cedar, and if they peered hard, jags of green the colour of moss growing by a waterfall. In their movements the eyes was like bees, in that they rested on an object, investigated it a spell, moved on to the next. They was presently resting on yours truly.

LATER, the meteorology coming on cool and the prospect of mayhem receding, he put leggings and a shirt on and put me off at a slow lope, him trusting my wind, knowing who I was now and what I'd done. Course, now he realized I was a Comanche nag and him being an Indian hisself, he commenced jabbering in ambagious fashion, and being of that age and seeing as no other males comprised our party to ridicule him, his talk turned to affairs of the heart.

He'd been in love with Looks At The Sky, still was, and my former jockey now become the major topic of the monologue, how beautiful and bright she was, way cleverer than him, and the clever things she did besides flesh hides and chop wood. How she walked pigeon footed and sat proud astride me and ate her meals all delicate (Jesus, this was getting tedious) and always kept her chin clean of grease and that thing she did with her hair, the way her top lip formed two mountains and a valley. He appeared blithe to the jug ears.

He never mentioned her demise up on the Purgatoire. Wonder why. But then the memory of it might have been as raw to him as it was to me and so he left that part untold. And all them stories was told in the past tense. But maybe he'd pledged his troth and she done jilted him. You can intuit my mental turbidity here.

So I kept the spark of hope well away from my mental kindlings she might be alive someplace, puzzling out some knotty problem, asking a moth for advice. Whatever the truth of it, she was still alive to that Indian as much as to me. But I have to say his talk tipped my mental equilibrium, my own memories bundling back like that. So I pitched him off. He got the mulligrubs and that truncated his circumambages for the rest of the pm.

When he spoke again he said, I will call you Yellow Crow.

TWO REASONS he might have donated that truncated nomenclature. In memory of his former sweetheart, or because he foresaw the full version unwieldly, especially in jeopardacious moments. Or a combination of the two.

We splashed across that Cimarron, though he chose a different ford than the one what'd smothered them sumpters, and I danced across without plugging my feet. Come the crepuscular he plunked an arrow in a jackrabbit and dug up some prairie onions. Herd of elk grazed off yonder, bunch of wolves watching from a knoll, in the nearabouts a party of deer drifted by, and he might have took me and gone off to shoot hisself one for his repast. But he never.

He led me off to a hollow and some fresh grass where he dug hisself a hole and built a fire therein, roasted them victuals. After he'd wiped the grease off of his chin, he commenced singing. His vocal chords exhausted, he rose and danced about in angular fashion. The limbs exhausted, he sat and watched the moon butting through the clouds, such you'd think the moon itself were dashing across the firmament. He conversed with a wolf howling off yonder. He went off into the plain and stood a piece and returned with a look of satiation on his face. He crumpled into a cross-legged sit, whereupon he commenced weeping for reasons unknown. He was athwart me by cockcrow, the moon long gone, clouds obscuring the stars, goddamn owl yipping off someplace.

We'd forded the Beaver, the plains rising and falling now in swells you scarce perceive, and I cock an eye on a bunch of low hills, a trio of furuncles and a pimple comprising the principal excrescences. I feel him relax on that blanket he flung over me. We are home, he mutters, and it clubs me what a long walk he must have took to get hisself a nag and prove his manliness, and I calculate myself insufficient booty for his efforts. Maybe he'd starved hisself and got a vision out of it. That'd be some recompense. Could be somebody dropped him off halfway.

We come to a coulee and he walks me down to the bottom where a creek flows clear and we follow it upstream. We fetch up at a bend where the bench knuckles out and he dismounts. He opens a parfleche he'd been carrying slung from his shoulder, his meagre possibles within. He extracts a twig brush and sets about applying it to my hide. So he'd figured he might as well make the best of it. He withdraws a strip of weasel fur what has brass wire woven into it and ties it to my bridle. He takes two raven feathers and ties them in my mane atwixt the ears. To the casual observer it must have looked like I possessed four of them items.

He attends to hisself. He claps the dust off his shirt and leggings, ensures his breechclout is decent. He takes a pouch and cups a hand and pours umbrous powder into it and stoops to the creek. The powder transforms to vermillion and he applies it to his face in the form of two lightning bolts. He ain't endowed with no mirror and the creek flows too fast to serve as substitute, so them jags ain't exactly the greatest examples of verisimilitude. Least he don't have to worry about his hair. He takes out a cavalry cap he must have purloined en route to nabbing yours truly, rubs his forearm across them crossed sabres and fixes it atop his braided poll, un-canted. We is all set.

It weren't like the first time. I didn't exit no narrow defile to get blinded by the sun. It were a cool day of scudding showers and shards of blue and clouds too big to spy resemblances, the hooping wind bending the grass. Them rivulets of herbage pointed the way and we followed.

We round the knuckle and pause beside a pile of ungulate bones. The tethered eagle regards me, a crop of tail feathers half-growed. He don't admit no acquaintance. And there they are.

Maybe two score of lodges arranged in two circles, off yonder the pony herd grazing peaceful, two boys on guard tossing stones at each other. They greet a rider coming in, a deer athwart his horse. Smoke is exiting horizontal out of smoke holes and fire pits. My nostrils catch its stink and that of roasting buffalo and boiling bones. Couple of females and the same of slaves is hauling firewood, a bunch more rubbing brains and grease into hides. Shavers run about firing blunt arrows. Two males inspect a pony. One is Cunning Bird.

Them bristling lodges, doors pointed toward the sunrise, smoke flaps ajar. By God. My old bunch going about their dailies, and I feel my spirits rise like a hawk on the wind. I can't say why.

MY REVERIE SOON COME TRUNCATED. The yappers clock us, commence eponymous activity, and come running. Two women look up from their labour and stare out. They yip and howl. Hears The Moon yips out a reply and holds his bow and that Army Coltses aloft, fires a shot and plants his heels into my flanks.

I twig his intent and leap into a dead run. My jockey, whooping now, I take him a full-chisel spin around the camp. Folks bundle out of tipis. The females have quit their choring and watch on, mouths ajar, clapping their hands to their heads, the exact combination of effects Hears The Moon intended.

He pulls me into a tight turn. He wants to flaunt the nimbleness of his new steed. Now nimbleness weren't never my strong suit, and my posterior hooves slither some in the mud. But I thwart that mire, and I even hold my head up a little to show it never happened and if it did, it were naught and anyway weren't my fault. Like I learned off of the gubernators.

My ginger is up now. I'm going to give them spectators the big finish. Off yonder is a bunch of cured hides, stacked ready for trading. They is about the height of a humano's hip. I'll go jump them bastards.

Hears The Moon, well he apprehends my intentions right off and whoops anew, digs his heels in to urge me on, like it's his idea. I am in rapid motion toward that stack, clods of prairie kicking up behind, my ears flat and my mane flowing, my tongue lolling out, when it clubs me. My earthly ain't never required much in the line of jumping. Maybe some when Looks At The Sky pedagoguerized me. But them impedimenta were little more than the height of a fallen comrade. In the general course of affairs, equines tend to detour around obstacles.

Jesus, what to do. Veer off? Dig my hooves in and commit my jockey to a solo attempt? But, goddamnit, that Indian hauteur sure is infectious. Weren't no going back now. It were death or glory.

Now you is sitting back in your upholstery expecting me to make an arse of myself. You know the only attributes I got to call on in this predicament is my wind and my gumption, and both of them items was redundant in the task at hand. But it weren't so.

I was whittling on whether to offer up a prayer to the Lord, realizing I was scant of time for the preliminary blandishments, when Looks At The Sky comes to me, big as life. You can do it, brother, she says. I know it. Show them as you showed me.

Well, I am so fixated on my former jockey showing up like that, who wouldn't be, that I fail to notice my hooves have recent departed tierra firma and the rest of me has followed suit. You should have heard the silence. Even the yappers have shut up and is agog. Their tongues loll out and their heads follow my trajectory.

Naturally, I attempt to maintain a graceful arc, and I believe to this day I made a fair job of it. But then my front hooves plug into that miry ground, the downside being my hindquarters continue progressing. I picture Hears The Moon's face in the mire, all his manly flauntations come to naught but abjection and mockery. But I feel his thighs and knees and ankles lock onto my flanks, his fists tighten down on them reins and grab a handful of mane, and despite my nose grazing the dirt and them posterior hooves grazing the hides and planting theirselves in advance of the anteriors, somehow that Indian remained athwart, and them near calamities and his equitatory prowess in negotiating them calamities only serve to garnish the display.

Well, you can imagine, them Comanche all started and howling and cheering and clapping their hands to each other and their thighs. Shavers was first to arrive and they slapped me and cavorted, getting atwixt my legs like they do. Hears The Moon gathered up a boy and sat him on my neck, like that fretful Cheyenne pa done, some step-relative or other. The men showed up trying to look unimpressed, though their crinkled eyes and upcurled lips let slip they was of the reverse temper. The females, their eyes shining, was grinning like Cheshire cats, whatever they is, my jockey mopping it all up like bread does gravy.

A further female comes shouldering through the melee, a sturdy arrangement with knobby wrists and elbows, muscles taught as piano wires. I see her fists is clenched. Hears The Moon clocks her and the triumph evaporates and his face and shoulders slump. He digs his heels into me, but he'd done left the fleeing option too late.

Fox Who Runs Straight yells, Where have you been you disobedient pup. She reaches up and drags him off and he thuds into the dirt, bends and shoves a forefinger in his face. You think I have nothing better to do than spend my days worrying about you? I thought you were dead. She opens a hand and tries to cuff him. But he sees it coming and deflects the blow with his forearm. She feints twice and he moves to parry, and you could tell they is well-practiced in this activity. She raises the other hand to strike, but this is just a ruse, and as he attempts to evade the blow she fetches him one about the ear with that previous. The Comanche all cheer.

You can imagine, the admonishment ain't going to go down too well with them marriageable females what was recent admiring on. She stares down at him a breath, hands fixed to her hips, and reaches down and grabs his shirt and hoicks him to verticality. She holds him out from her and takes him in, shaking her head, and I see them optics watering up. She says, My boy, and pulls him in and they bury their hands in each other's hair, her squeezing so tight I figure asphyxiation a danger. Both are weeping now, a finale what causes the spectators to jeer and flap their hands and walk off.

That night they held a big party to celebrate Hears The Moon's return, them Comanche always amenable to an excuse for a blast. Hears The Moon staked me outside his tipi, and I tried to shut my ears to the din, a futile endeavour when the singing kicked in. The whites would have needed no few barrels of busthead to unshackle such inhibitions, but not them temperate Indians. Later

Hears The Moon led a young female off into the trees. He looked right pleased with hisself, I tell you, sporting that forage cap. He looked over to me and grinned, and were Indians acquainted up with the gesture, which they wasn't, I swear he'd have given me the thumbs-up. So intent he was in his courting, he never looked behind and clocked that girl's ma following on, accoutered up with a cudgel.

FIFTEEN

Come the morning and they'd finally pried their bodies off of the buffalo robes, a quartet of males come doddling over. Two I recognised right off. They was Cunning Bird and White Antelope, that latter the sawed-off fellow what'd intended castration upon my person.

First thing White Antelope done was bend his back and look atwixt my legs, feel around at the part where my ballocks had once swelled proud. He sucked his teeth. Where the hell you get this clumsy knife job done, kind of style. He raised himself and nodded at Cunning Bird who nodded back at him, mouth downturned Indian style. Then it was the standard leg-rubbing, flank-feeling, chopper-scrutinising inspection in which the whole quartet took part, pausing and muttering at my various combusted parts, poking their fingers into my wounds, fingering my brand, going ahh.

An aspect of an unknown fellow struck me as familiar, and when he come inspect my choppers I tried to place him. His hair were blacker than all them others, as if an attempt at over compensation had been made. But the charcoal and grease had missed a portion, and ginger hairs poked forth. By God, it were the ass-fluffed speckled boy they'd got captive on my very first day as a Comanche, the one the females had fustigated into shape.

Well, you should have seen him. Weren't no way he could have looked more Indian, what with them braids and the tattoo and the face ruddled and the buckskins and a nice battle scar on his cheek, and I saw he'd lost that mudslide belly and them thin arms had knotted up with muscle. Well, there'd he'd been tearfully pondering his future and predicting it painful, and now here he were a full-fledged Comanche, and by his aspect I'd say he was finding the life agreeable. Even got a Comanche name. Best I can render it is, Used To Cry.

At the conclusion of the inspection they all stepped back and rubbed their chins or the rear parts of their necks. I ain't reporting no speech here, even though being Indians they was gabbling on. Reason being naught notable was said, save for, Yes, this is surely Yellow Crow with One Foot in the Snow. I'd know those short legs and the tree-stump head anywhere.

I let that slide, being more mithersome thoughts was bundling into my noggin. It was the demeanour of that bunch what worried yours truly. This weren't no big welcome-home for the lost hero. They didn't show up bearing armfuls of gewgaws to bedeck my person. Some aspect to my homecoming was embrangling their minds. Earlier I'd seen Slow Turtle perambulating about the camp, fully attired thank the Lord. I'd taken a real liking to that fellow after his display on the knob, and I hoped he might come say hello. But, though he cast a glance in my direction, and I saw he knew me, him being part of our adventure with the spirit Apache out on the Llano, he never did. You'd think he was avoiding me.

Well, that bunch, they finally said something notable, and that utterance occasioned the turbidity to enter my mind once more, and invited tiny birds to take residence in my stomach and start flapping about. They said, Wonder what Picks Herbs By The Lake will say.

I didn't know who Picks Herbs By The Lake was, although I

should have, having prior enjoyed the company of that individual. The name was delivered in a portentous thunderstorm-in-the-here-abouts manner, what had put the jimjams up me. He must be some big chief possessed of big puha. But then again, Picks Herbs By The Lake weren't exactly the kind of manly appellation a chief would want to strew about willy-nilly. Something sat askew. I was soon to find out what, being Picks Herbs by the Lake was off somewhere visiting relatives and was due back in a couple of sleeps.

AIN'T nothing to report about them days, bar I spent the time with the pony herd and bumped into my cousins, and we spent no little time nuzzling and thinking nostalgic thoughts about the Llano. I can relate a curiosity to keep you entertained.

A white trader and a pair of mules showed up and camped off yonder. He couldn't have been no Texan or he'd have already got ventilated and be fertilizing the grass. Even though he were wearing the skins of deceased animals to blend in, you might be surprised to find a white circulating unmolested in a Comanche camp back then, them Indians infamous among the whites for rapine and torture. But an Indian is obliged to be hospitable to them who ain't proven enemies, particularly if they show up with gifts. He got a mixed-blood along to do his choring, but evidently he weren't no hand at translating delicate negotiations, and the lexis of sign weren't ample enough neither, being they got Fox Who Runs Straight in to parley.

Turned out he wanted to ransom Used To Cry, return him to his white ma and pa and change him back into a civilised Christian, get him a mortgage and some life insurance, and they was prepared to pay a high price. A couple of chiefs was keen to trade. The trader had laid out coffee and sugar and tobacco as antipasti to the deal, big butcher knives, half dozen Coltses and likewise of Spencer repeaters supplying the spit to the handshake if I may mix my picturing, though ammunition to shove in them latters appeared absent.

The deal got stymied at the outset. Lay aside his Comanche ma and pa goddamn wailing at his possible departure, soon as he discovered he were the item subject to negotiation, Used To Cry took his horse and possibles and absquatulated hisself onto the plains.

All that preamble is by way of pry-barring in some intelligence about Fox Who Runs Straight, being her deeds and character is crucial to the understanding of pending events. You notice I interpolated there she were the interpreter. How can that aboriginal female be educated enough to translate English, I hear you cry. Well I'll tell you, being Hears The Moon told me.

The Texans killed her ma and pa while massacring a Comanche village down on the Colorado River, not the famous Colorado, another'n. They caught her trying to swim the freezing creek, waited till she foundered then drug her out, took her captive and put her to slaving in a white's home. That's where she picked up the lingo. You can imagine, she had a hard time of it, being Indian, frequent whippings and, when she come of age, what the whites called outrages but what moniker don't apply to an Indian. Bunch of times she escaped, got caught and drug back and fustigated. Way she got out was she got traded, like they was trying to do with Used to Cry, only reverse-wise. The Comanche paid a white woman and a white girl to get her back. Hell of a price. By God, the way they tell it, seemed like back then the whole economy ran on trading kidnaps.

Now I am in the bad habit of truncating Indian names for my own selfish ends. You won't find me engaging in such discourtesy with Fox Who Runs Straight.

THE SUN WAS HALFWAY down the sky, and Hears The Moon had come out to give me a brushing, affix sundry knick-knacks, daub on assorted pigments, them comprising couple of red zig-zags on my haunches and black circles around my eyes, and to the casual observer it must have appeared I were wearing spectacles. At the outset he'd said he was going to daub the wind on me to indicate my special magic. He stood back and scratched his head a stretch. Even dipped the dipped his fingers into the pot at one point as if to commence. Then he huffed and said, I am sorry Yellow Crow, I do not know how to draw the wind, so I got lumbered with the zig-zags and spectacles. Me adorned thus, Picks Herbs By The Lake showed up.

Hearing yours truly had arrived was the fly-twang on the spider web. I heard her before I saw her. That voice, by God, like an angry cook putting away frypans, and that buckskinned harpy is marching on, head inclined, arms preceding, them limbs held rigid and moving in time to the sway of her bosom. Jesus, she'd put some timber on during our interlude.

She'd got Cunning Bird and White Antelope in tow, them speaking mollifying words, struggling to keep up. There he is. There he is. How dare you allow it, allow that horse into our camp after what he did to me. Let me get at him. I'll put it right. She interlarded these phrases with pejoratives directed at the two males and remarks germane to my future survival on this earthly. The most worrying aspect were she had a big knife strapped to her considerable hip, and her chubby hand were moving toward it.

Hears The Moon, well he might have endured kidnap, Comanche inculcations, survived the cholera, snuck into a US Cavalry camp and purloined hisself a nag, a fine hat and an Army Coltses and outwitted the pursuers. But the sight of her in full charge occasioned the colour to drain out of his face to the extent you'd have mistook him for taibo. She got that knife evaginated and kicked through a pile of my apples.

I'll say this for that Shoshone-Ute, he placed hisself afore yours truly and folded his arms and jutted his chin out. The two males grabbed hold of them swinging arms and attempted to drag Picks Herbs to a halt, but imagine throwing twine around a runaway train. Hears The Moon, well that manly posture come to naught. She swatted him aside like a grizzly a gopher and attempted to gain possession of my reins. I knew then what she was about. For reasons hereunto unconfirmed she planned to stick that knife in and jugulate me to perdition.

Well as you can imagine, after all I done endured I weren't standing for this, and I snapped my head back and whipped away them reins and trotted off a few horse lengths distant. She weren't dumb. She knew she couldn't chase down no nag, what with her corpulence and all, and she stood there at bay, and had she been a buffalo, she'd have been harrowing the earth and tossing dust in the air.

We stood eyeballing each other, her examples bone-awling into me. She darted forward a few paces and I retreated a few paces. We reprised the action. I could keep this up all day. I saw on the sinister hand she'd cut off her little finger at the final knuckle, a deletion I judged scant sacrifice for the loss of a fine daughter. Because, for those of you slow on the uptake, it was Looks At The Sky's square ma, the very same, and she ain't mellowed none. Who'd have thought she'd have been nomenclatured up Picks Herbs By The Lake. Not me.

The males sought to turn the hiatus to their advantage. They spread their hands out and cocked their lips and heads and spoke unctuous words, and you'd have more luck farting through your drawers to extinguish a prairie fire. Me now being out of range, she turned on them. Why did you let that horse into the camp? Do you know what it put me through? My husband runs away and my only daughter dies on me. How am I supposed to manage? Get a rope round his neck and drag him close. She turns to me and spits out my new moniker, Death Horse.

She prattled on and the truth of it prys its way into my thick noggin. I were the one who carried Looks At The Sky to her death. She was fine before yours truly took her off. Turned out I was the only equine survivor of that jaunt up the Purgatoire. The rest of them nags had either never made it back or been dispatched to supply mounts for their deceased jockeys in the afterlife. They let me live, I'd be bad medicine. She waved that knife in my direction anew. I'd bring bad luck and pestilence to their band, she said, like I done poor Looks At The Sky. She done disremembered all the trouble I went to saving that girl from the spirit Apache.

Them males watched on as she completed this discourse, pretending they was listening, and seeing as she weren't progressing the persuading, she turned the ocular taps on. She dumped herself cross-legged on the plain, them eyes coursing, and commenced wailing, encoring the racket with further comments about how hard her life was now her daughter was dead and her husband alive but departed to locations unknown.

Well, there is only so much a soul can be expected to take of this, and while I distanced myself off a piece more, them two chiefs said they'd hold a council and decide what'd be done. I estimate that pair remembered my prior deeds and that is what saved me. Were I an uncelebrated nag they'd have inveigled me close and let her plunge that knife in and come the crepuscular I'd have been feeding the yappers.

I HAVE to report the outcome of the council weren't propitious to my prospects. When all was said and done I were only a nag after all, and them chiefs liked the quiet life. Hears The Moon, him knowing me best with Looks At The Sky demised, were the one delegated to do it.

I have to say, I considered that decision hard on the boy, after all he'd walked all that way to rescue me from the US Cavalry, proved his manliness, and then he put on all that entertainment.

But I reckon they figured Picks Herbs by the Lake would have performed the task in leisurely fashion, and what with my past heroics, I deserved to be done in quick.

Now I could tell you that Hears The Moon come to me one morning brandishing that knife, trembling and tearful, rubbed my ears and spoke nonsense up my nostrils, held that blade over me like Abraham done over Isaac when the Lord commanded he kill his firstborn son, and then Hears The Moon drops the knife and wails he just can't do it to me. He just can't. After all, you know I survived this peril and went on to become the only living survivor of the fight known as the Little Big Horn. But he never. He never had the merest intention of following that diktat.

He'd led a convoluted life had that boy, like Mrs Cash and the Cornishman and Pervis, and as I said in that hereunto, them types always saw some affinity between them and me. And let's own it, it were partly due to my theatricals that he enjoyed his first copulation with a female, which is no niggardly event in a sprout's life and one surely worthy of recompense, albeit he earned a cudgeling for it. So what happened was this.

Fox Who Runs Straight was quarter Cheyenne. Don't ask me how or anything about the step-pa or even if there was one, because I know nothing about them affairs. She decided of a sudden she wanted to go visit a grandpa what'd succumbed and was set to demise. They was camped not far distant, and the Cheyenne and the Comanche being on friendly terms in them days, all got agreed and the departure date set.

Fox Who Runs Straight left in the cold dawn a day earlier than agreed, and by sheer coincidence a day earlier than that set for my transferral to the afterlife. She took me and Hears The Moon along, and left Picks Herbs By The Lake to stew in it. I estimate the plan was that when they got back it'd be blown over, or maybe Picks Herbs by the Lake would have died of an infarction, her being fat and choleric and given to smoking the pipe. It was some risk she was taking, but when it come down to it, it never got to pan out like that.

Anyhow, all that forgoing is by way of enucleating how I become a member of the Cheyenne Nation. How I discovered myself amid the tac of falling leaves, from them big timbers along a creek the tribes called the Lodgepole, what the taibo call the Washita.

SIXTEEN

J esus but come the winter the aboriginal life gets tedious. Ain't naught to do but trudge about chawing cottonwood twigs. Compared to this, that last winter with the Cornishman were a riot.

By the time us trio showed up they'd been off on their fall hunt, so that entertainment not to say potential embarrassment was done and dusted, and it is the aboriginal way that, come the inclemencies, they all hunker down in their lodges under a pile of buffalo robes and come up only for air and to perform the necessaries, attend to their toilet, boil up some grub, engage in verbal intercourse, gamble, tonk on a drum, items of that nature. And, by God, did them inclemencies strike hard.

The Lord sent us a concatenation of blizzards. They blew in and maybe a foot of snow piled up, and the next day the snow would turn to mush and then it'd freeze nocturnally so come the morning it were a crust of ice and you best watch where you step. No few times my legs embarrassed me. That said, I must say them Cheyenne couldn't have abided in a better spot. Nestled in a horseshoe on the river we was, them big timbers sheltering, a bluff off yonder contributing likewise. Why, if you was inclined you could even paw through the snow and dig down to some tolerable chawing herbage. And I growed my shaggy winter coat.

This benign topography were famous among the indigenes, and strung out to the east of us was sundry bunches of Arapaho and Kiowa, more Cheyenne. By God, even some Comanche come in. When she heard about their advent, Fox Who Runs Straight stalked off to investigate, worried Picks Herbs By The Lake maybe followed our trail. But she saw no tipi circumscribed by irregular distance and heard no bellowing, so it weren't our bunch and we was safe from admonishment. Nevertheless, to err on the side of prudency she kept us distant.

As for her grandpa, the one who was sick almost to death, the one for whom we'd made the mercy dash, well he was a more lively example of the Cheyenne.

He appeared not to feel the cold like the others and spent his time sat outside his lodge fashioning arrows, tying lariats, chunking snowballs at yappers and polishing a knob-handled flintlock pistol. He conceded to wrap his lower portions in a buffalo robe, but them uppers was clad only in a shirt, the sleeves cut-out so he could flaunt his knotty arms. On his shoulder was an old bullet wound and he had got his woman to tattoo a border around it to render it more conspicuous, and below his eye a powder burn from misuse of the flintlock.

As regards his headgear, well that was the only dispensation them upper parts allowed the inclemencies. Buffalo-hide cap it was, taken from the neck part of the animal, the noteworthy features being two ear flaps what bestowed upon him the aspect of a trail hound. Now I supply these particulars, but they was only visible if you could distinguish him through the fumid currents puthering forth from his tobacco pipe permanently combusted.

That pipe were a riot. Weren't no Indian contraption what might serve double duty as a hatchet. It were wooden, in the form of a serpent caught in a squirm and you saw its scales and its eye and it tumesced out to the bowl wherein the leaves was conflagrated. I once saw similar fixed atwixt the teeth of Dutchman trudging west aside his ungulates. I remain ignorant as to whether this were the same item. That Indian, his mouth were absent two biting dontics, and I conjectured the teeth was removed deliberate to accommodate the pipe, being the refinement allowed him to slide the bit in and out without inconveniencing hisself to open the jaws, and likewise facilitated the efficient egress of smoke.

Once he'd struggled through the flaps of his tipi, that Indian seldom moved from his seat, what consisted of a pile of wore-out skins, and he owned a couple of taibo females to minister to his necessaries. I reckon they was mother and child, given the resemblance, and they'd bring him chuck and firewood, rawhide for lariats and fresh sticks to make arrow shafts, them latters if they wasn't straight he'd objurgate the females in a reedy whine and raise his hand in threatening manner, though I never saw him strike. Weren't their fault. How would them whites be experts in the aerodynamics of arrows? My ears recollect the sound of that arrowsmith when he applied the finishing touch to his creations, a gentle repeated rasp such as Cupid might make sharpening his love darts.

Now, I am whittling on whether to supply the name of that Indian, being to mustard up the tedium of those days I've already told you a good bit about him. But it is one of them convoluted affairs, so I think I'll pass. The salient point about that fellow is he was half-brother to the old chief of our bunch, an individual the more savvy amongst you might have heard of, him one of the more famous Indians. Up there with Crazy Horse and Quanah and Geronimo, Thunder Rolling Down the Mountain, them types.

What can I tell you about my brief sojourn that ain't equally tedious. Not much, and that's the truth. Were I still in company with the Cornishman I'd have been looking forward to Christmas and the concomitant presents, one of the fonder recollections of my earthly. But I was with the Cheyenne, and they was a bunch of damned heathens.

I passed my time yonder with the pony herd, and did my best to nuzzle in with that steaming bunch. Some was a mite standoffish, I guess them sensing the admixture of Comanche and cavalry in me, such cognisance embrangling their noddles. A curiosity to report, some had bells looped about their necks, and I figured this a Cheyenne fancy. I remained in bifurcated mind about it. It'd be a boon on the locating side come a foggy morning. But what if the US Cavalry happened to be noctivagant up on them bluffs. Remember, last time I saw goddamn Custer he were bent on restoring the Seventh's glorious reputation, and weren't no better way to accomplish that task than massacre a bunch of goddamn primitives.

My jockey, well he was as attentive as any adolescent devoted to his slumbers and the onanistic arts could be of a winter morning. Most days he come huffing over, a bulging blanket slung across his back, contained therein fresh herbage he'd excavated. That were right considerate of him, I tell you, and to show my appreciation I let him sing to me without wandering off. Given pending events, I reckon that extra chuck is what got me through those seasonal privations and permitted me to progress through my earthly and to that summer day up on the Greasy Grass, where I become the only living survivor of the fight known as the Little Big Horn.

I can now break the tedium.

WE WENT OFF ON AN EXCURSION. Now that event were unusual in itself. Winter coming on, them few Indians still out hunting and raiding was all now straggling in and diving into their snowy tipis. So what took them Cheyenne away from their smoky lodges and musky wives must have been a matter of some heft. This were it.

Them stragglers had reported soldiers tramping about the

plains. By God, they'd even decamped at the confluence of the Wolf and the Beaver and chopped down trees to build a fort.

Now these reports discombobulated them Cheyenne minds. What would them troopers be doing out on the plains, the winter coming on? They couldn't be down here to for reasons of chastisement.

I ought exposit here that to the Indian mind this'd be fighting unfair. The Comanche didn't snug theirselves into their tipis on the Canadian come the winter and expect a bunch of Apache to descend on them of a morning, them all spooned up to their women. It weren't traditional. Since times they done forgot, summer was the season for warring, when the plains was high with grub for your ponies and you could run about crashing your club into them skulls and sawing off scalps naked barring your moccasins and breechclout. But them Cheyenne was in for a surprise.

The whites' fondness for winter fights figured large in the aboriginal's demise. You probably don't know this, but in my dotage I was present up on them frigid Dakota plains, alongside a creek the Sioux called the Wounded Knee.

Anyhow, the majority ciphered it them troopers was up to something, but imminent attack weren't part of it. Why would you be out in all that meteorology when you could be asleep next to a fat woman. But me I'd come acquainted with goddamn Custer by then, and he didn't seem the type to let inclement weather thwart his plans.

Now that famous chief, I calculate he shared my doubts, because it were him who arranged our excursion down the Washita, to its confluence with a creek the taibo renamed the Cobb. There, a fort was located, likewise a general, and they was going down to parley and find out what the goddamn hell was afoot.

Don't ask me why Hears The Moon was selected to form part of this delegation. Could be he were distant step-kin to the chief.

Could be that chief thought he needed the experience. Could be they needed somebody to see to the ponies and fetch the firewood and smash the ice for water.

Come a mid-morning, smoke spiralling up vertical out of the lodges, the sun burning off the fog and glassing over the snow, that adolescent comes trudging over. He is wearing long Apache-style moccasins whereon he has sewn an extra sole, and a buffalo skin cap similar to the arrowsmith's. He slips that army bridle over my head and his pad saddle across my back, affixes his possibles, and we toddle on off to join the other bunch what is waiting, them numbering the sum of the legs and tails of two equines, a good moiety well past the bloom of youth. We slip out of camp, nobody about to pay us much heed apart from Fox Who Runs Straight who waves, biting her lip, sundry choring womenfolk who glance up.

I TELL YOU, forward locomotion in heavy snow is no trifling affair. Us bunch out on the Llano, them flakes start billowing down, well we'd be down in the breaks and we'd find some ravine or crack in the earth and we'd put our arses to it and stay put for the duration. So I'd attempted little in the way of snowy travel before in my earthly. Adjacent to the camp, we followed the trails of them Indians what had just come in, but further you got out, you just had to break your own trail.

We took it in turns. Hears The Moon, being the youngest and most easily bossed, were selected for the first shift, and I was soon sudorated up and huffing, even with my wind, and I doubted the ability of them ordinary ponies behind to make similar headway. Such proved to be the case, and here my famous wind disadvantaged me, as did my patient nature, and my trail-breaking duties got more frequent, and longer.

The snow, it clumped about my hooves and on my belly hair.

Icicles dangled from my mane and poked me in the peepers. The wind was such that the snow I kicked up flew off and got dumped ahead, one of the Lord's drolleries I imagined. You come to a creek, you have to break the ice to wade on in, and then chunks of ice come barrelling down it and crash into your legs. Come a point along the trail when I felt a drag on my arse end, like some yapper had affixed his choppers thereon. Ice was balling even on that fixture too, such that I could have swung it and demolished a doghouse. You getting the picture here?

This type of travel ain't exactly comfortable for the jockey neither, me plunging and high-stepping like that, and it struck me this trail-breaking malarkey was another reason they had brung him along. Them passing the pipe around. Yeah, let's take him. He's naught but a sprout and he got that nag what's supposed be famous for his wind. Yeah, let's let him do it.

Hears The Moon, he slapped my neck and cast forth doxologies, Well done Yellow Crow, I never knew a pony of such wind, you are truly a wonder, but they was cast upon stony ground and found no purchase.

The wind stirred them snow-laden branches and a slab of it fell onto Hears The Moon's neck. Well it is my experience Indians like nothing better than to witness the painful misfortunes of others and they laughed themselves to the extent one fellow fell backwards off his pony.

The retelling of the event and the allied derogations sure perked up them Indians. Throughout the trip that boy become subject to no little persiflage regarding his manhood and sexual proclivities, as humano males is apt when they band together. The discourse was tedious in the extreme and I won't delay you with the particulars, but that boy took it and went about his duties in cheerful spirit. Looking back now and knowing what I know, I don't begrudge them fellows taking their entertainment where they could, for the mood of that trip were in the main sombrous.

At least chuck weren't on ration. A panoply of beasts and

creeping things were using the timber to shelter from the inclemencies. Turkeys stood on branches as if waiting in line for opera tickets. They watched us pass by and the Cheyenne ignored them. They could have shot them easy, but Cheyenne ain't partial to poultry as repast, and come the crepuscular they built theirselves wickiups and a fire and they feasted on a roasted deer. Hears The Moon brought me a blanket of grass, and for dessert I chawed on them plentiful twigs.

If the trip was hard for that famous Indian chief, he didn't show it. He said he'd seen of over sixty of such winters, however many that is, and would see a good deal more and copulate with many more wives before his body died and his spirit went off for more fun. Despite his protests, the younger men doted on him and brought him chuck and arranged his robes, snuggled up to him when they retired so as to keep him warm, and he never neglected to thank them.

Them all snoring away, but shuteye for me was in short ration. You know my antipathy to arboreal features, and were I a humano I'd figure old Absalom for an ancestor. The wind, it soughed through them goddamn timbers, limbs creaking, branches cracking off and thrashing down, the topmost swirling about like they was trying to wrench out their roots and flee.

Come the night it quieted down. The hour before dawn, in the kind of glow you only get when a blanket of snow is reciprocated by a blanket of cloud, I watched the black shape of a panther step out the trees. It halted, one paw raised, breath steaming out, belly crusted with snow, and held itself still like only them felines can, albeit I knew those ears and nostrils'd be in full motion. It raised its head and sniffed the air and held still again, and then bounded on off through the snow toward a grove where I'd prior seen a herd of deer ensconce itself. If it made a sound, I never heard it.

I pictured them deer then, eyes popping, ears rotating, flanks quivering, knowing it was there, knowing its purpose, but not knowing when or which of them it would strike. Pity them Indians never saw that panther. They'd have took it as a great sign and used it to divine future course of action, maybe even changed the course of history. But they was all in the embrace of Morpheus.

Took us a good four of them winter days to make that trip, and that was hard travel, what in the summer you could do in two and take picnics. The snow thinned out some, and as we fetched up in the hereabouts of the fort it could have been applied by the Cornishman's sugar caster.

SEVENTEEN

I t weren't much of an effort. A rectangle of low buildings devoid of the carpenter's art, them logs dropped vertical into the ground topped by sod roofs. A marching-about square, in the middle of which stood a pole bearing an American flag, wind-torn to streamers. Off yonder was a stable, beyond that, snow-crusted tipis.

Being he is about to start talking, I will proceed to supply a description of that famous chief.

Tolerable tall and solid sums up the general impression, and I calculate him a good bit beefier in his younger days. The complexion, dark, the features strong, one of them aboriginals what looks like his lineaments been chiseled out of an antique piano leg and left in the sun to gnarl and crack, a face of colliding angles and planes what echoed the topography wherein he passed his life. Such picturing might lead you to believe them features was composed into a hard expression, but you'd be wrong. He looked out at the world through wind-creased eyes, and his lips carried the trace of a smile, and he carried his head inclined to one side, just a hair.

Now ignorant types might interpret these aspects as signs of ignorance and mental vacuity. Me, I saw a benign, curious character, a man who'd drunk in life, wiped his chin and burped. He'd survived its projectiles and directed his bare arse at them, weighed such events and arrived at a clear appraisal of his own position in it all.

Now, I've went off windy as an Indian in that last, and you might decoct it all down to one word, dignity. But I saw him fall backwards off his pony when that hunk of snow slammed atop Hears The Moon.

They was frying bacon off somewhere, and as they walked us in the Cheyenne made gagging signs. Hears The Moon leaned forward and said, Yellow Crow, you have been with the whites. Why are the always eating filthy pigs and why do their forts smell of boiling leaves? This is not the food of warriors. I treated the enquiry as rhetorical of nature.

Bunch of troopers come out to greet us, the sentry having yelled out, Injuns. But we wasn't whooping or waving spears and clubs, and this was a fort where other tribes come in for rations in exchange for roaming the plains free, so they was habituated to aboriginals knocking about and so wasn't firing guns at us, albeit them latters was pointed in our direction.

A man called Wolf Looking Back spoke a little white, and together with a bunch of sign he made hisself understood they wanted to speak to the general as a matter of urgency. A corporal took us off to a low building, and when they dismounted he tried to chivvy them inside. They glanced through the open door and declined the offer, wrapped their blankets about them and squatted down, adopted the edifice as windbreak.

Naturally, he made them wait, that general. Could be he was otherwise engaged. More likely he wanted to communicate to them indigenes their true station. Whatever. The sun had traversed a good segment of the sky by the time he showed up, a big steer-horn moustache, a nanny-goat beard adorning the chin part, disappointedly devoid of headgear, though to impress the savages he had donned a tailored army jacket fitted-out with silver buttons.

He entered the building, acknowledging his petitioners with a nod, a quartet of munitioned-up troopers tramping on in behind. The Indians, concluding it weren't no jail after all, followed.

Now me and my highly attuned lugs was tethered right outside, in a position such that I could spy through the window, which is right fortuitous for the telling of this tale and allowed me to see a fly-specked portrait of the incumbent Great Father, that mudslide nose staring out. The window glass was faulty and if I moved my head around it made his chin swell and the eyes bulge, and that fenestratory defect entertained me a good bit. Anyhow I can't render them Indian speeches verbatim. It was all a long time ago we all passed a lot of water since, and even if I could remember all them vocables it'd use up too much of the printer's ink, so you'll just have to be content with the gist of it.

Black Kettle spoke first, a geriatric half-breed same colour as the general's desk interpreting. He spoke slow and deliberate. These was weighty matters and he didn't want them whites to get the wrong end of the stick. He said he had always been a friend of the whites and he considered the whites friends of his. He said the Cheyenne had never raided in these parts south of the Arkansas. They had even left the Texans unmolested. At this point he might have appended, unlike some I could mention, but he nodded his head in the direction of a bunch of Comanche lodges and figured that sufficed. He conceded the raids on the Saline and the Solomon, but said the whites shot first. Then it was back to the old chain-of-command topic. He had told his young men not to raid, done his best to keep them at home, offered inducements, proffered threats, but — and he ran out of words at this point and hoisted his shoulders as much to say, But what you gonna do. He re-hitched the eloquence and said that the Cheyenne liked the Indians presently residing about this agency, the Caddo, the Wichita, the Kiowa and Comanche and such, said he'd like to move his band down here where it'd be easier to keep his young men quiet. He said all he wanted was peace. He paused. He never mentioned the Seventh perambulating about the plains building forts.

But maybe he never got the chance. An Indian standing to the rear had been fidgeting and rolling his eyes. You could picture the workings of his noggin. Goddammit, he ain't saying it right.

That Indian were an Arapaho and were nomenclatured-up Big Head, maybe Big Neck or Big Mouth, some large body part. Anyhow, it don't require no further comment. He pipes up, and Jesus did he rub soft soap on a cracked saddle. He called the whites Brothers, the General the representative of the Great Father in Washington, upon whom he only wished wealth and joyfulness and many children, and who once gave him a medal. He took the medal out and held it up for the general to see. Big Head said he was here because he wanted to pursue the path of righteousness, and anyhow he had never harmed a white in his life. He spread out his arms to indicate he were coming to the nub. The Arapaho and Cheyenne was south of the Arkansas like they'd agreed in the treaty, and yet here was soldiers following them on down and fighting them. The general must order the soldiers to stop. The general must write a letter to the Great Father to tell him to tell them to stop. He said he'd had a brother killed by the soldiers, but was prepared to let it go, him being a man of peace and so forth.

The General, I couldn't see him through the window, and I didn't know if he was standing or seated, but he listened to the discourse in silence, and then he cleared his throat and took a deep breath and I pictured that moustache begin to work up and down. What he said was, they was fucked.

Now you know there was more to it than that, but that were the nub of it. He had no jurisdiction up there. He weren't about to write no letter. No. They damn well could not move theirselves down here and mingle with these friendlies because they might bring the wrath of the US Seventh Cavalry down with them and his friendlies would get caught up in it. They best go on back and take the matter up with the Seventh. They is reasonable fellows. Had he a basin handy, I believe he'd have washed his hands in it.

As we left the fort I bet the old chief was pondering how you can make peace with an over-compensating yellow-haired man bent on destruction. He weren't to know Little Phil had spelt out his orders so there'd be no mistake. Locate and destroy Indian villages and ponies. Kill or hang all those deemed warriors. Well, at least they'd got some coffee and sugar and hardtack out the visit, so it weren't all bad. Wolf Looking Back turned and yelled to the guards, You should grow your hair long so that we can have honour in taking your scalps. Well, there is always one ain't there.

———

THIN SNOW EDDIED at our feet. It reared up like rattlers and fled as sidewinders. The blanketed old chief, he were a pyramid of white. It clumped about my eyelashes and in my hooves, laid a fresh skin on my breast. Hears The Moon was obliged to dismount and huff on my eyelashes, take his knife and chip the ice out of my hooves. I recollect hoping that in any upcoming mayhem the Lord smiled on that boy.

Travel was silent and as hasty as them conditions permitted, them having got the bad tidings and wanting to get back to their families. They camped in the crepuscular and was always up before cockcrow. Last night out the wind shifted south and they dug their fire pits out on a rise on the open plain and slept covered only by their buffalo robes.

Come the true dead of night, a lone elk commenced grunting nearby. It'd be an old bull, them spryer males done kicked him out the herd the rut done. The wolves'd be watching on, smacking their lips. The old chief, he pries hisself out from among them snoring bodies and walks out a piece. He empties his bladder, a laboursome sporadic endeavour accompanied by a deal of groaning. He wraps his robe tight about him and gazes up at a hole in the clouds and the stars contained therein. He loops off a rawhide pouch what dangles from his neck. I watch his silhouette extract small objects, examine each one in turn, before uttering a low prayer and replacing them. By dint of the darkness and the distance, I cannot supply the identities of them items contained in his medicine bag. He raises his head and chants out a further prayer at low volume, him being a considerate type and not wanting to wake his fellows.

As he returns, cotton-boll snow drifts down. He opens his mouth and darts to one side to interrupt a trajectory, sticks out his tongue, eyes wide and fixed on the flake. At the last instant he adjusts his head and catches it on his tongue and holds it there and allows it to dissolve. He closes his eyes and tears squeeze out. A smile curves on out toward his ears. I have to say thenceforth in my earthly, whenever them precipitations fell and I found myself at leisure, I engaged likewise.

Dawn, the air still, a fog sloughed in, the Washita and its timbers invisible, though them features only fifty horse lengths distant. They dally while the sun yellows the fog, and huffing steam we go crunching off through the frozen melt. They'd decided no soldiers would attack in such meteorology, and anyhow we was barely a day now from the camp.

They stayed up the plain, us nags plodding on, heads down, about broke-down now, even yours truly. The fog lifted and sunlight flooded the snow, turned it to gold, and it was the goddamnedest thing. Not one, but a trio of suns was on our flank, set in a horizontal line.

I'd witnessed such a wonder but once before in my earthly, as a colt out on the Llano. A day in the late winter, the day after a norther roared through, a flawless sky, the air so still not a hair on my winter coat was stirring, and here they was again.

How can I describe this marvel the Lord had seen fit to bestow on me and these men. The sun, still low, was flanked by two offspring. These lesser suns possessed a tail and wings of golden light, but the wings wasn't held horizontal. Picture a hawk forced to make a sharp turn, his wings extended out above and below. The upper wings continued on, curving until they touched their brother's, creating an arch what put me in mind of a bow petrified in the act of loosing an arrow. This arch framed the father sun. You might see it as some kind of portal, and I'm telling you, despite the dazzle, it looked right inviting.

Now you know I ain't of them types amenable to auguries from nature, thereof in these latter pages there has been a goodly crop, and I expect you've been skewing your maws at the want of nuance, but if that sight made an impression on my thick noggin, you can imagine how them aboriginals took it.

Agog about pegs it. Wolf Looking Back jumped off his horse and dropped to his knees heedless to the snowmelt. He spread his arms and sang out an exaltation, albeit him being but of tin ear it were a tuneless affair. The others, after a stretch of dumbstruck, they jabbered, the topic for debate the meaning of it all.

Accord were in short supply. Some said a glorious future lay ahead for the Cheyenne. The Sun God was beckoning them on and they had no need worry because his sons was in attendance as escorts. Others agreed on the glorious-future side, but said it lay on the other side of this earthly, and to get there they would have to die as warriors, their families too. An old Cheyenne called Little Rock piped up it was four winters to the day since his brother's daughter and grandchildren had been killed at Sand Creek, and maybe they ought throw that into the interpretative stew. They all shrugged at that. Hears The Moon, well that sprout had no clue, being in desperation he grabbed my lug and whispered in, What does it mean, brother? Jesus.

The old chief, silent as them others jabbered, watched out from that wind-creased face. He coughed, and they all shut up. He said he had seen this sign three times during his youth, up in the Powder River country. He said that one time it was at the end of a long winter and they were starving and the sun family had led them to a snow-bound coulee wherein a bunch of buffalo was drifted in. A couple of Crow had beat them to it and they had a fine old time taking their scalps and feasting on the cow they already done killed. The other two times they had tried to approach and enter the portal, but it was like chasing a rainbow, and no matter how hard they rode they never got no closer and then it vanished anyway so they had wore out their ponies for naught. He made the further observation that the sun family shone from the east, from where the white savages was flooding in from. Then he shrugged his shoulders, That's all I got.

What them Cheyenne needed was time to chant out songs and burn herbs and refer the matter to their spirits, but time were the one thing they didn't possess. The sun family faded, and they kicked us nags into forward motion, them all memories and forebodings.

Hears The Moon nudged me alongside Little Rock. A curiosity to relate about that fellow. He owned a pretty shield, colour of midnight, stars and a big crescent moon depicted thereon. The major decorative features was avian, in the form of a big bird surrounded by a bunch of smaller birds, all turquoise with red tails, and they was fitted with curious legs what terminated in eggs. Could be them pegs was items of hugeous symbolism, or the artist's talents didn't attain to the depiction of claws. But the birds was of a type I'd never observed in my earthly, so I'd doubt the intention were verisimilitude to nature. To complete the avian theme, feathers dangled from the shield, although I was disappointed to see they comprised those of a goddamn owl. Little Rock never let that shield out of his sight, and I judged it an item of great magic. Anyhow, to get back to the point, Hears The Moon said to him, Is it truly four snows since Sand Creek? and I figured him fishing for particulars, him being Shoshone-Ute-Comanche. But Little Rock merely confirmed and added, Ask me nothing about it. Henceforth he urged his pony into lope, and we all followed suit.

Sand Creek were a catastrophic day in the history of the Cheyenne nation and if you is ignorant but inquisitive you best go consult the history books. Even the whites was embarrassed telling it.

Late in the pm the ground rose gentle and we come up on the bluff what overlooked the camp. Us nags was all about blown and down to a walk, but they urged us into a trot to make that last rise, and as they looked out our knees was knocking and muzzles was scraping the snow. No combusted tipis and charred corpses greeted them, and yonder a bunch of shavers was precipitating theirselves down the slope on sleds. I heard the creaking as them Cheyenne all relaxed back in their saddles, the low sun performing alchemy on the snow.

I might have been exhausted in body but my curiosity was still quick, and I saw the sleds employed buffalo ribs as runners, and I pondered on my examples being used for such merriment come the time my own demise. I was musing such when from above I heard a whampf. I jerked my head around and Hears The Moon was scraping dirt-snow off the side of his face. Little Rock had leapt off his horse and despite his advanced years had launched a chunk. A trio more slid off their mounts and cahooted up. Hears The Moon had had it easy them last few days, them fathers and brothers and uncles burdened with more weighty matters, but now they made up lost time.

Soon they was all at it, hooting and yelping, saving for the old chief who assumed the role of spectator. Him being old and stiff from the journey, I figure all he wanted was to unfold that frigid body and dismount the one time. That role did not save him from a misdirected shot what glanced off his considerable nose. Like I said, I don't begrudge those fellows their childsome frolics.

The camp had clocked the commotion, and the women was ululating. The men looked up shading their eyes trying to look dignified, and children and yappers ran out to greet us. One runner, she weren't no canine or shaver, and were it a footrace Fox Who Runs Straight would have won the prize, albeit handicapped by waving and hooting and weeping simultaneous. Hears The Moon, well he heard his stepma's voice and him being a well-mannered boy, he decided he couldn't allow her to climb all the way up the bluff to greet him, though that woman fly enough to accomplish it, and soon we was plunging on down.

I'll leave you to picture the reunion of mother and son who'd feared they might never see each other again, not that I witnessed much of that emotional incontinence. Me, I was famished and soon as that boy leapt off I commenced pawing the snow for herbage to chaw. While engaged thus, out the corner of my eye I spied a Kiowa war party coming in.

Eighteen

B y God, if you owned the sensibilities to appreciate such sights, you'd say it was a right pretty night. Humanos is apt to construe pictures and scenes from the patterns in which the Lord saw fit to arrange his stars, and them characters was all in attendance, though the three-quarter moon shining obscured the dusty trail they followed. One night after he'd done performing the Old Testament, the Cornishman told me the whites' names for them patterns, but I done forgot all now. I would adjunct that the night was peaceful to boot. But it weren't.

The Cheyenne petitioners had bought us equines in close, them fearing trouble, and yours truly, I was located near to Fox Who Run Straight's lodge, which itself was maybe twenty humano paces from that of Black Kettle. But somewhere in the herd a bell was tinkling and it got right mithersome. Come the dusk a woman had stalked up casting glances about, and looped it off a paint mare and gone back to her lodge. Later the husband had come marching over, elbows crooked, her in tow, looped the bell back on. She heaped no few aspersions upon that man for this deed, and apropos any copulatory plans he got that evening, I ventured they was in a state of ruination.

Add to that goddamn bell, some nag had a cough and went at it all night. A colicked-up baby was wailing off somewhere, and a dammed canine were squeaking and growling out a heroic dream, interpolating a yap or thee when the deeds got particular rip-roaring. Downriver somebody was holding a party, them concomitant shrieks and yelps filtering up. If the Seventh US Cavalry was blundering about up there on them bluffs, they wouldn't be needing California Job and a bunch of Osage scouts to locate us. They'd just need to cock an ear.

Now, that Kiowa war party what'd trudged in. It weren't included to add colour.

By God, I don't know what offence the Ute had perpetrated, but that nation was getting it from all tribes, Indians in general not being of the forgive-and-forget disposition. Returning from raiding them latters, them Kiowa had cut the trail of a soldier column, and going by how the grass was tramped and rutted, a real big one. It was proceeding in Cheyennerly direction in apparent haste, well as much haste as a bunch of US cavalry can muster. En route to their tipis and wives the Kiowa had deposited this news on Black Kettle and his bunch.

All bar Black Kettle, them Cheyenne threw their hands up and the females commenced wailing, but Black Kettle told them all to shut their yaps. The old man was wore out from the snowy trail and the visit with the general. He told the Cheyenne males to come by his lodge later and they'd hold a council about it, decide what to do. No soldiers would be attacking at night, in the middle of winter. Why would they.

That council, well I could hear it where I was standing and it weren't no Quaker meeting. Even Black Kettle's cool head couldn't quell the men's remonstrations. Outside the lodge, despite the frigidity, Fox Who Runs Straight lingered. Maybe she figured her a survivor of a winter massacre she might have something instructive to contribute to the debate. She weren't asked, and the more she listened the more she huffed and stamped her feet and clawed at the stars and wrenched her hair.

The flap opens and the men stomp on out. She strides over and remonstrates. Are we moving? Why aren't we moving? My family was massacred at a place such as this. Murdered against the bluffs. We stay here and — but they interrupt her and tell her all is in hand, shoved her aside. We'll take care of it, kind of style. She cries out and wrenches out a clump of hair.

A period of gentle weeping follows after which she hoists herself up and goes to her lodge. Hears The Moon, Get up, she said. We are going downriver. Get up! They argue a piece, albeit their voices held in check being they don't want to wake the camp, the upshot to them words being Fox Who Runs Straight exits the tipi alone and gazes at the moon a spell, fists clenched. Then she stares up at the bluffs.

She clocks me and stalks over, looks me over a spell. She speaks, I trust you, Yellow Horse. But are too worn down. She goes off to the herd and selects a spryer example and stakes it outside her lodge. She looks back up to the bluffs, hesitates, and returns to the herd and selects another and ties it beside the old chief's tipi.

Around midnight, Hears The Moon comes traipsing over. He tells me the story of the council and the part appertaining to him. Brother I have been chosen to go to the soldiers. I am going with an old chief and he must tell them not to attack us, that we are at peace. I have been given a white flag. I must hold it up as we approach. For the whites this flag possesses great magic. He glances about before continuing. I am very frightened and I wish could take you with me because you have mighty spirit and bring good luck. But I fear further travel through the snow might kill you.

He got that about right. Always was considerate, that boy.

He tells me he is taking another pony along who, though prettier than me, does not possess my strength. Thanks. He got a shield in his hand. It ain't as pretty as Little Rock's, but it features the standard feathers and scalp locks, is painted red and yellow, the colours divided by a horizontal black line, a black half-sun setting thereon fitted with buffalo horns. It recollected me of Slow Turtle's. He says the old arrow maker gave it to him for good luck. Despite that he says he might not see me again and he thanks me for my brave deeds, not that yours truly remembered any of them items in particular, unless he means me jumping that stack of buffalo robes. He takes his knife and cuts a tuft from my mane, stuffs it in his medicine bag.

THE MOON SET. The wind shifted with it like it always does. I caught their stink. Them herd ponies caught it too and snorted and stamped. Ain't nothing on God's earth stinks like the US Cavalry.

They was up on the bluff, and I pictured goddamn Custer with a spyglass pressed to his bug eye. He'd have ordered silence, and I knew them troopers'd be doing their damnedest, but my ears reoriented and picked up the jangle of tack, a stifled cough, a hoof crump in the snow. One of his big hounds yolfed. I heard it whimper, then silence, and that was when he killed his dog I done told you about. Them slumbering Cheyenne, they was blithe to all this commotion.

They'd wait until dawn. In darkness, killing is a mithersome and confusing business.

Fog fingered on up out of the Washita, the morning now so still I could hear the hoarfrost forming on the tree branches, the snowmelt stiffen and creak. Above the trees, the morning star rose, the brightest I ever saw it, but too late to contribute illumination, a blush of light on its heels, the colour of a prairie rose. The light swelled and the fog turned the snow blue.

By God, but music bands is inconvenient. You got to tramp about toting that clatter, meanwhile getting derided by your fellows for avoiding the fight. You imagine them unfortunates toting the big drums and brasses along, although I guess life is easier for them that blows down a whistle. The time comes and you got to get set-up and get your fingers warm and pay attention to the man with the stick, all the time sitting atop a fidgety nag, and you better not play no bum note. Meantime, drawing attention to yourself like that, your trigger fingers occupied, there is always the chance you might stop an arrow from a sneaky savage.

Goddamn Garry Owen they call it. One of Custer's favourites, the overture to the United States Seventh Cavalry, God bless it. You should seek it out. Right lively it is. You'd think it a tune to turn men from dark thoughts, in lieu prompt a toe-tap and a jig, link arms and do-si-do, pull a cork or three, dwell on the cheerier aspects of life. Never seemed to me a tune apt to rouse men to massacre.

So Garry Owen comes busting through that dawn air, and the Seventh comes busting down the bluffs and crashing through the timber, pistols aloft, swords for the nostalgics, yipping and yee-hawing theirselves into a state of bloody frenzy.

I WON'T BE DETAILING no gore. The memory of the Battle of the Washita sits as heavy in my head as it did back then and the reliving of it causes me to feel discomposed in myself. Books about it ain't exactly on short ration, so I'll just supply such particulars you'll be ignorant of, being all them histories was written by the whites, the Indians being illiterate in matters of letters, though goddamn geniuses as plainsmen.

The Battle of the Washita. That's the first item in want of clarification. That is what they called it, the taibo, although if it was such an item then all them raids on the poor homesteaders up on the Saline and Solomon was all battles, and if you own a dictionary of words it might be worth you taking a pencil and finding the Bs and making an amendment.

Anyhow, here goes. I'll take a run at it, though it be a hedge snarled with briar and mesquite and cholla, a ditch on the far side.

At the exact point the musical accompaniment busts forth, Hears The Moon steps out of his tipi ready to go on his errand, holding his white flag and buffalo-sun shield. He stands agog a moment, trying to figure it out, then seeing the soldiers charging on he hoists up the flag albeit he never got no chance to wave it, and putting his faith in the magic of that bleached calico proved a serious error, being a soldier come by and shot him down where he stood.

That soldier was George Armstrong Custer. He let out a boyish whoop, having shot his Indian for the day, and he rode up onto a knoll, en route swerving his black nag to run down another. Henceforth, that knoll served as his podium and he directed the slaughter much as a musical conductor might direct the orchestra.

The old pipe-smoking arrow-maker exits his tipi, him needing to empty his bladder or having heard the band strike up, one of the two I guess. His pipe is lit and fixed atwixt his teeth and his head is already surrounded by considerable fumage which I guess obscures his view of what is shortly to be visited upon him. He waves his hand to clear the smoke and screws his fists into his eyes to get the sleep out, peers forth. He hoists that flintlock pistol and adds to the fumage, but the pistol misfires and I doubt that ball inconvenienced a trooper. They shoot him in the belly. He staggers back. His body folds. He kicks his legs some while his blood stains the snow. The force of the shot has ejected the curly pipe from his mouth, him lacking the dontics to keep it in place, and it smoulders on a pace or two off.

His woman comes out the lodge. She is grey-haired and knot-armed. She bears a sabre older than she. She looks down at her man. She turns and hoists the sabre high and shakes it at the chargers and shrieks out a challenge. The soldiers ride on by her. One doffs his hat.

Back at the band, the musician's spit has froze inside their instruments and Garry Owen is now issuing forth in a series of squeaks and farts.

Fox Who Runs Straight. Fox Who Runs Straight plunges out of her tipi and runs toward her son whose milky eyes is gazing up at the milky sky. His mouth is working but I don't hear no sounds issuing forth. She grabs his wrists and drags him to the trees. Jesus, it is astounding the strength a humano can conjure in moments of duress. She comes out the trees and sees the troopers coming on, but makes no move to dodge back in. You all seen what a killdeer does, a coyote approaching the nest. Fox Who Runs Straight shrieks and waves and runs across the open grass. She limps but I don't see no injury. A trooper rides toward her with a sword aloft. I don't see her again till later.

The old chief. He exits his lodge, a wife and kin bundling out behind, hoists his rifle. By God, he looked like he's dropped two score years. He fires off a shot, then clubs the legs of a trooper riding by. That trooper falls and the chief gives him one in the teeth and grabs his horse and mounts, dragging the wife up behind. He kicks the horse, but it is panicked, eyes rolling, and it takes a piece to get it into forward motion. They gallop toward the river, whereto a good portion of them Cheyenne is now running. Another wife, she stumbles out and gathers the pony Fox Who Runs Straight tied there, and dashes off after her husband.

They shoot the old chief in the back just as he reaches the river. He falls forward then rocks backwards knocking the wife off through whom the bullet has also passed. His foot catches in the stirrup and twists him around and that topographical face slaps into the mud and bounces. His favourite wife makes it to the river and they shoot her too. Their bodies get disturbed some as Seventh ride through.

The Seventh is thundering by now. A girl looses off an arrow at the exact instant a bullet smashes her breastbone.

A one-legged Indian jumps on a horse staked outside a tipi and rides off. A man rushes out that tipi and looks about for his horse. In all fights there is valiant acts and craven acts.

Gunfire coming in from all sides. They have dismounted and got in among the trees. Custer done got us surrounded. The bullets splash into the snow. Terror-crazed ponies charge about the village.

Fabridzio Capeesh charges by on a dun horse, glassy-eyed like possessed by Legion. He reins up and empties his carbine into a tipi, hard luck on anybody in there, jabs his spurs into them bloody flanks and departs. Yaaahh!

Tom Custer and his canted cap. A child is stumbling out of a tipi. His horse runs it down and it rolls twice arms flailing before it lies still. I don't know if he did it deliberate. A woman runs barefoot toward the river, the froze snowmelt cutting her feet. A trail of red footsteps.

A woman staggering out her tipi, a bullet in the thigh, the hole in her traded skirt blooming red. She carries her baby. That woman, she holds her baby out front for them troopers to see then clutches it to her breast. Plunges a knife into it and her both. A trooper reins up and shoots away half her skull, to be on the safe side I guess.

That's plenty for now.

Looks At The Sky and me out on the high plains. The prairie birds all singing out and the flowers blooming, buffalo calves butting skulls, so it must have been high summer. Bunched clouds resembled bouffanted ladies. A squall had blown through, not that such precipitation ever bothered her none, but she dismounted and told me to shake myself.

I can't explain it to this day. I began to spin and dance and kick like a colt, feeling the sun drying the water off of my back I guess, the droplets exploding off my mane and tail. She gets sprayed. She laughs her clanking laugh and slaps her thighs. Her bag of possibles gets flung off, the pad saddle works loose and that fine antelope skin and its red spot of paint somehow slips out and flops on the wet grass. I even roll on my back and kick my legs in the air, and I ain't performed that act in polite company since I was a foal up on the Llano.

She don't get mad nor nothing, her stuff getting strewn about. When I get a hold of myself and back up on four legs, she picks off the dirt and grass, flattens her hand to a blade and scrapes off the rainwater and replaces the antelope skin and saddle. She slaps my neck. Rubs my ears. Blows up my nose what makes my rear dexter quiver. Talks nonsense into my ear. She plucks a patch of sweet grass and shoves it atwixt my choppers. Says, There Brother.

Later she was walking me along and we flushed a gang of sparrows. They was drinking at a pool the squall had left. She slid off and bent to drink, scooped up a palm-full, then froze, staring down at the hand. She fingered the agua therein and put her hand back to the puddle and let the agua flow back. She squatted down on her haunches and studied the pool.

You might call them water striders, pond skaters, Jesus bugs, but that pool was crowded, them all strolling about. No few was piggy-backing in a prolonged act of copulation to the extent it was a goddamn orgy in there. Where the hell they had all come from that day out on the dry high plain, well only the Lord knows.

Looks At The Sky touches the water and looks at her fingers. She touches the bugs with the pads of her fingers, as if to press them under, but then releases. She scoops up a handful of water and holds it up to the sun and watches as the droplets cascade from her fingers. She opens her hand and presses it onto the water, flat as a duck's foot. After a spell of kindred activities she rises and says to me her eyes wide, Water, Brother. It has a skin. It is a very weak skin, but it heals quickly.

The sun setting, a sickle moon rises on the opposing horizon. We depart, and a bunch of antelope come in to drink.

They'd have made a fine couple, her and Hears The Moon. She could have told him what she saw, and he could have told her what he heard.

DIN. I flatten my ears to it. Shouts and shrieks and screams humano and equine, dog barks, ordnance cracking and banging, hooves pounding, lodge poles smashing, goddamn bugles, humanos crashing through ice-fringed water, cries of infants.

Stink. Blood and cordite and faeces from split guts, burning tipis and lodgepoles, whiskey.

Custer watching on, arms folded across the pommel. The flag-bearer at his side, it hanging limp, that big golden eagle concealed.

Ain't much fighting in the village, less than you might expect, them Indians more intent on fleeing. Men and boys make a stand, trying to cover their families' escape. A man is pumping a ramrod, drops it and raises the gun to shoot. A man owns a repeater, is on one knee with it hoisted. I see him shoot a trooper off his horse, and another, then take a bullet in the hip, one in the chest. He falls belly down, cheek flat to the snow, eyes wide, taking it all in, his hand reaching out and his fingers digging at the snow.

The ponies. Most was in panic now and had shifted theirselves off toward the trees. Some was bleeding out, heads down and moaning. Me? Yours truly? Well you know me and my famous calm, my goddamn composure what served me so well in my earthly. I'd moved off some but I still lingered close to the camp. I can't say why. Maybe it were knowing Hears The Moon was laying there alone. But the recollection of them motives is now as foggy of the day.

Fog and gunsmoke mingle. My eyes sting and scratch at the murk. The camp is near clear of Indians now, least the live exam-ples. The fight here has taken no longer than it takes you to eat your breakfast. The killing is down at the river. Mopping up, they calls it. Comes a point where the soldiers line-up and pour fire under the bank. I figure a bunch has sheltered there, believing in their desperation that wall a sanctuary.

Couldn't have been no fun for them Cheyenne dressed in their night attire taking refuge in the river like that. Some tried, but it must be hard to defend yourselves when you are waist-deep in flowing water, chunks of ice clunking into you, the kids all bawling. Course, them sharpshooters all made sure they hit no non-combatants.

Dead and dying lay around the village amidst a litter of discarded blankets and robes and clothing tramped into the blood and mud. Scouts is taking scalps. Couple of troopers follow their cue. Soldiers are pointing Coltses and dispatching groaning males, and it don't require no mortal injury or a full set of hairs about your privy member to be deemed worthy.

A tipi blazes. It is a marvel how long the smoke hole maintains its function, them flames licking at the lodgepoles. Soldiers are slashing open the remainder, firing shots, delving, dragging out dead, wounded and alive. The males they kill. Aught they consider valuable, they pile up. They break down the tipis and apply the torch, former occupants watching on.

Jesus but the telling of killing gets tedious.

A bunch of troopers is herding women caught in flight, all bemired and bloody. Fox Who Runs Straight, her head is gashed and she must wipe the blood out from her eyes. She glances over to where her son lies. She wails and tears out a chunk of hair. Least them Osage scouts ain't visited them parts yet.

Them troopers deposit the women before Custer atop his knoll. He is drinking steaming coffee out of a cup his striker just handed him, a biscuit in the other hand. The women huddle, the troopers watching down from their mounts, their hats pushed back, the butts of their carbines resting on their hips, barrels pointing at the sky and smoking. Custer's eyes range over the women. The women sway and sing their death songs. Even them raised to it, the sound unnerves. Custer's lips move, and the troopers lower their rifles and prod the women off, out of range of them cabbage ears. To add weight to the command Custer has jagged his hand in the direction he wishes them to depart. He forgot about the coffee and it splashes onto his britches and onto the neck of that nag, who snaps his head back and snorts.

California Job, trotting over on his mule puffing on his corncob pipe, a trio of troopers in tow, eyes smiling. He wears a hat comprised of a deceased rodent. They trot on by me blithe and proceed on to a bunch of ponies off yonder and attempt to round them up. But them ponies ain't having it. The stink of them taibo is making their eyes roll, and they dodge and scatter. The men regroup and debate. A trooper is sent off, proceeds on to the women what is bunched up singing songs.

I know what he is about, them ponies won't be ordered about by no whites, but they will by the Cheyenne. That trooper jaws with a lieutenant a spell, and they nose their horses into the women, swinging their quirts and poking their carbines, cut four out. One is Fox Who Runs Straight. They move off a piece but then she stands and folds her arms and spikes her eyes into them and spits out words. That trooper what been sent, he plants the butt of his carbine in her face and goes select a more docile specimen.

You can tell by the snorts and stamps and eye-whites them ponies know something amiss, but they let themselves get gathered, them women now doing it. They pass by and gather me too. I discover myself next to that pretty black with the white star and socks of my subterranean days who got stole away from Tom Custer that night. But he is in terror and don't recognize me.

Some might say the Lord made a mistake, giving man dominion over the beasts of the field and the creeping things like he did. Not me. I ain't one to question the Lord's wisdom. But the whites interpreted that ordinance in sanguinary fashion. They exterminated all the buffalo and beavers and wolves and panthers and grizzles off of the plains knowing there'd be no comeuppance. I even hear tell they shot all the mustangs, to mince up as lapdog chow, make room for more cows. Me, I don't believe it. Even the whites got to have their lines in the sand.

I broke off to philosophize because I was stalling. This next part is the hardest.

Here it is. The best thing is to just vomit it all out and be done. If you lose the sense of it, well it can't be helped.

The drive us horses to the base of a steep bluff, more of a wall and ain't no way a nag could climb it. Soldiers is banging in posts and stringing ropes out. So they done made us a corral. They keep bringing more ponies in and I ain't never been corralled with such a big bunch. Custer arrives and picks out the best of us, gets them led off. Officers follow on and do likewise. Them remaining don't settle. They skitter about much as the space allows and toss their heads and moan. They seek each other out and nuzzle and butt, organize theirselves into a single mass of horseflesh. The mass starts to whirl like water spiralling down a sump, them all casting white-eyed glances at what is afoot.

Officer gives an order and half-dozen troopers duck under the rope. They got lariats and long knives. They is stripped to the waist. They rope the pretty black with the white star and socks and the knife goes in and the blood fountains and they drag him to the ground for him to bleed out his flanks shuddering and go get another. They all go at it now working in pairs. The ponies scream and kick and pitch. They try to jump the rope and get clubbed back. I try to get away from it, get myself as tight under the wall as I can. It goes on. They rope and stab, rope and stab, rope and stab. But the work is slow, them horses all crazed and bucking and hard to rope making the work dangerous.

They see me. Me standing calm not like them other panickers, an easy kill and they come on. The noose flies toward me and I dodge it because I is fly staying off of the corn and oats and I is a goddamn Comanche steed the finest light cavalry but one has hold of my mane and the other clubs my knees trying to bring me down and another comes at me with the knife and he raises it. I whirl my head around and it clubs his head and knocks him down into the bloodmud and the knife flies. They got do better than that. Goddamn better than that. I am Comanche. I ain't going to be sent under like some swayback at the abattoir, after what I done already survived.

It goes on. They make little headway. Officer gives an order. Troopers line up and check their loads. They line up on the bluff above. Officer tells them with the knives to get out and they get out looking like they bathed in blood. Officer tells the troopers to take aim. Officer tells the troopers to fire. Bullets smash in. The ponies buck stamp kick and bite. Officer gets mad. Troopers don't want the task and some is firing high and some don't fire at all and some is weeping. Officer berates his men and some fire but others stand head down.

Custer, Custer shrieks at the officer. Custer snatches a carbine out a trooper's hand and shoots a pony through the head. He shoots half-dozen more, he shoots a dog what come sniffing. He don't always hit the head them ponies all whirling about and tossing their heads and one time he needs three. He hurls the carbine at the trooper. That's how it is done you snivelling wretch. Get to it.

Now they kill, their manhood embarrassed into it. Most is glassy-eyed and stiff-chinned clenched teeth some laughing. Some got their eyes shut. The earth is dead horses and them dying pawing at the bloodmud. I ain't calm no more. I ain't composed. I am panicking with the best. That jaw shattering and them teeth flying into my face is what does it. Bullets smash into the wall horses slamming into me they fall a leg flung up and a hoof kicks me in the teeth but now ain't space left to buck and kick you got trample them down what you have to and horses is left droop-headed islands among the dead and wrenching bodies and smoke. It goes on. Looks At The Sky. I rear and paw at the wall trying to climb kick down dirt and stones. A grey tries it gets to the height of me but they shoot her down neck thuds into bloodmud kicking air. My white sock red with her blood. It goes on. Pony kicks through the cordon and charges off toward blazing tipis sprays blood. Looks At The Sky. Dim light. It ain't ending. I look off into the shooters eyes gunsmoke-blinded and bloody, see him. His eyes is shut and he is aiming high. A bullet hits me in the haunch and I scream and he opens his eyes. All that din and he heard me. He sees me his mouth drops open and he shouts words my deaf ears don't hear. Ducks under the rope. He ducks under the rope. Bodies as stepping stones through the bloodmud he comes kicked in the hip sinks down pushes up on his carbine sergeant screaming Get back you fucking bastard and his foot slips trapped between juddering bodies wrenches it out the slime, comes on, comes on, he done ducked under the rope, comes on, waving, Mouze my Ansum. Mouze my Ansum. It's one of ours. It's one of ours.

NINETEEN

L ooks At The Sky, she talked to an otter one time. Talked to an otter, sprawled on a rock, belly-up, sunning itself. A poppling creek, snowy Christ Bloods watching on. We'd snuck up on it, her slung along my flank Comanche style, ready to fire off arrows under my belly. She dropped into the grass and that otter never moved. I can't explain it.

I thought her about to apologize for taking its life and skin, but instead they conversed. She began it softly, like that first time she rode me. I never caught much of what the otter contributed to it save for sundry squeaks. By the time that otter tired of her jabber and slipped into the creek, I had wandered off to chaw on a clump of herbage. She strolled over poking a finger in a jug ear and reported the otter had revealed the magic of swimming under water.

She mounted up and we followed the creek to a spot where it pooled out by dint of an old beaver dam yonder. She stripped off and dived in. She surfaced and whipped the water from her hair, laughing at God knows what, and said, You should come in brother.

I proceeded in up to my knees. It were half tolerable. Me, I only swim in times of emergency.

She took a bunch of deep breaths, arched her body and dove under. She was under quite a stretch, and I saw that she was attempting to swim otter-style, her body waving, mimicking the currents and eddies of the creek, though them gangly arms and legs couldn't help but mar the effect. She stayed under so long I admit I begun to fret some. Then she surged up and her head broke the water skin, gasping and coughing and I knew she'd sucked in a lungful. When she done she beamed out and called over, See Brother? See how well he taught me?

Yours truly, I can make no remark germane to her progress in matters sub-agua. I'd never witnessed her attempt such activities prior so cannot vouch for the quality of the otter's inculcations. All I can report is come suppertime there was fish roasting between a mesh of twigs, and she weren't in possession of no fishing pole. Comanche generally don't eat fish, considering it poor fare fit only for inferior tribes, so I guess it were a new experience for that sprout. The piscatorial repast she pronounced tolerable but the tiny bones was mithersome.

YOU CAN GET AWAY with a lot in the confusion of battle. Ahithophel must have inveigled me in with the spare horses because when I'd regained my wits, there I was. There you go my Ansum. Your wound isn't so bad. I'll be back soon. I recollect them words.

A smutty sun had rose above the trees, though you could scarce see it through the big smoke. The smoke from burning tipis ascended vertical. Ammunition and powder bags exploded.

The officers rummage the heaps of belongings for souvenirs, Custer down off his knoll, making sure he gets first pick. He selects hisself Little Rock's shield. I'd recognize them birds and crescent moon anywhere. They say it now resides in a museum of American fauna, alongside its owner's scalp.

They herd the captives together, no males is among them, commence driving the dirging women and kids onto waggons.

You recollect them Indians downriver, Arapaho, Cheyenne, Kiowa, sundry Comanche who hate to miss a fight. They have heard the commotion and now they appear on the bluffs and begin firing in. They hit naught of import, them distant and the smoke roundabout. Custer, he sees the odds shifting, decides to flee.

He gets the band to strike up another ditty, them instruments now thawed out, and we march past the bonfires, the stink of charred flesh and hide fouling the air, a soft breeze stirring the glowing embers of bows and arrows and lodge poles and saddles, unburnt parts of blankets and moccasins and shirts and cradles and people poking out. We march past a piebald laying on its side huffing out its existence. He has ate all the herbage within the stretch of his neck, in his death him discovered an appetite, maybe wanting to take his leave engaged in a familiar act, and a half-moon of cropped grass is about his head.

We march east toward them other villages. Custer is trying to make them indigenes think we is about to wreak similar destruction on their families. He keeps them Indian females and kids between us and the bluffs, kind of shield. Them Indians see our course and scatter back to their villages to ready their defence. Come nightfall Custer turns about and we head back the way we come. We don't see no more Indians on that trip. I admit it. It were a cute move.

THEY CUT out a bunch of women, examples that weren't too gashed and dirty, and stood them in line. Officers dusted theirselves off and posed alongside, got their pictures took for posterity. A mix-blood scout sorted through the females and picked out the prettiest, Fox Who Runs Straight among them, led them off toward the officer tents. Custer strolled through the bunch holding up chins and squeezing rumps, picked out one called Young Grass That Shoots in Spring and took her off. She were Little Rock's daughter. The others perused the remainder and made their selections. Later, squeals and shrieks arose from them tents, and them cries weren't exclamations of ecstasy.

Next morning, Fox Who Runs Straight. I'll say this for her, looked like she'd put up a good fight. Later the mix-blood procurer, well he and a trooper took her into the scrub, figuring it was their turn now. They come out bloodied, and the trooper holding his crotch, he said, Goddamnit, you said squaws rape easy.

The whites said the Indians was vermin what needed exterminating to make way for white enterprise. If they was vermin why did they fuck them? You don't fuck a rat or roach. Forgive my coarse parlance here but sometimes you just got to say it like it is.

I ain't saying they all took part in it. I witnessed acts of mercy during the fight. Saw an officer hoist a bloodied boy on his horse and take him off to be with the womenfolk. Trooper searching the scrub found a woman and child and shouted back, Ain't nothing here. But I seen it throughout my earthly. Men what been engaged in killing their fellows, it gives them a hell of a hard-on. You figure it. I can't.

A SOUTHER BLEW. The men removed their big coats and eased back in their saddles and smoked their pipes. Scout come and reported bunch of buffalo drifted up in a ravine and Custer took his remaining hounds and went off and shot them.

Yours truly during this return? Well I were in a poorly state. The snowy trip to the fort had wore out my body, and now my near massacre had broke my mind. My bottom lip flapped about like a landed burbot, heedless to my brain instructing it to stop. I even went off my grub, that's how bad it got, the flesh falling off of me. In the end I could scarce keep up with the troop, and I discovered I didn't give a damn if they left me behind. Goddamnit, but sometimes this life can't be tolerated. The wolves could have me. I lost interest in headgear, and never regained it.

I halted and put my nose to the snow. Sergeant come and encouraged me with a stick. He nodded over to the women and children and said, I ought to butcher you to feed them savages.

I estimate he didn't want to be delayed, being he left me behind. Adjacent was a bunch of trod-down scrub. Soft and springy it were and it looked right inviting. I'll lay myself there a spell. What is the worst that could happen? I crumple my knees and flop down. I note my mind is wondering what it's like to get et by wolves. Figure they'd start at the arse end. A bee floats by, woke by the souther I figure. He finds a shaft of sunlight and bends a stalk of grass. Hell I don't know if bees got lungs or not, but his body pulsed like the effort had wore him out. A teaspoon of syrup would sure perk him up. Take a whole boatload for me. I lay my head down and them twigs is as springy as they look.

Some item is chawing on my tail. Ain't the choppers of no wolf. There'd be more than one of them canines. I knew who it were, them crunching teeth, them rotating jaws. Done chawing, he butted my arse end and, me not paying him the required attention, come bit my neck. Thenceforth he proceeded afore me and emptied his bladder, and his stinking piss splashed my muzzle. I'll get you for that you bastard mule. I hauled myself up and started on after him. But he was sly. He maintained hisself two paces ahead so my choppers only clacked air, proceeded to bugle out copious and pungent flatus offensive to my highly tuned nostrils.

AHITHOPHEL COME SEARCH ME OUT. I hear footsteps clump up behind and a hand run along my flank and continue on to my rump, that former quivering at the touch of it. I don't look around because I know who it is, by the weight of hand and tenderness of touch. Ahithophel's burred-over voice bubbles up like warm molasses, Mouze. My Ansum.

He is at front of me now, and them tears is coursing down them pastry cheeks. Speechless he is at the weight of it all. He has his arms about my neck and is hugging me and scratching my mane and I feel his tears on my neck and I want to feel embarrassed for him but that inclination gets smothered somehow. I can't say why.

He steps back and looks me over. By God. My Ansum. By God. For half a breath I think he might doxologize the Lord but he never. He raises the cap to scratch his head and the wind blows the pompadour up and it flaps, but he don't notice. Jesus but he got thin. He walks around me for an inspection, sees my wound and catches his breath. He runs his hand over it, By God, he says, By God. But we came through didn't we, my Ansum. We came through.

The Cornishman, well along with my bane he kept me going rest of that trip, though his mind weren't in no better state than mine. He got the blacksmith to take the bullet out. He'd come see me and plant that dough face in my neck. How are you Mouze my Ansum? He found an apple one time, the Lord knows where, and shoved it atwixt my choppers. Keep your strength up Mouze. I can't have you dying on me. Soon after the fight he said, I never signed up for this. I never signed up for this, Mouze. Later he said, I shot him. I killed him, laying there. I took his future. His unborn children.

Well he was always one to state the obvious, and he didn't supply no further particulars. You'd think he'd have rent his garments and railed at the Lord as the cause of it all, but he never.

I guess for those of you short on imaginative powers I ought supply an explanation as to how he fetched up on the Lodgepole Creek that day and come to be my saviour.

He stood a'front of me tousling my mane and I could see them waters was about to bust forth, his wobbling lower lip the outrider. He hangs his head and mutters, the voice all cracked, You were right all along Mouze. But them ocular damns hold, and the feelings come busting out in locutatory form. First you were kidnapped, he says. It broke my old heart, you seeing me through all those times. I called out for you that morning my Ansum, and you weren't there. I borrowed a mule and searched all over, he says, and I believe him.

The farmstead goes to perdition. A late frost burns the crop just sprouting. Then the rains fail. Somebody tells him to try dynamiting the sky. I ain't making this up. A new scientific theory was going about, and Ahithophel, he believed in science, and dynamite.

He builds hisself a kite and lights the fuse and sends it on up and they heard the explosion back at the city. Precipitation duly shows up in the form of hailstones what mash the crop. The grasshoppers come to finish the leftovers. You can imagine, he had no grain to share with the glass-eyed fellow and the stiff-hatted fat man, and the grasshoppers ain't obliged by eating through their briefcases and the paperwork contained therein. They call in their loan.

They weren't homesteaders, he says. They weren't even locals. They weren't even the ones getting the land. They were lickspittles, for speculators back east.

Tornado come and blew off the door to his hole in the ground and sucked out the moveables. He was away taking solace between the thighs of Mrs Barrels at the time and when he got back they was strewn all over the prairie, that crystal sugar-caster smashed, the China teacup vanished. The hogs and poultry was vanished too, sundry scrap metals, although that goat still abided, chewing on his big bible.

In the end even Mrs Barrels jilted him. Troubadour banjo player took up residence in the town, of stable pompadour, a set of expensive dentures and a twinkle in the eye. Made a tolerable living in the saloons, knocking out Buffalo Gals, Silver Dagger and Dinah Blow Your Horn, and soon it were more than his banjo he were twanging on.

He weren't never the same after that fight weren't that Cornishman. We got back to the fort and you'd see him wandering about muttering nonsense to hisself and to the sky where his non-existent Lord resided, and it weren't long before his comrades started putting distance atwixt. His eyes changed to them of a clay doll's and his speech held no destination. The officers upbraided him for slovenly attire, and he'd stand to attention and Yes Sir and they'd tell him to get his shoulders back and get his goddamn head up and didn't he know this weren't no two-bit outfit this was the Seventh United States Cavalry and he better shape up. They slapped his face. Custer ordered him bucked and gagged.

Mundane duties was his lot, them officers figuring him good for nothing intellectual, and you'd generally find him tossing dirt out of a hole. Come dusk he'd take a bottle and go off into the plain and sit gazing off, and I hoped he was watching them big rollers sweeping into Nanjizal.

I GOT some loose ends to tie up appertaining to them events on the Washita. These remarks may include some philosophizing.

Custer never punished the perpetrators of them raids up on the Solomon and the Saline. He was just marching about in the snow and struck the first village he stumbled across, and he wouldn't have found that if it weren't for them Osage scouts. Custer came in from the West, and the old chief's camp was furthest west, so that were that. You got a fox been after your poultry. You go out and shoot the first fox you see. Yeah that showed him. He won't be back. Peering down off them bluffs at cockcrow they couldn't have known who we was, and Custer didn't care what Indians we was as long as we was Indians. He were more intent to ascertain our strength. Making sure he outnumbered us a five to one.

It sure was hard luck on that old chief, that Indian being the most peaceable of the whole bunch. In the end they resorted to lies, saying how they found booty in his camp, former property of them poor rustics. From what I saw that day they was more interested in acquiring souvenirs than collecting evidence what'd stand up in a court of law. Aught devoid of monetary or curiosity value went on the bonfires.

Speaking of lies. That woman who took her and her baby's life in lieu of allowing soldiers to gain possession of it. Well back then, certain officers'd take an aboriginal infant away from a burning village, take it back east and raise it up as a novelty, dress it up like a doll and arrange dinner parties and when they was on the port and cigars trundle it out for gawping purposes. Maybe take it down to the lyceum and give a speech about it, take a stick and point out features of interest. Imagine that.

Custer lied saying that infant weren't no aboriginal. He said it were a captive white baby and the squaw done killed it out of spite, the goddamn savage, and ain't you grateful we is cleaning them out the plains for you. I'd rejoinder in my experience Indians raiders don't take infants captives. They is too troublesome, all that wailing and crying. The Comanche poked a lance and was done with it.

Custer wrote in his memoirs that they tried their damnedest to spare the women and the children. Well, Indian boys and no few girls are expert in the use of bow and hatchet and are tolerable fair with a pistol, provided they can find a solid object on which to prop theirselves. Maybe Custer decided they weren't going to take no chances that morning. What I saw, they was shooting at any males not wearing a blue uniform, canines included, and pouring fire into groups of folks engaged in the hostile act of sheltering under a riverbank. And I never saw nobody waving no white paper about offering terms of surrender.

Tom Custer, he got shot in the saluting hand.

———

DAY COME California Job barrels in on his mule waving a paper envelope, It's from the ginell for the ginell, he yelled out. Custer got the whole bunch of us to stop and he read it out, the message relayed back to them out of earshot. I can't remember it verbatim so I'll give you the gist, although individual words have wormed theirselves into my memory and gnaw there still. It were from Little Phil. He complimented Custer, which is why Custer read it out loud I guess, on his energy and rapidity in killing aboriginals given the recent meteorological contrivances, and congratulated him and his men on efficient and gallant services rendered. Well, I'd agree it were efficient.

I can adduce an amusing particularity here to lighten the mood. As Custer read the message a horse located directly behind was experiencing difficulty. Evidently something was sitting awry with his bit and he kept poking out his tongue and licking at his nose and tossing his head about. That nag owned an uncommonly prodigious tongue, and allied to the gravity of the words the effect was comical, especially when the tongue shot out at the word, gallant. Troopers tittered and Custer paused and looked out, whereupon they tightened their lips. Lucky for that nag Custer never clocked them posterior events, or he'd have ordered it shot.

We fetched up at the new camp they'd been chopping the trees down for, what'd puzzled the Cheyenne so much. They called it Camp Supply, I guess after some General Supply someplace, though I never heard of him.

We halt about a mile out to form up, Custer telling the troopers to ferret out the best uniforms they can find. The Osage go out front. They paint and feather theirselves up. How do I look, you hear them say, henceforth subject to derision or approbation. Sundry booty adorns their persons and their ponies. They fix Cheyenne scalps to their lances and hoist them erect. The scouts come next, California Job puffing on his corncob pipe trying to look blithe. I seen him turn aside and rub extra dirt and grease into his hair and beard. Then come the women and children and baby captives wrapped in blankets, then the US Seventh Cavalry, God bless it, fronted by the band. Don't ask me why they formed up in such manner because I do not know. Custer, he located hisself at the head of them wretched captives, displaying his trophies I guess. The boy toots and we lurch forward.

Puffs of smoke sprout from the fort, and the reports of them welcome-home shots come following on. The Osage take their cue and fire their guns at the sky, but them fellows never know when to stop. The fort doors swing open and two officers come galloping out in their best bib and tucker to escort us in, buttons and sabres twinkling in the low light. They have no little trouble locating Custer, him having plumped for the buckskins and resembling a scout, them officers perscrutating for gold trim and shiny buttons. He is chagrined by this, you can tell, and he has to holler out, Hey, over here, and still they is obliged to look twice. They salute him and say, The General's compliments, further gubernatorial blandishments.

An Osage breaks formation, shrieks and waves a scalp about he claims as Black Kettle's. The band strikes up Garry Owen. The troopers fire off their weapons. Canines is running out the fort and yapping. Jesus knows how they got there so quick. They bee-line for our yolfers and a fight breaks out. The Osage is still firing, throwing in whoops for harmony. At the fort somebody is stringing up last-minute bunting and another is combusting firecrackers. The din spooks a bunch of resident army nags and they charge out the fort and come thundering past.

You have to admire them captives. Notwithstanding their

degradation they are determined to show no sign of their injuries, be them physical or psychological. They hoist theirselves and their blankets up and harden their faces into items akin to geology, their expressions, how can I express it? Closest I can get is, grief held in abeyance, all bar the shavers and the infants what is agog or wailing.

The spectators is now all cheering and tossing headgear about. They carpentered up a platform special and Little Phil is stood on it, a couple of lackeys at his shoulder. You can see Little Phil's eyes sweeping the Seventh. He is looking for Custer, and that latter must sure be lamenting ordering his striker to fish out the buckskins. The officers sabre-salute the general. He tips his hat, but his eyes pursue the search. Custer, he stretches up in his saddle, circles his arm about as if releasing a knotted tendon. Finally he takes that big hat off and waves it. Little Phil clocks him and nods, and I calculate if it weren't for them moth whiskers you'd see a curl to his lips. Like they is cahooted-up in some conspiracy and, goddamnit, they pulled it off.

Well, this all has a kind of summing-up concluding-remarks kind of style to it don't it. Narrative strands getting tied up, lessons learned, protagonists sent off into the sunset. And yet here we all is, still one and a half nags' legs years from the Greasy Grass, a fight of which I was the only living survivor. I'll bet you is hoisting a corner of your lip thinking, How long is this joker going to go on for?

TWENTY

You know what, I been thinking the exact same thing myself. We all know them individuals what never know when to shut their flytraps and how mithersome they is, you trying to stay polite. I once saw a man cornered by a garrulous female feign a choking fit. Got his face to go purple and everything.

Yet events remain to be staged. Characters is waiting in the wings what elucidate how life was back then and explain why it is now. I have a fancy to philosophize further and get an item or three off of my chest. And I done told you I am the only living survivor of the fight known as The Little Big Horn, and if I don't enucleate on that you is apt to feel you done been thimblerigged. Like going to the circus anticipating apes and getting costumed canines. Ain't nothing worse.

Three women shelled out healthy kids on that winter trail. I speculate they went to school someplace and became good Christians and learned their letters and how to guide a plow and never learned how to pilot a half-wild pony with their knees and shoot an arrow through a buffalo going full chisel, what would have been prodigal pedagogy anyhow, them ungulates soon shot the hell off the plains.

We took the women and kids on up to Fort Hays and put them in jail, although what crimes they committed was beyond my noggin. Folks came and gawped through the bars like you would at a zoological park. Shavers threw stones. Soon their eyes grew dull and their hair lank and their clothes lousy. They pressed to the bars whenever modestly attired females wandered by.

They got some lumber in and carpentered up a bridge over Big Creek. It sure saved travel time and the expense of swimming lessons for them troopers going over to that burgeoning city to get turpituded up.

Served double duty as gallows did that fixture, to the extent it got dubbed the Hangman's Bridge. Turn of the year four soldiers of the Tenth US Cavalry was dangling therefrom, the prairie wind twisting them bodies making the ropes creak. Their crimes was unknown to me. Some said it were a lynching. I searched the faces to see if erstwhile castrator Pervis of the culinary nostalgics were suspended there, me become habituated by then to bloated corpses. But them faces swoll purple, the tongues poking out, made identification an uncertain affair.

I got a new jockey, a heavy-limbed, toe-jamming cow-licked New Englander of English Midlands extraction and meagre philosophical abilities who responded to every quandary, conundrum, deadly jeopardy, jigsaw puzzle, poker hand, exotic repast, putative aboriginal assassin, with the remark, Arhh, it's a bugger. You distinguished him at long range by his stiff-legged walk, feet set wide apart, and I surmised maybe he was possessed of sensitive ballocks prone to chafing. His equitatory abilities was pitiful. I remain unapprised if sensitive ballocks was the cause of that deficiency being as I never saw them items in the flesh and there were always a McClellan between him and me. He expressed his negative verbs with, I, he, you, don't got to — goddamn ignoramus. He got a powder burn on his cheek due to a mishap testing a fusee in a former life, a blemish what occasioned him to be nicknamed Flash, though he swore his name was Ken. Said he was a trained gunsmith, but no trooper of my acquaintance ever vouchsafed a gun to his care. He wore boots what squeaked when pressed into motion. By God, you wouldn't believe how aggravating that can be. That's all I got on that individual.

You is asking what happened to Fabridzio Capeesh. He departed the Washita undamaged, at least bodily, but it sure took the ginger out of him. He learned enough English to convince everybody of cobbling skills acquired in a former life, and thenceforth spent his days attaching extra leather to cavalry boots. The change of vocation perked him up no end. Even grew a bushy moustache and waxed the ends into horns. He'd cock an eye on me and say, Comay va, Trasandatino? Twist his moustache horns and wiggle his top lip, Kay pensee? Bellissimo, no?

GODDAMN CUSTER, him burning that a Cheyenne village and returning trophied-up, well that restored his reputation. He become a celebrity. The big injun killer and plainsman. When he weren't absent back east attending to personal affairs, gubernators, moguls, mandarins and nabobs, dukes and princes, a tsar or an aga or two for all I know, come visit and he'd put on the buckskins and that hat, the red cravat, round up his hounds and take them out on excursions to reduce the local creation, take home badges of manliness in the form of buffalo heads and elk antlers and panther pelts, maybe a grizzly if they was lucky and that latter's nose ain't seen them coming.

One time yours truly got roped in. I had recent enjoyed a bowl movement and was standing leaning into the wind trying to catch some shuteye, when the wind dropped away and I about fell over. I jerked awake to see a waggon coming on. Bunch of bowler-hatted panjandrums debouched theirselves, puffing on cigars thick as whip handles, waistcoat buttons defying the laws of tailoring and engineering, them all talking like their fellows was located some distance away.

One fellow were doing most the talking, thumbs jammed behind his suspenders, rocking back on his heels, his cigar bigger than anybody else's, so I figured him the big chief. In corporeality I'd say he were the exact antipode of a buffalo. All arse he were, that part tapering up to a torso a consumptive poet might be proud of, surmounted by a tiny head, a derby hat fitted atop, canted. He suggested a spinning top at rest but somehow maintained perpendicular. But when it comes to enterprise and commoditizing, athletic ability counts for naught. He puffed on that cigar fitted in the corner of his mouth and bossed everybody like he was Cyclops Ben Cowski hisself, though I doubt he could have pushed a freight train up a hill. I recollect his name was Bowker, something of that ilk.

Our party comprised what, maybe half dozen officers, half dozen panjandrums and similar of enlisted men to perform the drudgeries. Ken Flash come and got me curried up and polished up my tack, said, Arhh, It's a bugger, led me out. A waggon conveyed such dignitaries adjudged too fat to ride any distance, Bowker comprised, and come the time a beast were held at bay I expected they'd be propped atop a horse and led forward for dispatching and posing purposes. So it might turn out tolerable trip for me after all. Behind, a couple of waggons toted their picnics, and beyond them a brace of soldiers drove a sprung buggy, a quartet of furbelowed females as cargo, brung along to witness deeds of manliness, already with their bumbershoots erected against the sun.

They got the band out to send us on our way, them big-nostriled chargers all prancing to it, yours truly among the spare nags. Garry Owen. A shudder went down my flanks and the urge rolled over me to turn and run for it. A panjandrum shouted up, Hey lookie fellas at that nag's jaw what's flapping. If you fancy being a mogul seems ignorance ain't no impediment.

Soon as we'd gone any distance, Custer sent off his dogs and they ran down a number of jackrabbits what they brung back legs jerking atwixt their slabbering choppers. The panjandrums applauded and complemented Custer on the aptitude of his dogs and expressed wishes they owned similar.

Scout comes chiselling in says he's spotted a herd of three-score or more buffalo yonderward. Well, the panjandrums is excited as Texans en route to a cockfight and they lever theirselves out the waggon, although I see a couple is persiflaging to conceal their anxieties. Maybe they was just banking on the picnic. A brace of troopers bring over the horses. They may not be the fleetest or most nimble in our bunch but they is sure the sturdiest they can lay their hands on. They keep me in reserve, me not being pretty.

The troopers supply arse-shoves when required, and Bowker's horse already splay-legged expresses disgruntlement at his new duty via grunts and snorts. They check their guns, and Custer trots over and issues final orders, showing he is the one bossing even though they be panjandrums. He advises them on the natural habits of the buffalo and which part of it is best to shoot at. He says, Good Luck gentlemen, and Bowker kicks his horse and his bowler hat flies off, and a trooper is ordered to go fetch it. They hand him a scarf and he ties it on such you'd think him suffering from the toothache.

They ain't obliged to ride far. The troopers have chivvied the buffalo as close as they can and are blocking escape routes. But ain't no avoiding a measure of equitation and the panjandrums lean back and blunder down the declivites and hang on tight up the inclivities. A nag steps in a prairie dog hole and dumps his jockey.

The chase. They dig them spurs in and bounce up alongside them slowest and winkle out a revolver, point it in the general direction. Them officers, Custer included, have already shot down a dozen or so, to show them how it is done. The panjandrums commence firing and a curious detail ensues. Evidently a bullet has creased a cow's spine and severed some cord located therein, being she is progressing along dragging them dainty rear legs behind, them pegs plowing the prairie. At least now her calf can keep up. She ain't providing enough sport though, so a trooper is sent to perform the dispatching duties.

Bowker, he evidently got ambition because he gone after and old bull, scarred and tufted from many battles, and slow. He jogs adjacent, puts three or four slugs into diverse locations, whereupon the bull, him being a veteran of such encounters, swerves and hooks that sturdy nag in the belly. That latter lets out a shriek. Bowker ejaculates likewise, him now airborne.

Well you can imagine, witnessing such doings, visions of own buffalo days with the Comanche come bundling into my mind. Me and Looks At The Sky, we made a fine team, and watching the efforts of them army nags, I judged my qualities as a buffalo horse had been harshly judged and the subsequent deprecations was unmerited.

Well the Lord, him being possessed of the ability, he must have read my thoughts. He ain't one to tolerate nobody thinking well of hisself, so he decides to teach me a lesson like he done old Job. I get picked as replacement for that hooked nag what is lying wheezing off yonder with a trooper pointing a Coltses at its forehead.

Bowker, he lies on the plain wiggling his arms and legs like a flipped turtle. They hoist him up, him belching profanity, and an officer glances about to check if the females is in earshot, but they is off a piece sipping lemonade. A soldier removes his cap and claps the dust off Bowker. Bowker he says, Get the fuck off of me soldier boy, and shoves him aside.

Now, I expect him to spurn the opportunity for further chase, especially when he cocks an eye on your truly being led over. I cough and stumble some, an attempt to convey I am a bumble-footed steed he best not entrust his safety to. But you have to hand it to that mogul. That old bull done got his dander up. Like he been bested in some big-money deal by a rival he considers inferior. He ties his hat back on and regards me from head to hoof. He says,

Is this the best fucking sonofabitch you got? He don't wait for no answer. He yanks my reins out of that trooper's hands and commences the mounting process. That trooper puts his shoulder under his arse and shoves. Bowker don't say thank you.

He wears big showy spurs as you might expect, them types insensate to vulgarity, spurs what put me in mind of the degenerate. He plants them into my flanks. I feel the blood trickle, but I set off at my regular pace. The bastard ain't going to boss me, and for a moment I consider pretending to step in a prairie dog hole and dumping him afresh, but my pride don't allow it.

Like you'd expect, them four slugs ain't worrying that bull none, but he is old and wore out and we gain on him quick. Other examples is more conveniently located, but Bowker wants to get his revenge on this particular ungulate. I get on the bull's flank, remembering how Looks At The Sky taught me. I even come in from the correct side, by God. I sure hoped she was watching this. Bowker puts a couple more in. That old bull veers toward me and thrusts them horns. Naturally, I am expecting it and dance away right nifty. You should have seen me. We lose a little ground and Bowker puts a couple more into the haunches, thinking it will hamper his progress. Goddamn novice.

I haul him alongside again. My bellows is blasting, Bowker's heft now telling, to the extent were I still in possession of them items I do believe I'd have busted a ballock. I feel him fiddling about for another revolver and I think, Jesus, I hope he don't shoot me out from under him like Custer done them others, thrice. He's got that gun out now and puts four more in. He manages a get couple in behind the shoulder. The old bull jags toward me and I veer off again. But Bowker, he ain't alive to the manoeuvre.

I feel him bouncing up top. I envisage daylight blinking between my back and his arse. I know he ain't balanced right, and them pigeon knees ain't clamped on, that's certain, and only the non-shooting hand is grasping the reins. So only his massive arse and the laws of gravity effecting it is keeping him aboard. But now them conjunctures ain't enough. I slow to a trot but he crashes off anyhow.

The old bull is standing off yonder now, head down, flanks riven by scars inflicted by generations of young pretenders he done bested. His knees tremble. Blood is foaming out the nostrils. So least Bowker got a lung shot in.

I wander back to see if he wants to remount. A trooper is hauling him up. He strikes me in the face with a stick he calls a crop. He drags another pistol out his pack, a big old Navy Coltses. He checks the loads and marches on off to the bull, stands close, but not too close, fires into it. He empties the gun, the buffalo flinching at each shot, blood measling out. The bull stands. Bowker demands another pistol. He puts four more in. Even puts out an eye though he been told not to aim at the head end. The bull totters. His knees crumple and he thuds down. Dust and grass fly up and is carried off on the wind. Bowker stands over it, utters a curse word, and empties the gun. The buffalo wheezes on, the one eye gazing out, what I done to deserve this, kind of style cursing his luck it weren't wolves. Bowker stomps off. Says, Get me a fucking half-decent horse, by Christ.

Well, he sure showed that dumb ungulate.

———

THEY BAGGED THREE DOZEN BUFFALO, the only humano casualty a panjandrum who got his gun caught in his shirt sleeve and ventilated his forearm. Nobody shot his own horse out from under him like Custer done, three times. Nobody cut out the hot liver and chawed on it seasoned with bile.

They fetched out the camp tables and the folding chairs and set up the cold cuts and the beer. Prandials concluded, they took their scatter guns and went off burping to see what else was worth de-existing in this Eden, as one of them panjandrums called it.

Come late in the pm, the troopers was told to take the deceased animals and parts thereof and create a tableau. They laid the buffalo's tongues in a line to create a foreground and lead the eye in, piled the rest up behind. Bowker told a trooper to go off and saw the head off of the old bull. He placed it atop, pride of place, and I have to say that old bull didn't look too disappointed by it. He retained his tongue, and it poked out in an attitude of mockery, such that they said it ruined the effect. They tried, but the tongue refused to be pushed back so they cut it out too. Bowker said, My taxidermy man can easy make a fake, a remark they all considered hilarious and guffawed loudly thereto, though yours truly failed to see the humour. Bunch of wildfowl, sundry pigeons, three buffalo birds, couple of sacks of prairie chickens, sack of quail, an owl, two hawks, three herons, two dozen sparrows, half-dozen meadowlarks and the jackrabbits completed the confection, sundry further creeping things I forgot. Telling it now I remember they shot a bunch of crows and ravens and snakes, but these was deemed unworthy.

The camp chairs was set up and they sat, the females centre, them nimbler panjandrums standing. Photography in the offing, Custer shoved his way to the front. He stood in semi-profile, chin jutting, hat on, what blocked an officer's face too junior to protest. The photographer took their picture and they all laughed. He said he had to do it again because a mallard's wing had begun flapping. They all threw their hands up and mock-complained and uttered jocularities and laughed again. He ran forward and tossed the mallard aside and told them hold still, took the picture again. They all cheered, that wing flapping on.

The troopers built a fire, went off to get the wine and the beer and dainties took out the waggons, and the panjandrums feasted on the choicest parts of their kills, toasted their current and future triumphs.

Lubricated up, they bested each other in sporting tales and owned examples of taxidermy, the usual salacious topics being off of the agenda what with ladies present. Them latters listened demure, making sure to enunciate admiring haws where appropriate. Bowker, he got the fat cigars out and offered them round magnanimous, told jeopardacious tales of shooting elephants and rhinoceroses out on safari, whatever them items is, the voice relentless as a spike hammer, them all listening intent like he was Jesus and it were the Last Supper.

Bowker combusted up a fresh cigar and settled back in his stick chair, its quality of construction under severe test. He expounded on them exotic beasts' sporting merits and weighed them against those of the buffalo. Firing a glance at Custer he said, It is doubtless a matter of degree, but I judge the lumbering buffalo inferior quarry. Now, the rhinoceros, he is a worthy adversary. His fellows all nodded and puffed out smoke like Indians at council.

Custer, he tried to hide it, but I saw his cigar droop and the anger flash behind his eyes. He shifted in his chair like he got a biting insect peregrinating his crotch, the company too polite for him to scratch. He bit on his pouty lip, and the tiny eyes darted about, him whittling on it. He ahemed some and come back with, It is a pity, sir, I whipped all the naked savages. I am sure you would find them a more worthy prey. Having fired it off, he admired its flight, looked about for concurring nods, and failed to hold down the corner of his mouth. But Bowker had got onto the topic of hippopotamuses by then, and he and the myrmidons never heard him say it.

Later Bowker sends a man to fetch a flat leather box, the corners reinforced with yellow metal. He opens it and calls Custer over. He hands the open box to him, says, Colonel, in gratitude for a marvellous day's sport.

You know, I never did figure that bastard's true rank. Some called him colonel, some called him general, although now I think on it, them latters was generally of the lower ranks. Anyhow, forgive the divarication. You'll have to go check the history books

At the colonel, Custer's face contorts, but he regains hisself and takes a hunting knife out the box, twirls it about in his hand,

217

holds it to lamp light. Ahh, he says, Made in Sheffield England. A fine blade, sir. Silver bolster and butt catch the light. He smiles and puts the knife back in the case. He sits hisself back down and places the case on the ground. When he raises his head that pout is back in evidence. He got a stone in his boot, and his striker ain't around to pull it off for him.

Naturally, I was employing the device of metaphor there. I cipher it out this way. It done clubbed him what he is. He might be a famous war hero and Indian killer and village burner, but he ain't them panjandrum's equal. No sir. He's frozen his arse off on them winter plains, risked injury and even death to his person fighting indignant aboriginals, albeit that risk of the minor variety, even killed his pet dog. But such deeds count for nothing against whipping a business rival, cornering a market, buying low selling high, buying up the cheap land what he just done cleaned out for them. Personal enrichment of the monetary kind, and the flauntation of the consequent gewgaws and furbelows, trumps martial exploits every time.

You get down to it, it was them panjandrums what was doing the real extirpating. They had spied their chance and poured their money into the plains, and now weren't no road back. They invested in the ironworks and railroads and reapers, threshers and drills, seed companies and flour mills, invested in surveyors, developments in hydrology, barbwire and abattoir mechanicals, cow killers and hog suspenders. To extract a profit they needed them plains sterilizing. Custer, he were the hired help. They give him the cutlery as a tip.

Well that's my take on it anyhow. But I know as much about enterprise as Nose Like a Bear did about implements of husbandry.

Next day, them panjandrums done waved cheerio, Custer spies a wolf yonder. He larrups off after it quicker than an Irishman spotted a barroom, couple of yolfers in tow. But as you know by now wolves is quicker than they look and cunning to boot. The lobo already got a start, the party is soon lost among the swells.

Custer ran a good horse into the ground that day. We found it laid out, head thrown back and mouth gaping teeth, the wind drying the sweat off it and stirring its mane. Custer was sitting on the carcass, smoking his pipe, ahoying, attempting nonchalance. Said it had stepped into a prairie-dog hole and broke its neck. I knew that nag. It weren't no ex carthorse. I looked about for sign of rodent holes and saw Custer was lying. It goes without saying but I'll say it anyhow, no deceased wolf was in evidence.

You'll be wrinkling your noses here, thinking the previous sporting episode a bagatelle included in this volume purely for entertainment purposes, a daub of light against all the shade, so to speak. Chiaroscuro, Fabridzio Capeesh'd call it. But I'm telling you, the odorous Mrs Bacon Custer, her always with the odour of old flowers on her to disguise her true stink, was one of the females sipping refrescos on that outing, and she related the very same in one of them doorstops she wrote justifying her husband's existence. You go check on it. Although I expect she accentuates aspects at variance to them I picked on.

Out on that trip Mrs Bacon Custer said the plains air were, Like champagne. I expect she was attempting versification, like them types with no proper work to do is apt.

Bacon. Old Noah called his son Ham. So that's alright then.

TWENTY-ONE

First time I ever got loaded into a cattle car, and let me tell you, me being an denizen of unbroken horizons and steepling skies, it were not to my taste. You imagine being shut into a confined space with a bunch of sweating, defecating, urinating nags, every last one of them afflicted with the malady of halitosis, the floor all slick with shit and piss. Add to that that the car jolting and lurching about, the sun pounding down, no water from cockcrow to cockshut unless it rained and you stuck your tongue out. I bit and barged my way out to the truck walls and rested my weight thereon and poked my nostrils out the chinks, felt a mite better for it. Nevertheless, something about the motion of that vehicle gave me the goddamn colic.

Henceforth I was to enjoy many a railroad trip at the hospitality of the US Cavalry. Worst of all was them boxcars. Back then the custom was to pack us in tight to stop us biting and kicking each other. You can imagine, no spare air in there, you arrived at your destination and you piled out and there'd be a deceased nag or three laying the floor and they'd drag it out, sell it off for chow.

Why is I joggling on a railroad train at this juncture in my earthly? Well, the Cheyenne and Arapaho now whipped in them parts, though the Comanche was still marauding, they shipped us off to the mysterious orient for duties appertaining therein.

Luckily, we wasn't on that railroad train for long, otherwise I do believe my condition would have declined to that of a lead miner's ass. We debouched therefrom and proceeded on to that big muddy river and to a wharfage, and a steamboat snubbed to it.

The foredeck were occupied by sundry crates and bales and stacks of firewood and sailors enjoying tobacco in multifarious forms. The sailors rearranged the merchandise in dilatory manner, and a wide board was let down and we was herded aboard and packed in tighter than a ballet dancer's privy parts.

Now, on the way down the main topic of discourse had been whether the boiler would explode. Steam boilers was always exploding back then, and the troopers told each other stories of flung body parts and strewn giblets, generally concluding the discussion with, Hope to Christ ar'n don't blow up. Ken Flash said, Arhh, it'd be a bugger. Naturally, they located us nags adjacent to them big kettles, them figuring in the event of catastrophe horseflesh might serve as a tolerable blast absorbent.

Well, least it weren't no cattle car. I barged my way to the outside so I could observe the water. The mechanicals hissed and clatterwhacked and a big whistle blew somewhere up top. They unhitched the boat and we jumbleclunked out into the stream and I felt the breeze on my face. I remember thinking the voyage might be tolerable, if we don't detonate.

FIRST THING WAS we got stuck. Hung up on what they called a sandbar, and the sun traversed a good segment of the sky before they pried us off. The captain objurgated a boy in obscene manner, him tasked as lookout but otherwise engaged in chunking pebbles

at a turtle. I figured him in for a fustigation at the Captain's conve-
nience, but he remained blithe, and I conjectured beratings and
beatings quotidian fare.

I recognised that boy. He were the boy me and the
Cornishman gave a ride into town that time, him of the flour-sack
trousers and the tumbleweed hair, what had returned the favour by
appropriating the fruit knife. I looked about for the Cornishman.
Maybe he could whack him in the head and get it back. Maybe he
could whack him in the head anyhow. But the Cornishman
weren't in evidence, and I doubt he'd have recognised that boy
anyhow, him half-crazy by then.

That boy's prospects had sure improved. Though he were still
unshod, he looked like he'd et a decent meal or three. He wore shirt
and pantaloons what bore no publicity for feed companies, though
the shirt looked like it been stole off of Giant Porter's washing line,
and while snugged by string at appropriate points it still billowed
in the wind and might serve as a sail if the boiler blew up.

The riverbanks was lined with goddamn trees, doubtless
gadflies resident within but it satisfactioned me no end to see how
the river liked to chaw away at them. No few places the river had
gouged the earth out and the trees had toppled in. Some was fresh
toppled, the foliage still green and optimistic. Some had lain so
long they was like skeletons, and bleached arms reached out like
they was bent on dragging us under. At such tree-wrecks you'd see
men with saws engaged in dismemberment, and further on we'd
pass such timber for sale as fodder for them hungry kettles.
Cordage they called it. I know not why. Probably appertaining to
Frenchmen.

You wouldn't think it, but trees is a major feature of riparian
travel. Not only branches but whole trees was floating about or
caught up, birds and turtles loafing thereon. Them upturned roots
and branches strained out lesser vegetation to form tangled mats
what reminded me of Ahithophel's pompadour. You'd think a wig

salesman had passed by suddenly apprised the bottom done fell out the market and got rid of his stock. But they was slow times and my noggin whittled on such trumperies.

Those tangles formed the last resting places of the deceased. Some tragedy at a hoggery had occurred upstream going by the abundant swine strewn. That or maybe Legion been cast out, again, and I wondered why they didn't blow the whistle and hack off a side of bacon. But them visible obstacles wasn't the most dangerous. You'd see a roiling current, an eddy, a whorl like a knot of writhing snakes, and a fellow at the front would clang a bell and holler back and tell the driver to steer clear, and you'd hear the branches scraping along the bottom of the boat.

Perils galore it were. Chunks of ice was barrelling along, it still being the thaw up in them northern fastnesses, to the extent you'd think you was floating along in a chocolate cobbler. They'd take poles and fend off the smaller chunks, hope for the best with the bergs, though once the mechanicals got going we outran the buggers.

We come to another big river, turned dexter-wise and soon we was passing by the big city where loquacious Pervis excised my ballocks, them steamers still tethered up, folks scurrying.

They stopped to take on cordage and passengers, unload acquisitives and load acquisitives. They roped off us nags and put passengers in with us, and I bottomed it out them humanos was scant of enterprising savvy, and this was where it got them, travelling livestock class. Well, I guess if they want to improve their position in society it is up to them to progress their business acumen, albeit far as I ever saw such acumen amounted to naught more than hortatory skills allied to disregard for the prospects of your fellows.

A couple of tamed Indians was among them parvenus, a male and a female, and they stood apart next to the boilers where no other humano lingered. They wore Indian leggings and moccasins, but whites' topcoats and hats, hoping to blend in I guess. A couple of malefactors looked at them askance, muttering insult sparse of imagination. Smirched up with grease and slovenly in their comportment, I conjectured them buffalo hunters. Goddamn filthy savages, was all I heard, those fellows' volume making sure them primitives did likewise. One spat sputum in their direction, and I thought it might kick off. But that were the sum of it.

We proceeded on down that river a spell and then we swung sinister-wise into another river the whites called the Ohio. Swamp reigned in them parts, as did crooked shanties, and where planks was in short supply old cow hides served as walling, washing strung out, though how it might ever dry in that rank air I held no clue. Going by the fetid stink I ventured the natural processes what digest vegetation was suffering a dyspeptic complaint. Wraiths stared out the shanty doors hugging knob elbows. Clabber-faced boys and men fished from tiny boats or stood slack-armed, watching us watching them. Motionless shitepokes ignored us. Even the canines was languorous and they layed about like jetsam, or is it flotsam, and could scarce blink the blowflies away.

I was glad we didn't dally in that dismal place what with the tribes of gallinippers massing for attack. Ahithophel visited and experienced a moment of the old lucidity. He gazed out melancholy and said, Look Mouze, and pointed to a sign nailed to a shanty. They call that one Elysium. How about that. Must be an educated fellow denizened there.

Now as I alluded to in that previous, a curiosity exists about a steamboat in motion. Everybody stops to look. They whoa their plough horses, hold off pounding corn, stop playing tag, plunk the felling axe into the half-bit trunk, delay shouting, Timber. I saw a man in the act of slaughtering an ox hold still, the hammer raised in both hands, the ox snubbed to a trunk chewing on patient. He could have been old Lot's wife, only with a big hammer. Pair of canines engaged in the act of copulation even turned their heads to watch us clank by, maybe confirming we weren't about to blow up and fling rivets.

We was well into civilization by then and cabins and houses was showing up regular, squared-off, black-corduroyed fields, yeoman staggering behind implements of tillage, picket fences confining beasts, all that free lumber about. You'd go past fields what was all stumps of mighty trees what had stood till late, such that if you was fixing to open an al fresco confectionary you could save yourself the expense of purchasing tables. The Cornishmen, him owning no dread of high explosives, could have absconded hisself from the Seventh and started a new career as a stump dynamiter, if he still had his wits.

I didn't spot no prairie lumberjacks in them parts. Most of them settlers was applying the axe to its intended purpose, which was fine by me, and I determined that the axe and its distant cousin, the saw with two handles, was both fine inventions. Logs was everywhere waiting to be hauled off, droop-necked nags standing by in harness thinking, How'd it come to this. Sometimes you'd think a big wind had blown through and knocked all them ancients flat, and if one of them giants from old Noah's day been circulating, he could have stood them all back up on end.

The more impetuous enterprisers took a different tack. To hell with all this chopping. I'll burn the bastards down. One dusk we saw a big smoke and flocks of birds in flight, sparks flying. We got up close and you felt the boat tilt as the sailors and passengers went to gawp and exchange remarks. Each bough, branch and twig was black outlined in red, and the flames reflected back from the water till you thought the very waters themselves was aflame and the boat were about to be combusted. Well, I did. The wind tousled the crowns and the glowing cinders leapt up toward the moon and blinked out. Despite the chill you had to turn your head from the heat and content yourself to listening to the crackle and spit, a thrash when a big limb gave up.

If ever somebody wanted to get off they stopped and got out a little boat and a man rowed them to shore. One time the Indians wanted to disembark but the boatman refused to share the boat with them, and they was obliged to wait till we come to a jetty.

A male and female embarked, bodies jack-knifed by an excess of manual labour, him a dome-crowned flat-brimmed hat with inexpertly barbered grizzle poking out. Her a bonnet, the hair below the colour of new wool. They was both dressed in black, and I estimate they was funeral-bound. The hands was all knobs and declivities, and his carried a valise and a ladder-backed chair with a straw seat. Her examples carried a walking stick and a basket of live poultry. I cogitated on how the chickens might comport theirselves during the obsequies, but my noggin bottomed it they was most likely repast for the wake.

The woman settles on the chair and I figure maybe she is cousin to California Job being she takes out a corncob pipe. She bangs it three times on the rail to knock out the dottle, suggesting a prior life as an auctioneer. She inspects the bowl and grunts and her man hands her the pouch without being told to do so.

I tell you, maybe it is the tedium of the journey, but all round-about is watching this pair like is Chinese acrobats and they is about to ascend the flagpole with their legs extended horizontal. She ignites a Lucifer. She does so by trapping the match in the crook of her forefinger and flicking her thumb nail. She glances about to see in anybody is impressed, I know I is, and combusts the pipe, sucks on it, making a papping noise. I don't know what comprised her mundungus but they was of such stink I conjectured even California Job might pass.

She puffs on it a stretch, the fumes obscuring her man, her eyes roving about her fellow travellers, although I have to admit to assuming the presence of them features being in lieu of orbs was slits. Picture the navel of a seated naked fat man, pair of them. That inspection concluded, she sticks her thumb in the bowl and hands the pipe back to her man. He takes it and hands over her knitting.

Now, I had never witnessed such occupation prior in my earthly. It was the goddamnedest thing, them needles clicking to the extent you figured sparks might fly, the fingers whirring you'd have more luck observing courting houseflies. Her man stared beyond his fellows at the brown water drifting by, holding the ball of wool, colour of same. I don't know how she done it nor the future purpose of the cloth she was producing, but you watched the garment grow before your eyes. Scarf maybe. Some form of headgear for them born insensitive to style, Apache maybe. Mercy hood for them convicted of capital offences.

Later, when she done knitting and had re-combusted her pipe, her man took out a metal contrivance in the form of a keyhole escutcheon, a big one. He put it to his lips and commenced twanging, banging his foot to a rhythm personal to his head. The spectators hummed along, trying to locate a tune, waved fingers and tapped feet so as to fix on a beat. They longed to chorus in. That's how bored they was, but them rhythmic endeavours was in vain. The old lady commenced to sing. Now you all is expecting me to say she had a voice like rusty nails pried out of barn siding, but you'd be wrong. Sonorous of timbre it were, plangent the Cornishman would peg it, the sound of breath applied across the aperture of a bottle, and it rendered the spectators wistful.

ABORIGINALS. Well saving for that unpopular pair of the ill-matched costumery, I didn't see no further examples on this trip. Weren't none ranging the bluffs waving lances and displaying posteriors, but neither did I observe any what had took up the horticultural life. To embark on that latter you'd require folding currency, savvy of jurisprudence and the guile to keep your fiscal arrangements cloaked, maybe insurance indemnification, and Indians was illiterate in such vexations of enterprise.

I did see a frame house proceeding west along the bluff. I ain't talking parts awaiting erection here. It were the entire edifice, roof, doors, windows and all, and a curious sight it were too, such that Ken Flash was moved to utter, Ooh, arhh. I whittled on what provided the locomotive power, steam out the frame being none were issuing forth. But my bemuddlement were by dint of a trick in the topography. A score of oxen emerged from behind a knob hauling a carriage for which they must have gone to the wheel-wright with a bulk order anticipating a discount, multiple whips cracking above their backs, nostrils blasting out clouds of steam into the miasma presently swelling about the rooty banks.

Apropos the general temperament of the steamboat passenger, it was of dismal cast, what with the incremental travel and the monotonous scenery and the constant prospect of exploding. One evening a couple of malcontents shot at turtles and sundry wild-fowl. The captain got a man to come down to tell them to desist on account they was disturbing the knobs up top, like the clatter-whacking mechanicals was the strums of Orpheus. But they was wily fellows bent on entertainment and no sooner had they put down their rifles they began singing hymns.

Well, the knobs up top could not complain about doxologizing the Lord and soon they had a bona fide choir going, albeit tran-spired no few ears was of the tin variety. They kept the repertoire popular. The word Rock was repeated in a variety of keys until they succeeded in rendering Rock of Ages in agricultural style, them all cheering at the end, and a robust Nearer My God to Thee went down a storm, though it left no few in a tearful state what needed comforting. See Gentle Patience Smile on Pain was judged too sombre and shouted down. Blest be the Tie that Binds, not everybody knew the words and it petered out, notwithstanding some inventing their own. Running short of ideas a fellow started up John Brown's Body, but for reasons political he was threatened with a beating and only made it to mouldrin. Autonomous choirs then formed and sang independent songs, and a kind of competi-tion broke out to see who could sing the loudest. Them songs wasn't all devotional in nature and I do believe libations was being consumed about this point. Although it weren't Christmas, they buried the hatchet and rounded off the panegyrics with, Hark! The Herald Angels Sing. They all haw-hawed and pounded backs and shook hands and declared the event a triumph and continued the voyage like they was total strangers.

TWENTY-TWO

They disembarked us in a place called Kentucky, birthplace of the boy sharpshooter who failed to hit Slow Turtle even though that Indian painted a bullseye on his chest and wore a shiny conquistadore's hat. Or was it Tennessee. Kentucky was all low hills and shallow valleys, swagged and clumped with goddamn trees. I took an instant dislike to it. We ever come to a flat spot where you could see an unbroken circle of sky, my heart soared like a hawk.

Transpired we was police horses now, the Seventh dutied to regulate the activities of a new religion they called the Klu Klux Klan. Has a kind of ring to it don't it. The most notable feature about the creed was the outfits. The adherents garbed theirselves up in white sheets and pointy hats, to put the jimjams up the heretics I guess, but to me the effect were comical. They dressed thus when they was celebrating their esoterica you understand, not when they was en route to the feed store or spending an evening at the billiard parlour.

Turned out the heretics was the black humanos. But no matter how righteous they was they'd never be allowed into the church because they bore the curse of Cain, or was it Ham, the one who laughed at his pa Noah when he intoxicated hisself and stripped naked, and the curse of Cain or Ham or whoever was that their offspring was black-skinned instead of the proper white, so they could never be allowed in anyway. I admit I may have confused the details here.

Anyhow, the Klu Klux Klan, who was all white, believed the blacks to be an inferior species, like the Comanche does Mexicans, and being they couldn't enslave them no more, like the Comanche was still doing them Mexicans, by dint of the big slaughter what had outlawed the activity, they was hanging them up from the trees what grow in them parts, and had the Klu Klux Klan been operating out on the treeless Llano I do believe their religion would never have had a chance. I hope you is getting all this. Anyhow, our job was to stamp on it.

Well it was like chasing Indians about the plains only these Indians was white and lived in houses and towns and had trees and privies to hide in if caught unawares, and anyhow could not be distinguished from the good whites unless they was caught red-handed sporting the white sheets hoisting a black man. Their chief, he got hisself nomenclatured up as the Grand Wizard. Well good for him. Everybody knew who he was but he never got caught cracking a whip over a prone black man, so he was alright.

Course, had Custer applied the Indian policy we'd have shot the first whites we stumbled across, destroyed their town and acquisitives, raped their women, and got the bunting strung up. But things was different in the orient. They knew who the culprits was. That weren't the difficulty of it, and we'd go along with the local sheriff who arrested them felons peaceable and they got put on trial and then they was freed by the judge who hisself was a Grand Titan or some such. Jesus but you humanos like pecking orders.

Goddamn Custer, you could tell his heart weren't in the task. Drinking cobblers with a bunch of cigar-combusting dignitaries one time, him not me, I heard him apologise for, This goddamn pointless duty what serves only to persecute those in whose hands lies the future prosperity of this great state.

I would have been no-wise surprised if he hadn't got the odorous Mrs Bacon or to tailor-up one of them pointy-hatted costumes for hisself, if only to wheedle himself into Kentucky society. Can't imagine there is much to it, cut the head hole and the arm holes, the conical hat being the most challenging aspect, making sure you get them eye-holes in the right place so you ain't running about blind and is able to pick out a tree with a suitable branch. Now I cogitate on it, there's probably more to it than you'd think.

The Custers owned a couple of servants who was nifty with needle and thread, both of them black females, both of whom they spoke to like they was toddlers and referred to as darkies, though I never saw them administer no whippings. That pair might have scrupled at the task I guess. Could be they'd have engaged in acts of sabotage, omit the head hole maybe. Put the eye holes too far apart or too close together.

The black folks, they lived in shacks they called shotgun houses. I remain ignorant as to why they was nominated thus. White folks was domiciled in them shacks too, so the enterprising life weren't working out for them, but I guess for the system to work you got to have them that loaf all day and own parasols and build stables fronted by Corinthian colonnades, whatever they is, and them that get shafted in the shotgun houses. Every humano can't sit about drinking cobblers and chawing syllabubs all day. You got to have somebody to do the goddamn work.

Talking of liquor, the poor folks they wasn't gumtionless, and they enterprised by making their own liquor and selling it. Moonshine they called it, nomenclatured thus because they brewed it nocturnally, reason for the nocturnality being it were an enterprise whereof the gubernators disapproved. They disapproved of it because they wasn't getting their cut.

Somebody'd take a bribe and we'd go off into the middle of the woods to a bunch of gadflies and a shack located therein, a thread of smoke twisting up. You'd find a slabbering canine or three posted as vedettes, generally chain-limited. If the proprietor was present the officer read from a piece of paper while the former vituperated or wrung his hat or both. If he were absent, they skipped that part and commenced smashing. They took a sup first, just to confirm its nature, and always confiscated a number of bottles, to serve as evidence. The troopers, well they obeyed their orders but was sullen about it, and I do believe they'd have preferred latrine duty. These was their own kind they was impoverishing.

Custer, well such duties was a good bit below his station, and we didn't see much of the bastard on this oriental sojourn. He spent his time and government stipend at the racetrack and the stud farms, him considering hisself a fine judge of horseflesh and looking for investments, a good deal of them latters being with the turf accountants.

To digress, we went to arrest a man at a stud farm one time. He weren't present or was hiding under the hay or some such, so our visit were fruitless, but Jesus, I never realized the life them stallions lead. Eating hay all day and admiring the view, until such time arises you get led out to the dripping mare. Life is all gravy for some.

It ain't all it's cracked up to be though, and it wouldn't be the life for yours truly, me being no exhibitionist. Thing is, they don't leave you to it and let nature take its course. You get put to the mare. That's what they call it, and always an audience is present.

So this stallion gets led out, the member atwixt his legs connoting a leaky fireman's hose. A couple of fellas is holding the mare and a bunch more is standing about spectating. Don't ask me why. Talk about pressure. Well a bunch of neighing and snorting and stamping and sniffing takes place, but he don't get to it. His member is still dangling. Verbal encouragement follows. You can imagine the efficacy of that tactic, and they walk him about the paddock to relax him some. They lead him back and shove his nose up the mare's nethers. Well this applies the starch, if you get my purport, and he rears up on his hind pegs, and I think, Yeah. You go to it fella. And don't make such a goddamn palaver about it.

The problem now, well, how can I put this and respect your tender sensibilities. His member, it is waving about like a drunken trooper's sabre brandished at cigar-store Indian, and his first stabs go awry. Remaining on the bibulous theme, picture an inebriate applying a key to a lock. They allow him a few more prods but he ain't getting no closer to sheathing his bumbershoot, so to speak. This could take all day.

The boss, he is looking at his pocket watch. He says goddamnit, and marches over. Risking a hoof to the head, he grabs it with both hands and shoves it in, strides off wiping his hands on his pantaloons. The spectators all cheer. I had some embarrassments in my life, but Jesus.

That were one of the more entertaining days. The troopers spent a good bit marching about in squares, holding their rifles out for the lieutenant to look at and polishing up their shinies. My jockey précised it thus, Arhh, it's a bugger.

One day after we had cut two black men down and destroyed a whiskey still, Ken Flash said he wanted to go to church. It's all such a waste, he said, and you can make of that what you will. I never knowed he were a god-fearing man and he went up in my estimation. He parked me outside a chapel more akin to a shack and I cocked a fetlock and listened to them all doxologizing the hell out of the Lord via the medium of song.

Propped in a lean-to yonder were a carving of a man getting tortured to death. Naked he was and nailed to a fragment of carpentry. Defying the laws of gravitation, a piece of drapery covered the man's tender parts, and you had to admire the way the artist had arranged the swag so as to conceal the privy appendages yet still display the lean belly and scalloped thighs. Right curious were that image. It clubbed me then it were an image of the Lord when his pa who is also the Lord sacrificed him to pay for humankind's sins, and I wondered why it lay neglected in a shack ready for the bonfire.

I don't know if they was similar god-fearing, but the James Gang was running about Kentucky concurrent-wise, and had we clapped eyes on them ruffians it may have gingered up the visit and this episode some. But we never did.

———

THE SIOUX GOT STIRRED up on them northern plains, that tribe being almost as belligerent as the Comanche and not taking much persuading, and the whites barging on and finding gold, or pretending to and printing up enticements. We got loaded back on the steamboat and floated back toward the bosom of the Hesperides.

To describe the reverse trip to the Missouri would be tedious in the extreme, but I am disposed to relate one episode what might arrest your intellects, assuming you is possessed of them items. If you is a type reading this for the mayhem, then feel at liberty to flip the pages.

The goddamnedest Indian you ever saw embarked. Got on with a lot of dreary whites, he did, conspicuous as a Klan Wizard attending a circumcision. He sure weren't tailored up like them Indians on the outward voyage. Coutured up in whites' gear he was, but from silk-banded stiff hat to leather shoes wherein I could observe my reflection. Full complement it were, worsted wool suit and waistcoat, charcoal with white stripes, watch chain, though I never saw no watch, calico shirt with a stiff collar I saw chafed his neck, and a purple necktie made of a shimmering thread.

The tailoring hung about his frame pretty good, though it stretched here and there, that frame being expanded some compared to that of the regular Indian unless they is Comanche who like their grub, and I ventured he'd developed a taste for white grub like pork belly and deep-fried dumplings, duffs and pandowdy and such. He carried a book to boot, a heavy tome under his arm. Picture a preacher en route to administer corrective carrying his bible unholstered. Now, if you was aiming to fashion up an exterior with the express intention of attracting the attentions of malefactors, this'd be it.

You should have heard him talk, as he was obliged to upon boarding, to a sailor who knuckled his hips and looked him over, his mouth skewed like he was ejecting a corn kernel from a gap in the molars. The Indian said he had a ticket to go up top with the knobs, but the sailor wouldn't allow it, said there was sure to be ructions, said he'd best stay downstairs with the nags and the rustics. But my ticket clearly states Second Class, he said, in an accent like them West Pointers.

That accent knocked the sailor off his gubernatorial stride. He took a step backwards, pushed his cap back, his mouth working but the words fish bones in his gullet. He couldn't have been more embrangled if yours truly had addressed him. He rubbed the back of his neck and managed to cough out, You got stay down here, and that's the end of it. Who you think you are, you goddamn —— red bastard, at which juncture he directed a, Beggin yer pardon ma'am, to a buttoned-up type who clucked. His concluding remark were, You stay down here or you — get off. A burly come over carrying a length of pipe and said, You got trouble here Tarp? To imply pending violence he slapped the pipe against his palm.

The Indian spoke. No sir, no trouble here. Just a misunderstanding regarding my ticket. If you let me pass I shall be content to remain down here with these persons and animals. I told you. He could have got a job selling insurance no trouble.

Well alright then, said Tarp. And see that you do. He leaned over the side of the boat and ejected a stream of spit from a gap atwixt his front teeth, an act what recollected me of an eaglet I once saw squirting defecation out the nest. The Indian touched his hat and squeezed through, them making sure his fine suit grazed their oily vests. The burly watched him go and said, Jesus, whole damned country is going to hell.

I figured he'd have his braids tucked under his hat, but he got hisself settled against a rail adjacent to the kettle, took it off and his head was shorn as a July sheep. He pushed the surviving hair back though it merely bristled up and he looked at them others looking at him. He nodded a greeting. They ignored it and carried on looking. He replaced the headgear and opened the book and read it. His lips remained motionless and he didn't employ no forefinger to follow the lines.

How come yar'n all dressed like that? A man, his apparel deceased wildlife, a hat that had once enjoyed life as a racoon, the tail still extant. He was short on dontics and owned a nose that to a rustic would prompt thoughts of plowing. He leaned his chin on the business end of a muzzle loader subject to extensive usage.

I have been to college, Sir. I am returning to my family.

The man chawed on a plug, bringing his mind to bear on this intelligence like a team of oxen requested to pivot in a buffalo wallow. Betokening mental turmoil his brows corrugated and he pulled an earlobe. He placed the rifle butt on a cranefly wandering by at his feet and said, How come... How come yar'n all been to school?

My family was killed when I was a boy. I was fortunate to be adopted by a man of kind heart and some means. I did well in my lessons, so they...

The man adopted a simper and repeated the first sentence back to him. Then he said, Well boo goddamn hoo for you, and looked him over afresh. Well I'll be a goddamn son of a bitch. Hear this? They is educating Indians now. What next? Sending skunks to kindergarten? He looked around at the audience to see how it flew. It got a laugh, but I didn't reckon much to it. The cranefly was waving its legs. We is all doomed now, the man said. All doomed, I tells you. They is going to beat us to death with a volume of Plato and scalp us with the razor wit of Eureka.

That were a better jibe, but it appeared to exhaust his knowledge of the ancients. He sauntered over, pressed his face up to the Indian's. What trarbe r'you, boy?

Choctaw, Sir.

Well they ain't educated the goddamn stink out of you Choctaw, that's for sure. He flipped up a hand. The Choctaw's hat fell off and landed in the smuts. He said, his face still up close, Maybe there is another lesson I could learn you.

You got to hand it to that Choctaw. He come back with, Teach, Sir. Not learn.

The man's brows furrowed anew. When he got it puzzled out, he said, Why you stinkin' ... and he raised his musket for clubbing purposes.

Clewt? Clewt? Well, by God, it is you. The Cornishman, struck by a moment of clarity, the man wrenching his head around. How the hell are you, Clewt? You know me. It's Ahithophel. We worked that claim out in Colorado. Pikes Peak or bust we was, remember? He was holding out his hand. And we were certainly busted. Naught but mundic. But they were lively times, by God. Remember Abednego? Old Abednego? Never gave up on a garment? Gone now. He —

Clewt squinted out. Phil? That you? Well I'll be a son of a bitch. Goddamnit. Well look at you, soldier boy. Ahithophel extracted a bottle and held it out obvious, as you might an apple to a hog you is aiming to deacon. He extended an arm around Clewt's shoulders, chivvied him off to reminisce.

And that were that. The cranefly, it never recovered from his injuries.

I'll break off here being It just clubbed me in the telling I ain't intelligenced you up on old Abendego. Abendego shot hisself. Weren't no suicide, him scant of the pondering abilities incumbent for that action. You recollect how his hobby was to de-exist creation. Well while chasing a gopher one day he contrived to get his shotgun tangled up in a thorn thicket, I guess like that ram what saved the boy Isaac from his pa's sacrificing knife. Not wanting to climb in and get hisself pricked or further damage his attire, he attempted to pull it out barrel-first. They found that goddamn symmetrical hat off across the prairie, untarnished. The erstwhile prop for that item, they never did find that, but its absence sure truncated them hortations.

AHITHOPHEL SHOWED UP LATER, stink of whiskey but sober. I figured he got Clewt into an innocuous state and come back for a goodnight natter with yours truly. But he went directly to the Choctaw, who was still reading, his hat smutty but back in residence.

Excuse me sir, said the Cornishman. Would you mind my enquiring what you are reading. I am a devotee of literary arts myself. Jesus, here we go. I braced up my noggin to file away some new vocables.

The Indian looked up, wary until he saw who it was. Why, it is Dickens sir and, please, may I thank you for your earlier intervention. You saved me from bruised knuckles and your friend from some embarrassment. I estimate now that Indian was the politest individual I ever heard engage in the act of sustained locutatory intercourse. Infectious, ain't it.

Ahithophel, please. Phil is fine, and Clewt isn't a friend of mine, we just carried out exploratory excavations in Colorado once. Which Dickens is it, sir?

James, please. Hard Times. He riffled the pages and sighed. I confess, while I understand the words, Dickens errs to prolixity, which renders the tale somewhat opaque, especially to one ignorant of the towns of northern England and their mills. But I am interested in learning about other lands and the customs of the inhabitants. He directed his eyes at the Cornishman. Ahithophel, King David's councillor, if I am not mistaken? A rare name indeed.

That it is, James, and I see you are familiar with scripture.

Well, they went on back and forth like this no little, them trying to out-polite each other it made you want to vomit, and I'll fetch out my editor's pencil to save you the tedium and get you to the salient part. I calculate now they was weighing each other's intellects, see what they was up against, so they didn't find theirselves cornered in ignorance and embarrassed.

I thought Ahithophel might engage in nullifidian discourse, but he never. The intellectual soundings concluded, turned out all he wanted was to listen. That educated Indian embrangled his mind, just as it'd done old Clewt. He wanted to know what he was, and how he come to be so. What it meant that he'd killed some.

The autobiography. Family in Indian Territory wiped out by vengeful settlers. Adopted by a god-fearing couple but nonetheless friendly for all that. Excelled at his numbers and letters. Gone to college, quarter white and fair-skinned for an Indian so they let him in, got a hard time of it from his peers. Wanted to be a doctor. No chance. He talked on and his accent attenuated, the words rounding off and falling out slow and regular like clods from an undercut riverbank, the Indian in him coming out.

Did you not find college so difficult, said Ahithophel. I saw he wanted to add, being an Indian, but he never.

Being an Indian, you mean? An ignorant savage? Ahithophel cast his eyes in the direction of his boots. Do not worry, friend. You will be subject to much mockery for conversing with me. To answer your question, no, I did not. I found it extremely easy. I can quote Hamlet's soliloquy and calculate the annual compound interest on a 1500-dollar loan at seven percent and tell you that Michelangelo painted the Sistine Chapel in 1512 in the mannerist style. You hand me a rawhide cord and I will tie you a lariat. I can draw a bow and hit an apple at fifty paces and every morning I praise the Sun for allowing me to live. My Choctaw name translates as, Brave With Horses, because when I was a boy I dragged my sister from under an ill-tempered mare which had shied and fallen.

My grandfather lived in a frame house and owned thirty negro slaves to tend his fields. What does all this mean? Am I as you are? This is what you are asking of me. I do not know. My name, James Lee? It means nothing. The name of Christ's apostles is the sum of my knowledge.

He wanted now to be lawyer, would probably end up being a schoolmaster on a reservation. The old ways was fucked. That is what he said. The fight against the whites has long been lost. They are skilled in speculation and enterprise and transaction. They have instituted a legal apparatus to defend business and profit, and their lands are burgeoning. My people barely conceive the meaning of those terms. I must educate them before it is too late and everything is taken away.

It was quite a speech, and you ought congratulate me for remembering it. Maybe the old noggin ain't as perforated as I thought. He finished it off with the sockdologer, Let me ask you a question, sir. How does it feel to kill me and drive me from my home? You come from England and pass through a land where my grandfather and his grandfather were born and hunted and farmed, where I am not permitted to reside. You come to kill me.

Now yours truly, I considered this query a step too far, them getting along thus far like a house on fire.

Ahithophel, well his eyes spouted tears. He talked into his chest. It is shaming to me, sir. I never intended any of it. It is all an accident of contingency. He snorted up his snot. And those paltry words are all I can offer you, sir. He said, I wish you good luck, and left.

AHITHOPHEL COME SAY GOODBYE. Said he'd talked to a fellow well-acquainted with the Cornish man's mining prowess and had offered him a job in the Kentucky mines chopping out coal. He was going to step off first chance he got tomorrow, get mixed up in a crowd and head back east. He'd done with Indian killing. He showed me a bundle containing a change of clothes. He rubbed my ears and scratched my neck and shoved an apple atwixt my choppers what I rendered to mush.

He quoted Job at me. It went like this, Hast thou given the horse strength? Hast thou clothed his neck with thunder? Canst thou make him afraid as a grasshopper? The glory of his nostrils is terrible. He paweth in the valley, and rejoiceth in his strength. He goeth on to meet the armed men. He mocketh at fear, and is not affrighted. Then he said, I'll never forget you, my Ansum.

You know, when we was getting massacred in the bloodmud, I wondered why Looks At The Sky didn't come to me like she done before in trepid times. Truth be told, I got a good bit offended by it. But, her being smart, she knew I'd be alright. The Cornishman, he were there to save me.

The Cornishman, he should have stuck it out with the pilchards. This life ain't made for kindly types, but somehow they got to navigate a way through it best they can like the rest of us. By God, he even blubbered over that wolf. I see him now underground laying on his side in a puddle, chopping at the rock, the candle sputtering, whittling on old Ezekiel and excogitating on Aristotle, whoever he is. The Lord, he don't like it if you spurn the life he got laid out for you, think you are better than it, and he teaches you a hard lesson. And the Cornishman was atheist and goddamn nullifidian.

Well, I hope you enjoyed a restful time in that oriental interlude. Yours truly, I was I was licking my hairy lips to get off the boat and out from all them goddamn trees and into them windy plains. There's many see those receding horizons and feel discomposed in theirselves, wish them gained and passed. Not me.

TWENTY-THREE

Now you is expecting me to tell you about my part in the
Seventh US Cavalry's expedition into the sacred land of
the Sioux, albeit as I understood it the Sioux had only
recent kicked out the Crow and Kiowa. The land reserved to them
for time in perpetuity by solemn treaty with the United States
Government, meaning they best keep their ammunition dry and
them vedettes posted. Maybe you is expecting me to descry the
lofty peaks and crystalline lakes and tall timber and verdant pasture
and beaver and elk and electrified skies of that aboriginal idyll, the
whites all contemplating them features and figuring how to
convert them into folding currency. The famous Black Hills I'm
talking about. The stuff of aboriginal legend, where they went
questing for lodgepoles and grizzly claws and elk teeth and eagle
feathers and visions, held their big councils and danced their acroa-
matics. Where old Sitting Bull got serenaded by an eagle what told
him he was to be leader of the nation and was in for hard times by
dint of it. Well, if you is expecting all that, then you is about to get
shafted.

I never clapped eyes that topography in my earthly so can make
no comment apropos its nature, Elysian or purgatorial. But where

mountains abide sooner or later goddamn trees show up, hordes of mosquitos and buffalo flies resident therein, throw in a panther and a grizzly, so I don't believe I feel no lacuna dwells in my earthly by dint of it.

I am, though, cognizant of the Seventh's mission in the Black Hills, to go find gold and lots of it, or pretend to. Then send runners off to the print shop and get posters and pamphlets and banners printed up and sent off back east. To the newspaper office to insert a notice or three. Custer, he even took along a brace of reporters to write it all up. That way the whites would shove in and scare off the buffalo and chop the lodgepoles into kindlers and fill the lakes with mercury whatever that is, build a stinky town or three with names like Deadwood. The aboriginals will get indignant, well wouldn't you, and Custer, well he'd just have to whip their arses. It ain't the apogee of augury to foresee such engrenage.

Us bunch, well at that time we was otherwise occupied up on the Milk River, but the news even reached them godforsaken parts. Trooper rode in and unbuttoned his jacket and extracted the bum fodder. Boys, you heard about this?

Gold! Big strike in the Dakota hills. Pull on a stem of grass and it comes on up with it. Riches Untold! Come get your share! He folded the paper and looked around and said, First chance I get, I'm going over the hill. Any you boys coming? Ken Flash, he said, Erhh, aarrh.

Here's a feature I never bottomed about the whites. Yours truly, I discover an item that is going to make me richer than Crassus hisself, whoever he is, an item what means I don't have to spend another day of my life in futile toil, me I'd stay dumber than old Zechariah. The whites, they cast aside their tools and leap on a mule and chisel off to the nearest town, get the band out and toss their hats in the air and perform corybantics. You figure it.

Anyhow, like I said, I can say naught about that Black Hills expedition. What they did was separated us bunch out from that bunch and put us on another goddamn train and we got sent east. What a bugger.

Well admitted, there was some north in our orientation, but there was me anticipating the big skies and the circle of the earth, them horizons unsullied by goddamn hills and trees, cloud shadows racing across the hooping grass and the wind whipping my mane, and here I was packed into another lurching boxcar, the floor greasy with turds and piss, the plains disappearing behind me.

Now army life consists to no small degree of dallying at uncongenial locations for reasons withheld, and we finished wintering at a snowy fort located on the fork of two big rivers. They said one was the Mississippi, but I can't vouch for it. I know the rivers was iced and giant jags barged up onto the banks and into the trees, great groans and wrenchings chorusing in, two boats, a jetty and a fancy buggy wedged in there. The fort I want to call Fort Smelling. But that can't be it. Snow-crusted tipis and their blanketed denizens was roundabout, similar of trappers whose boats had got iced-in and should have been debauching theirselves in lower latitudes and was miserable about it.

We lingered at that godforsaken spot a couple of moons, and it got tediouser than a Cheyenne camp of a winter. Tell you how boring it got, I got the yen for humano conversation. Imagine that. But in that regard Ken Flash were as much use as an arse without an aperture. His curryings was silent and dilatory, his locution limited to phrases like, Hold still, Shift your goddamn leg, and, Ahh, it's a bugger, at some unshared mental turbidity. I can't say Ken Flash was ever unkind to me, but he never blew up my nose or bent my ear and related a conversation he'd had with an otter. You think back on all the picturesque characters what have gingered up this tale, well he is the cornstarch, the boiled rice, the oatmeal mush. Humanos can't all be charismatics. It's my experience the majority is the reverse. You been lucky so far. Here's an instance of the limits of that humano's imagination. Now, obviously he couldn't make no headway with Trasandatino, so he gave me a new name. Buck.

I am rambling here. The memory of that damp melancholic place is enfeebling the zest of my storytelling.

Come a day when a souther sloughed in and the tree birds commenced tweeting and skeins of geese honked north and got shot at for it, they loaded us into goddamn boxcars. But my heart sang like a lark when I clocked we was proceeding occidental. Out the chinks I saw the herbage greening up, and though the sky was still jowled gray, it owned a luminosity, something akin to a full-moon night when the sky is plated over but the cloud glows so you know the orb is present. I learned later the prairie around them parts was pocked with multifarious lakes, and these waters reflected the meagre boreal light back up to the sky. Ain't no detail to write home about I know, but I am eking out the events here.

We halted and they let us clomp out and get some of that fresh grass, and after they quit complaining of their sore arses, the troopers, them being parvenus to these parts, talked of prior martial events roundabout, massacres perpetrated by the Santee and the subsequent admonishments, all a decade ago. To show the savages how civilized they was, the whites put the most guilty through the full judicatory process, and hung forty of the hostiles just south of there. Allowed them to smoke their pipes and sing their songs to the martial drumbeat, then pulled the lever. Done them all simultaneous.

Him being a craftsman hisself, it even impressed Ken Flash. He remarked the gallows what expedited it must have been an engineering marvel. All them folks on board, you wouldn't want it to be collapsing at the crucial moment and injuring nobody, and you'd want all them trapdoors opening in harmony so as not to leave nobody standing there with his thumb up his arse, his peers all kicking danglers.

Carpentered in the form of a bandstand it were. That way the spectators could all get a good view. They got the band in to play along, and enterprisers, spying an opportunity vended toffee apples and toddies. Puffing on their pipes, them troopers all agreed it must have been a fine Christmas present for them homesteaders.

Anyhow, weren't incumbent upon us bunch to worry about no whooping aboriginals descending on our railroad train. The Indians was all mundified from these parts, and peeping out through that chink, I saw the swains was tolerable advanced, big slabs of black earth exposed and riven, barns, shacks and mechanicals, rootling hogs, horizontal trees.

THEY ONLY DRUG one deceased nag out the boxcar, a chestnut with a white blaze. We'd fetched up at a river fort, a wheezing steamboat tethered hard by. Adjacent stood a bunch of storehouses tall as church steeples and the steamboat was getting loaded with such contents as resided therein.

The goddamnedest thing, it weren't no humanos tottering about under loads. It were a mechanical performing the labour. A big timber swung across from which dangled sacks and bales and crates, and it lowered them items onto the deck. Don't ask me how it all worked, but whenever motion was required a boy struck a knock-kneed dun at which encouragement she plodded around in a circle, constrained by a wheel whereto she was attached, and looked right surly about it. I fretted we too was going to be packed onto that steamboat, but it blew its whistle and clatterwhacked off north. We was foddered up and at noon the boy tooted Boots and Saddles, what I'd learned by then.

As Ken Flash cinched the saddle I glanced about at my fellow equines. I recognized nary a one. Few of the bunch what had whipped the Cheyenne was left, and I'd never noticed them go. I guessed they maybe gone claudicated or got wounded and abandoned, got sold and was now atwixt the shafts of some horticultural mechanical, maybe feeding lapdogs or soaping the thighs of

247

fine ladies back east, gluing the joints of a fancy credenza together.

Now if any river ought have been nomenclatured up the Canadian it was that effort. I ventured it was the first river of any consequence I encountered what flowed north. Now I come to think of it, that Purgatoire got some north to it, and the Ute Creek, near where I got my first battle wound, so I guess that's me busted on that compass point remark.

Now I say it flowed north, and the land of the Frenchman were indeed the destination of its waters, but I don't know what lay in ambush up there being it sure were reluctant to arrive. It flowed north, south, east and west, touching all point of the compass en route, and it recollected me of the ambagious discourse of that Cheyenne chief what was so afeared of the floating ballcock, an item I was yet to witness in destructive action and had almost forgot about. Now the whites, being whites and maybe Frenchmen to boot, they spurned the Canadian and called that river the Red River, like all them other Red Rivers.

We followed the steamboat north. I say north, but naturally we didn't follow the course of the river, which would have multiplied the distance tenfold, and indeed there was times when we saw that boat chuffing directly towards us. Our pace, well it sure weren't one to get the grass waving, wherever we was bound. Despite that, on account of its meanderings we was gaining on that steamboat and by the end of the first day we overtook it. At that stage the boat was a good bit distant, it enjoying a westerly course, otherwise I do believe a deal of persiflage would have issued forth. In lieu the captain gave permission to fire off a couple of shots so the sailors was sure to be apprised of our location.

I mentioned the captain there so I might as well intelligence you up. It were the Irishman who'd recognized my wind and piloted me in pursuit of the kidnapped chef and who was later aboard when we fled Slow Turtle's magic in the sandy knobs. That one, though he paid me about as much heed as the Comanche would a Whistler.

He weren't gubernator of our bunch. The incumbent of that job was a brooding fellow of dark hair and dark eyes who later was to feature large at the fight known as the Little Big Horn, of which fracas I am the only living survivor. Our Gros Ventre scout soubriqueted him up as, The Man With The Dark Face, which, lets own it, ain't the acme of inventiveness, and weren't strictly accurate anyhow. Me, I saw a boulder-headed baby-faced fellow. You could imagine a favourite aunt pinching his cheeks and chucking his chin, chortling, I going to eat you all up. Yes I am. Yes I am. Who's going to eat you all up then? Who is? I am. I am going to eat you all up. Yes I am, &etc.

That said, bar for when he was inebriated and he sang saucy songs, that major was cold as a hibernating toad.

Being a mechanical and not needing no rest, while we pernoctated that boat overhauled us. Come the morning them troopers slavered down their chuck and got mounted up, sans the usual non-com encouragement, and a race developed what was the only event that brightened that trip to the frigid north, though us late in the primavera by then. Day come we thought the implacable clatterwhacker finally done outpaced us. Then we exited a bunch of trees and saw it hung up on a sandbar trying to grasshopper off. Goddamnit, you had to admire the whites for it, getting that big boat to walk along like that, but it was slow progress, and as we surpassed it, the troopers all cheered and tossed their hats in the air and made obscene gestures.

The further north we got the callow began to talk of Indian attack, especially such examples as might be perpetrated by the pitiless Sioux. Way they talked you'd think the Sioux was Odin and Mars and Thor and the Comanche rolled into one. A boy even pulled out the line, They say they is the finest light cavalry what the world ever see'd.

Had I been cursed with the powers of speech I'd have rejoindered, You all ain't seen the Comanche ride, or some similar pearl, but I wasn't so that were that. Another who fancied hisself more inculcated assumed rejoindering duties and came up with, I'll think you'll find the Kalmuck Tartars can outride any filthy savage, what shut everybody up, except for Ken Flash who said, Arhh it's a bugger. But not one of them boys had rode against the Comanche, so I'd say they was ignorant, a mental condition what generally don't prevent a humano expressing an opinion. Anyhow, turned out it was in these hereabouts the slumpen general had won his spurs as Indian burner. Drug a big bunch of artillery out into the Dakotas he had, and blasted them to perdition.

Now, I figure we got to the point where you is all wondering, what is this joker doing hiking up to the far-flung fastnesses of the American empire, when out on them plains heathen primitives remain to be exterminated. And you know what? I was asking myself that very same goddamn thing.

Now, I'll preface the following comments by stating the nature of the affair is without the compass of my noggin and I ain't to be trusted on the particulars. You best consult the history books if you is finicky about the motives and methods.

The American whites wanted to draw a straight line across the territory to keep out the Frenchmen. That's the way I understood it anyhow. The straight line was to run from a big lake in the oriental all the way to the Rocky Mountains, hundreds of miles in the occidental. But it ain't as easy to draw a straight line across all that territory as you might think. You have to consult the stars. You have to perform arsmetrick calculations and write down the answers in a book. You have to look through a magic brass tube like the burly sergeant done prior to Mac relieving him of his dontics at a man located on a distant ridge waving a flag about and write it up. But I am in way over my head here.

Anyhow, our job was to be the protection for them thin-armed scientifics. We was to be a mobile strike force, ever prompt to administer instant chastisement to any aboriginals what might take sanguinary objection to the line-drawing, and you can see the flaw in that stratagem right off. Remember them summers we spent on the prairies chasing will-o'-the-wisps about? And up here was now high summer. Weren't no snow-bound Indian camps we could noctivagate up to and annihilate while they was knuckling their eyes.

Anyhow, come a cloudy solstice we fetched up at a fort where the straight line was to start out from. The steamboat beat us to the fort and the sailors leaned over the rails and reciprocated them prior maledictions. We ignored the sailors best we could and turned sinister-wise to make rendezvous with the scientifics. We never saw no indigenes for a good moon or so.

TWENTY-FOUR

Two goddamn summers we spent up there, proceeding hesperian-wise at the pace of a porcupine, and they was the dreariest most mithersomest experiences of my earthly, and I refer you back to that winter Cheyenne camp.

Them mithersome aspects. First off was the topography. Admitted there was stretches of dry plain, but likewise were stretches featured of swampy ground, what the locals called muskeg. Now you see a stretch of fine herbage ahead, you think, I will proceed on without danger to my person and chaw on that herbage. Not up in the land of the Frenchmen. To the neophyte, muskeg looks like grass, until you step on it, and then you'd go in up to your hams, maybe your neck, maybe even higher, but it never fooled me.

We come upon a beast of the field ensconced thus, one the ignorant might identify as some species of elk. What drew us to it was it bemoaning its situation with a series of loud aw-aws. Now I own capacious nostrils, but my hairy orifices weren't naught compared to them this beast possessed. Big top lip to boot what overhung its lower counterpart to the extent that were invisible. It were a confection not to impart confidence in its intellect, an estimation I judged authenticated by its bemirement. The most notable feature to it were its antlers. Now, how can I describe them, being they weren't like nothing I'd ever seen out on them southern plains. They featured the standard prongs, but they was mere terminations, and giant leaves would better give you the picture. Maybe they served as sunshades, but all them trees roundabout, that don't fit.

A trooper shot it, but it was too much mither to drag out, and they was deficient in the roping department, so they left it there, so I never got to find out how they'd adjudicate it as repast.

Goddamn trees grew around the swamps and on any watercourse we come to, on the flanks of low hills the locals called mountains. If recollection serves me correct, one was called Turtle Mountain, so that gives you some clue as to the stature of these eminences. Where you got hills and goddamn trees and still water, you get the habitués, gadflies and buffalo gnats and mosquitoes. They partook of us nags severely, our flanks rippling like grass in the wind, our muscles shuddering like the gunnels of an overloaded steamboat departing the dock, if you will allow me to mix my picturing there. They bit inside my ears and inside my lips and inside my nostrils and the corners of my eyes and on them tender parts where my legs connect to my torso and by the end of the nights my eyelids was so swoll I could scarce see out. My hide, well tie a couple of eagle feathers in my mane and I could have been a Comanche steed painted red for battle.

I ain't dumb. Left to myself I'd have found mire, even ordure, and rolled in it like my ma taught me. If they'd corralled us up we could have stood nose to tail and engaged in reciprocal swishing. But this was the US Cavalry and they tied us to a rope in a straight line, our posteriors all staring out over the prairie. Reason being, at the gadflies' first visitation a couple of nags had run off maddened and was never seen again, and they done spoiled it for the rest of us. It was a done deal and we was stuck with it, wherefore the Frenchmen got a fancy phrase I done forgot.

You might not know this, but an equine can die from such usage. It happened on that very trip to a gray with black ears and haughty demeanour, and a couple more nags was hors de combat a good piece, wordplay intended. My stolid jockey, I got to hand it to him. He boiled up a stew of tobacco leaves and sumac and turpentine, threw in a dozen or so rattlesnake heads, a lizard or three, couple of rusty horseshoes, and he rubbed it on me like it were the finest emolument. He said, Ooh arhh, if it don't work I'll sell it to the primitives as whiskey.

By God they was onerous days. The Comanche, they was leery of trees as Absalom, but we ever found ourselves caught out in such localities, well Looks At The Sky, she'd never allow me to be used thus. She boiled up herbs the square ma kept a sock of, threw in buffalo grease and ashes and painted that on. Just lucky, I guess, I weren't never vain about my appearance.

I said sock there, and you might be sniggering thinking I misspoke, meaning stock. But taibo socks served as fine repositories for aught you wanted to hang up and keep dry, and was always on the shopping list when they went off raiding.

The meteorology provided the greatest relief. That summer were a stormy affair, and come the post meridian you'd see the clouds bunch up and wrestle theirselves purple, jags of lightning, and come the crepuscular and the pluvials rodding down them gadflies'd be off using tree leaves as bumbershoots. Then you might get some shuteye, or entertain yourself watching troopers splashing about chasing tents in their underwear.

Here's a curiosity. Any groves or forests what obstructed the straight line, they didn't detour round. They chopped the bastards down, which was fine by me. Cut a straight line a trio of horse-lengths wide over the whole of that Turtle Mountain they did, and over any further asperities what blocked the view. And don't imagine it weren't the feeble-armed scientifics doing the labour. They stood about superior and watched burly derby-hatted fellows do it they'd brung along special.

Now, even when those trees is disposed of, you can't take a brush and a bucket of tar and paint a straight line on the prairie and on up the mountains and on through the swamps. It just ain't going to endure. So them burlies built a line of mounds shaped like tipis only in miniature, out of whatever lay to hand. Stone if no excavating was incumbent, dirt and sod otherwise.

High summer we Seventh camped on a river they called the Mouse, but what the Frenchmen had appellated up different, them being contrary fellows. I do not recollect that French appellation. We'd still clapped eyes on no indigenes, and I speculate our dark-faced major had wearied of trailing a bunch of noisome navvies and hoity-toity scientists and decided to settle by that sweet creek where he could drink whiskey while the troopers went off to make inroads into the local creation. If there was trouble, the thin arms could fire off shots, send a messenger, combust the prairie. But the straw what prompted the decision were an episode yours truly were germane to.

A stiff-hatted fustianed fellow strode over one day and opened the cavity below his waxed moustache. You there. Yes, you fellow. Care to lend a hand with this vital work to secure your country's border? Naturally he weren't addressing yours truly. Ken Flash was occupied firking a stone out my hoof. He looked up and around to confirm the enquiry was addressed to hisself. Marching about in squares was scheduled for later, so he shot a glance back at the sergeant who was snoring such that you could have balanced a feather on the exhalations, shrugged his shoulders and said, Errh, arhh.

We trotted off toward a grassy furuncle, Ken Flash bearing a flagpole such as a Comanche carries his lance. I guess he thought it'd only take a minute or two.

Half a morning later we toiled to the summit. Out on the prairie, topographical features is apt to appear closer than they is. I might have mentioned that prior. Ken Flash dismounted, positioned his forage cap so as to shade his eyes and peered back the way we come. I chivvied off a basking rattler and grazed the herbage what was already browning over. Its taste was bitter and its texture dry, such that it caught in my thropple, but I forced it down, one eye on my jockey.

He held up the flagpole vertical like they told him, and to his eyes he held a pair of brass tubes they had loaned him. He shifted to the side a couple of paces and peered back afresh. He shifted a trio of paces more. I squinted back and my highly refined peepers distinguished them scientists waving their thin arms about directing his movements. Ken Flash said, Goddamn bugger it, and shifted back a couple of paces. Then he stood motionless, peering back, the flag rippling in the breeze.

Now, I ought enucleate the circumstances what led to subsequent events. The night previous he'd caroused with his comrades until the small hours and drunk a considerable amount of whiskey of inferior quality. Withal, for a number of days prior he had been suffering from looseness of the bowels, brought on I venture by drinking that swampy water. On the trip to the furuncle we'd already halted twice for him to lower his britches and squirt. Conjecturing the errand to be but of brief duration, he had omitted to bring his canteen, and now, for motives beyond the compass of my noggin, he'd tossed his cap onto the grass, some paces off.

The breeze fell away. The flag hung limp. The sun pounded down. Ken Flash watched the scientists through the magic tubes, gripping the flagpole. Sweat beaded his face, and he stole a glance at the cap. I speculate he was loath to go retrieve it lest it be a critical moment back there and he ruined a calculation, occasioned a scientific to break his pencil. Any rate, the upshot was he tottered a spell and his legs buckled. He said, Arhh, bugger, I do believe I am taking a faint, and maintaining faith in its sustaining properties, he clung onto the flagpole. But such faith proved founded on sandy ground. It and he toppled. He said, Arhh bugger, again, and I grant on this occasion it were the mot juste. I heard a loud fart, the timbre thereof communicating it weren't entirely composed of gaseous substances.

He layed there a spell, me forcing down the herbage. He weren't in no jeopardy, though him hors de combat. The scientifics spying through their tubes they'd have seen the flag fall, and once they'd double-checked their arsmetrick they'd be sending out a rider to come see.

An Indian was beside me. Only the Lord knows where he'd come from, and he must have owned superior stalking proficiencies to outwit my highly attuned lugs and nostrils. I put it down the fact he'd arrived from downwind, the breeze carrying off the footfalls of him and his pony. But, merde, if you will pardon my French. Maybe I was losing my touch.

That pony was a fine animal, a paint with a blue eye and a flaming mane the colour of Looks At The Sky's hair, and were he possessed of the ability to smirk he'd have done it. He contented hisself with a snort and a disdainful shake of the head. Now, the Indian. I don't know what tribe he was, but he sure weren't no Comanche. He'd have been leading me off to recommence my life as a Lord of the Plain by now, my jockey's hair part of my adornment, maybe that latter's privy member stuffed into his own mouth. Certain Comanche consider that embellishment a fine joke. But not everybody gets their sense of humour.

Ain't no Comanche in the frigid north. They got more sense. This was a tamed local Indian. Maybe had took up the georgic life, got his kids going to Sunday school. Assiniboine maybe, Gros Ventre, maybe Arikira wandered north, the holes in the face showing he's survived the smallpox. Probably he'd come out riding his fine buffalo horse to remember the old days, though he wore a calico shirt and worsted pantaloons. As homage to the former life he had cut the crotch out them pantaloons and a breechclout preserved his modesty, bar for when the wind gyred. He maintained a fine pair of grey-streaked braids, crimson ribbon and brass wire wove in, medicine pouch about his neck, a brace of black smears below the eyes. So some wildness remained within.

He dismounts and strolls over to my jockey and prods him with a moccasined toe, grimaces and jerks his face away at the stink. He approaches yours truly, en route speaking gentle words in a strange tongue, and holds his hand out flat like there'd be grub in it. But when I inspect it is devoid even of a lick of salt and I done been betrumped. He takes my bridle and scratches my muzzle and rubs my ears. He sighs and says further words, the tone thereof I'd describe as irked but resigned. Then he bends and hauls up my jockey, shoulders him like he would a fallen comrade, dumps him aboard and lashes him on. A final phrase issues forth, and I conjecture it was something of the ilk, Horse, I'm afraid you've been landed with a shitty task.

You can imagine. It is humiliating for a white to be rescued by an aboriginal, specially a soldier belonging to a nonpareil force of Indian killers. With considerable hauteur that Indian walked us into the camp of the US Seventh Cavalry. The troopers woke up and went for their rifles, and he dropped the reins all insouciant and left me and my cargo there without a word, save for a nod in the direction of the Gros Ventre.

The dark-faced major, well he combusted his wig. He stomped off and objurgated the scientifics for inveigling his man into menial duty, said he was a trained cavalryman, goddamnit, who must be in a state of constant readiness for martial action. You get the drift. He got the sergeant to throw a pail of swamp water in Ken Flash's face to wake him up long enough to be told he was on latrine duty for the foreseeable. And that were that. We made that camp by the Mouse, and never another survey flag was raised by the Seventh. Such were the denouement of the contretemps.

COURSE, being a gubernator it were all bluster. The rapport with the spectacled scientifics declined a good bit, but he couldn't let them go off on their own into the wilderness and get massacred. So a pair was always ordered to follow on, and if me and my jockey was dutied we'd find a hummock and he'd dismount and we'd both chaw on the herbage and catch some shuteye. With the wind blowing away the gadflies, I admit, it weren't the Llano what with the country all rumpled, but they were tolerable days.

We saw our first wild Indians. I'd like to say we cut their sign and tracked them to their village whereupon we hoisted the guidon of the mighty Seventh and rode in éclated-up and issued advisements against molestation. But Indians always know when you are in their country. We moved camp one day and that same evening bunch of Sioux showed up for a courtesy visit, asked for tobacco and coffee, a sack or three of flour.

Whites always disparaged this activity. The begging of the indolent, they judged it, and added it to the bone heap of reasons why the aboriginals was in need of correction and extirpation. But Indians, they was always giving each other gifts, and could never cipher out why the whites was always so withholding. You walk into an Indian camp in a confident manner with your munitions visible but holstered, an Indian is obliged to throw another chunk of puppy into the pot and share his fire, let you smoke his pipe, and he won't wipe it on his shirt where you done put your lips. All you got to do is listen to his stories, and then he'll usher you into his lodge where he's thrown a buffalo robe on the floor so you can pernoctate in luxury. Out on the morrow trail he might massacre you and take your horses, but that is different affair, entirely.

Naturally, them Sioux asked them what they was doing in their country uninvited. When the whites told them they wasn't building no railroad, they was merely drawing a line to keep out the Frenchmen, you saw them heave a sigh of relief, and one of them said, Can't you build a big wall while you is at it. I never fathomed the import of that enquiry at the time. Now, all this leisure time on my hands, I estimate it weren't directed at the Frenchmen, who, let's own it, was thin on the ground up there, laying aside our example who bossed the aboriginal scouts called Pierre, and I ain't being lazy there, his name really was Pierre. That Sioux, they was hoping a wall might keep the US Empire and its whiskey traders out, preserve the last of the buffalo.

Speaking of dumb ungulates, it clubbed me I'd not cocked an eye on an example for many a moon. To say I was missing them bovines would be stretching the point, but I tell you, to circulate those graminaceous prairies and see only their skulls and chine gave me a queer feeling inside. I can't explain it. But on the plus side, I guess their absence kept the wolves down to manageable numbers.

Then come the day, perched on one of them hummocks, watching the cloud shadows racing each other, the wind in the occidental, my lugs picked up the boom of a Big Fifty. A moment of silence followed, save for the wind rustling the grass and a trio of ravens cawing dispute over ownership of a deceased skunk, then another boom, and another. He'd got hisself a stand going, that hunter, and I pictured them beasts standing about observing their fellows spouting blood and dropping to their knees.

That hummock featured a curiosity. Somebody had dug down through the black earth to bare rock and created a depression in the shape of a man, had placed a boulder where the head should be. Roundabout the rocks was incised with carvings of birds and edible prairie creatures, which to an Indian is a fair portion of them latters, particularly with the buffalo dwindling. My jockey regarded these items and said, Arrhh, heathen hocus-pocus.

The scientifics built their mounds among the mounds of festering buffalo, and I expect the birds and the coyotes and the maggots picked the bones clean, and the bleaching sun got to work, and now them bones is dust and is fertilising the grass and if you was to pass by you'd see verdant patches growing taller than the rest and were the buffalo still in circulation they'd bumble along and chaw on it.

We progressed on to some live examples. Indian scout come chiselling into camp bearing the news, and the troopers and even the scientifics went off to sport and come back with humps and tongues, heads for the taxidermy man. They shot wildfowl off of a lake. You might not know this, but come the high summer wildfowl lose the ability to fly. Them scientifics would know why or be in possession of book to tell them, but I remain ignorant on the matter. All I know, impaired thus, they might be able to float about in the middle of the lake to avoid the foxes and coyotes and badgers and such, but it leaves them at considerable disadvantage on the firearms front, and no few sodden avians was left floating about like dishrags.

Ken Flash turned loquacious, Arhh, Back in the old country they got a gun specially manufactured for the slaying of ducks, sure wished we done got one now. Of such length it is impossible to hoist to your shoulder and you done got place it lengthwise on a boat and lay down behind it and quack. Arhh, it's a bugger. And you should see the size of the shells. Take fifty, maybe a hundred out with a single shot. Another wag piped up, They ought invent an aboriginal version, which got a good laugh.

They owned a mowing machine, them scientists. Any time they come upon any decent herbage they got a burly to hitch an unfortunate equine to it. The grass sprayed up into the wind, the moiety of it departing off to Mexico, and they piled the remainder into heaps. Them ricks was insurance against dearth of fodder on the return trip, and I considered it an act of hugeous optimism, what with mounted Sioux circulating and the winter coming on.

The geese honking over, a norther blowing a particle or three of snow about, we ascended a step in the prairie and topped out in broken country of ridges and washes, cones and coulees, banded riven dirt like mine tailings, wind-bent half-growed trees, and black bitter ponds. We fetched up at an outlook of scoured rock and sour grass. They said off yonder was the Missouri and the forts, but all I could see was a distant bristle of lodges and the streeling grass.

The inclemencies coming on, the scientists holstered their brass accouterments and we turned back.

I smelt it before they saw it and they exclaimed Jesus Christ. The prairie was aflame. A line of fire and a curtain of black smoke, but you could have pictured that for yourself. I guess if you is being charitable you might put it down to a lightning bolt or a neglectfully disposed dottle, but yours truly, I'd wager a basket of apples it were an indigene fiendishment.

Now, them callow in affairs of the wilderness, they see a curtain of smoke and fire progressing on, they will spur their horses and try to outrun it. Dumbest thing you can do. Your nag will tire and you will be consumed. Me being of generous disposition, I'll allow you the benefit of my multifaceted experience on the high plains. That way you'll be apprised of the correct procedure if you is ever caught in such a fix.

What you got to do is trot toward it, and when you believe it is about to engulf you and truncate your earthly dreams and desires, you got to fight every instinct and put your nag into a gallop. Naturally, you'd need an equine possessed of my sang-froid. Your average nag, he or she clocks them flames appropinquating theirselves and it's no-thank-you and their eyes roll like tombola balls and they sprint off flat-eared contrary-wise, no amount of cajoling and fustigation on your part making a jot of difference. You got a nag like me, well it will leap that thin line of flame, being that is all it is, and lope on off into the charred ground beyond, discommoded by naught but a singed hoof hair and smoked nostrils.

I did that for my jockey that day, him by then knowing my gumption and giving me my head, though he never twigged my former life as a Lord of the Plain, and the other nags saw me improve my situation and followed suit.

As you can imagine, the fire consumed the ricks we'd left providential. You saw them flames licking the sky from miles off and I imagined them generally solemn Sioux staring out from some lookout, chuckling at their sabotage. The fires, together with the meteorology-blasted herbage, made for a hard trip home, and they left behind maybe half-dozen saggers and tremblers for the wolves. Me and the mules, we did alright.

Well we wished them scientifics and their confreres bon voyage and after a half-moon of trudging occidental-wise we put some south in our course. Under a pressing stone-grey sky speckling us with sleet, we caught up with a waggon rattling along, four sumpters hauling, brace of riders flanking on wore-out nags. Weren't no implements of tillage or domestic trumperies attached, no children peeping out, so it weren't no settler waggon, that and it was headed east. Being entertainment were thin on the ground, our bunch adjacentized itself.

The two riders comprised a white spectacle-wearer shivering under a mackinaw jacket what I conjectured concealed thin arms, and a wolfskin-jacketed example of duskier hue riding an Indian pony, blithe to the meteorology. I figured him the guide. That pair exchanged neither a word nor glance our whole visit. The driver, well it is hard for me to supply the form and lineaments of that individual being they was smothered by hugeous buffalo robe and a muskrat cap of like proportion, ginger whiskers concealing the greater portion of his face.

The Irishman enquired of the driver what he was doing so late out on the blasted plains, the inclemencies coming on. The driver concurred. Thank you for your concern, Captain. I was so enraptured in my work I failed to notice the progress of the season, notwithstanding the entreaties of my sagacious if generally taciturn native guide here. Me, I erected my auricles at the prospect of expanding my lexis.

The Irishman said, May I enquire the nature of your business.

Ginger Whiskers was up and out of his seat before the Irishman's sentence sailed out from atwixt his lips. You certainly may captain. I'd be delighted.

I said the waggon was rattling along, and it weren't no fancy wordplay, for such was the cargo's auditory manifestation. Whatever rattled lay under a tarp in shallow heap. Ginger Whiskers hauled off the tarp and tossed it aside with as much flourish as a tarp will allow. He clapped his hands together, and if he'd been a Frenchman he'd have said, Voila!

Now at such junctures I am in the habit of employing a device to arouse your curiosity, that being, and it were the goddamnedest thing! But I'd say this was the least goddamnedest thing my eyes was obliged to rest upon my entire earthly. Naught but a heap of old bones it were. I say old bones because they wasn't sun-bleached like the buffalo bones laying roundabout, and I'd go so far as to say their prior owners had enjoyed the subterranean life a good piece prior to exhumation, being they was dirt coloured and had dirt attached.

I spent the summer bone-collecting in the Badlands, Ginger Whiskers said, and extended an arm over the heap. They range from the Triassic to the Cretaceous. The Irishman nodded. I could tell he was trying to think up a supplementary question, but lucky for him no supplementary questions was required to stimulate further discourse.

Ginger Whiskers hauled a bone of some heft to the surface. This example here is the humerus of a mastodon. The Irishman scratched his whiskers as though cogitating and said, Ahh, indeed. He weren't making a bad fist of it.

Ginger Whiskers clattered on through the bones, and it weren't the sound of old bones knocking together, but of rocks colliding. This is the horn of a rhinoceros. Ken Flash said, Ooh, arrgh. He'd heard of a rhinoceros. This here is the jawbone of a tiny horse which once frequented these parts. Me, I pricked my ears up and quit scratching my nose on the waggon boards. Well, it wouldn't have served old Samson for Philistine-smiting, but I weren't about to deny the nature of it. Now, all these bones he was extracting and clacking together, the dirt never fell off, and I saw it too were rock.

Ginger Whiskers opened a small wooden box, Now here is the

piece-de-resistance. Whatever it was, it was wrapped in waxed paper and he enjoyed a good deal of ceremony unwrapping it. Behold gentlemen! They all went Whoaahh!, though they was yet to be intelligenced-up on the nature of it. Somebody even whistled. Yours truly, I conjectured it some tine broke off an antelope horn, maybe off a rack of antlers. Ginger Whiskers begged to differ.

This, gentleman, is the fang of a giant cat as big as a ruminant which hunted these environs countless eons ago, and I think you of all men will agree with our taxonomy of it as, a sabre-toothed cat.

He passed it to the Irishman who examined it as long as he thought polite. Yes, I see the resemblance. Do you mind if the men look at it? He passed it around and further expressions of wonder issued forth, Wow, Jeezus, Uhm-uhm, Well I'll be a goddamn sonofabitch, Holy Mother, Zookers, Bugger me, Ooh, arrgh.

As we bid farewell the Irishman asked Ginger Whiskers, The savages, don't they bother you and your small party?

He laughed. No Captain. They consider me quite insane. They call me Crazy Badger.

———

Naturally, it all being mumbo jumbo to me I remain unable to supply any enucleation of that display and why he was hauling them stone bones about the blasted plains. I supply it merely as an entertaining interlude, although I admit to being joyful them sabre-toothed felines wasn't still in circulation. Now the Cornishman, he'd have opined on it for sure. Could be it even tallied with his nullifidianism.

The grass turned from brown to grey, to white, then to grey with white patches, and we fetched up at a fort located by a salty water the Sioux called Spirit Lake but the whites improved to Devil's Lake. Make of that what you will.

TWENTY-FIVE

B y God, first time ever I was glad of a stable. You know me. I like to inure myself to the elements so I remain fly and ready for life's inevitable tribulations. I resisted, I truly did, stood in the lee of it for many days as the blizzards roared in, but the winter up there knocked the Llano example into a cocked hat. You get a norther out on the Llano and couple of days later you'd be paddling through the snowmelt seeking shade. That winter never quit. I heard an explosion one time and Ken Flash said, There goes another. Aarhh, it's a bugger. That were the sum of his intelligence on the matter, but a trooper said later it were so cold the trees was exploding.

The wind contrived to blow from all four quarters of the compass contemporaneous and secreted snow in the privatest of bodily locations. I felt my arse sagging one day and looked about to see my tail clumped with ice. Where was all the goddamn gadflies when you needed them. One swing of that tail, assuming I could have got it into motion, could have clubbed hundreds of the bastards to smash.

Day come when my breath steamed out and turned instantly

to ice particles what fell to the ground. When I breathed in I could scarce expand my bellows, and when I did it were like the horse combuster had miniaturized hisself had took up residence therein. Frost rimed my eyelashes and I looked out from under their white fronds. My chin, it grows a little beard in the winter, not up there with that of the buffalo you understand, and I never grow the hairy knees of them ungulates. But anyhow the point of that interpolation is the icicles hanging from it was the straw what done it. I had to own it. My old shaggy coat just weren't up to the task.

I swallowed my hauteur and entered that frowsty stable, pretended I'd wandered in accidental and feigned surprise at finding myself located therein, them flatuous nags all huffing and chomping hay. That bunch'd never spent a winter with the Cheyenne chawing cottonwood twigs. You could almost chaw on the fug in there and it was a right soporific ambience, I can tell you, so I found myself a chestnut mare of solid proportion and inveigled myself adjacent. When she'd got used to my stink, I leaned in and fell into the embrace of Morpheus.

A winter like that, you can understand why gophers and bears and marmots sleep it out, you really can. A toad can freeze solid. You can play baseball with it. But leave it out in the spring sun, the ice will melt out and it'll wipe its eyeballs and lurch away in search of sexual congress. The cold recollected me of Abendego and one of his habits. Come a bout of frigidity he wore his clothes inside out. To outflank the vermin, he said.

I towed a cart about the fort. That ain't a notable event in itself until you supply the fact that conveyance was bereft of wheels. In lieu it ran along on wooden slats, and I was recollected of them Cheyenne shavers sliding down the bluff on them buffalo-rib runners on the eve of their destruction. When I first got hitched I previsioned ponderous progress. But once you got it in motion it glided along like you was fitted with the wings of Pegasus hisself, until you come to an inclivity. They say the country of the

Frenchmen extends many days travel north from there and gets even more frigid, and up there they got teams of canines to haul them conveyances. I give due credence to the part about the dogs, recollecting them Comanche yappers what hauled miniature travoises, but I never believed the part about it being colder.

The officers, most of them absquatulated back east. The dark-faced major claimed to have sprained his ankle and weren't seen again till next summer. No few times the snow piled up against the stable and the troopers was obliged to come dig us out. I looked forward to them drifts. Chinking out the insinuating wind, them precipitations rendered the stable even more snug, and as further perquisite they forced the cancellation of any marching about in squares.

The lake froze over and the troopers chopped holes and spooled in fishing lines, maybe dislodged an aboriginal incumbent to save the hatchet work. A trooper fell in and froze to death and they hoicked him out, him all clenched up like that wolf Ahithophel poisoned. They covered him in a tarp and left him by the lumber pile till spring when they could hack into the ground and bury him in a round hole.

The soldiers was obliged to saw up their beef and apply the axe to the bacon, smash their beer into manageable chunks. I watched a pair of wits hand a frozen duck egg to a neophyte and tell him to crack it in the pan. He got his own back. Wrapped an egg in a snowball and mashed a corporal's nose, for which act he was manacled and ordered to tote a log about in his underwear.

For all I know they kept a store of them eggs ready to pack into artillery as ammunition to repel Indian attack, and I pondered on if disembowelment by duck egg was considered an honourable death for a warrior. But slow times like that your mind shuffles such trifles about.

I imagine you is getting itchy eyeballs. This ain't getting us any nearer to the Greasy Grass, goddamnit. If I want mundanity I can look out the window. Well, you got be goddamn patient. You'll get to find out how the Chosen One met his demise, being I am the one and only living survivor of the fight and hence possess the only optics to bear witness to the event.

After the big fight they made me celebrity. You know that? I got pampered worse than a Comanche's favourite buffalo horse and told I'd never again be compelled to charge into bloody battle. I got invited to fetes and parties, Sunday school openings, got fed apples and carrots, them latters always a let-down when you is anticipating the formers and I judge it an act of cruelty. I got slapped by gubernators and petted by spinsters and pinched by shavers and my picture took.

They showed me them pictures one time, and once I ciphered out what in goddamn hell I was supposed to be looking at I was a good bit crestfallen. They never captured my sandy colour, but they always managed to exaggerate my butcher-block noggin and sawed-off legs, which deficiencies by then I'd recent forgot, me being a hero and such.

Hero. Goddamn merde de cheval, if you will pardon my French. They didn't know me from Adam before the battle, and thenceforth proceeded to invent stories about who I was and where I'd come from and prior valiant deeds. I could have got massacred on the Washita or froze or starved to death on occasions unnumbered were it not for my own gumption, and nobody would've give a fig about it, well maybe Mac and the Cornishman. I wish them two had met and become friends, Looks At The Sky too, albeit that'd be stretching it.

Anyhow, my celebrity. Humanos can get right sentimental and I expect they wanted to extract something affirmatory out of the fight, expunge the picture of all them eviscerated troopers what had somehow got whipped by a bunch of bedizened primitives. Look at that nag what done survived everything. Maybe we can make it too. Hand me that bar of soap would you.

Being already on the booze to aid my recuperation, they was desirous I enjoy the whole cornucopia of life's pleasures. Plug of chawing tabbaccy were the first dainty, and they eased me in gentle by dipping it in molasses prior to shoving it atwixt. You know me, when it comes to molasses you can put me down as a Comanche, and I sucked and slavered on that plug, rotating it about my chops till that inky nectar was gone and the plug were feathered up like a rope end. Then I chawed down. Jesus Christ, Mother Mary, and all the saints in heaven.

I never tasted a goat turd in my earthly but I'd imagine chawing that tabaccy plug is thereabout. It finished amidst the straw and turds, and I figured they'd toss it in the trash can, but a fellow come over and rinsed it in the trough and bit off a chaw and didn't even look bashful about it. That prior invective is an Irish example I learned.

They sparked up a cigar and shoved that in. Go on Comanch', stick with it, you'll love it. Ain't nobody likes it at first. They got the photographer in to record the event for posterity and he said, Hold still goddamnit, to me, and, Say cheese, to the men, and it went off, and in some drawer someplace resides an image of yours truly puffing on a cigar. He were obliged to be quick. Weren't no time to figure no correct exposure. I never did figure why a humano would want to place a miniature bonfire atwixt their choppers, and my suspicions was confirmed and I coughed and the goddamn smoke burnt my highly refined optics. I shook my head and the cigar shot off and plunked into a pile of straw, and a trooper was obliged to throw a bucket of water on it.

They tried real hard with the tabaccy, believing I guess its curative properties would aid my recuperation. I venture had they got the chance the pipe would have been next, maybe got a straw hat and poked holes in it for my auricles, charge ten cents for admission.

But at the denouement of the cigar episode, the blacksmith barged into the stable and said, That'll be enough boys, and heaped further objurgations upon their persons. When the photographer objected, he fetched him a sogdologer about the ear, and that were the finish of my smoking days.

This blacksmith, he weren't the kindly fellow who'd first shod me up them summers since, though he were no less kindly. Maybe blacksmiths is all kindly. I wouldn't know. I only met two examples. Maybe he weren't even a blacksmith. There's a lot of remembering going on here.

Going by his name and throttled accent this fellow were a Dutchman. Gus they called him, and transpired he'd been detailed to look after me, me now a celebrity. Gus, he were a survivor of the dark-faced major's fight, and I figure by dint of it he were right doting toward me. Always had an apple for my choppers and a pat for my neck, was diligent in his curryings. I'd even say he were my best currier since Looks At The Sky.

We got our picture took together, me and Gus, my tail motionless on a rare windless prairie day, him holding my halter and looking right proud about it. He'd even took the trouble to uncrumple his forage cap so the crossed swords was visible. I guess you might find that picture if you peruse the histories and we was deemed worthy. Gus, he were a middling sort you wouldn't look twice at. The only item on the debit side, he favoured a big moustache in the style of goddamn Custer.

I recollect he liked declaring, I am a Prussian, to any who called him 'Dutch' and would listen. Told me he'd worked as a desk clerk at the coalmines and watched the ponies when they got brung up once a year to get the sunlight and had always liked horses and once he got to the Land of Promise and found hisself unemployed had determined to join the US Cavalry. Like Looks At The Sky and Ahithophel and Mac and Mrs Cash and Hears The Moon, he told me his innermost thoughts, most of which I done forgot, maybe because he spoke half them thoughts in the Prussian lingo.

This I do remember. Early on he comes with a bucket of mash and looks about to make sure we are alone and his optics lubricate up and he sobs a spell, his head on my neck. He rubs his eyes on his sleeve and snorts and says, We come through it Comanche, you and me, didn't we. We come through it. We're a lucky pair. I'll take care of you, and you can take care of me.

———

TOWARD THE END of my convalescence Gus left the stable door open, said, Go on Comanche. Enjoy yourself fella.

I were like a housecat confronted by a puddle. This can't be right. Figuring it dilatory behaviour on his part for which I personally might get objurgated, I loitered by the door and sniffed the air and contented myself with observing the mundanites of the fort, snorting derision at them nags marching about in squares. My wounds both psychological and physical had took a toll on my ginger, and it took a couple of days for me to edge out. I glanced about shifty, raised my head and twitched my nostrils. They all was going about their quotidians paying me no mind. I'd noticed tufts of herbage sprouting about the margins of the bandstand and they looked right tasty. Why not take a stroll over to confirm.

Naught of a wrathful nature descended upon me, and thenceforth I extended my ambit. Naturally, I scrupled to approach strangers lest I got a quirting and drug back, but it were the goddamnedest thing. All and sundry was intent on shoving apples and sweet biscuits and sugar lumps atwixt my choppers and washing the mush down with booze, slapping my neck so it got to be mithersome, pummelling my arse like I was Old Henry Clay hisself. How you doing Comanch? They taking good care of you?

Now you can imagine, such pamperings spoil you, and I commenced taking liberties. Come marching about in squares time I discovered that locating myself out front and high-stepping put them other nags off their stride. If I caused a surfeit of chaos some trooper would wag a finger and chide, but weren't never no malice. Sergeant Mickey, he hobbled over one time, tapped the side of his bent nose and said, Now Comanch, you behave yourself, and they'll be a wee drinkie in it for you.

Sundays and high days, the inclemencies permitting, they set up the camp chairs and the band climbed up onto the bandstand and the officers put on their plumes and their wives erected their parasols and they sat theirselves down to enjoy a musical concert. Me, I'd atwixt myself between and chaw on the herbage and swish my tail about, enjoy a bowel movement I'd saved up special, especially if they come to a largo mosso.

A favourite was to jerk my head up of a sudden, erect my ears and stare off into the distance rigid as a prize-winning pointer. I'd hold the posture, and soon, well they just couldn't help theirselves. The band looked up and played bum notes. The audience turned around expecting to see heathens lined up on the bluff waving sharps and blunts, and by the time they turned back I was chawing herbage again.

I have to admit around this time camp hygiene and ditto personal went all to hell. I acquired a reputation for overturning trash cans while perscrutating for apple cores and liquor dregs, for wandering about with coffee grinds, bacon rinds and crushed egg shells arranged about my face, maybe an apple-peel earring. I never owned no looking glass but I figure bloodshot eyes completed the confection. By God but they was good times.

The only real trouble I got into was when I barged into a picnic table fresh set up for a visiting general. I was attempting to get my hairy lips around a cream-filled brandy snap, a dessert what got all bases covered. Made a right hurra's nest of that table I did, but all that happened was Gus wagged a finger, though he was grinning, and shut me in the stable till the general'd gone, and even then the general come visit and got his picture took.

Years hence Gus got killed by a stray bullet on the Wounded Knee Creek, which is about as ridiculous as life can get. You survive the Greasy Grass and all them ensuing winters chasing Indians about the rumpled plains, to get killed by one of your own in the last ever Indian massacre, the wires buzzing the news to the Great Father before the blood had stiffened on the corpses, him reading the telegram illuminated by the incandescent light bulb. I witnessed Gus's life fade out, the snow dusting over him. I'd not kept my part of the deal, and that day my bottom lip took to flapping again and never did quit.

TWENTY-SIX

I went off divaricating there. My mind, bemired in the tedium of that winter, returned to the aftermath of that day on the Greasy Grass and my subsequent celebrity. I have only a few more episodes to relate before I get you up in the Powder country, which is right pretty if you is featured of them sensibilities and the meteorology ain't too inclement.

Spring arrives late up in the frigid north. The grass greens over and the prairie birds start singing a good moon later than they do on them southern plains, and we was only a half moon from the longest day by the time they rousted us out of that fort to renew our mission as lightning response unit to the thin-armed scientifics.

The trip west we took in leisurely fashion, and I believe them officers viewed it an opportunity to hone their sporting skills going by the way they kept charging off and the distant sound of munitions. Nobody worried about Indian attack. Down in the sacred Black Hills the Beau Sabreur was finding gold and the Sioux would be heading down there to remonstrate, so that took care of them, and later we'd be entering the land of the Blackfeet and they had been whipped into friendliness. No few of them troopers got the mulligrubs, them picturing their comrades strolling along though them meadows in their suspenders, picking posies and nuggets of gold out the verdure, the band along for serenading purposes, an endless supply of tender venison, ample opportunities to snabble a shovel and abscond.

We was to rendezvous where the Yellowstone strikes the Missouri, at the fort located there, wherein years later Sitting Bull would surrender. It was tolerable flat in them parts, the trees thinning out nice, the sky doming over. When we arrived, plastered on the blue was a cloud in the form of an owl run over by a waggon wheel. My spirits lifted at the sight of it and I wished I believed in omens.

They call the Missouri the Big Muddy, but up there its waters was green as sage brush. The Yellowstone, it comes in muddy, and for a stretch the waters run parallel, in the manner of shy paramours before they decide to go copulate. The rivers mingle and the Missouri takes on the colour of the Yellowstone. You'd think it'd be the reverse. I remain ignorant if such conjoining was by dint of the season or is a permanent state of hydrological dynamics up in them parts.

Heaped on the wharfage was a mountain of snow. By God, they'd even figured how to monetize them precipitations. We got close and I saw it weren't no snow but a pile of buffalo bones. A man had clumb to the top and was grinning, waiting to get his picture took. The photographer shouted, Hold still, and the grinner shouted back, Wait, and he cocked his hat and fixed a fist to a hip, acts what dislodged no few of them bones. So some entrepreneur had sent myrmidons out on the prairie collecting, and now them former denizens was waiting to be floated back east to be converted into currency to buy trumperies. Good for him.

Were midsummer day by the time the dark-faced major had arranged affairs and we trudged off along the Missouri heading for the Milk. The troopers had taken final advantage of the fort's flesh-pots and was hence steeped in begrudgery, the mud clumping about their boots, a thin sleet blowing in doing naught to mitigate their mood, them all pulling their collars up and their hats down. The environs of the fort, they was littered with sagging tipis and broken Indians squatting by meagre fires and from under their blankets they stared out at us as we went by.

Brace of trappers chased on after us and complained the Indians had run off their horses and what was we going to do about it. To add emphasis to his grievance one fellow grabbed the halter of the major's horse and become subject to a salty rebuke and a slash from the quirt, that latter likewise hungover. The major not the horse. He denied their importuning and we nosed through a herd of beef cows what was too dumb to shift until lashed, and we was out on the open plain. Rest assured I ain't going to describe this trip in its entirety which was over undulating prairie and not flat at all and left me discomposed in myself.

Somewhere up on the Milk we tramped through an old Indian battleground populated by good Indians. Arrow-spiked ex-warriors was strewn about in various stages of decomposition and attitudes of agony. Naught but skin and bones is a dictum of the whites, and such they was, the former stretched taut but perforated by the action of beak and fang. It were only a marvel the wind hadn't carried them desiccated remnants away. Skulls was studying dirt and sky, elbows and knees performing contortions, and feet and hands lay scattered where the prairie creatures had quarrelled over them. I was recollected of that fight me and the Christ Bloods witnessed them summers since, and I conjectured that'd be the state of them boys round about now.

The troopers and scientists rootled about for souvenirs, half-dozen arrow heads, the point of a lance and a brass bracelet their booty. They squatted amongst the cadavers and posed for photographs. A scientist got out a pair of tin snips and set to work taking samples. I got two skulls, three femurs, a pelvis and a humerus, he declared. Should do me, and he wiped his snips on the grass.

They talked about what brand of Indian they was. Whittled it down Piegans killed by Crow or Crow killed by Piegans. Nobody thought to ask the aboriginal scout who were the only likely expert. They praised the Lord for Major Baker and the US Second Cavalry, who by their valour down on the Marias had made it safe for us to travel unmolested through the territory, though him a drunkard and later reviled for his actions by cissy politicians and snivelling old-maid newspaper editors, cosseted females crying into their scented hankies what'd never planted a high-heeled boot west of the Mississippi.

The higher up the Milk we got the less agua there were in it. Herbage was likewise scanty, and the Gros Ventre said a plague of grasshoppers had been through. We wasn't yet arrived at the point where the line-drawing were at, and already they was fretting about forage. Days come when them troopers spent most the day on Shankses leading us nags. Me and the mules did ok.

We fetched up at a bunch of buttes the whites called the Sweet Grass Hills, at the foot thereof we made camp. Streams flowing down the hills provided lubrication to the plentiful herbage, but I calculate it must have been a famished humano who first tasted that grass and pronounced on its quality. To my equine palette it was bitter as embers. Goddamn trees festooned them slopes, but least they didn't dub them asperities mountains.

It was back to the duties of the previous summer, them lazing about, drinking spirituous beverages, marching about in squares, escorting waggon trains, nursemaiding scientifics, de-existing local wildlife, me getting bit by gadflies. I'd describe the attitude of the officers as laissez faire, and apart from the necessary duties of marching about in squares and holding their rifles out for the lieutenant to look at the troopers was given considerable carte blanche. Well we is back in the land of the Frenchmen after all. Speaking of them officers, that Irish mercenary never did show up. I conjectured the ennui of the mission had done for him and he'd gone off to find paid killing someplace.

One day my jockey shot hisself an elk calf for supper. I was watering at the creek and my eyes was forced to watch the blood-streaked water flow by, the ma elk bleating on, and the telling of the vignette transports my mind to another bloody creek.

TWENTY-SEVEN

Me, ankle deep in the Little Big Horn, on my lonesome, save for the blowflies massing and the vultures circling, the tugging coyotes and fluttering greenbacks.

I say I was on my lonesome, but the dark-faced major and his boys was still fighting for their lives up on that hill where they'd fled, and it was like a goddamn highway, Indians going back and forth to fire off a few shots and returning to camp for refrescos and a smoke. They paid me no heed. They'd seen my wounds and considered me busted. But I shifted myself into the brush, just to be on the safe side.

A trooper was hiding there, weeping. He clutched two tin kettles shot through with holes. So he'd been sent down to get water for them thirsty boys up top, a task they wouldn't be getting no volunteers for, and he'd got his leg shot to buggery for it. A sergeant he was, Irish fellow, and it were by dint of him I expanded my repertoire of blasphemy. Oh Jesus. Oh Holy Mother Mary and all the saints and angels in heaven. I swear I'll never sin again, by Christ. I swear it on my mammy's grave, God rest her soul. I am probably over-egging it, but you get the gist. He felt his leg and winced and wept. Oh Jesus. Oh God. Oh God, I am so sorry, so very sorry. Don't let me die in this savage land.

Immersed in his own suffering like, he never clocked me, and so he never became a member of the ample fraternity what all claimed to be the first what found me.

That afternoon the Indians fled and the next morning Terry's boys showed up.

―――――

TWO TROOPERS SPLASHING ON, their horses eyeball-rolling at the stink of death. Hey, look what we got here. Least this'n is on four pegs. What you figure we should do, Red, or some such goddamn truncated moniker. Red proposed putting a bullet in my brain forthwith. Roundabout sundry nags was clinging to the latter stages of existence and you'd hear the reports as their agony got terminated. One fellow was going about with a blacksmith's hammer.

Red, he put the muzzle to my white star and said, Least your suffrins is over now boy, and pulled the trigger. The click in lieu of the bang communicated it were an empty chamber, and the other fellow, him of kindlier eyes, held Red's arm, and said, Hold off reloading there, Red. Maybe it's a sign. He stroked my muzzle pulled an ear and said, He ain't much to look at, but let's give the fella a chance, and he went to fetch a hatful of unbloodied water. The salient part to it is before he shoved it under my muzzle he extracted a bottle of ardent spirits from his saddlebag, uncorked it and poured a slug in. Such was the inauguration of my life as a rummy.

At first I were indifferent to the taste of it, and I wondered why the humanos was so enamoured by it, but then my highly-refined peepers blurred over and my butcher-block noggin felt like it was about to float off and somebody better be ready to catch it, and I clocked my wounds wasn't hurting so bad. My head now being so light, I even managed to raise it and I nosed about the saddlebag wherein he had restituted the bottle, but it were buckled down tight.

I imagine they medicamented the Irish sergeant up likewise, being he was off yonder getting his leg sawed off. It were the goddamnedest thing. All the time I'd been adjacent he'd never quit blubbering and calling out for his mammy. Now, the saw rasping, he was blithe as old Daniel shoved in the fiery furnace. When they'd done and tossed the leg aside he said, You might as well take the other'n off while you are at it, kind of joke I figure. But he grimaced it out, and I saw the porridge face and the blue veins and cavern eyes glinting tears.

To provide him a means of conveyance, they skinned a recent-deceased nag and cut the hide into strips and lashed poles together to form a species of platform, a confection they called a litter. I do not know why. They tied it on a mule and hoisted the Irish sergeant, Ready boys? On two. The mule swung his head contemporaneously to attend to a flea bite, and his muzzle bashed the sergeant's bloody stump. The sergeant gritted his teeth and, you got to hand it to him, save for a single malediction he issued not a murmur. Ensconced atop, a distracted comrade slapped his bad leg and said, You'll be grand now Mickey. The way that mule joggled off, I calculated that prognostication founded on sandy ground.

They trudged me north down the Greasy Grass, keeping my exsanguinated body topped up with booze. I imagine it were a hard trip, but I recollect little of it, save for keeping my head down and plunking one foot afore tother, at a pace even them hereunto mentioned bier-toting clog-wearing Gila monsters'd be embarrassed by. I remember my nostrils getting irritated and realizing the air were full of smoke, and thinking that'll be the aboriginals combusting the prairie to thwart pursuit. Mickey's mule, he wandered off to a patch of acorns and bent to chaw, and Mickey slid off and got deposited atop a cactus.

This part might have been a dream. Trudging on in the dark

through broken country, stink of burning in my nostrils, din of the groaning wounded, the flames of bonfires guiding us in. A steamboat blowing its whistle. The whistle startling the mule, who shied and dumped Mickey into a ravine and they had go fetch him. Grass strewn on the deck to the height of my knees.

Being I made it as far as the Big Horn River, I guess they figured they might as well chuck me on the steamboat too, and they located me at the rear by the big kettles. The sergeant-toting mule, well he must have been wearied by then being he dropped to his knees and expired. His one-legged cargo slid forward, and I envisaged him destined for further discomfort, but an alert boy clocked the event and grabbed him by the shoulders. But when they carried him aboard they banged his head on a stanchion and he had to get that bandaged.

So me, him and a bunch of other wounded got shipped back to civilization. Apropos my multifarious wounds, on the boat a single-toothed crimped-face man had presented hisself. He canted his bowler hat and pronounced, I am an experienced veterinarian practiced in all the chirurgical arts appertaining to the equine. I will be happy to render assistance to this unfortunate creature for a minimal fee. I saw he was lacking a digit and one ear lobe and figured maybe he done practiced the trade on hisself. Them excisions looked neat enough.

Well they allowed it, and by God was I glad of that busthead. Worse than any pending probings and diggings was the way they roped down all four of my limbs, five if you is counting my head. In moments of sobriety, his not mine, he extracted a ball and two arrowheads, and hacked down to another ball before quitting on it, sudorated up, and declaring, It ain't adjacent to naught vital, him already pocketed the fee and not looking to impress by then. He placed the bloodied ball and arrowheads before my eyes for inspection. Look what I dug out of you boy. You sure is one lucky son of a bitch.

So come time to disembark, and I was so tanked they had to lay me on a waggon to get me to the fort, the very same two moons since I had set out from, auspicated-up by a goddamn owl. Back at civilization, another fellow claiming the skills in the veterinarian arts fetched up. He wore a canvas apron and half-moon spectacles and emitted no stink of tangle-leg, and them items communicated to me confidence in his abilities. He weren't no better, but he dug out maybe a dozen projectiles over the coming half-moon. They didn't cut out the final ball till a couple of summers hence.

You all know I never was much of a hand at getting my wounds treated, and even being a good bit soused I squealed and whimpered a good bit during and after them ministrations. I were unsteady on my pegs to boot, frequently tumbling and barging into solid objects, but I estimate now them effects could easy have been by dint of the liquor. So they hoisted me up in a sling, tied my halter to two horizontal ropes and pulled them tight so I couldn't swing my head about. I estimate they believed the sling a mercy to me, and they left me deposited therein a good stretch, my hooves grazing the floor. I expect they believed it'd be a paregoric and allow my wounds to heal and the pus to drain out and prevent further damage my tibulations and bargings might cause. But Jesus, the indignity, spraddle-dangled like that, them other nags passing the stable door opportuning theirselves to squint in and snort derision, goddamn dock-tailed miniature canine what stopped by daily by to cock his leg in my direction.

I'd say it took a couple of moons for me to get enough strength to locomote without tottering, and my recuperation were adjudicated right speedy. Yours truly, I put it down to the liquor. Every day they brung me a hearty breakfast of corn mash soaked in whiskey, and sooner or later a trooper showed up with a bucket of beer. Weren't long before I was leading life of Riley, whoever he was. Were around then they started me off on the tobaccy.

GETTING RID. Well all through that fall and winter nobody rode me. By spring they figured I'd got enough strength back, and me being a celebrity then, they wrote out a roster and schedule.

I knew something were afoot. Weren't no whisky mash and bucket of beer that morning. Gus showed up early and picked the coffee grinds off of my face and curried me up and raked the dung out of my tail. I had pretty much hit rock bottom by then. He trotted me around in a big circle and made me drink a pail of unsullied water, activities arranged I estimate now to ensure me fully sobered up, that colonel not wanting to risk his offspring chunked off by an drunken equine. Gubernators present, weren't no first-come-first-served, and numero uno on the roster was the Colonel's daughter.

The saddle was cinched on, and I tell you, it was a right queer feeling. First time since the big fight, of which I was the only living survivor. She showed up in a furbelowed frock and a hat what resembled a Comanche shield minus scalps and eagle feathers augmented by a nipple located centre-wise. A group of folks was watching on, smiling, heads cocked, hands clasped, trying to ingratiate theirselves.

She rubbed my ears and said, Oh Comanche, like she goddamn knew me, and I saw lachrymatory activity in the corner of her eye. Jesus. She gasped and said, You are such a hero. I refer you to my prior remarks on such remarks. Gus held my reins and they put a box down on the dirt and she could climb up easy, and it were the goddamnedest thing. When they brung it over I'd noticed a peculiarity about that saddle. In lieu of a single pommel it featured a pair of horns, and off to the side was what I can only describe as the male member in a state of mild enthusiasm. Anyhow, she didn't cock her leg right over but somehow arranged her bustled posterior so both pegs dangled over the same flank.

I sure hoped we wasn't going on no buffalo hunt. Lay aside I was feeling light-headed by dint on my libatory deprivations, that saddle seemed no-wise secure to my mind and I pictured her sliding off and tossed about among the hooves and horns. A female in a lace apron and lace hat then trotted over and arranged my jockey's frock so it formed a kind of curtain down my sinister side. She handed her a parasol, even opened it for her, so chasing ungulates was off the agenda, unless she planned employ it to club a calf to death.

Now the Comanche might have sat side-wise and gone chiselling off whooping to display manliness, but I conjectured that weren't the motive behind her seating arrangement. I never did fathom it, and the best I can propose is on a prior outing she'd suffered chafing to the privy part, and wanted to stymie further abrasion and consequent septics. Nip it in the bud, you might say.

Gus grabbed my ear and said into it, Now you go easy today Comanch' and gave my neck a hefty slap, and a tweeded fellow come over and told Gus to shift out and took our picture, me and the furbelowed female, and I imagine if you ever find that image you will see the blur where my noggin should be. Them was heady days and I never could behave myself. A companion joined us, similar attired and mounted on a snooty bay mare, and together with a surly trooper we trotted off and I figured some entrepreneur had come along to clear away all the buffalo bones being they had a nice picnic on the unsullied prairie among the flowers and the twittering birds while I stood with my tail up my arse wondering what Looks At The Sky would have made of it all. Unseen by that pair chattering about frocks, in the sky a hawk struck a dove and transformed it into an explosion of feathers, which don't never get boring.

Ain't nothing further to report of that trip. The Indians had all been exterminated out the country by then, so weren't much likelihood of attack and them females carried off to get their coiffures mussed up. I can, however, adjunct an epilogue.

Couple of days subsequent, another officer's daughter showed up. She were tiny affair but she didn't need no box to stand on to mount up, and she strapped on her own saddle and it weren't fitted out up with no surplus protuberances. She weren't wearing no window drapery neither, but wore a shirt and a pair of cavalry pantaloons turned up at the ankle and tight around the hindquarters, and in lieu of the Comanche shield she wore a narrow-brimmed slouch mashed down. Under it she'd tucked an explosion of curls, but they still poked forth.

She slapped my neck once, scratched my muzzle and said, Alright Comanche, Let's get those cobwebs blown away and sans warning she kicked me into a gallop. We chiselled off down the trail along the river, then she knee-nudged me off up the bluffs. She leaned forward and shouted, Why Comanche, somebody taught you well. You got that goddamn right.

Jesus, those bluffs. In no time my joints and bones felt like neglected steam mechanicals. My bellows was pumping and the suds was flying off me. Now unbid my legs stopped galloping and in lieu my heart took up the gait. What in goddamn hell.

You know it. My life of sloth and turpitude done caught up with me. I'd lost my wind, and that was the only thing I ever got going for me. I resolved forthwith to renounce the dissolute life and return to abstinence. Grass and water and apples. That'd be me henceforth. You never knowed, they might run short on nags and take me out on them frigid prairies chasing aboriginals again, which is exactly what they did.

My jockey, she noted my fagged state and slowed me down, and I am ashamed to say we attained the summit of them bluffs at a walk, albeit a fast example. She slapped my neck. Been a while, hasn't it Comanche. My fault. I should have realized.

She dismounted and walked me a spell, and I dallied and chawed on a patch of sweet herbage and she allowed it and took her hat off and leaned her head back and let the wind blow through her curls so as to put me in mind of a waterfall when a trick of the wind drives the droplets heavenward. She went off into the tall grass and squatted, her location evident only by the cloud of steam issuing forth, and I speculated she was draining her bladder. On her way back she took out a cigar and struck a match on her rump and lit it and snorted twin blasts of smoke out her delicate nostrils. She said, You won't tell anyone, will you Comanche.

That ain't the interesting part to the anecdote. We cantered down the hill, and I maintained that gait until we reached the environs of the fort and felt right cocky about it. My jockey, she come rigid in the saddle and said, Uh-oh. Christ, here we go.

I spied ahead the furbelowed female appropinquating, crook-elbowed, which ain't never a good sign. She'd eschewed the nipple-shield and plumped for the bonnet.

The opening salvo was, How dare you ride..., and it declined from there. My jockey dismounted and they remonstrated a stretch and then the furbelow reached out and pulled out a curl. I mean right out. It had all been all finger-wagging up to that point. My jockey, she stared at the detached curl a spell, then tore the bonnet off. She threw it to the ground and jumped on it and proceeded to lead me off. I estimate she figured that were the full-stop and close brackets to the argument. The furbelow grabbed my reins, and for a stretch there ensued a tug of war, my noggin yanked back and forth until I commenced to feel lightheaded. They dropped the reins and began rolling about in the mire, and that was when Gus come over and pulled them apart, though it were like picking apart two cockleburs.

The upshot of this were the Colonel issued a judgment old Solomon would have been proud of. You can read it in the history books. The parts I remember go as follows. Henceforth, the nag known as Comanche will not get rid by no persons whomsoever, nor be obliged to perform whatsoever any kind of labour. He shall be treated in kindly fashion by all. Something along them lines. The kindly parts and the labouring parts was fine by me, but I sure enjoyed that curly-topped female's equitation and I was good bit irked our incipient affiliation come truncated.

As alluded to earlier, that ordinance proved about as trustworthy as the part in an Indian treaty that says, Yours in perpetuity.

I already told you I was present on the Wounded Knee Creek that frigid day to witness the end of it all and Gus laying there.

Around the time of the summer solstice Gus scrubbed me clean and slung a big black braided blanket over me what about touched the ground, cinched on a polished saddle and attached to it a pair of cavalry boots, likewise polished. He arranged the boots reverse-wise. I remain ignorant to this day as to why. Maybe the Irish mercenary owned Comanche ambitions. Outside, a big parade was formed up sombrely attired, and I was led to the head of it. Gus yanked on my reins and said, Now you got to behave today Comanch', understand? and looked into an eye a spell. I nodded my head but it were pure coincidence. My days of bibulous revelry, though, was over by then, and they figured they could trust me, and me being led along, nod my head randomly was about the best I could do on the high-jinks front. The band kicked up a solemn tune. The beat thereof put me in mind of them Ree death songs, and me and Gus marched about in a square. The band played more solemn tunes. The wind whipping his plumes, an officer clumb up on a box and gave a solemn speech, tolerable brief, and the band played us out with goddamn Garry Owen.

I led that parade every year until Gus went and my old pegs give out, them appendages by then having led a hard if lively life.

TWENTY-EIGHT

Well this tale is taking about as many switchbacks as that river we raced the steamboat along.

Back with my feet in the bitter grass of them Sweet Grass Hills, events was about to ginger up. The boy was tooting Boots and Saddles. Rider had come larruping in proclaiming hostiles en masse to the north-west, and they all shook off their hangovers and checked their carbines and we went chiselling off, picturing eviscerated scientifics. Us nags got a right sweat on, but when we fetched up the scientifics was sat outside tipis enjoying refrescos.

Bunch of tamed Indians they was, Blackfeet, and by God they was a poor bunch, gaunt faces all perforated by the pox, trail-worn tipis, knuckle-backed coulee-cheeked offspring, barely enough horses to go around to the extent a brace was afoot, which is about as poor as an Indian can get. Said later they was off north to join more tamed Indians and go after the buffalo, if there was any left.

Soon as they clocked the Seventh rattling down on them, two chiefs leapt up, the soup flying, and rummaged in parfleches. When we reined up they was holding up squares of paper, writing thereon. The wind blew one away and he had to run and fetch it.

They was letters of recommendation from white chiefs. One chief even had a medal from the Great Father like that windy Cheyenne chief got, but he never talked up no floating ballcock, and truth be told at that point in my earthly I'd abandoned hope of ever witnessing that item in devastating action. But I figure the sight of them scientifics sampling Indian chuck had already decided the major against bloody chastisement and he looked like an infant what had his rattle took away. He'd even got the sword out ready.

Now them Blackfeet knew from prior experience that whites' credentials and medals ain't no guarantee against massacre, but they'd fished them out for inspection anyhow. One fellow waved a New Testament at the major, although what good he thought that could do I remain ignorant, and his possession of it, like its contents, was subject to interpretation. It had a hole in it and for all we knowed he'd scalped a preacher. The major, he revaginated his sword and gave them articles a perfunctory glance and was about to wave the incumbents away when one paper in particular caught his eye, such that he was moved to read it aloud.

To whomsoever it may concern. Be it know that this Indian is a dumb and filthy specimen and on no account to be trusted. He is to be shot forthwith and his verminous body quartered and burned. If you pay no heed to these words, your goods and chattels will be stolen and you will be relieved of your scalps. You have been warned.

They all had a good chuckle at that. The major handed the paper back and told the Blackfeet they better behave themselves or there'd be trouble. The chief rejoindered with we have been behaving ourselves and what mayhem do you expect our poor bunch to cause anyhow and would you like to share our prandials, the latter invite the major declined with a wrinkled nose. The chief asked him being he was in the hereabouts drawing a line to keep out the Frenchmen, couldn't he keep the whiskey traders out too what was ruining his tribe. My jockey, he were dared into trying that whiskey one time and he went blind for half a day.

As an parenthetical excursus, the less ignorant among you might know in them frigid parts is a trail called the Whoop-Up Trail, its terminus being a fort of that nomenclature. Now maybe it is eponymized thus after some general the Frenchmen got called General Whoop Up, but I'd doubt it, such a name being a good bit outre, even for Frenchmen, and I remain of the outlook Whoop Up was named by dint it were the turpitudinous location whereto them rotgut peddlers and buffalo hunters retired to celebrate their profits in debauch.

The major said weren't nothing he could do about the whiskey traders. He was there to protect the scientifics, who them Blackfeet was presently poisoning. He weren't there to stymie the progress of commerce and enterprise. He turned to the scientifics and said, Gentlemen? and extended his arm in the direction of our camp. They said they'd finish their refrescos and be along directly.

WHAT ELSE CAN I tell you of our second summer in the frigid north.

The optimists got the mower out afresh and sent the navvies to stack the hay at intervals of a day's ride and it all got stole. A buffalo herd of moderate proportion bumbled by and they went out and shot at it and it stampeded through their best water. A trio of troopers tired of the languor and went over the hill, literally and figuratively. Ken Flash chawed on hardtack and broke a tooth, examined the hardtack box and bawled out, This bugger got 1861 writ on it.

Me and him got sent off to the Rocky Mountains to defend the scientifics' final efforts. He spent a good few days flâneuring and fishing and napping by a clear lake in a peak-fringed valley, staining his chops with whortleberries and chewing through stems of grass, while I got suppered on by the gallinippers and terrorized about to death by a grizzly en route to a burgeoning chokecherry bush. That tree never stood a chance. The bear ambled over and broke off a limb and dragged it through its teeth, one end to tother. The leaves was left attached or spat out as mush, and any berries what wasn't caught atwixt the choppers was gobbled up where they lay. It was the goddamnedest sight, and I observed it from considerable distance.

It sure must be hard drawing a straight line through a mountain range with all them knuckles and knobs, inclivities and declivities, and that was where the scientifics chucked in the sponge, and Voila, the Seventh's mission ceased. I conjecture they figured the mountains would serve to keep out the Frenchmen, them latters all being constantly surfeited up on soft cheeses and fine wines. But I ain't to be trusted on that aspect of it.

We went back at the buttes. By God shuteye were hard to come by. The wolves decided to hold a convention, so that was the night out the frame for sleeping purposes. The days, well the first snows dusted the buttes and they was filled with clacks and chocks as the Bighorns fought for copulation rights. Imagine the sound of two rocks chunked together. Two anvils maybe. You wouldn't think sheep could make so much din.

Vis-à-vis our sojourn in the frigid land of the Frenchmen, that is the final curiosity to report. Shortly I'd be located in a more southerly portion of them rumpled plains, in the Powder River country, what the Cheyenne say is right pretty, although goddamn Custer was there to spoil the view. I were en route to my date with destiny at the fight known as the Little Big Horn, a fight of which I was the one and only living survivor.

Now, here I been reminiscing about my dotage after the big fight and realize I might have led you astray and not rendered credit where due. Now if I'd munched through an apple for every trooper what claimed to be him that found me that fly-blown morning on the Greasy Grass, I have been demised by the colic by now.

Weren't no white anyhow. Were an Indian.

Directly after the big fight the women arrived to cut up the bodies like they do to stymie progress in the spirit realm. One wore a fancy buckskin shirt with antelope-skin panels, though its best days was long departed and maybe she figured it suited to the bloody if celebratory task. A fair amount of glee were involved in her knife work, to which I'd say she was entitled. At the application of the knife one trooper leapt up, him feigning death, and for a few seconds they exchanged blows, until she terminated it with a bone hammer she carried for that express purpose.

By God. Somehow she'd got out of jail, spurned the horticultural life, and trudged off north and joined the Cheyenne up there. The wearer of the fancy shirt were Fox Who Runs Straight.

She caught sight of me, stood and stared. I knew she couldn't place me, and her reduced to one eye now by some mishap rendered identification a risky process. Still, if observed from the favourable side a white male would still consider her a handsome prize, and I figure it lucky for her that day she were on the victorious side.

Her head cocked and her jaw dropped open, recollecting me of her stepson. The eye brightened and she come over. She stood off a spell her eye ranging over the cavalry saddle and tack. She reached out and pulled and plucked at them items, as if the act would explain my presence. She walked about me and inspected me like Walks Slowly and Humps a Lot done all them summers since, though she never felt my legs save for my bloody white sock. She stood back and said, You are Yellow Crow with One Foot in the Snow, the horse of Looks At The Sky Too Much who died of the sickness on the Purgatoire with whom my son Hears The Moon was in love. You later became Hears The Moon's horse and jumped over the buffalo hides below the Antelope Hills. But you were murdered against the wall by the Lodgepole River. Now you are here. I do not understand.

I tell you, no matter what the circumstance, Indians ain't the type to stint on personal history or truncate nomenclatures. I'll adjunct that eavesdropping at that moment were a trooper's ear she was holding onto and done forgot about.

She walked about me again and examined my wounds, me wincing at every touch. She tossed away the ear and hurried off, returned with a trooper's hat brimming with water, no wordplay intended, and a bunch of fresh grass she must have walked a fair distance to gather. She held out the hat while I drank, and was right patient as I drained it, and I tell you it were the sweetest most quenchsome water I ever tasted in my earthly, though I couldn't swear it were untainted by the juice of life. She tossed the hat aside and packed my worst wounds with the grass. You won't read in no officer's report they found that ministration.

She said, Come, and tried to lead me off, and I expect thenceforth I would have resumed the aboriginal life. I got myself into forwards locomotion, stumbled and staggered a piece, but truth was my strength had drained out like beer from a barrel used for target practice. But Fox Who Runs Straight, she was a stubborn type. She called to a couple of cronies, who looked up from their work and jutted their chins, arms all bloody. They rolled their eyes and picked a way over through the cadavers. I saw their arms was bloody not by dint of their current occupation but because they'd slashed them in grief. So they was already in a bad mood.

Them three women shoved, barged, hauled, and imprecated me down to the creek, them other two protesting continual in Cheyenne, and I estimate had they their way I'd have finished in the cookpot roiling along with some goddamn yapper. But Fox

Who Runs Straight, she were right persuasive, and I was spared such final indignity.

They got me down to the creek, and them actions saved my life for the third time that day I'll never forget. Fox Who Runs Straight grabbed my ear and whispered, May it go well with you Brother, and went back to her labours. To get called Brother by a Comanche is about the highest accolade a nag can get.

Life gets so peculiar it becomes impossible to bottom. I do believe all them incapacitating wounds saved my life for a fourth time that day and allowed me to go on to my life of boozy celebrity. Laying aside the cookpot, let's say I had resumed the aboriginal life. A winter or three hence I'd have found myself on some frigid prairie, demised by vengeful troopers, my body dusted with snow, Indians scattered about in attitudes of frozen repose, wolves circulating.

Anyhow that's the how I become the one and only living survivor of the fight known as the Little Big Horn.

But it ain't the why.

PART THREE

THE FIGHT KNOWN AS THE LITTLE BIG HORN, OF WHICH FIGHT I WAS THE ONLY LIVING SURVIVOR

TWENTY-NINE

At least my goddamn bane weren't sullen. Well, not right off. You imagine, he hadn't sniffed my derriere or chawed my tail for three summers and no sooner he saw me he perpendicularized his ears and bounded toward me, legs kicking out such to put a spring colt to shame. I'd prior spied him standing blithe with a leg cocked while a cowbird picked the ticks out his auricles, and I'd inveigled myself behind a dun mare hoping for concealment, but she chose to clomp off at the inconvenient moment.

I readied myself. He'd announce his advent as per usual, slam into my flank so I'd be fully apprised of it. But the ground, miry as it was, he made his turn and his posterior legs slid out from under and skittled my own examples.

He were first up, chawing on my mane and lugs. I raised myself, him butting and barging, what rendered the raising endeavour unduly prolonged. I got a bite in, by God. His reckless conduct could have broke my legs. But that that bite registered about as much a .22 slug on a bull buffalo, and he rotated hisself and proceeded to scratch his muzzle on my haunch, leaning his weight into me like he always did, and once he'd relieved hisself of that itch he set to work on my tail. I never did understand what he found so goddamn tasty in that appendage.

I ought enucleate these prefatory remarks. We was up on the Heart River prior to the US Seventh Cavalry's summer campaign against the wilful Sioux. A right sullen camp it were too, and the history books they go big on it, how the troopers was wandering about with the mulligrubs them all presaging their deaths. How they was visiting the chaplain and was making wills and writing letters to beloveds and betrotheds and vouchsafing keepsakes to friends and strikers for them to extract years hence and polish on a sleeve and gaze out wistful to remember an old friend curtailed.

Now I cannot comment on them privy matters, but far as I could see the number of voluntary visits to the chaplain was about the same as they always was, zero. Contrary-wise, visits to the camp demimondaines remained steady. So nobody was believing this might be the last chance I get to profligate myself in debauch. So I dispute the history books. I'll allow the camp were sullen, but no more than any bemired army camp at the fag end of winter, and I'll adjunct the troopers perked up at the prospect of going out to chastise aboriginals. It got them out of digging latrines and marching about in muddy squares and holding rifles out for the lieutenant to look at, escorting thin-armed scientifics about.

All them histories, they was written long after them boys was left eviscerated and flyblown on that ridge, and their comrades looked back and interpreted minor events as portents of doom. Oh yeah, now I think on it, it was unusual foggy for the time of year. My dog took to howling at the western sky. Never done that before. I saw a forage cap trod in the mud. I bust my sword opening packing crate. They never ascribed naught auspicatory to them events at the time, and them scribes as wrote it all up, history being generally like chawing on sawdust, proceed to invent and exaggerate further to ginger things up. You won't catch me doing that.

Apropos those history books detailing our expedition into the heartland of the Sioux, I'll add a word of caution. I expect they is full of sensation and hearsay, based as they are on the half-a-life-time-since memories of cheesecloth-brained old soldiers, superannuated Indians what, let's own it, have their own take on reality, and anyhow don't want to admit to no felonious action and wind up culprits liable to retribution.

Getting back to the omens, yours truly, me being part Comanche and amenable to omens, I did experience a disquietude about this trip, and so I began to look about for confirmatory portent.

The day of our departure for a start. It was right gloomy. Fog blanketed the camp. A thin mizzle soaked my ragged coat, my winter hairs by then dropping off in clumps, and had a stump been adjacent I'd have been engaged in some serious abrasion. We paraded around the camp, flags and banners raised but hanging slack, the troopers sodden, goddamn mud balling about my hooves, parading to show everybody we was off to put an end to the Sioux and their primitive lifestyles. The band, it was present and struck up goddamn Garry Owen. The last time I heard that tune was down on the Washita before the curtailment of my career as a Cheyenne Indian. There goes another portent.

The officers was all waving and tipping their hats farewell, tall in the saddle, goddamn Custer on his special-occasion horse, Vic, a sorrel with a blaze, three white socks and snooty with it. I even felt my jockey hoist hisself erect. Off to battle, they felt good about theirselves did them orphans and misfits, failed farmers and thwarted migrants, that Springfield dangling, a Coltses strapped to their hip, a hundred rounds of ammunition to shove in. They was a member of a proud outfit with a fighting reputation. Undefeated to boot was the Seventh, albeit they'd only ever fought primitives. Them boys was off to fight for progress and enterprise and God-ordained destiny, expurgate them naked heathens off the plains to make way for the lawyers and tax clerks and insurance salesmen. Yep, they sure felt like somebody. I ought addend the Seventh was short of nags on that trip and three-score of them proud boys had to walk all the way to the Powder.

The womenfolk all out to watch, wringing hands and biting lips and dabbing eye corners. The officers dismounted to kiss goodbyes, and them ocular floodgates bust open when the band kicked up The Girl I Left Behind Me. The troopers remounted and the women propped each other up and picked them up what'd took a faint at the weight of it. Meanwhile shavers was marching up and down banging tin drums and shouldering wooden rifles and saluting. A scamp or two pointed their rifles at the Indian scouts and went, pyow-pyow.

If them wives was open to portents, well they was about to get one writ large. After they'd dug a couple of waggons out the mire and got the beef herd in reluctant motion, the column snaked out the fort toward the wilderness. Soon them in front, headed by goddamn Custer and Vic, was well ahead, and by dint of the fog we lost sight of them. Then they ascended the bluffs and clumb out of the fog, and at the same instant the sun came out and lit them up, and there they was, floating above the clouds, refulgent in golden light.

As omens go it weren't a subtle example, and if you wanted to modify it for them of calloused sensitivities you'd only need to get them twanging on harps. Well the white women started wailing, and what with the scouts' wives already well progressed in ululating, the band banging away, me and my lugs was goddamn glad to get away.

They say the odorous Mrs Bacon Custer later wrote in one of her spouse-doxologizing doorstops that the troopers was reflected in the sky, so as to give the impression of twin columns heading out. But that idle woman was always given to flights of fancy.

Me, I saw an owl sat in a tree. Big fella it was, colour of prairie grass in the fall. Curious to see one out in the diurnal like that. It had ears like a mule and the moustache of Little Phil and eyes of finest gold. My bunch of Comanche believed owls was portents of doom and'd do their damnedest to conjure powerful medicine to thwart it.

Looks At The Sky, she shot an owl once and claimed she suffered a run of bad luck for it. Maybe that was why she died of the cholera. Who knows. Her being of curious mind she apologized to the owl and dismantled it to see how it were constructed. You might not know this but an owl has the goddamnedest eyes. In the form of cigar stubs they are, and she bottomed it that was why an owl must move its entire head when obliged to study an item and appears to be in a permanent state of startle. It can't swivel its eyes like you and me can, which makes you wonder how they communicate exasperation. Later she sewed the owl's wings to the shoulders of her shirt and said, Brother, these will allow me to move silently so I can approach game and evade our enemies. Well good luck with that.

This ain't getting us up to the Greasy Grass.

That owl watched us depart. It rotated its head twice to get a better fix. It retched twice and ejected a stool. I'm glad I never acquired it, but to egest out of your mouth like that, that's quite a trick, one to sure render that hatch in your union suit redundant. You paw the mouth-turd apart you find fur and white bones and skulls and tiny white teeth. The owl shoved its head under its wing and was gathered into the arms of Morpheus. That's all I got on the fatidical owl.

Custer, well he weren't suffering no presentiments of doom. As the Cornishman were born to wield a pick, so Custer were born to molest aboriginals. At the head of the column, his big hat canted and a turkey feather planted therein, the red scarf around his neck to show everybody where his head was lest they be blinded by the light reflected off it, he was happier than a boy on Christmas morning with a toy train. I venture he was anticipating aboriginal captives and picking out a squaw or three, him soon out of range of the odorous Mrs Bacon.

To make extra sure he got hisself noticed, he wore his tasselled buckskin suit. Naught unusual about that you are thinking, but this were a white example augmented with beaver-skin trimmings and must have cost him a good bit to get tailored up. That whiteness did not suffer well the privations of the campaign, but that spring morning as he ascended above the clouds and the sun caught it, you'd think him old Enoch, the Lord receiving him to heaven in glory.

Curious aspect to the buckskins, the grizzled scouts and windcreased plainsmen who Custer so wanted to be, by then they was eschewing the hides and going for the flannel shirts and twill pantaloons. Consult the photographs of Indians taken contemporaneous and you'll see they too was plumping for such apparel, save for them studio examples where they was bedizened and propped up to convey the Noble Injun. By God, the world of fashion is capricious.

Could be Custer'd made the sartorial effort to compensate for the tonsorial depredation. The golden tresses, well they was now a distant memory. When newly arrived at the fort I saw he'd allowed the rear hairs to grow long, and if obliged to go hatless for extended period in the presence of ladies he'd comb them strands forward to construct over the bald part so as to suggest the prow of a ship. But before we departed he'd shaved it all off, which is the other option I guess, and he kept his hat on for most of the trip, until some Indian knocked it off. In my entire earthly I never met a bald Indian, and weighing it now, could be why Custer was always so resentful toward the aboriginal.

So we got up onto that rumpled country, and by God did that bastard love the plains. He could race his fancy horse until it was blown. Jesus, he could even shoot it in the neck and have it fall from under him and his striker'd bring up another. Three times. Didn't matter any how many sudorated equines he left splay-legged and slumpen on the prairies, nostrils drizzling lung blood. Yep, the plains was his playground, stuffed with game both quadrupedal and bipedal he could send to perdition, take heads and horns and scalps to nail on his wall back east.

Custer, he even took the time to learn taxidermy. I bet you didn't know that. I passed by his tent and there he was extracting eyeballs from a badger. Naturally, he got an audience to watch him do it, and least it weren't no indigene he were doing it to, but I wouldn't bet against it. Back then there was such characters as made boots and bags out of aboriginal skin, purses from female privy parts, and it'd just be a matter of increased labour to stuff a whole example.

He'd brought his kin along for the jaunt, invented jobs for them to do. Besides Tom Custer, him now a fixture in the Seventh, was brother Boston, a thin-armed fellow with bacon-rasher whiskers, the mien of a consumptive poet and the cough to go with it, him likewise well-advanced on the balding front, which may have accounted for his melancholy demeanour, and nephew Autie, a square-headed wire-lipped sprout, still furnished with hair and opting to divide it down the scalp in a straight line like Uncle Tom.

Soon as we was out on them rumpled prairies they all went off on japes and I do believe they viewed the campaign as a sporting trip. Aboriginal game yet to present itself, they shot the heads off prairie hens, reduced hawks to explosions of feathers, blasted vultures off of survey posts, converted badgers and coyotes to limpers. Their chine was abundant, but the buffalo was gone, so tongues and humps was off the menu, but soon as any four-legged beast presented itself they larruped off after it, goddamn yolfing deerhounds in tow. On such occasions Custer rode Dandy, not so fancy as Vic being a dung colour, but nimbler-footed and gump-tioned, so there'd be less chance of him falling off.

Custer shot hisself a bear he claimed a grizzly. We trotted by just as he was getting his picture took, it laying there with its mouth propped open, him on one knee, hat tipped back, look-what-I-did on his face.

Now I retain considerable expertise on the appearance and stink of a grizzly bear and I can testify it weren't no grizzly. Were just your standard bear, though I admit it were a large example and tawny of colour to boot, and I don't figure Custer was in much jeopardy stalking that bear, being its teeth was worn down to stumps, least them still present, likewise the claws, and one eye were absent.

I wasted a good few words there about goddamn Custer. Be advised, henceforth I ain't going to be giving Custer no more publicity than that horse-abusing popinjay already got.

FOR THE UNEDUCATED AMONG YOU, I guess now we got going on this trip I ought elucidate the reasons behind this expedition into the land of the Sioux, that blessed Powder River country bosomed atwixt the Bighorns and the Black Hills, wherefrom them Sioux evicted the prior aboriginals.

Curious aspect was, weren't no talk like them summers since en route to admonish the Cheyenne. Back then it was all about the fiendishments them boys had perpetrated on the shoving rustics, how they had run off their cows and trod down the corn and scared the poultry out of laying and outraged the womenfolk. Up on the Powder they talked up no particular crimes for which the Sioux was due chastisement, never read out no newspaper articles whipping up vengeful sentiment. The only thing they conjured was the Sioux's refusal to give up the Black Hills, and their reticence to get herded onto the reservation to eat reesty beef and mouldy flour and get their kids peddled rotgut. Though way I saw it, via the implacable machinations of enterprise them Black Hills was already gone, whether they touched the white man's pen to paper or not. Like the bum fodder said, you could pull up a plug of grass and shake gold out the roots.

Best the campfire philosophers could come up with was of a more theoretical nature. You can't have a bunch of filthy heathens living wild and free stymying God-ordained progress, were the gist of it, and generally in such discussions one fellow is bolder than the rest, maybe he's read a newspaper or three, got a slick tongue to boot, and he'll puff out his chest and open his maw. Our Boanerges were a rug-headed Baltimorean, and he stuck his thumbs behind his suspenders and opined something in the region of the following. I'll append that owing to a gap atwixt his front teeth you should hear his sibilances expressed with a whistle:

To the white man time is money. He labours all day to create the comforts of life and turn a little profit. He cannot sit up all night to watch his property in the event some lazy thieving Indian comes along and steals the fruits of his enterprise.

He got a lot of haw-hawing at that opening salvo what served encourage him further. He combusted up his pipe and puffed on it to lend gravity.

The Redskin has had his day, friends. Why, hasn't Bad Hand MacKenzie whipped the Comanche, and they are the vilest most verminous of primitives. (Haw-haw) These that are left are a pack of whining curs that lick the boots of those who smite them. (Haw-haw) God has ordained the white man to be master of this continent, and the safety of our frontier settlements can only be secured by total annihilation of the Indian and their filthy whelps. (Haw-haw) Better they should die than live like the miserable wretches they are. (He jabbed his pipe stem at the audience at this juncture.) Why, wasn't it Jefferson who said, They are beasts of prey and must be pursued to extermination. Yes comrades, history will show the Indian to be a mere footnote to the irresistible advance of the Caucasian. The time has arrived for the glorious hives of industry to usurp the filthy wigwams of indolence and throw heathen barbarism into oblivion.

Well, it were some stemwinder and they all haw-hawed, but I'm not sure how much purport his audience extracted out that filthy-wigwams postscript. Nevertheless, the Baltimorean were right proud of it, and he leaned back and gazed off, as if the words was arrows and he was admiring their flight.

Humanos too dumb or too lazy or too fearful to articulate their own runty opinions just adore a fellow who'll do it for them, and I do believe were we located anywhere else but the blasted prairie a round of applause would have bust forth, and I remain of the outlook that Baltimorean would have went on to become a noted gubernator or used horse salesman, had he not got his belly opened in the fight known as the Little Big Horn.

A beanpole fellow, bandy legged and featured of a neck to tempt a wringer, witnessed the approbation the speech garnered and craved his share. He stood and removed his hat for gesticulating purposes and spat out a gobbet of tabaccy to make room for the vocables. Yeah, tarm fer Manifest Destiny to overspread the cont'nent allotted to the wart man bar Providence. Let's go god-damn whip them god-damn red niggers to god-damn perdition whar they god-damn belong.

Two items here. I can't offer no remark on the veracity of the Jefferson citation, whoever he was. Second, the Baltimorean fired off the filthy word twice. All I can say is the Comanche I sojourned with was the most pernickety bunch you could ever wish to meet, bar for when they was covered in gore. And if you is one partial to the ironies of life, I'll supply that at the instant of the second filthy, a louse exited his ginger neck whiskers and traversed an ear to the sanctuary of the side whiskers.

Oh, and a third item. The Comanche getting whipped. That was news to me.

THIRTY

We climbed into high country, riven by dry creeks and featured of meagre herbage and crumbling geology. Badlands they called it. The dirt creeks debouched into a north-bound river, cottonwood and willow fringing. Fronting the river was bluffs banded grey and yellow and white, and they recollected me of them Llano canyons, though the dirt there is redder and the canyons is deeper, looking like the earth been turned inside out, and the rivers there generally ain't lubricated by no agua.

This was my kind of country. You looked hard enough, agua abided. Creeping things was going about their dailies, and a dearth of trees denied hiding places for bears and panthers and gadflies. Tolerable grass only added to the appeal, and I figured they was Badlands only from a white's eyrie, dubbed thus because they impede the march of progress and hold no prospect of personal enrichment. Seeing them bluffs, I deprecated myself for my craven- ness in never going back. But my kin, they'd all be bleached bones by then, and their progeny wouldn't know me and wouldn't allow me in, me now steeped in the stink of humanos.

On the portents front, I glanced off and saw a snake engaged in the act of consuming a gopher. The gopher's tail and rear legs were sticking out the gape and was somewhat agitated, being I guess at other end he'd be observing the digestive juices. Now you'll be saying, Where's the portent in that? Well as you know, gophers is generally dirt coloured, but this example were a curiosity to divert the gaze of a scientific, struck as it was by a case of albinism.

While we was loafing about waiting for the scouts to report, Custer berated a black man with a bible name, Asa, Isaiah, Ashurbanipal or some such. He weren't wearing no uniform, so I figured him a scout loitering for reasons unknown, but transpired he served as interpreter.

You might find it strange, a black man cahooted up with the US Seventh Cavalry up on them folded plains, helping them locate aboriginals to exterminate. But after he got freed from the tobacco farm he'd wandered north, married a Sioux, got aboriginaled up and for some years had lived the wild life. Yet now here he was tracking his in-laws. That's in-laws for you.

I remain ignorant of the motives for the berating, but the day previous Custer had got us lost, and we tramped about in circles a good bit so maybe that appertained. Custer'd be blaming him for bungling his orders to the scouts. Like I said in the hereunto, you got to watch out for the gubernators. They will betrump you any chance they get.

Anyhow he got him on his knees and struck him with his quirt, You useless nigger, he said, said he wished it were the old days so he could send him back to the plantation for them to kindle a bonfire about his ankles. In lieu Custer told him to take his boots off and condemned him to Shanks's for the rest of the day, and I saw his feet later and they was like mashed beets. You might notice I ain't reported no goddamns or bastards in that episode. Custer, he weren't one for malediction. He believed it impolite, speech fit only for brutes.

Day or so later Custer and his dogs went off after antelope and they had to send a detail to go find him. You won't find that wrote in no history book.

We scouted upriver for Indians, found none, got ourselves lost again and stuck in a snowstorm. Being Custer had promised the scouts they could take all the scalps and horses they wanted once we found the Sioux, I'd doubt them Ree and Crow was doing it deliberate. Yours truly, I was sure hoping the meteorology didn't decline further. Custer left a bunch of good cavalry nags froze to death on that Washita campaign, and gave about as much thought to it as to the bugs us nags was mashing under our hooves. But we was scant of horses on this trip, and come the night when the snowmelt froze on our coats, a norther biting in, Custer ordered us to be whipped, the idea being keeping us nag's in continual motion would maintain our blood in a liquid state. Which it did.

Us bogged down a couple of days, I could shuck out a picket pin easy by then, even worry away a knot. So, I went off and pawed through the snow and found some decent herbage, chawed on windblown cottonwood twigs, whereof them other nags was ignorant as a repast. They watched me in a state of embranglement and never partook theirselves, and I estimate they never twigged the nutritional advantage, wordplay intended. But that owl had done give me the willies, not to mention that gopher, and I do believe it was such provident actions what contributed to my survival of the forthcoming privations and permitted me to serve out my earthly in luxury.

We struck west towards the Powder, jagged country, deep ravines and high ridges and god-chopped rocks, stumbled past burning stones, black smoke billowing off on the wind, don't ask me how, and the blacksmith said we should halt and collect a mess of it for his forge. When we get back we'll file a claim on the land, open a mine, make a killing, a couple of officers said, colloguing up, their backs turned to their fellows. It clubbed me that last time I'd seen rocks on fire was when that degenerate about abused me to death. Another bad omen. Hope you are keeping tally.

I ain't going to detail the tortuous progress of the bumbling waggon train through that country. Go back to the slumpen general's campaign against the Cheyenne them summers since if you want the full maledictory picture. One time, I spied a brace of indigenes observing us from an adjacent ridge, but even my highly refined orbs failed to discern if they was laughing at us or not, although their shoulders was jerking.

Meteorology, well it is a fickle mistress and we toiled on under a pristine sky scratched with clouds what put me in mind of lambswool caught on barbwire, and I can afford you no further resemblances to break the tedium. The troopers' faces and lips blistered up. Them with heavy whiskers mocked them without and I finally saw the practical side of them fibres, and with his ridiculous moustache Custer never need worry about maintaining his lips in a pliant state ready to go slaver over them captive squaws.

We got lost again.

WHILE WE IS BLUNDERING ABOUT HERE I guess I ought apprise you up on the jockey whose vertebrae I was currently joggling. When we arrived at the fort on the Heart, Ken Flash, he got give a nice new sorrel. The workings of army gubernators are akin to water moving under ice, so I remain unable to supply a reason for his usurpal. Goddamn Custer were about to arrive and one of his peccadillos was to have all the nags in a troop coloured the same, so maybe that appertained, but I can't figure how. Anyhow, they gave me an Irishman.

It was Irishmen galore in the Seventh back in them days, and now you are thinking, at last, the return of the handsome soldier of fortune. But you'd be wrong. This effort were a lanky, crook-shouldered fellow, who in all my acquaintance of him never did raise the back of his head to the perpendicular, and maybe a life spent among low beams accounted for it. To burnish the effect he looked out at the world from under heavy brows, black they was, but by some freak of nature the scalp hair were grey as old snow, though him still young. I figured maybe life's vicissitudes was what accounted for the disparity, him being a destitute alien, newly resident in foreign country and engaged in exterminating its natives.

'I dug peat for a living,' he said one day, and you go figure it because I never did. But he talked mostly about cows. His folks was herders and milkers, and he spoke of them goddamn bovines like they was old lovers. Maybe they was. You can imagine my interest in that topic, and I never did understand why humanos is so partial to the discharges of the bovine tit. His main aim in life was to be recumbent, and thus engaged he'd talk to his fellow Hibernians about misty mountains, soft rains, cows and grass and colcannon and poteen, sundry Marys about whose nethers they'd rummaged. They called him Davy. I never saw him after the big fight.

BEING no aboriginals was obliging us by flaunting theirselves to get shot at, the dark-faced major got sent south on a scout. Now you whites have a phrase: to thrust your nose disjointed, or some such. Mumbo jumbo to me, but you'd say that was the effect the mission had on Custer. You could tell he was itching to go on that scout, find the Indians, whip them and get his name in the papers. Naturally, him being a gubernator, he went about camp saying it were all a wild goose chase and anyhow he never wanted to go in the first place.

The rest of us followed the cloudy Powder north to the Yellowstone, and you won't believe it, but a steamboat awaited us thereon, loaded with ammunition and liquor. We done trudged and got froze and burnt through all that wilderness, and all the time we could have travelled in idle luxury. But you just had to admire the whites for getting that technology up there in that wolf-trod wilderness, though I'd bet it had walked most of the way. They'd plated the wheelhouse in boiler iron, so I guess them sailors was suffering the harbingers too.

A saloon in the form of planks set on barrels were already set up, a wall of canned comestibles serving to segregate officer and trooper, and they descended upon it like grasshoppers upon sprouting corn. By the middle of the afternoon the ambience was that of an Irish wake, a goodly number already unconscious and sun broiled. Fights had broken out and concluded, the combatants now locked in embraces and exchanging expressions of love. Them sober enough was forming a queue outside the cabin of the two demimondaines what had made the voyage and was about to get amply remunerated for their sand.

Next day, the meteorology still obliging, they got the band going and the good crockery out and the officers lazed by the river nibbling dainties and humming Bonny Jean of Aberdeen and Mollie Darling and I'll Twine 'Mid the Ringlets. Others made inroads into the local creation. The men, least them as was able following the debauch, wrestled or played baseball or knocked a stake in the ground and pitched horseshoes at it, swam in the river. Davy and another Irishman detached a waggon board and thereon performed a straight-armed dance of considerable vigour, their knees attaining the height of their nipples while their faces maintained an attitude of utter disinterest. Troopers less limber played cards or went fishing. I don't begrudge them boys their amusements.

Custer, he weren't no big drinker and he made an example of two worse hungover. He got a couple of barrels fitted with leather straps and got them boys stripped naked and suspended them barrels from the shoulders so as to conceal their privy parts and thenceforth paraded them about camp. I admit, it were a comical sight, though Custer being Custer, he allowed it to go on till their shoulders was bleeding and their thighs abraded to mush. You won't read about that in no history books. Such humiliations was routine and deemed unworthy of comment.

Yours truly? My forebodings vitalised my appetite and I packed in the grass and my belly bolused up and for a spell I feared the colic and getting the paraffin poured down my throat. But my forebodings drove me on and I couldn't help but keep chawing. Them other nags dozed and butted and barged each other and regarded me like I'd lost my wits. My bane? Well him off with the mules, he weren't vicinified to disturb my gluttony, albeit one time I did hear braying and saw a pair of ears rotated in my direction, and I conducted myself as deaf and blind.

Speaking of mules, bossing this whole shebang, even Custer, was a real general, not like Custer, General Terry. I ain't being disrespectful. They all called him Terry, even the men, and I calculated him a paternal type desirous of an informal ambience about the camp. You'll have to look in the history books for Terry's cognomen, as I never heard it. I don't intend to describe this individual being his notable feature was that he had no notable features. Anyhow, Terry decided the best policy was to dispense with the blundering waggons and proceed on with pack mules. But a flint resided deep in the hoof of this strategy. Terry, he never considered the fact them beasts was draught animals, habituated to rub of tongue and shaft and squeak of axle, and the troopers, they weren't no arrieros, and had about as much idea how to balance a load as I had to grasshopper a steamboat.

My bane, well he were one of the first up for packing. You got to recall he were the exception in all this. He were born to be packed. That demised eagle-shanty dweller you all forgot about, he toted his gear across the blasted wilderness and up onto the Llano, Comanche trade acquisitives all over the high plains. But as that trooper lugged that aparejo toward him he maintained a stolid ignorance as to its function. The overture to it were the bridle, an item he also professed nescience of. By then I known that mule's acquaintance a long time, but I never knew he could draw his lips so far back, and his yellow teeth articulated hostility to the tack such it took two troopers to twist his ears before they got it on.

Henceforth he embarked on the Spiral Dance, completing a series of circles of such perfection to confound old Euclid hisself, and in the end a comrade was enlisted to grab hold of the tail, which as you know is the act of a neophyte and he got chunked on the knee and had to hobble off for medical attention. A little further dexter-wise and that troopers ancestorial prospects would have got terminated. But that were shortly to happen anyhow.

They got him settled, but I knew he were just playing along. It could have been a trick of the light, but I swear the bastard winked at me. As they were lashing the pack on he swoll out his belly. An old trick, and you all know why, and in their ignorance they considered the aparejo cinched tight. He even let them load it with boxes of ammunition. The troopers cocked their hips and pushed their hats back and regarded. One said, I don't get what all the goddamn fuss is about.

My bane, he stood, as if pondering his new situation, the wind whisking his tail, some muscular spasm rippling his flank. He nibbled at a flea bite. He twitched one ear and gazed out fixedly, and I followed his gaze but observed no particularity worthy of his thrall. I'd doubt he was composing an elegy to the evanescent plains. Off in the bluffs a raven croaked.

Well it were that day up on the high plain atwixt the headwaters of the Purgatoire, when he distributed them Comanche acquisitives about the grass, and I ain't going to repeat the description of it, albeit it was right entertaining and I am tempted. I'll adjunct that the act was a good bit more lively, him having a bigger audience, and it was truly a marvel the altitude he achieved out of them posterior legs, and if you was a poetic type you might say the pirouette had a brutal grace to it. The hee-hawing was such I venture them Sioux and Cheyenne camped over the divide held off stirring their cookpots and hoisted an eyebrow.

The salient feature here is, like I said, he was one of the first up, and them other mules all observed the display. I ain't never seen quadrupeds so rapt, and I guess them waggon-trained beasts concluded this the appropriate comportment when strapped with carpentry apt to wear holes in their backs. So them waggon mules, well they was already pretty used up, but they demonstrated theirselves ardent disciples of their new prophet. Others owned aspirations for the racetrack and omitted the dance and sprinted off to locations unknown, ropes trailing behind, troopers chasing, a picket pin or three thrashing about threatening a braining. Others wouldn't budge at all.

Them mules was nothing but trouble all the way up the Rosebud and over the divide to the Greasy Grass. If matters was reversed and the Sioux was trailing us, they could have sat back in their saddles and crossed a leg across the pommel, followed the trail of comestibles and accouterments and never been obliged to poke a turd to determine its age. They could have stocked up on ammunition, if they possessed any single-shot Springfields, although generally the Sioux favoured a Winchester, and bows and arrows and hatchets.

I ain't included this mulish episode for tawdry purposes of entertainment. Thinking back on it now, I do believe my bane was a wormy spoke in the wheel of Custer's humiliation that day, them troopers up on that sweaty ridge all running out of ammunition. Custer even sent off an Italian musician back to the mule train with a message, Quick! Bring up more ammunition. But it were a long trip and he never made it back. A further aspect to it, as the campaign dragged on we was obliged to camp early every day to allow the mule train to catch up, them beast dawdling in generally around sundown, and you can figure that hour it being about the time of the solstice.

So you might say my bane saved the Sioux and Cheyenne from massacre that day. You figure it. If them mules had never delayed us, Custer could have arrived at the Greasy Grass at the time he schemed, in the dawn twilight. Catch the Indians at their toilets like he did on the Washita. Thin-armed scholars have argued at some tedium about why Custer got massacred. But I'd bet ain't one of them idlers done argued the case for some contrary Comanche mule.

———

FOR REASONS WITHHELD, we marched up the Yellowstone. En route we stumbled upon our first Indians. These was the good variety, located as they was atop scaffolds and swathed in hawk-pecked blankets and well along the road to decomposition.

Custer and his kin got first pick of the souvenirs. Autie, he rode about yelling, Look what I got! I got me a bow and six arrers and two pair of beaded moccasins. My ma will sure love these baby ones.

An officer took down the baby, unwrapped it and took measurements and made notes and drew pictures in a book. Custer inspected a scaffold painted red and black, decor the scouts said betokened a brave warrior. They kicked the scaffold down and stripped the warrior, regarded his stretched skin and gaping mouth and sunken eyes, and scratched their chins. They took the knick-knacks his kin had left to help him through the spirit life. Bone dining utensils and items of personal grooming figured large. So he were doomed to spend eternity with stained fingers and hayrick hair. Then they divested him of his moccasins and threw him in the Yellowstone, along with the baby.

Them Crow and Ree scouts. Now given the chance they'd massacre a Sioux family and ride off gleeful like they been out berry picking, but they hung back from this activity, muttering to each other out of clouded faces. The wind soughed through them scaffolds, them tattered wraps all flapping. You can imagine the ambience, and I figure the men sensed it.

———

Upriver we found a trooper's hat, and nearby the balance of him, a bleached skull and a torn overcoat, a trio of brass buttons still in situ. Them items lay adjacent to the charred remains of a fire, and sticks lay roundabout. The sticks hadn't been reduced in dimension for combusting purposes, and the Rees said he'd been beaten and burned to death. The troopers was by then trail worn and sullen, but whether true or not, that adjudication put the ginger into them and Davy said he wished he'd pissed on that warrior's corpse.

On the flats where the Rosebud flows into the Yellowstone we camped under glowering clouds, and waited for the dark-faced major to come up trumps on the bad Indian front.

The steamboat huffed up and the generals held a meeting on it. Custer exited pulling at his ridiculous moustache. One of his yolfers trotted up for a stroke but he ignored it, and he strode off bearing the mien of one owning a personal raincloud. From the sounds coming from the rear of the boat them lesser officers was engaged in a lubricated poker game. They all got inebriated and they say Tom Custer got totally busted, albeit as it panned out his prodigality was to count naught against his future advancement.

From the front of the boat came further sounds of inebriation. They originated with dark-faced major, who'd arrived while I was off packing my belly with grass and cottonwood twigs. Slumped on a bean sack he was, singing. Them lyrics was a good bit slurred, but I have managed to sieve these examples from my silted memory: *I'm Captain Jinks of the Horse Marines, I feed my horse on corn and beans,* and, *Four and twenty virgins came down from Inverness.* Ain't it shocking how your mind leaks so many events but retains such trifles. He took a swig and sang a dirge that began, *At dreary midnight's cheerless hour.* It made me flatten my ears, but he didn't get far before his head dropped to his chest and he commenced blubbing.

It just clubbed me. The dark-faced major later got his epaulettes tore off or put on trial or some such. A fellow officer's daughter were going about her toilet and he got caught peeping though a chink in the curtains, which if you think on it must be right embarrassing, albeit I'd bet a barrel of apples she'd left that chink deliberate. I don't know why I adduced that episode. Generally I ain't one for tittle-tattle.

You might be wondering what the dark-faced major was doing there on that steamboat, being the last you heard of him he was off scouting the Tongue for unfriendlies. Well he ain't done met them in person, but he'd stumbled on a big trail. Substantial numbers, is what he said.

And here is Custer decocted. He objurgated that major for all to hear, called him a snivelling coward for not following the trail to its authors and serving up divine vengeance. They say he even calumniated him in an article he wrote and sent to a newspaper back east. But you know Custer by now. Last thing he wanted was for the dark-faced major to go and whip the hostiles and return to plaudits, the Beau Sabreur stuck on the Yellowstone watching baseball games and fishing competitions. Perpetually seeking to abase your rivals, all seems a wearisome palaver to me. Anyhow, Custer got his way. Us bunch, we was to be sent off to follow that trail, all the way to its terminus.

Overnight a big hailstone smote my hindquarters and interrupted my chawing. If it were portent, I couldn't cipher it.

THIRTY-ONE

G oddamn Garry Owen, again. Terry on a knoll watching us trot by, his nag opportuning hisself to lift his tail and engage in a bowel movement, and I pondered if it were another omen I should include in my burgeoning tally. To add to the cacophony, a drum was tonking away yonder, the Rees singing their death songs, what chunked a whole heap of wet buffalo chips on Terry's valediction.

Thank the Lord this trip I wouldn't have that goddamn ditty blasting into my lugs again. We left the band behind along with their musical instruments, although we took some of their white nags along to replace our own what was already busted. Maybe if you is a superstitious type you might interpret that jettison as another spoke in the wheel of defeat. For the first time the Seventh would hurl itself into bloody battle without no musical accompaniment.

It were now omens galore if you was looking, like I was. While I was getting saddled up a big kerfuffle arose by the river. Such was the thrashing I thought it a mule engaged in drowning. Then I saw beak and pinions and wings beating water. I didn't believe they got alligators up there, but it could be some outsize dontically-advantaged fish getting revenge on some shitepoke, though I admit piscatorial knowledge weren't my strong suit back then. You never knowed what curious creeping thing you might encounter up on them boreal parts. You ever seen a wolverine?

It were then I clocked the hook in that bird's beak and the strength exploding out the wings, and it clubbed me. It weren't getting drug under. It were dragging out. It thrashed a good bit, body lurching and bucking, and come the point I was certain it would chuck in the sponge. Then it broke free and the claws emerged, and clutched therein was the biggest goddamn fish you ever saw. The bird beat the air now, droplets cascading, arching its body in the effort to ascend. That fish, it hadn't done quit on life just yet, and it writhed and jerked, but them talons stayed clenched. The general colour of it were silver, like most fishes are, but as it struggled the sun caught it and it dazzled white, such as a canted pane of glass might on a sunlit day. I'd say it was the whitest thing I ever saw.

That fish's ongoing resistance, well I guess it were an impediment to that hawk's progress being it leaned down and tore a hole in its head, and henceforth only a tail twitch bore witness to its former existence.

Now you tell me. Is it me, or was them omens auspicating theirselves up into a regiment of indubitability? The Comanche, they'd have shrugged their shoulders. The auguries was betokening it weren't to be their day, and they'd have departed the campaign accordingly. Weren't no shame to it. Me, I was stuck with the Seventh.

Anyhow, an officer shot that hawk to get a fish breakfast. In an instant its lines, its heft, its vigour, vanished, and it slapped shapeless into the grass, dead as old Pharoah and just as wet. Short on the gundog side, his striker trotted off and picked up the fish, held it up by the tail for admiring purposes, and it traded the cold waters of the Yellowstone for the hot grease of the frypan.

It were noon when we left Terry on the knoll and started up

the Rosebud, the main cause of the delay being the fustigation of the mule train into order. They'd butchered members of the beef herd to take along, although Custer delighted in galloping about on shiny Vic bellowing, You'd better take plenty of salt along, boys. There's hard riding ahead and you'll be dining on horseflesh before we are through. You might consider that tactless comment, all us nags standing about with our big lugs pricked, but Custer, he didn't go big on empathy.

Yours truly, I was so stuffed with grass my swinging belly hampered the motion of my posterior legs, but my discomfort was outweighed by my smugness. My auguries was right all along. Custer just confirmed it. We was in for a hard trip. Broke-down horses would get et, and I weren't about to be one of them. On the Powder we'd left a couple behind for the wolves. Custer, he was a goddamn horse abuser, and I'll spit in the eye of any bastard what gainsays me. If I was possessed of that ability.

Before we'd cleared camp them mule's packs was already littering the prairie, hardtack and ammunition busting out, and I saw Terry's head and shoulders slump, just a hair, though he shook hands with Custer and wished him good luck. One of Custer's cronies called out, Now don't be greedy Custer. Save some redskins for us, and Custer come back with, Don't worry. I won't, which as rejoinders go, is about as recondite as you can get.

On the meteorological side, it were a cold fresh-rinsed lemon-sky day, the wind shoving us out the north and I'd say the mood of the troopers was likewise bright and brittle. Custer had gone about yelling, There isn't any bunch of savages the Seventh can't whip, and I'd say most of the boys believed it. I tell you, a good portion of them boys believed Custer some kind of genius, Cump Sherman, Abe Lincoln and the Lord Jesus Christ rolled into one. Next day we struck the Indian trail.

Holy Mother divine. May God have mercy on us all. They was my peat-digging jockey's remarks at the sight of it.

A hundred horse-lengths wide I'd estimate it, could be a thousand given my talents arsmetrick. It followed the broad bottomland and you'd imagine the Lord had sent a bunch of angels down to mow the grass, such was the quality of grub remaining for us nags. So we wasn't about to find them Indian ponies famished like they was on the Washita. Where the bluffs crowded in and narrowed the trail, the travois poles had tore up the turf you'd think a rustic had been through with a team and plow, and the sun now pounding down and a parched wind stirring, we was about to eat considerable dust.

They cast their eyes about that trail and it were the first time I saw them troopers bite their lips and exchange fretful glances. Course, it weren't no surprise to yours truly. I'd been observing Indian sign all day, including a couple of bunches of grass suddenly sprout up atop a ridge. Weren't long before we fetched up at entire villages, any rate their sign.

The scouts counted the circles of flattened grass and kicked through the old fires. Broken bones lay scattered where they'd sucked out the marrow, fragments of deceased buffalo, a cracked cook pot and broken utensils. A line of buffalo skulls all painted red was arranged so they was all staring off east. Don't ask me why. The officers paced over a big area of pounded grass and scratched their chins. Me, I knew it was where they'd held a dance. Yonderward were a bunch of wickiups, where the adolescents had camped away from their mas and pas and told dirty stories. Souvenirs was scant and the Custer family was crestfallen. They estimated more than four-hundred lodges, and that was just the first of a bunch of erstwhile villages we tramped though.

Custer charged about. We have them now boys. Won't be long before we flush a covey or two of these primitives and you'll be drinking deep from the cup of Artemis.

It were then I finally decocted it. That man was a fool, and I won't be denied. And worse, he fooled them boys by means of a fancy hat and tasselled buckskins and imperious demeanour. You should try it. Put on some swanky duds, exude a confident air and talk loud and in a fancy voice, you'd be surprised how many will go along with you. Even to destruction.

The primitives, they all knew we was in the field and bent on taking their scalps and massacring their ponies. Yet these aboriginals wasn't behaving according to regulation. They wasn't fleeing like them Cheyenne did at the advance of the slumpen general and his canister shot and haemorrhoids. They was strolling along, camping when they pleased, picnicking and picking prairie flowers and playing shinny and attending to manicures, and didn't give a damn who found their toothpicks and dottles.

The trail departed the river and wove its way up the inclivities and we followed it. I head a ruckus behind and saw a mule tumbling into the ravine, legs kicking air. As he hit bottom the ammunition boxes bust open and we waited for the bang. But weren't none, and the dust blew away and revealed my bane struggling back to verticality.

He shook hisself, huffed a spell, kicked each leg out to confirm function. He snorted and twitched his giant lugs and commenced to climb back up. By God, you had to admire him. That beast would do anything to dispose of his burden including throw hisself off a cliff. He took his sweet time climbing back, taking frequent pauses to regain his breath, dallying to admire the scenery, enjoying a bowel movement, and I feared an officer might order a .45 calibre propelled toward his person, but we'd broke down a brace already that day. He clocked me and issued a bucolic greeting. I turned my head aside and affected ignorance of our acquaintance.

Goddamn Custer pushed us hard that day, and nags' necks was drooping and knees knocking at the end of it. Me, I was doing okay. We pernoctated on a flat amid the stink of wild rose, overlooked by riven hills and timber what might have concealed the

Sioux and Cheyenne nations combined. The men chawed on hard-tack and raw bacon and looked glum about it. The Irishmen talked of Bad Hand Mackenzie and how he'd whipped the Comanche and they was the toughest Indians of the whole bunch, and if the Fourth could do that then the Seventh could whip the goddamn Sioux.

In the Llano canyons he done it, Bad Hand, massacred 1400 Comanche ponies. Imagine that. I don't know how many that is but it sounded a good deal more than Custer knifed, shot and bludgeoned to death on the Washita. They say Bad Hand went insane later. By God, it were only by dint of Picks Herbs By The Lake's dyspeptic disposition I weren't still a Comanche and present at that massacre. But ain't no way to outwit what the Lord got planned for you.

Davy took his hat off, raked a cowlick and said, I dunno if I could do that lads. I was brought up with horses. The others looked at him and chambered insults. He saw his manhood about to get mocked and he says, Course, I'll massacre and scalp as many of the feckin reds and their pups Custer can put in front of me. Them others, they un-cocked their insults and say, Aye, you worry too much. You'll be feckin grand, Davy. Feckin grand. Later Davy brung me a hatful of mouldy oats, and said, Sorry lad.

Weren't no grass about, what with the Indian ponies chawing it all down you'd think a Mexican and his sheep passed through, and anyhow fearing horse theft they got us nags tethered to a picket line, although them Indian boys sure do enjoy a challenge. I finished up them oats still famished and congratulated myself on my providence, stuffing my belly like that up there on the Yellowstone.

You won't believe this but a bunch of officers went to Custer's tent and serenaded him. The whites invented a word for them types what's done fled my noggin. You saw his shadow shift inside the tent as he put his hat on and drew the flaps back, and he stood there nodding his head and listening without a jot of embarrassment as if it were the most natural thing it the world. Imagine that.

It were around then the Irish mercenary came dawdling over. Recumbent Davy secreted his whisky bottle and jumped to his feet and saluted. The Captain, he shot a glance over at me and said, I'll be taking your horse, trooper.

So now you know. That's how it come to be. He rode out the fort on the Heart River on a chestnut Kentucky thoroughbred, a beast currently in need of a bale of late-summer hay and a month in a straw-lined stable. Yep, he'd done remembered me and our lively time together in the sandy knobs all them summers since chasing after the kidnapped chef and getting insulted by yellow-painted Slow Turtle. He'd spent all day inspecting sign of a thousand aggrieved indigenes and knew we was soon to go up against them. Now he needed a nag possessed of wind and gumption and calmness under fire, and he knew yours truly were the exemplar of such qualities. The debit side was he'd took up the habit of wearing buckskins, like Custer, so we might get shot at a good bit more.

He strolled over and slapped my neck and his bent-up words issued forth. How you doing there boy. Remember me? You'll get us through this, won't you, Comanche.

Well there you go. Ridiculous ain't it, him ignorant of my history as a Lord of the Plains, and I guess if you was the analytical type you'd say him donating that name adds a circularity to my tale. He were likewise ignorant of its meaning. Yours truly, in my whole earthly I never wanted to fight anybody all the time. And a goddamn curious name to bestow when you is soon go into battle against aboriginals. The battlefield is confusing enough already. We get separated and he starts yelling out Comanche! Comanche! them soldier boys is apt to soil their britches thinking them Lords of the Plains is en route.

THAT WORD JUST CLUBBED ME. Arse-lickers.

That camp grew eerie quiet as it settled, such that them engaged in the activity could hear the lice crack between their thumbnails. Game had vanished, the Indians done et it all, and you heard nary bird tweet nor rodent squeak. A rattle as a lone magpie picked through the bones of an old camp across the creek, the moan of the timber as it sieved the wind, that were the sum of it. I ain't inventing this to crank up the tension. That's how it was.

Maybe it was that ambience compounded to the wearisome day and my lengthening tally of portents what induced my nightmare.

It started promising. Me and Looks At The Sky chasing cloud shadows, her grinning teeth and flaming hair. But then the clouds turned purple and bunched up into fat humano faces whose nostrils shot lightning bolts at us. I say us, but I looked round and Looks At The Sky at that juncture had departed to locations unknown. I fled. The country heaved before me like crusted quicksand inhabited by tribes of writhing snakes, the lightning exploding all about me, me blasting and foam flying off of me, my eyeballs swirling red. The plain beneath me transformed into a herd of buffalo and I was running across their backs and I felt proud of myself galloping over them dumb ungulates but then I broke though and tumbled down legs flailing and buffalo falling about me.

Now generally speaking, when you fall in a dream, that's when you jolt awake. But me, I never. I was locked into it, and even though a creature dwelling in a corner of my noggin kept tugging at me telling me it were a dream, I couldn't wrench myself free of it. I tumbled a long time. Until jagged rock rushed up to meet me and my limbs exploded and was cast to the four winds and I was surrounded by buffalo in a similar state of dismantlement. I looked up and a big bull was falling directly towards me. It filled my vision until black was all I could see and then the bull changed into Custer and them shattered buffalo laying all about me changed into them poor wrenching shuddering nags on the Washita. Custer, being Custer, he righted hisself and floated down and landed on his two pegs. He were dressed like a circus Indian, a beaded band about his head, a vertical feather plunked in back, his face all rouged up and charcoal rubbed about his eyes to show he were a bad Indian. He produced an axe, a big double-bit bugger, and strode toward me over them heaving bodies squelching and raised the axe above his head and I saw he'd shaved off his ridiculous moustache and his top lip was red and puckered like that of a harlot and he had a hang tooth like a gravestone what grew monstrous and yellow of a sudden like his hair and that tooth thrust out his maw and impaled me and it was it what did for me not the axe.

Jesus. Dreams, eh. I'd had nightmares off and on since the Washita, but this were a humdinger. Such visions is apt to send you crazy. Old Pharaoh owned magicians to interpret his dreams and he still got plagued on and finished drowned in the Red. Yours truly, I got my wind back, worried off my tether and went off to perscrutate for herbage and mud to roll in, what with the gadflies thronging. I found patches of both down by the river atwixt the deadfall. The mud, well it were a good bit soothing but the grass topped up barely one leg.

Custer, he came doddling over, and I pressed myself further into the trees so as to avoid admonishment. He looked about to make sure nobody was watching, and commenced weeping.

His shoulders jerked and he chup-chupped such that he put me in mind of the girl we took from the Texas horse farm all them summers since, her later traded for a bunch of blankets and iron-mongery what got shucked off by an ornery mule on a pristine day up on the headwaters of the Purgatoire. He sank down on his haunches and pulled his head between his knees, what was quite a feat of limberness I can tell you, and rocked back and forth a spell. I shifted a hoof and a twig snapped and, goddamnit, he looked toward me.

You know, it just clubbed me now in the act of telling it. I figure Custer was possessed of defective vision and, him being Custer, was too vain to admit to it and wear eyeglasses. Why on this very trip, the same day we plunged into the valley of death, the scouts took him up to a lookout and showed him the vast Indian village snugged along the Greasy Grass, and he claimed he couldn't see it, and insulted them scouts saying they was inventing the magnitude of it as an excuse to go home to their wives, and you need to know, your plains Indian's optics is second only to yours truly on the far-sighted front. Maybe throw in an eagle. Now, Custer stared into the timber wherein I was ensconced, directly at me, even knuckled his eyes and squinted and blinked, and I was sure my white star would give away my presence, though I held still as a snipe. But he never saw me.

What that snapping twig did was haul on the bit of his sentiments. He erected hisself, huffed half dozen times and rubbed his face. He looked at the stars and again looked about to see if anybody was watching. He put one hand on his breast and stretched out the other to the hills and cleared his throat. A hiatus occurred at this point, and you have to hear the following versification sprinkled liberally with such items, and he adopted a right snooty tone to go with it. This is how I heard it.

There is a side, to the affairs of man, which, taken at the flood, leads on to fortune! (He clenched his fist at this juncture and thrust it at the firmament.)

Omitted, all the voyage of their life, is bound, in, shadows, and mysteries.

On such a full sea, we, is all now afloat.

And, we must take, the currant, where it swerves.

Or lose our dentures.

Like I said, right peculiar how such trumperies stick in your mind. You can imagine, all them declamatories sailed over my head like ordnance fired by new recruits, and maybe you can make head or tail of that mumbo jumbo because it long since defeated my butcher-black noggin. Whatever it was, it sure elevated his mood and when he finished he looked right pleased with hisself. So I guess you'd say he returned to his regular demeanour.

He pulled his big hat down on his head and turned to leave and, as if struck by another thought, he stuck his finger in the air and spread out his lips to form a smile. If I was to interpret that smile I'd say it was meant to convey bitter sarcasm. Et two, Benteen? he sighed, and repeated it. Et two?

You have to check the history books for that one, but by then them beef steaks was in short supply, and I figure maybe come suppertime that Captain done et more than his share.

ON THE PORTENTS FRONT, that next dawn the unique example was a single ruddy cloud in the act of obliterating the morning star.

Weren't no trumpet toots to injunct them to wake up and put their clothes on and eat and drink, saddle us nags and mount up. We was about to attempt silent locomotion like we did with the slumpen general down on the Beaver. But the plan got shafted from the get-go, by dint of when they got loaded them mules they all started hee-hawing like they been inculcated up to do, every last one.

My new jockey cinching up my girth, me swelling my belly out, one of his fellows come dawdling over. What in Chrissakes you doing with a nag like that? he says. You could use that head to pack an earth floor. It were a new one, but I considered it a poor analogue.

Trudging along, the Irish mercenary aboard, the acrid dust blistering my lips and burning my eyes and no immediate perils to occupy my mind, I thought on Slow Turtle and that snooty paint mare and Looks at the Sky's square ma and the curly-lipped adolescents and White Antelope and Cunning Bird and I wondered if they'd been among them Bad Hand killed, although my thwarted castrator would have got his just deserts. I was tolerable certain the square ma would have took a good few taibo with her, and I pictured her covered in gore, clutching the jawbone of an donkey like old Samson done, surrounded by a pile of bluecoats. But it didn't matter how many bipedal Comanches Bad Hand massacred. Without their ponies they was finished.

Such musings weighed heavy, and I felt discomposed in myself. I guess Slow Turtle could have made it, maybe rekindled his bullet-defecting medicine and was presently disporting hisself naked someplace. I recollected him painted yellow, his acorn member and crimped ballocks and inset nipples, and my cast of mind elevated.

THIRTY-TWO

Discarded Indian knick-knacks, trash and accouterments was such now, it was like marching through a continuous dump. It being the beginning of summer, I figured they must be going for the simple life and having a clear out. But them paraphernalia was only the antipasti. The sun were about a quarter up the sky when we come to the main dish of that penultimate day.

The augury to it was a bunch of rocks rising out the valley floor tall as a fifty humanos, like the Lord had got halfway through building a mountain and said, I'll just set these here a spell while I go for refrescos. Now as you know I ain't much of a hand at spotting resemblances, but these was undeniable, and it was the goddamnedest thing. Them rocks was a family of giant prairie owls stood on the grass, standing sentry against a colossal coyote or hawk or some such. Yep, goddamn owls again. I admit that when we got closer they was more akin to squat Indian chiefs at council, a few females throwed in, but by then my noggin was bent on interpreting the innocuousest items as a portents of doom.

Going by the amount of aboriginal artwork thereon, these rocks was a sacred place. The Rees circumambulated muttering and pointing out depictions of various vintage. They paused and all yelped simultaneous and pointed. My jockey, he wanted to take a look and he urged me forward, although I admit I was no wise desirous of adjacentizing myself to them harbingers. This picture showed a bunch of spider-legged troopers, their heads hanging as though the necks was hinged, and it weren't no vintage example.

Now you'd think that'd be enough bad medicine for the day. But as prior alluded, them geological owls were just the overture. Soon we fetched up at whatever the antipode of an overture is. Now, how to supply a likeness. A trooper called out, Hey, look at that giant wickiup, but that don't do it justice. A giant spider froze in the act of stretching its legs. Yeah, now we are getting somewhere. A big pole were at the centre of it, banded in paint the colours of nature, and lesser poles leaned in toward it, so picture the ribs of an upturned basket, plus the big pole. Give it a span of what, dozen or so horse lengths, and suspended from the big pole, for us to discover and ponder, were a white man's scalp.

The scouts said it was a special lodge where they'd held the Sun Dance a moon or so ago. Now I ain't never observed no Sioux Sun Dance and hence remain unable to descry the particulars of it, but they say it is a sight to behold, them braves all dangling from strings and streaming blood. Sun Dances, they was like buffalo hunts to them memoir-writing adventurers and white captives. Weren't one of them fellas didn't witness the dance and describe the gory particulars. Some even claim to have partook, so if you is titillated by such doings I expect you can read about it all there. I'll footnote the following so you can weigh the onerousness of the affair. The Comanche, now them Indians bent over backwards both literally and figuratively to demonstrate a manly indifference to pain. But they never took up the Sun Dance.

The whites back then leapt on such indigene ritual as more ammunition to bolster the extirpatory approach. Indians was all heathen savages still practicing the primitive rites of the Stone Age, whatever that is. By God, if we divest them of their land and enterprise the hell out of it we'd be doing civilization a favour. But going by my earthly, religious types of any creed is apt to perform painful acts to flaunt piety.

It were one of the Cornishman's favourite topics. If his mouth had been fitted with sleeves he'd have been rolling then up. Them holy men and saints what went out to live the desert and starved theirselves and struck theirselves with sticks and applied red-hot pokers to their breasts. So as to spite the sin of Onan, one fellow opted to sleep perpendicular in a thorn thicket. Another went down to the smithy and got the blacksmith to forge him a chain so he could whip hisself with it. You might think he'd go directly to the hardware store and get hisself a chain straight off of the counter and commence without delay. But he wanted a bespoke chain, the bespoke part being the hooks fastened into the links. That way each lash fetched out chunks of flesh and rendered him more bloody and hence more holy for when he paraded hisself about.

There was the fellow who lived in a birdcage at the top of a pole and got dry crusts and gristles throwed up and lived in his own filth, and I figure you'd be best advised to squint upwards if you was planning to pass asunder. A saint gouged out her own eyes to discourage a beau she fancied, which you'd think'd do it, and numerous males, so as not to be lured from the true path by the temptations of the flesh, got a hammer and chisel and sat spraddle-legged on a stump, underdrawers about their ankles, and excised their own ballocks.

I sure hope them fellas took the trouble to give them chisels a final strop. As victim of it personally, it ain't no task you'd be wanting to take two or three swings at. And you best take care not to get your thumb caught atwixt, albeit creating another pain might distract you from that other. And you'd be provident to have a receptacle handy for collection. And what are the chances of them orbs rolling directly in? They could go rolling off down some prairie dog hole, and then where would you be?

Up to your armpit risking a rattlesnake bite or a peck from a goddamn owl, that's where. Whittling on it now, I'd say the whole endeavour is shot-through with potential mishap. One fellow, maybe hoping to obviate them potentialities, took a different tack. He held out his privy member for a viper to chaw on.

And didn't the Lord hisself watch his son get nailed to a tree and take all day to die so you humanos could get your sins washed clean. Jesus, but that final example got the Cornishman's mustard up. Some fellow does you some wrong, something bad, he'd say, like fornicate with your wife. That fellow, he shows up one day wringing his cap to say he's sorry. He never meant to do it, says It's these ballocks the Lord done give me, they is like having an evil spirit swinging between my legs and I ain't got no say in it. And you say, Alright, I'll forgive you. But first, see my boy over there playing on the swing, just hold on a spell while I nail him to that barn siding yonder and watch him die. And remember, it's all your fault I have to do this.

To get back to the point and them Sioux tearing lumps out their persons, as the Cornishman exposited, all religions is apt to demand some kind of pain and suffering somewhere along the line, and I don't see why you got pick on them Sioux. Least they got an edifying vision out of it.

Weren't just the scalp they left laying about to put the jimjams up us. Buffalo skulls was perched on poles and laid out in patterns. They'd painted three big rocks red and laid them in a line. You'd scarce pass a patch of sand without a picture drawn in it. Jesus knows what they all purported. To their brothers: This way to the big fight. To us bunch: You are about to get your beans knocked in with a bone hammer.

Custer, he was as pervious to such signs as my bane was to Pythagorean trigonometry, and maybe they knew it being the Indians left examples more perspicuous in nature. A pile of rocks. On one side lay a bull buffalo skull painted red, on tother a doe skull left sun-bleached. A sharpened stick descended from the summit and penetrated the eye of the doe.

The Rees poked about a former sweat lodge. You got it, them Sioux had dallied to take a sweat. They waved for Custer to come see. Now I was a fancy officer's mount I got the chance to go too.

They'd arranged the stones around it so the wind wouldn't blow it away, and even my noggin could decrypt what they'd drawn in the sand, soldiers, tumbling from the sky like grasshoppers, into an Indian village.

Custer, he said, You see gentlemen, even the ignorant heathen knows we are going to fall upon them like locusts and consume them. He snorted and stuck his boot in the sand and ground out the picture.

Now I don't know if that were bravado on Custer's part or he genuinely believed we was about to whip the Sioux and Cheyenne nations, but he was generally can-do of nature I wouldn't discount the latter, neither the possibility he was deluding hisself, a habit gubernators is prone to engage in. At best it were a mootable point. But nobody seemed keen to moot it.

Them Crow and Ree scouts slumped in their saddles and muttered dark thoughts and held their palms to the sky. They'd got a different take on it, and I believe a moiety of the officers and men and their sidelong glances was beginning to doubt.

Yours truly, to me it were plain as the ball on the end of Custer's nose, and whittling on it I was recollected of my religious inculcations. The Seventh had travelled deep into the northern quarters, into land of Magog, but the protagonists had got switched around. It were Gog with his hooks in the Seventh's jaws. He was drawing us forward to the place he wanted to fight us, so he could smash us, our swords and our bucklers, whatever they are, leave our corpses for ravenous birds and the beasts of the field to chaw on.

At times like this officers generally go off and have a confab, and while thus engaged they plant a flag in the dirt. Don't ask me why. Anyhow they was confabbing and the wind gusted and blew the flag down. An officer went and plunked it back in. It blew down again. This time they didn't notice and them blue and gold crossed sabres lay a good stretch slapping the dust the Indians had churned up. Officer clocked it and told a boy to take a stick and work a hole in the dirt and try again. It worked after a fashion, but the boy had dug his hole cock-eyed, and the flag only accentuated the error.

The Comanche, they'd have been back in camp twanging eyebrow hairs by now.

———

THE TURDS TOLD IT. We was almost upon them. When we first cut trail, the beetles had been at their labours and them apples was dry and crumbling. Later they was crusted over but still holding moisture within. Now, the pony turds yielded to the merest touch. There's quite an art to it. The scouts rode in and said they'd seen a big smoke in the west, and it weren't no prairie fire.

We kicked through dust ankle-deep now, dust what seemed to entirely composed of biting ants. My eyelids swoll and cracked as did my hairy lips, and whenever we made one of the frequent goddamn halts for the scouts to report, the gadflies descended.

Out on the Llano one time, me and Looks At The Sky, trailing a buffalo herd and chawing on their bitter dust. My eyes swoll and crusted up likewise, and I admit I complained a good bit. Looks At The Sky slid off and extracted a pouch and shook out fragments of tree bark into her palm, added water and worked them into a mush, said, Here brother. This will shut you up, and smeared the unction onto my burning eyes. It was like snow on a fresh brand. I don't expect they get such bitter dust in Hibernia, wherever that is, and there ain't no call for such cures.

You can imagine, the dust tortured the troopers likewise, but least they had grub. Grain for us nags was gone, or was way back with the mule train getting spilled. Our only fodder was cactus and sagebrush. I will chaw on sagebrush at a pinch. The flowers ain't bad but the greens is bitter and too much is bad for the nerves, and them features was already frazzled. A number of my fellow equines was already sagging and I didn't give much for their chances. Custer weren't about to have no epiphany and turn into Saint Francis.

The trail got even bigger. Trails and tracks was piling in from all directions save north where Terry was. Even my noggin could see we was on an aboriginal highway, and you follow a highway, sooner or later you fetch up at a big city. Custer, the great plainsman and Indian fighter, his interpretation departed from mine. The trail was dividing, he said. At the advance of the mighty Seventh the Indians was in a state of terror, and was scattering into small bands.

I do believe this thought infused the panic into him. You all know my opinion of panic, and the strife it will deliver unto you, and I remain convinced such agitation were another spoke in the wheel of Custer's defeat. If the Indians scattered thus, they'd be impossible to chastise, and Custer wouldn't be able to get his picture in the papers in time for the Centennial. So he drove us on even harder.

The highway, well it took a turn off the Rosebud up toward a divide of wolf-teeth hills. The scouts said beyond was the valley of the Greasy Grass, what the whites called the Little Big Horn.

WE CAMPED. The Rees and Crows rode off to scout what might be lurking in them wolf's teeth. The troopers collapsed exhausted amidst the stink of rose and plum and crab-apple blossom, the tinkle of robin song and chortle of blackbird. Across the creek, a thin smoke spiralled up from the embers of an Indian cook fire. Nags tore at scant and seared herbage, and when they raised their heads to look for more, gaunt faces stared out.

The mood of that wearied camp? You knowing half them boys was to get eviscerated on the morrow. Well I'd say a moiety was morose, wondering whether they was going to be up for the fight or would prove craven, maybe picturing themselves champing on the muzzle of their own Coltses to avoid capture and wondering if they'd feel any pain when it went off, henceforth getting chopped up by the womenfolk, all the life they'd miss out on. But in any joint endeavour you get your melancholy types.

On the other side of the psychological coin was them talking the fight up. A grand day lay ahead. They were going to get their names wrote down in the history books. They was going up against the last big crowd of hostile aboriginals the American Empire would ever see. It was the final chance to get scalps and souvenirs of what'd soon be a bygone age, them lawyers and insurance brokers all shoving on. You might not believe this, but on the day of the big fight, troopers ordered to the rear to guard the mules, they wept at the prospect of missing it.

The Indian scouts, they wasn't divided. An officer asked them for a prediction, and unbid a Ree performed a dance depicting dodging many bullets. Them hoppings and gyrations needed but little deciphering, and another life he might have enjoyed a theatrical career. The dance concluded, that Indian uttered not a word and in lieu cocked his head to one side and shrugged and spread his palms out. Looking back now I conclude the act one of sarcasm. He went off to join his fellows smoking pipes and wailing out death songs, located the key and chorused in. You can imagine the effect them dirges had on morale, and the Irish mercenary went off and told them to shift theirselves distant.

Now a bait I dangled to hook you into this tale was Custer's arse bones poking my hide, and you been thinking, Here we is on the eve, and they is all about to get massacred. He done shafted us. Well here it is.

Custer, I figure he sensed forebodings in the camp and reckoned he ought ginger the boys up. He chose me to administer that ginger. Naturally, he looked about for Vic and Dandy, but they was off distant getting fed oats and apples dipped in molasses and chilled spring water and sugar lumps. So he searched for an alternative, that invisible top lip curling as he regarded our sagging knock-kneed bunch. His eyes paused on me. The ridiculous moustache twitched and the nose wrinkled and moved on. But them optics cast about and returned, and he strode forward. Jesus.

So much for my goddamn providence. Had I been gaunt and knock-kneed like them others, he'd have picked another victim. Anyhow, that's how my sore back come to get prodded by the arse bones of the great horse abuser and Indian burner George Armstrong Custer hisself.

By this juncture, the Irishman had relieved me of my saddle and the stirrups appended thereon, so Custer was obliged to leap aboard. The first attempt I'd dub a fiasco, him sliding back to ground, and I venture in Custer's equitatory experience a mount featured of a hide slick with old sweat and blood were terra incognita. He tried again. He took a run up and jumped, and a hiatus occurred while his hands were pressing down on my back and he cocked his leg at right-angles. For an instant I thought he might make it, so I shifted my rear end as you might if a rattlesnake reared. In the end his striker had to come and shove on his arse. Custer made out he got a gammy leg.

I hoped he might surprise me, but he sawed on my reins and dug in his spurs, and proceeded to gallop me about yelling, Brace up Boys! Brace up! Tomorrow you'll all be heroes. We have the red devils now. Just beyond the divide in their feculent wigwams. This time tomorrow you'll be bathing in blood and glory! And further such nonsense.

Such was my nervous despond, I didn't realize it then, but you know it and I now know it. Yours truly missed his chance to divert the course of history. I could have picked out a likely rock, hoisted him vertical, cracked his skull, and saved all them boys' lives and ditto of no few nags. Him demised or witless, we'd never have gone charging off into the valley of death just so he could get his picture took with souvenirs. Them other officers more prudent, they'd have followed the plan, corked off the escape route and got them Indian nations trapped against Terry advancing from the north.

Now you is grumbling at this juncture, Yeah, but that'd mean them aboriginals would have got massacred instead of the troopers, and a damn sight more. And I would rejoinder, You can take your yeah-buts and shove them up your posterior aperture. Read your history books. The Indians got obliterated anyhow. Like I said, my being the only living survivor of the fight known as the Little Big Horn allowed me to be present a number of winters hence at them wind-blasted tipis along the Wounded Knee Creek, where the Seventh served up their revenge cold, both literal and figurative, and Gus got killed. I survived that fight, albeit I'd describe it a pretty one-sided affair. Firing canister shot into a ravine crowded with humanos ain't the acme of military strategy. The Indian victory that day on the Greasy Grass only served to delay their abasement, and served only to ginger up them artilleried whites, though I admit the Indians extracted a day of joy out of it, and Sitting Bull, he went on to star in Buffalo Bill's Wild West show where they re-enacted the fight, albeit some might consider them recompenses small beer. And think of all the idleness at the print works and the poverty among thin-armed scholars by dint of all the books what'd never got wrote.

I mentioned artillery there and it just clubbed me. We never had any that day. Yet we left brass napoleons and howitzers on the steamboat. I never saw no floating ballcock neither, so maybe it weren't up to rough usage on the plains, but by then I were convinced that windy Cheyenne chief invented it just to put the willies up us. Anyhow, Custer being Custer figured the glorious undefeated Seventh didn't need no fancy munitions to whip the primitives, which is a curious outlook if you think on it. Canister shot is right discouraging to massed attack.

I'll footnote Custer's equestrian acumen. Coarse and mediocre is how I'd describe it. Not a patch on Looks At The Sky or any other Comanche of my acquaintance. I never saw him slide under the belly of Vic or Dandy going full chisel and fire off them fancy pistols, stand erect or ride reverse-wise relying on magic for navigation. I calculate myself lucky during our union them fancy pistols wasn't strapped on, else I might have got shot. I'd go as far as to say Fabridzio Capeesh were his equal.

I AIN'T ENUCLEATED my own cast of mind that fateful eve. Well what do you think, me witnessing all them portents and a campaign veteran to boot. Why at the very moment I got unsaddled I looked down and there was a party of red ants carrying a family of white maggots off to their burrow for reasons I'd wager disagreeable. I knew it. I believe some of them boys knew it. Maybe even goddamn Custer hisself knew it, but'd never admit it. Forgive me for quoting that windy Cheyenne chief yet again, but we was fucked.

Not that I were panicking. You know me. A cunning plan was forming in my head, a plan of such cunning and guile, Looks At The Sky herself would be proud of me, albeit I admit that Indian were generally of that disposition in my company, her blessed with low expectations of life.

As they picketed us nags and rolled out their bedrolls I estimate the troopers all thought they was in for their regular slumbers. But I knew Custer. He knew them Indians was close, and he wouldn't quit now till he was burning tipis and massacring ponies and jangling the braids of a female, no matter the cost to man and nag alike. Soon as I heard the first snore, I'd put my cunning plan into action.

Truth be told it weren't much of a plan, and it don't bear close scrutiny, but I'll tell it. I'd worry off my tether and wander off from the camp a piece, pretend to chaw on a piece of herbage blithe, and edge my way out from them somnolent guards. There I'd stamp my feet, to discourage a rattler. Yep, that'd be it, to discourage a rattler. I'd cough, what with all the dust in my thropple, even let out a nicker or three. I knew somewhere out there a boy'd be watching on, looking to make a name for hisself. He'd sneak in and wave his blanket and I'd trot off tail-hoisted to reconvene with the aboriginal life.

By then I'd piled all my ante on Custer losing the fight, you understand. If he'd have won, I'd have finished massacred along with them Indian nags and never have progressed to my life of boozy luxury, although I might be getting my ramifications awry there.

Me being the only living survivor of the fight and hence present therein, you all know them intrigues come to naught. You know how many times in my life I'd got kidnapped with no say in it. The one time I were actually desirous of it, were my cunning scheme what got kidnapped. The Indian boy, he never got a chance. That first snore I mentioned, well it never rattled out, and never got a chance anyhow what with all them frogs croaking out for copulation and the goddamn coyotes yipping in the wolf's teeth. If you was the reading-before-bed type, the light was such you could have still been turning the pages, when Custer got us rousted and saddled-up.

So that was me shafted. How now to advance my prospects. You can get away with a lot in the ruckus of a camp preparing for battle, so when my jockey went off for a confab I stumbled down to the creek. The Comanche, when they know they are in for a hard fight, any sweet water they come upon they drink till their bellies bulge like that of a puppy dog afflicted by intestinal worms. I was ignorant of the character of the agua up on that wolf-teeth divide, so I figured the prudent action was to emulate them Lords of the Plains.

———

NOW I DON'T KNOW what offence the Irish Captain occasioned during that confab, but when he found me he yanked my reins and directed me to the rear. Transpired his role in the Seventh's advance to glory was to trot back and fustigate them mules along. That man had been raised by gentlefolk, but if you heard them vituperatives directed to toward the mules, you'd peg him raised by a brothel madam in a hell on wheels.

Were good and crepuscular when we fetched up at the mule train, whereupon the present incumbents reported they had just chased off a trio of Indian boys prying open a box of fallen hardtack. I never knowed an Indian risk death for a bite of maggoty hardtack, unless they were starving, so they must have had some project in mind for that box.

The light was leaking away, but enough lingered to illuminate the mules, and by God I wished we'd dallied an hour for the darkness to blind me. Jesus but they was sorry bunch, fustigated to hell and half-starved, muzzles scraping the dirt as they toiled up the inclivity. Them what was able was wandering off to chaw on scrub, and got struck for their trouble.

I looked about for my bane. I can't say why. Upon my advent I'd expected a pair of ears to spring up and a hee-haw to echo about the valley, but no such salutation issued forth. It took a good bit even for my eyes to locate him, him resembling just about every other mule in that train, bar them humped-backed dirt-nuzzlers deceased among the scattered comestibles, a gang of twilight sparrows feasting thereon.

I'll say this for him. He'd made a fair attempt at shucking off his pack, being half the load was absent. The debit part was the remainder had slid under his belly, and was playing havoc with such gait as was remaining. The legs was leaking blood, both anterior and posterior. His belly remained invisible, and I shuddered to think on the condition of it. I guess his back was getting respite, but the whackers had got him sussed by then, going by the glistening welts thereon. He'd been beaten a good bit more than them others, and they'd shaved off his tail to identify him as a troublemaker, so he couldn't even beat off the gadflies. Where the pack had ground his hide to bone, blowfly were investigating.

I turned my head aside. To expunge the picture of him I imagined him them summers since, after we just rubbed out the spirit Apache, splashing about in the Canadian tormenting the willdfowl. I looked back and nickered. I can't say why. A single ear flicked up and rotated toward me. The neck muscles tautened as he tried to drag his head up, and slackened as he failed. He opened his mouth but no sound came forth, only blood. An eye blinked. I remain ignorant to this day if the other were in concert. My jockey jabbed his spurs into me, and last I saw he was plunking one foot before the other, muzzle to the dirt, the need for fustigation long departed. If it were all an act, then it were a monstrous burlesque.

BY DINT of our new location at the rear we et more acrid dust than anybody. Even before the dark closed in I could scarce see to the end of my muzzle, and we was obliged to follow the jangle of tack and rattle of munitions and farts. If Lady Luck smiled on me we might get lost in the wolf's teeth and I'd miss the fight.

We proceeded on until the eastern sky smudged over silver, my jockey slumped in the saddle, dreaming of misty mountains and dewy grass for all I knowed, so it was left to yours truly to follow that stinking column.

We dropped into a hollow and bumped into the forward troop. The Irishman woke up and dismounted and gave my reins to a menial and went off to determine the reason for the halt, them roundabout all grumbling out their ignorance. Approaching mortal combat, any information what might affect their future prospects remains unavailable to the common soldier.

Were little cheery about our situation. Best I could extract out of it was to congratulate myself on my providence and bloating my belly with agua while I had the chance. Any we'd stumbled across had tasted of rotten eggs and fire. A maggoty buffalo lay in one such hole, and some nags was so desperate they partook, them as wasn't quirted back. Me, I hadn't descended that far yet, but I did consider it. Only because that water might render me unfit for service and they'd leave me behind and I could toddle off someplace. Knowing my luck, the beef now finished and the bacon departing likewise, most likely they'd jugulate me and salt me away.

The sun well-up, and us no sign of an advance, the troopers cursed the lack of shade and breakfasted on wormy hardtack and collops of raw bacon washed down by tepid dirty water. Like I said, you got to watch out for them gubernators. Give them the chance, this is what they reduce you to.

Me, I spied a sagebrush dexter-wise and leaned over for a chaw. In my haste I butted a nag's head out the way, and she shrieked an objection I considered improvident given our location deep in the Land of Magog. A sergeant hissed back, Keep your goddamn mount quiet soldier or I'll slit its throat myself. I admit now. My egoistic behaviour proved to be my shame.

I chawed on that bush a good bit, and when I leaned back that nag swung her head out the way to avoid further injury. It were then I caught sight of her eye. I say eye. In lieu of any orb was a scab about the size of a hen's egg weeping blood and pus. The bolus suggested some creature dwelling within trying to bust out, and I saw it was inhabited by tiny maggots. I recoiled, but I couldn't wrench my eyes away. She turned away and I was freed of the sight of it. I knew that dappled gray. She were down on the Beaver all them summers since chasing the Cheyenne about. I whittle on it now and I estimate me, her and my bane was all what remained of that party.

I allowed my eyes rove over her and wished I hadn't. She was blown. Couldn't have been no blowner, nostrils bubbling blood, shuddering legs and palsied flanks, rasping lungs and sudorated neck, and all we was doing was standing still. He weren't supposed to, we was supposed to be ready for instant action, but her jockey had eased the saddle off to give relief. I ain't about to describe her back.

I looked over my equine companions. Sagging necks and trembling legs, bloodshot eyes, swoll lips and tongues about sums up a goodly portion. Vic and Dandy yonder, they pranced about spry as colts, with their private supply of grain and agua and obligation to tote naught more mithersome than Custer's skinny arse and fancy guns.

You need to know how it was back there. Back there in that feculent sun-raked ravine, a multitude of terrified horses and men, pissing and shitting. Stamping eye-rolling horses fighting for twigs, tearing at their reins to reach a poisoned wallow. Seared mat-haired men, squat on haunches gnawing raw meat and scratching at lice-infested chitlins, staring gum-eyed at the gnarl-timbered wolf's teeth for what might engulf them. This is what they do to you.

Quarter day we skulked in that hollow, waiting for Custer to make up his goddamn mind, hiding from Indians who all knew we was there, the solstice sun cooking us, the gadflies guzzling our blood. Ants climbed my legs and did battle with the gadflies and won and bit my tender parts.

Move out. The dappled gray's legs buckled and she went down. Her neck whiplashed and her bad eye struck a rock and yellow splashed out. Enough. Enough with this goddamn shit. We slogged up out that ravine and up to the wolf's teeth and I knew, by God. That bastard strutting popinjay weren't going to do that to me just to get his fucking name in the papers.

THIRTY-THREE

I t ain't like you seen it in Buffalo Bill's Wild West. Humanos don't arch their backs and fling their arms up and stare aghast at the heavens when they die. You get the odd arm-flinger, but mostly they stumble, slump, crumple, kneel, crawl on hands and knees, squirm and kick legs.

Move out. What prompted the order to depart that stinking ravine was a Ree scout come chiselling in flailing an arm. He reined up and rode in zig-zags, sign intended to convey hostiles had been located. Custer, he spoke to him a moment and departed in a state of joy.

Up onto the divide we went, the wind-bent trees stirring memories of them recent demised Comanche. Not that they hoodooed me. I didn't see no stiffened corpses frozen in death agony. Them Comanche, they was dancing.

Into the valley we went. Don't be picturing no charge. Half of them nags could scarce raise a tottering lope. The terrain, I figure Lord got tired of creating that day and just dumped some acrid dirt and raked his fingers through it. That'll do her. I'm off to get doxologized.

We divided. Custer sent a bunch off west with the white-haired

Captain. I know not why. We trotted past a burning tipi, glowing fragments breaking off for the wind to carry away. Inside, the flames was consuming a dead Indian on a scaffold. Off a piece, a scout was chawing on the picnic his family had left to sustain him to the afterlife.

Custer talked to the scouts. They threw up their arms and gesticulated down the valley. He prodded a finger and called them Women. Troopers wrenched on the reins of stamping gyring nags, them all frantic to get down to the Greasy Grass for a drink.

We divided. Again. Custer took a bunch off north up the bluffs. We followed the dark-faced major toward the creek. The major had opted for a straw hat to keep the sun off. We fetched up at blue-green agua. The Little Big Horn. The Irish mercenary and the dark-faced major talked. Meantime I bent my head and drank deep of that limpid creek. On the skin of the water a grey feather edged with blue floated by, a ladybug adopting it for canoe. Dry as the dust on a moth's wings was that feather, although a droplet lodged on its upward sweep looked set to burst and ruin that ladybug's voyage. Looks At The Sky were the one told me about water skin, and the thought occurred to me that Indian hadn't visited in a good bit.

The Irish mercenary sawed on my reins and we headed back the way we come. I remain ignorant to this day why we made that detour. We'd continued on down the Greasy Grass, the future would have turned out different for us both.

Took us a good bit to catch up with Custer. He'd glimpsed glory and gone off at a lick. The trail weren't difficult to follow, strewn as it was with dead and blown nags and superfluous outerwear, the sun now slamming down. We heard a crackle of gunfire from behind and my jockey said, Sounds like they made the charge, Comanch'. They better leave some for us, eh fella. It weren't yours truly he were trying to ginger up.

We found Custer up on the bluffs, spectating. He'd took his buckskin jacket off by dint of the heat, and Binoculars was pressed to his eyes through which them tiny orbs was watching the dark-faced major's fight. What he saw I do not know, being the valley were naught but a cauldron of dust and powder smoke. We sat there a good piece like that, him watching on, to the extent his minions looked at that big village downriver and exchanged furtives. Somebody said, Look, the red bastards have already fired the grass. But it weren't no smoke. It was dust, arising from a vast pony herd, and the fighters sprinting toward it to get their mounts. Custer watched on blithe, giving the dark-faced major a chance to show how brave he was.

Remember, I was at the Washita, albeit on the aboriginal side, and Custer had hatched a similar plan. He knowed by then this weren't no isolated village outnumbered five-to-one like Black Kettle's was. But down in the valley, seemed like the dark-faced major had got most of the warriors occupied. So Custer'd charge into the village, exterminate any adolescents and old men what resisted, burn the lodges and accouterments, massacre as many ponies he could and scatter the rest, kidnap women and children and hold them hostage against reprisal like he done them years since, proceed unmolested to glory. Let Terry downriver mop up the rest.

But this weren't the Washita. It weren't no sneak attack. Them families wasn't asleep, snugged in their snow-plastered lodges, believing theirselves safe because they'd touched the pen. The grass was high and their war ponies weren't enfeebled by a diet of twigs. For days them Sioux and Cheyenne had known we was approaching, was fully apprised they was the intended quarry, was even proceeding blithe to it. Now they was ready. That's my take on it.

The village were now in tumult, dust flying up, folks scurrying, children crying. Custer muttered, Goddamnit, they are scattering. His glorious victory were about to get thwarted. Sure, some women and kids engaged in fleeing preparations, but most of the turmoil was ponies stamping about ready for the fray, men gathering their best mounts, collecting weapons and charging off to join the fight upriver. Custer sent the Italian trumpeter off with a note to get the mule train brought up with more ammunition. That trumpeter said, Si, prego, and galloped off on the errand that saved his life.

We divided. Custer and his bunch galloped off toward a coulee, scouting for a ford I figured. Last words I heard Custer say were to the Irish mercenary, Hold this position. Come on when you get word.

Were then Brother Boston came riding up and asked for directions. He'd come up short on souvenirs and didn't want to miss out this time. He got directed and loped on off after his brother.

A crackle of gunfire came from the coulee and Custer chiselled back out with a diminished bunch, went off downriver and sent an officer and men off to try another coulee. Us bunch, we waited.

We waited a good bit, maybe the time it takes for the disc of the sun to traverse a lodgepole. The Irishman nudged me up on a knoll for a reconnoitre.

How can I picture the scene. Try this. A hot spring day, you come upon a swarm of bees departing their hive, a mass of bodies with no space atwixt and they is all climbing over each other. That's how the Indians was trying to cross the Greasy Grass to get at us. I heard a sound like the applause of giants. It was the ponies tumbling into the river, their bellies slapping the water. The Irishman said, Jesus Christ, and wheeled me round.

HE TELLS the men to get into defensive positions. When the soldiers dismount, their legs is trembling. We is in a gouge of stony ground but they take tin cups and plates and spoons and hack out deeper depressions, pass the whiskey around.

We wait. In the valley at the dark-faced major's fight, firing is now sparse and is ascending the bluffs toward a hump off south.

Something has gone awry down there and them boys is firing backwards.

Shots come in from the sagebrush, first the spit and pop of knotty juniper on a campfire, then a hailstorm against a tipi wall. I knew it wouldn't be long, and soon them arrows is raining down. Nags get hit and shriek and tear at their reins.

I said before in a dismounted battle one in four men holds onto the mounts and the rest do the fighting. Up there it was one in eight and it were impossible to hold them terrorized nags. Me, the Irishman kept me hard by, got his striker to hold me, that latter curled in a little ball at my feet. I flatten my ears to the din and try to remain calm, hold myself as still as them fizzing bullets would allow. An arrow pierces into my back and a bullet strikes a haunch. But you are equal likely to shift into the path of a projectile.

It didn't take as long as you might think. Another picture. Imagine a river, a big stone in the middle. A beetle sunbathing atop. Up in the mountains a warm wind has melted the snow. The agua, it swirls around that stone and rises and rises and ain't a goddamn thing that beetle can do about it.

The Irishman, he tried a tactic or two out the manual. Feathers popped up out in the sage, painted faces and torsos, and snuffed them tactics out. Rifles blazed and pruned the sagebrush and sprigs flew up. Couple of Sioux boys rode about in the open to demonstrate manliness and got shot for it. The horse holders shot their charges to make redoubts and lay down behind, and the survivors stampeded off and caromed through us. So the Indians was among us now.

A trooper grabbed a sorrel as it fled, managed to mount the pitching body. He wrenched at the reins trying to turn it to his purpose, but all it did was go around in circles, and the Indians shot him in the leg. The horse made up its own mind and careered off down the hill toward the river, him hanging on by the neck.

A lull, and you hear the cries of the wounded, the sifting wind, the sparrows chirping in the chokecherry bushes. The survivors take a sup of whiskey and pry the jammed shell cases out their rifles. A kerfuffle hard by, and two mounted Indians come busting through and tap the heads of half-dozen troopers with a knobbed stick. The soldiers fire, but them boys' magic was strong. They said later Crazy Horse were in that pair, but I never knowed that Indian to recognize him. Then it busts out anew, and I guess the lull was just so they didn't hit one of their own.

I only see two suicides in our bunch. Most fight till they is engulfed. One boy throws his gun away and rolls hisself up in his blanket. Another stands tall and blasts his pistol till it runs dry and henceforth yells threats and throws arrows back at his assassins.

The Irishman, dodging about behind me, his striker down there dying, I realize he is using me as a goddamn shield, and a couple or three intended for him thud into me. I flinch some, but hold still, save for that bottom lip what has commenced flapping. The sun obliterated by the dust and gunsmoke, I can scarce breath and see. The Irishman shouts something at me, but I am deaf now on account of the roaring gunfire and the shriek of eagle bone whistles.

I feel his weight come on my neck. A bullet has destroyed his knee. He looks about at them other dead nags forted up. He yells, and this I do hear, I got to do this Comanch'.

Goddamn him. All my earthly has arrived at this. Me a goddamn redoubt. I picture my sun-bloated body and the blowflies assembled thereon. The hot muzzle burns my white star and I catch the stink of my burning hair like when they done branded me them summers since when I pictured myself on the marble road. I close my eyes.

Something slams into me, throws me into him, knocks the wind out of me. It ain't no bullet, maybe the Sioux acquired artillery. Last thing my eye clocked was a pair of pricked ears and a nodding head, and I figure a stampeder done it. Why weren't its ears flat like the rest of us? Whatever it is, the blow has knocked the Irishman's shot awry. He is down on one knee now, hoisting his carbine. An arrow strikes him in the belly and a bullet strikes him in the chest, so that immediate worry is taken care of.

You might think me stone-hearted there. But the Irishman, he were gentry and weren't forced into it like them destitutes and aliens bleeding their lives out hard by. He could have been back home in the soft rain and mists and the soggy grass, ambling off in his rubber boots to pat his favourite polo horse. But he was here, on this seared smoked ridge in the god-scratched wilderness, fighting natives who'd never insulted him personally and who'd never heard of the Emerald Isle, and even if they had, wasn't planning to visit it and massacre his family.

I swivel an eyeball to identify what object struck me and saved me. But it ain't my eye what identifies it. The wind carries his stink up to my charred nostrils.

He is on his knees, at my feet. My bane, shot through the neck. To this day I do not know if it was the Irishman's bullet intended for me what did for him. Somehow he's shook off his pack and come looking, caught sight of me and issued his standard salutation. He is looking up at me, his sawing bellows and blasting nostrils attempting recompense for the life juice pumping out, a whistle issuing forth from the hole what felled him. His head wilts and I am minded of a prairie daisy left in a dry vase on a July day. He slumps. His last breath sighs out, and you might say it were a trick of the light, but I know it for a fact. As the head slams down, an eye winks at me.

As if my wounds and the flying projectiles hadn't given me goddamn enough to contend with, now there was me feeling rotten about myself. I'd treated that mule with naught but indifference at best, goddamn contempt at worst. Now the bastard done saved my life.

I had scant opportunity to consider my feelings, such as they are. Most of the boys is all dead now, but a survivor has hold of my reins and is attempting to mount, one arm dangling. I spin about, being in no mood to get ridden. He plants the butt of his rifle against my shoulder what numbs me and I hold still.

I can supply no description, only state that he was a heavy fellow. He yells Yah! like he is expecting me to chisel off, but the best I can manage is a skewed trot. He digs his spurs in and whacks me with a gauntlet, but by God, that is all he is getting out of me.

We head for a knoll yonder where another fight has broke out, pass a trooper punching his bloodied fallen mount. The horse, you got to hand it to him. He tries to do his duty, tries to rise, even arranges its front legs and heaves. The soldier hauls on the reins and heaps profanity upon it and kicks it in the belly, over and over. You can't judge them boys too harshly. They was as panicked as their nags and out of their heads with the terror.

We is making slow progress towards that other fight, although I am overtaking a few limpers fleeing afoot. The Indians, they seen us flee, but they ain't in no hurry. Arrows zip by. So they ain't aiming to hit yet. They hurl dirt and stones. But they ain't out of ammunition. They is being disrespectful. A crowd blocks our path, and the other three sides is populating up. He kicks me and slaps me with that goddamn gauntlet. It could be a quirt threaded with glass shards. I got nothing left. They is hurling insults now and closing in. They tug at his britches, insert a knife. Jesus. Jesus Christ, he whimpers. He shifts in his saddle and I hear him draw the Coltses and the bang what sprays his brains to the firmament.

Them braves proceed on to the battle on yonder knoll, spitting on his corpse as they pass. You can imagine, ain't no scalp to take.

SO THAT'S YOURS TRULY, left alone up on that ridge, reins dangling, dripping blood. Behind, screams as the wounded are dispatched. Ahead the battle is hotting up. I ain't seen goddamn Custer for a good bit now and I figure he failed to kidnap hostages and that'll be him on yonder knoll, making his stand. Below

Indians is queueing up. There weren't enough room for everybody on the battlefield that day, and I am sure some boys must have gone home disappointed. Them yonder troopers have already slaughtered their nags and is firing out from behind. The incline, well it looks like last spring somebody planted Indians and they is all now sprouting up.

I spy Vic. He is the only nag standing. I figure Custer is holding off killing his favourite until things get real desperate, and sure enough there the Beau Sabreur lies, one hand clasped to a bloody stain on his bespoke shirt, the other clinging on to Vic. You got to admire that nag. He rears and snatches the reins out of Custer's hand and departs through the smoke and I never saw him again, though I expect he finished fertilising the prairie.

I'd like to tell you Custer died snivelling for his ma having previous soiled his underwear. I'd like to tell you the Indians drug him out alive from under a dead trooper where he'd hid his quaking body, that he genuflected and whimpered for his life. But I can't. Like I said, the part of his brain what ought have told him to be afraid of battle, that part were absent.

I can't report he died no hero neither, his guidon fluttering adjacent, a pile of cadavers roundabout, him a boy again playing Soldiers and Indians with Tom and Boston. So don't picture him standing one leg cocked on a fallen nag, sighting along his pistols, the barrels jerking up as he picked off the whirling savages, Come on boys! We have the red devils now! That ridiculous moustache.

I'd wager but few witnessed it, otherwise occupied as they was, but I'll tell it.

Like I said he were already shot when I saw him. Shot in the valley for all I knowed. It were Vic's hasty departure what did for him. Rearing up to snatch those reins away a front hoof flicked out and caught Custer under the chin. His head snapped back and that were that. They get overrun and an Indian strolls over and puts a bullet into his temple, as you might dispatch a doe.

That Indian. That Indian carries a shield, painted red and

yellow, the colours divided by a horizontal black line, a black half-sun setting thereon fitted with buffalo horns. In the remotest reaches of my brain a chine of memory stirs, and though my eyes is burning and rheumy, I roust them for a final effort. The dust and smoke thwarts me, but then it clears some.

By God. On a day of goddamnedest things it were the goddamnedest of all. He'd filled out some, and his face was painted red with black eye sockets, but I saw it weren't no Sioux or Cheyenne or Arapaho. It were a Shoshone-Ute-Comanche-Cheyenne, and he carried a buffalo-sun shield and were short that earlobe the Comanche cut off all them summers since. And if you ain't guessed it by now I'll supply the name. Hears the Moon.

It was as big a surprise to me then as it is to you now. Last time I saw that boy he was getting drug into the brush along the Lodge-pole Creek by his heartbroke stepma Fox Who Runs Straight, subsequent to receiving the honour as the first indigene shot in the Battle of the Washita, and by Custer to boot. But I admit, I never witnessed no funeral exequies.

I let out a neigh, loud as I could muster. I can't say why. He never heard, what with me distant and enfeebled, the din of battle and him otherwise occupied. He never took Custer's scalp, that pate no longer worth the mither, and he went off and applied his knife to the circumference of another.

That fight lasted about half the time the Irishman's did. Them imbued with terror of Indian torture suicided theirselves. Others tossed their guns away and held their hands up. One boy smiled and offered his gun to his onrushing assassin. They must have been neophytes to the plains, and the Indians met their actions with astonishment, contempt and brutality. Last I saw of Hears the Moon he were engaged in a fistfight with a comrade over souvenirs. By God but that boy had growed up.

He ain't going to show up again. That afternoon was the last I ever saw Hears the Moon. He weren't down on the Wounded Knee Creek them winters hence, so maybe he got demised prior or plumped for the life of reesty beef and sandy flour, maybe even learned his letters and arsmetrick, him a bright boy. I remain ignorant if he knew it were Custer he was plugging, what with that latter's famous yellow locks and buckskin jacket absent, and minus his big hat Custer were a runty-looking fellow you wouldn't look twice at. But if he did, he never admitted it to no thin-arm later come asking.

A FEW MORE HOOVES remain to be filed smooth, knots to be teased out the tail, circles painted around the eyes. For one, I ain't yet told you the actual bona fide reason I become the one and only living survivor of the fight known as the Little Big Horn.

My multifarious wounds and my dwindling life force. I knew there were a trio of arrows sticking out my back and posterior parts, and numerous agonies betokened the presence of lead. All wounds aggregated, they said later I had a good baker's dozen, however many that is. My torment you can take as read, but being there weren't nobody to cry out to, it weren't worth making no fuss, save for my flapping bottom lip over which I held no sway, but watching my blood spot the grass were sure diminishing to the spirits.

My tongue was swoll up with the thirst by then, and I limped off into a ravine in search of agua. It were like sacrificing day in the Old Testament down there. The humanos, they was all silent, but a horse or three was still snuffing and pawing at the ground, though them all recumbent. I tried to pick my way down, but the defile steepened and corpses is hard to get any purchase on, so I started back up.

I headed back to where my bane had fallen, my bellows sounding like that pit saw I witnessed with the Cornishman. I sniffed about him. I nudged him. I remembered the Comanche taking him at the eagle's nest shanty, how he veered off the trail if he scented an acorn, how that rear dexter flicked out if inveigled into a gallop, how his incautious if joyous bray saved Looks At The Sky's life from the spirit Apache. I pawed at the ground by his head. Who can say why. He weren't about to spring up and chaw on my tail like the old days.

I wandered off a piece and stood and dropped my head. Blood drizzled out my nostrils and I tried not to ponder my prospects. What was the Cornishman's valedictory bible verse? He rejoiceth in his strength. He goeth on to meet the armed men. He mocketh at fear, is not affrighted.

My strength now were naught to rejoice over. Jesus but my legs wanted to chuck in the sponge. They was already well along the quaking trail and now my knees commenced to knock, so I splayed them out, thinking that would further their sustaining powers. I had determined not to lay down, least not of my own volition. But the wind stirred and began to bump me about. I tottered and rearranged my legs some. But it wouldn't be long. My posterior, the one with the white sock, it buckled, so I let it hang, and stood on three.

You get your legs arranged right, and a tripod is a right stable construction, but I am now leaking blood like a panjandrum-shot buffalo calf, and I hadn't had a sup of water since I filled my belly in the poppling Greasy Grass, back when everybody was still quick. The prairie, it became my greatest enemy. It gyred and tilted so as to throw me off my feet. The scrub appeared as the finest straw piled high beckoning me down for a nap. I admit to being tempted, but that goddamn prairie, it weren't going to outwit me.

Another rear gave out, and I dropped on my haunches, sat like a canine a spell, which is about as humiliating as life can get. I get my bellows to suck in a deep breath, and grunting to shame a hog I hoisted myself back up onto three pegs. But it was over. I knew it, and I sunk back down.

So this were it. Me and all my multifarious nomenclatures, Yellow Crow With One Foot In The Snow, Bastardo, Mouze,

Rab, Trasandatino, Yellow Horse, Death Horse, Buck, Comanche, this is what my earthly travails had led me to. Expiring on the rumpled northern plains, what was never my home in the first place, choking on my own tongue, sat spraddle-haunched like goddamn canine, blowflies staking claims on my wounds, my bones about to fertilize the herbage for some goddamn cow to bumble over and chaw on. Even my bottom lip had figured to hell with it and stilled. All it needed were a goddamn owl to show up. I looked out and my optics was no longer highly refined, my vision closing in as if peering through them scientifics' brass tubes, and a foggy dusk were settling in, somehow pierced by stars falling toward me. My knees hinged and my head slumped and I fell sideways. The grass prickled my tongue. I coughed up blood and one eye watched it pool out. A longspur steeled up and sang.

Looks At The Sky Too Much, she come to me and said, I have a memory for you, Somohpah.

Somohpah, I done forgot that one.

She was right fond of me was that Indian. That said, ashamed'd be is too big a word for it, but you could always tell she were disappointed I weren't no speedy nag, a great buffalo runner she could prance about on afore that snooty paint and them curly-lipped compeers.

So, picture us up on a knoll, a blasting day of cloud resemblances and sun dazzle and whipping grass, the plain flushed green all bee buzz and bird tweet, elk and buffalo and antelope grazing, lolling wolves, cloud shadows racing each other to the Christ Bloods. A shower has blown through and deposited agua on my posterior and now it lies in transparent pebbles. Looks At The Sky, she is off a piece, has located an ancient tree stump she knew was there and said a prayer to her spirit. She scrapes out a hole and places therein the spirit Apache's scalp and his child's moccasin, puts a coyote-proof rock on top.

She leaps back aboard. I feel her stretch up in the saddle, the wind rushing about my ears. She is looking behind. She yells out, Get ready brother!

Yours truly, I am already ready. I stamp and snort and curvet in anticipation of it. We engaged in this activity before.

Hup, hup, hup. Yeeee-hi!

She don't need to kick me and she is already laying along my neck. The pebbles fly away as we plunge down off of that knoll kicking up plumes of dust and I am already at full gallop. I rotate my highly refined optics to check on the progress of that cloud shadow.

Yeeee-hi! Her grinning teeth and flaming hair, ears flapping for all I knowed. The first time I ever wore that gifted antelope skin atwixt me and her, the spot of red paint.

Go Brother. Go.

And I go. I glance at down at my legs and them appendages is a blur. I swivel my eyes. Now that is curious. That cloud, it ain't gaining on me like it generally does.

Yeeee-hi!

I am blowing good now, and this is normally the part where the cloud shadow swallows me and Looks At The Sky reins me up and feigns pleasure and surprise and tells me never mind I did good. But something right peculiar is going on down there with my legs.

I look down, and it is the goddamnedest thing.

I swear. My blurring hooves ain't touching the herbage. I can scarce feel the whip of the stems as they graze my ankles. I dislodge nary a prairie flower. You know prairie dog holes never bothered me none, but now it ain't even incumbent on me to look.

I glide along a good piece like that, blithe, observing the scenery. I don't recall a single knee-nudge from my jockey. I nod a greeting to a sparrow. I nicker at a coyote looking down a hole.

That cloud, well I figure it figures, To hell with this, I got go rain on somebody, and it veers off. Looks At The Sky yips like a wolf pup presented with a leveret, Brother! Brother! You did it!

She lays along my neck and talks nonsense in my ear and I think again on that gift atwixt me and her. Maybe there is something to it. Who in goddamn hell are you to say.

A WOMAN APPROACHES with a big knife, a bone hammer and a determined look in her eye. She wears a fancy buckskin shirt, though its best days are long departed and maybe she figured it suited to the bloody if celebratory task. Sewed into the shoulders is panels of contrary character. Edged with beadwork they are, of exquisite quality. The panels are antelope hide, and the woman, she possesses only a single eye. I raise myself up to meet her.

Editor's Note

The manuscript concludes with a number of random annotations, but these are frustratingly undecipherable.

Further Reading: in endeavouring to authenticate the events described in the text, the editor has amassed a considerable library. A select bibliography may be found at www.williamfagus.com